TORTURE
to her
SOUL

J.M. Darhower

This book is a work of fiction. Any references to historical events, real people, or real places are used fictitiously. Other names, characters, places, and events are products of the author's imagination, and any resemblance to actual events or places or persons, living or dead, is entirely coincidental.

Copyright © 2014 by Jessica Mae Darhower

ISBN-13: 978-1-942206-02-6
ISBN-10: 194220602X

To anyone who has ever fallen in love with the last person they should ever give their heart to.

This is for you.

Prologue

Secrets are a funny thing.

You keep them bottled up, hidden thoughts nobody else hears. It makes it hard for others to get close to you—for them to ever really *know* you—when you hold the deepest parts of yourself back, only letting people graze the surface.

But some secrets, I think, are better left unspoken.

Sometimes secrets have the power to kill. The power to *destroy*. We each hold nuclear weapons inside of us, our fingers always hovering over the buttons for detonation. Most of us press them. Some of us don't.

I wish I had that kind of restraint.

I envy those who keep everyone at an arm's distance.

I'm weak.

Too fucking weak.

I let her get too close to me.

I heard this saying once, long ago, that I've never forgotten: *three may keep a secret, if two of them are dead*. I've spilled many secrets in my life, secrets that always ended up with somebody dying. Sometimes because of me, and other times... well... *because* of me. I think about them when I lie in bed at night, see their faces when I close my eyes, relive the moments the buttons were pressed and everything around me imploded.

I'm a haunted man.

Darkness surrounds me.

Figuratively.

Literally.

It's dark.

It's that heavy sort of darkness, the kind you can feel when you breathe, the denseness filling your lungs and slowly suffocating you. There's no relief in this darkness... only more torture. Sweat coats my skin as the summer humidity clings to the air, making it hard to find a shred of comfort. I toss and turn, restless, in and out of sleep, losing seconds, minutes, hours...

Every time I look, the clock in the bedroom reads something different, the glowing red numbers taunting me.

11:43 pm

12:11 am

1:45 am

2:09 am

Rolling over onto my back, I squeeze my eyes shut, throwing an arm over my face, trying to force myself to stop looking at that damn clock. It dictates my life and I hate it. I fucking *hate* it. The silence is strained, the noises from the old house settling exaggerated to my ears. There's nothing peaceful about it.

Another creak.

A wooden floorboard groans.

The bed shifts suddenly.

I move my arm and open my eyes, my gaze hitting the ceiling when I'm jolted. I find nothing but darkness above me, the glow from the alarm clock in my peripheral.

Slowly, turning my head, I look at the time again.

2:45 am

Another noise.

A loud click.

My heart skips a beat before hammering hard in my chest.

I know that sound.

It's not normal.

Unnatural.

The cocking of a shotgun.

I sit up, blinking rapidly, desperately seeking out whatever's in the darkness, but it takes too long for my eyes to adjust. No, *her* eyes adjust before mine, and she sees it... she sees the predator.

She realizes we're the prey.

"Naz!" Her voice is a panicked scream. "Oh God, Naz!"

I'm frozen. It's only a second. Just one second delay until my vision finally adjusts. I stare at the familiar face—a face that smiled at me hours ago, like there was nothing but love between us. A face, I realize, of a man who held secrets. A man I didn't really know.

The face of my best friend.

It's only a second, but it's a second too long.

A second of hesitation that takes away everything I love.

BANG

The noise explodes into a fiery light that jars me, thrusting me to consciousness. I sit straight up, once more smothered by the darkness. I gasp for air, sweat pouring down my face. I blink rapidly, the scene greeting me again and again every time I close my eyes.

Blink.

Blink.

Blink.

Fuck.

No matter how much I try, I can't forget it.

I can't stop seeing it.

I can't stop *reliving* it.

The bed beside me shifts, and for a moment I convince myself it wasn't real. It was just my imagination. That's it.

It didn't actually happen.

I'm okay.

She's not dead.

But when I look over, it's not Maria's eyes that regard me, not her face I see, and reality comes crashing down all over again.

It wasn't a nightmare.

No, it was a memory.

Karissa eyes me cautiously in the darkness, but she says nothing. She doesn't try to console me or ask what's wrong. She doesn't have to.

She probably already knows.

She knows me.

Sighing, I look away from her as acceptance sinks in, instinctively glancing toward the stand beside my bed, seeking out an alarm clock I haven't owned in twenty years. I wonder what time it is now... wonder if it even matters anymore.

Time stopped at 2:45 am that day.

I've been stuck in the darkness ever since.

I'm going to tell you a secret.

A secret I've never told anybody.

I, Ignazio Vitale, have always been afraid of the dark.

If you tell anyone that, I'll kill you.

Chapter One

My life is a case study of gluttony.

If you're looking for an apology about that, you'll want to look elsewhere. I'm not sorry in the least. Everything I do, I do it in excess; everything I have, I have more of than I'll ever need.

What can I say? I don't deny myself anything.

I've killed over a dozen men in my life. More than two dozen, if we're being honest here. I stopped counting long ago. I kill, and I hurt, but until recently, I only ever really loved once.

Maria Angelo.

I thought she was it, thought she was the only one who would ever reach me, the only one to beat through this battered armor I wear. I thought my ability to love ended with her, and I was fine with that. I live my life in excess because it leaves me satisfied. Love, on the other hand, hurts like a son of a bitch.

I know.

Believe me, I know.

I watched love die right in front of me, gasping, struggling for just one more breath life wouldn't grant. I decided, at that moment, that I'd rather just die than feel that again.

But then *she* happened.

I pause in the doorway of the kitchen and casually lean against the wooden doorframe, watching as Karissa cooks. Or tries to cook is more like it. Oil splatters into the air from a pan on the stove, some chicken frying away, the outside of it blackened nearly beyond recognition. A pot in the back boils over, the burner hissing when the liquid hits it, as smoke rolls out from inside the oven.

"Shit, shit, shit," she chants, popping the pink earbuds out of her ears and draping them around her neck. Grabbing a set of potholders, she yanks open the door, trying to fan away the smoke. It quickly consumes the air around her the same time loud beeps start blaring through the room.

She casts an angry glare at the nearby smoke detector before pulling out a baking sheet and throwing it on the counter, spouting another string of curses at whatever it is. Biscuits, I assume, although they look like lumps of shit.

Appetizing.

I walk over and reach up, popping open the smoke detector and pulling out the battery so it'll stop making noise. Karissa glances at me, offering a timid half-smile in place of any words.

Words are a rare gift from her these days. She showered me with plenty of scathing ones before they dried up and we entered the drought stage.

I wait it out, but her silence is deafening.

Frustrating.

Downright torture some days.

She walks around here with those earbuds in her ears, music blaring as she blocks out the world. If she can't hear me, she can pretend I'm not here. If she can't hear me, she thinks I won't waste my breath trying to talk.

She turns back to the stove, to her burnt food. She's usually better than this, but something has her frazzled. I'm not sure what it is.

"Everything okay, Karissa?"

She clicks off both burners as she mutters, "just fucking wonderful."

My jaw clenches at her tone and I force myself not to react. I don't take to disrespect well, but she dishes it out some days like I'm starving for it.

Hell, maybe I am.

Maybe I deserve it.

But I don't like it.

At all.

Instead of pushing her for more of an answer, for a *better* answer, I just walk out, leaving her to salvage a dinner she knows I won't eat. She does this every day now, part of a routine she settled into this summer, a routine she doesn't often differ from anymore.

She's predictable, borderline robotic as she fights to keep her emotions from showing around me, like if she does the same things day in and day out, maybe I'll grow complacent and overlook her presence. Like maybe I'll forget about her. Like maybe it's the key to getting away. She doesn't realize that's how I catch people. They think they fade away in the bustle, when they stand out more to me that way.

She's distracting herself, with these disastrous dinners, these routines, but it doesn't keep her from thinking. From *over*thinking. Strained silence fuels the most morose thoughts. I know. Believe me, I know. And that just makes it all worse.

She's a ticking time bomb.

Tick.

Tick.

Tick.

It's only a matter of time before I clip the wrong wire and she explodes.

Heading into the den, I take a seat at my desk and pull out my cell phone to call a nearby Chinese place. I order whatever the special is today and request some *Beef Lo Mein* without any of the vegetables, Karissa's favorite.

I can hear her moving around in the kitchen, banging cabinets and throwing things. I just lean back in my chair and listen to her chaos, absorbing the impact like it's made with her fists.

I didn't set out to love her.

I didn't even plan to like her.

But it happened... we happened... and I'm still trying to figure out how to deal with that.

The delivery guy shows up in less than thirty minutes. A new one every time, different places whenever I order out, so nobody can predict where I'm eating from that day. It's not fool proof, but it's certainly proven safer than eating something Karissa makes.

I pay for the food before curiously strolling toward the dining room. The light is off, but Karissa sits at the table alone. The glow filtering in from the kitchen shows me she has a plate in front of her. She shifts the food around with her fork, not eating it, as she once again has those earbuds in.

I'm not surprised.

Another part of her routine: she won't admit defeat.

Wordlessly, I pull out the carton of Beef Lo Mein and set it on the table beside her before I make my way back into the den, leaving her with a shred of dignity, letting her eat whatever she wants in peace.

Dealing with people.

Finding things.

My specialties.

I sit in the den, my feet propped up on my desk, leaning back in the leather office chair as I scarf down my dinner. My eyes are trained on the laptop, on the stock ticker scrolling along the screen. I have some of my money invested in various high-profile businesses, legitimate dealings that keep me off the government's radar, but my focus right now is on the little ones, the barely existing penny stocks nobody cares about.

Chop stocks, they call them.

You find one, invest, and con a bunch of others into putting their money in, convincing them it's the next big thing, and then as soon as the price skyrockets, you pull your money right back out. The stock will plummet, since it's shit, and everyone else loses out, but you walk away with a pretty profit thanks to the suckers.

It's illegal, and I don't do it, personally, but it comes with the territory.

Finding things.

I've always been good at orchestrating schemes, finding a way to get things, to make money, but it wasn't until I started working for Ray that I really honed my skills. I have connections all over the world now—if somebody needs something, I know a person, or know a person who knows a person who can get whatever it is. It goes hand-in-hand with dealing with people, when it comes down to it. If people are terrified of you—of what you're capable of—they'll never cross you or turn you away.

That particular skill of mine wasn't discovered until later... until the world I built crashed down around me, leaving me a ruthless shell. When you've got nothing left inside of you except for darkness, it becomes easier to snuff out somebody else's light.

And that's me. I do what I want, take what I want, and make no apologies for any of it. After all, I wasn't born this way. The world made me who I am, and the world pays for that mistake every day. There's only ever been one thing to evade me, one person to elude me, one clever enough to stay ahead of me all these years.

Carmela Rita.

Johnny was easy to find. He took the same route Karissa is taking now: predictability. He played it close to the chest, settled into a routine, buying a house and working a shitty nine-to-five job, hoping to fly under the radar by becoming nothing. Fitting, really, since he *was* nothing.

Carmela, on the other hand, shook up her routine, living a life of chaos, of impulsiveness. Whenever I got close to her, she fled, switching tactics, moving on somewhere else.

She's a lot like me, I think.

She's smart.

But I'm smarter.

It's how I know this isn't over, that killing Johnny hadn't ended anything. I wish she would run again, disappear into another life, create another existence somewhere and never look back, but she won't.

I know this, because that's not what I'd do.

Carmela's full of darkness, too. The only light in her life now brightens my home, and she'll come for it. She'll come for Karissa.

God help her when she does.

Speaking of the light of my life...

My eyes shift from the laptop to Karissa when she walks into the den, barely making a sound as she curls up on the couch and grabs the remote control. She turns on the television, keeping the volume low, as she flips straight to the Food Network. A notebook lays open on her lap, a pen tucked between her fingers that she absently shakes as she stares at the screen.

She takes notes, like it's important.

She jots down recipes, like she needs ideas.

And she studies... and studies... and studies, her nose stuck in that notebook half the damn day, like there's going to be some sort of test at the end of it all, like she's going head-to-head with Bobby Flay or Rachel Ray or whatever obnoxious host she's watching today.

I close the laptop and finish eating, my attention on Karissa now. I watch her, dissecting her like she dissects whatever's being cooked, breaking her down into tiny fragments like the ingredients she jots down in her notebook.

14

TORTURE TO HER SOUL

I wonder if she knows how much I've done this, how much I've studied her, how well I know her inside and out. I know her sighs and smiles, the meaning behind the crack in her voice and the goose bumps on her skin. I can tell when she's happy, when she's sad, when she's furious all by the gleam in her eyes and the pep in her step. She's an open book, an energetic, emphatic woman, and no matter how hard she fights to keep her emotions from showing, I know what it is she thinks of me.

I know she hates me.

I can see it. I can sense it.

It's written in the tension in her muscles, the way she folds into herself when I'm close, the flush of her body whenever I dare touch her. But I know she loves me, too. Because a fire wages beneath her skin, and not all of it is fueled by anger.

Every now and then she'll forget she's supposed to despise me, she'll forget she's not allowed to want me.

She'll forget I'm a monster.

And all she remembers in the moment, all she knows, all she cares about, is that I'm a man, a man who went through hell, a man who loves her, who swore he wouldn't hurt her, and for the moment she'll let herself believe it. She'll forget I'm the bad guy and remember what it felt like when she thought I was the hero.

The one who would drown so she could stay afloat.

That's what I cling to.

That's the glimmer I look for when I study her.

It's not there today.

She's scowling, every inch of her tense, her jaw clenched. She knows I'm looking at her but refuses to so much as even acknowledge I exist.

I smile, watching her.

She's trying to hurt me, but all I can think is she's so goddamn beautiful when she's pissed.

My cell phone ringing distracts me from the moment. I pick it

15

up from the desk, not bothering to look at it as I answer. I know who it is from the sound it makes alone. "Yeah."

"Ignazio!"

Ray's already three sheets to the wind. His voice doesn't betray it, strong and steady as always, but he called me by my first name. He doesn't do that when he has his wits about him.

"Yeah," I say again, sitting up straight, dropping my feet to the floor.

"We're over at Cobalt," he says. "Come on over for a bit."

"Yeah," I say, standing up. "Okay."

I hang up, slipping my phone in the pocket of my black slacks. I could tell him no... I'm probably the only person who could deny an invitation from him without serious consequence... but the air in the house is too stifling for me to stay here. She needs space to get over whatever it is that has her so upset today. I know she'll be here when I get back.

She'll be here, because she knows if she isn't, I'll just track her down and drag her right back.

Slipping on my shoes, I fix my tie before grabbing my coat from the chair. I put it on, fastening the button as I start for the door. "I have things to do."

Karissa says nothing, doesn't even look at me, but she heard. The way her face twitches tells me so, as she bites down on the inside of her cheek.

"I might be late," I say, strolling over to the couch, stopping right beside where she sits. "Or I might not."

Another twitch. More silence.

I stand there for a moment, contemplating, before leaning down and pressing a kiss to the top of her head. I don't bother trying to kiss her lips. She won't resist me, she never does, but I'll get nothing in return today.

"Call me if you need me."

A grunt, soft and throaty, like she fought to restrain words and instead only offered the sound of annoyance. Annoyance at the fact that I'd dare think she'd ever need me? Or annoyance, because deep down, she realizes she already does?

Either way, I smile again, laughing to myself as I walk out.

∽ᑺ⌒ᐝ

The Cobalt Room is an upscale social club deep in Manhattan, not far from the campus of NYU. It's the sort of place people admire from the outside, a grand old structure that belongs in the pages of a historical magazine, but very few ever get to step through the door. It's membership required, by invitation only, and to get invited these days, you have to get through Ray.

He doesn't own it, but he certainly controls it. He runs most of his business out of a back office, tucked away behind the elaborate bar and swanky entertainment rooms. He hangs around out front, commanding the crowds with his open personality, but when you get pulled into the back, you know there's hell to pay.

I don't bother to flash my ID when I step inside. Kelvin, the man working the door, knows me—he's one of us, after all. He works here most afternoons for Ray, moonlighting weekends a few blocks away at the little nightclub called Timbers. He was working the door that night, the night Karissa went there with her friend, the night I decided to make my move.

Kelvin sent word as soon as she showed up that night. He recognized her face and knew she was my mark. They all knew, frankly... every one of Ray's men know exactly who Karissa is.

Kelvin nods, bowing his head as I pass, maybe out of respect but more likely because the guys don't like to look me in the eyes.

Few people do.

The street soldiers, cruel thugs who lie, cheat, kill, and steal, shy away, whereas little Karissa, half my size with barely any physical strength, never hesitated to stare me straight in the eyes, like she was reading my soul with just a glance. I thought at first she just didn't see

17

it, didn't see what I was, but after a while I realized she saw it—she just didn't mind it so much.

Didn't mind that there was enough darkness inside of me to rid the world of every stitch of light.

Nobody ever looks at me that way, with that sort of openness, that sort of trust and affection.

Not even Ray.

Except for when he's drunk, maybe. And drunk he is tonight. He grins when he sees me approach him in the private bar area, grins like he's the Cheshire cat and he found an Alice to fuck with. "Naz!"

I nearly flinch when he says it. He catches himself right away and doesn't apologize, instead shrugging his shoulders and scrunching up his face as if to say, 'ah shit, you caught me.' He waves his hand, wordlessly telling the guy in the plush leather chair beside him to vacate, and I slip into the seat the moment he's gone. I motion toward the waitress, telling her to bring me my usual—a bottle of cold pale ale, still sealed. She brings it without question, without hesitation, and I use the bottle opener on my keys to pop the top off.

"So we cashed out the frozen food stock this morning," Ray says right away, lounging in his seat. "Almost a quarter million profit."

"That's great," I say, relaxing in the chair. "I take it my drinks are on you tonight then?"

"You know it," Ray says, holding his glass up—scotch, on the rocks—to clink it against the side of my bottle. "You keep it up and I'll buy you an entire brewery."

Laughing, I take a sip of my beer. "I'll hold you to that."

"I know you will."

Spirits are high and alcohol flows freely. Ray laughs and jokes, his mood infectious. I humor him, smiling, trying to relax and push everything else from my mind, but thoughts of Karissa keep seeping back in.

It looks like we're just hanging out, but this is work for men like us. Plotting, scheming, talking, socializing… it's the part of the job I hate. It's not that I hate people in general. I don't. Not really. I'm just happier when they're not around.

Except for her.

Goddamn Karissa.

Always my exception these days.

She never should have been.

It's past midnight when the women arrive. They're not usually invited, not allowed inside Cobalt, but when Ray gets a hankering to celebrate, everyone indulges him.

Prostitutes. They call themselves escorts. I call them whores. Most are nothing more than girls with too much make-up and not enough brains.

Brandy, Ray's meddlesome blonde girlfriend, shows up and squeezes into the seat with him, draping across his lap as she nuzzles into his neck. She once sold herself like the others, but Ray took a liking to her and kept her for himself.

His own little baby doll, he calls her.

Everyone else starts to loosen up, while my muscles grow tenser, the alcohol in my system doing nothing to quell my growing unease.

It doesn't help that Brandy's little friend perches herself on the arm of my chair. She's new, obviously, a first timer around here. She looks down at me, smiling, her pupils like black marbles. *Stoned.* "Hey, handsome, you looking to party tonight?"

I stare at her, my expression blank, as her leg brushes against mine, her foot rubbing my calf. Brandy takes notice and scrambles to stop her friend, drunkenly stammering, but Ray clamps his hand down on her mouth to silence her, his gaze fixed on me, that grin back on his face.

He wants to see my reaction.

Sometimes the man makes me feel like one of his play toys.

I finish my beer—my fourth, as it is—and set the empty bottle down on the table beside me. Sitting up, I motion for the girl to come closer. She leans down, smiling seductively, thinking I'm going to kiss her collagen-infected lips, but I bring my mouth to her ear instead. "I'll slit your throat if you ever touch me again."

Her expression must be horrified, based on the way Ray wildly laughs. I don't care. I stand up and head for the exit, not looking back. "See you later, Ray."

"Bye, Naz."

This time I do flinch.

It's not the name itself that bothers me. I've always preferred it to Ignazio. But hearing it reminds me of the man I used to be, the man I was before. Naz had hope. Naz was full of love.

Naz died a cruel death.

I told Karissa to call me Naz. I said it in a brief moment of weakness, because she looked at me with so much light in her eyes, so much innocence in her expression, that I thought for the moment it might've been a reflection of the old me.

Blissfully ignorant.

I lost my way then, forgot who I was, and I still don't know how the hell to get back from there.

It's after one o'clock in the morning when I get home. The house is dark and quiet. I pull my jacket off when I step in the door and loosen the knot of my tie, sighing. The den is empty, television off, remote control sitting on the small table on top of Karissa's notebook. I push the remote away and grab the notebook, picking it up to read the top page. A recipe for some sort of potato dish with notes on the bottom: *how to cook the perfect steak.*

I toss the notebook back down when an envelope peeks out of the side of it. Curiously, I pull it out, seeing it's addressed to Karissa from NYU.

It's wrong of me, but I look; I pull out the paper and read through the letter.

Dear Ms. Reed, yada yada, whatever whatever, you lost your scholarship so we're going to need you to pay.

A bill for damn near twenty-five thousand dollars.

TORTURE TO HER SOUL

I let out a low whistle as I shove the paper back into the envelope, returning it where I found it in the notebook.

No wonder she was in a bad mood.

Chapter Two

"Do you want—?"

"Nope."

I stall, mid-question, and stare at where Karissa sits on the couch, notebook on her lap as she watches yet another cooking show. *Same shit, different day.* I can faintly hear music playing from the earbuds draped around her neck, making it possible to talk to her for the moment.

"Can I at least finish my question before you answer?"

She says nothing, jotting something down that she sees on the screen, acting once again like I don't exist.

Taking a deep breath, I ask, "Do you want to go with me to—?"

"Nope."

I try to push back my frustration, but it comes pouring out of me in a groan.

The woman is unbelievably infuriating.

Shaking my head, I walk out of the den, not bothering to ask for the third time. Grabbing my keys, I head out of the house, slamming the door behind me.

She got to me.

I try not to let her.

I try to stay calm and collected. I'm trained to keep my emotions from showing. But she alone knows how to get under my skin.

Once again, she's my exception.

Always a goddamn exception.

The drive into Manhattan seems to crawl by this afternoon. I crack my knuckles and my neck as I sit in the busy traffic, trying to work the stiffness from my body, tension that seems to grow more and more every day. Instead of getting better, instead of things settling down, it feels like we're stalled at the starting line.

Patience has always been a strong suit of mine—I spent almost two decades tracking down Carmela, waited years to try to get back at Johnny—but I'm nearing my tolerance limit with their daughter.

I head to Greenwich Village, parking the car in a garage near Washington Square, before making my way around the block. NYU student services, on the first floor of the building: *Office of the Bursar.*

The building is brightly lit, surprisingly busy for it being summertime. I wait a few minutes to be acknowledged, stepping up to a middle-aged woman sitting behind a large desk in the lobby of the office.

"I need to speak to somebody about paying a tuition bill."

The woman starts rambling about how the student can make payment arrangements online, giving me the usual spiel, but I cut her off. "No, I need to make a payment, and I'd like to pay it all. Today."

An hour later I walk back out, twenty-five grand poorer with only a printed out receipt to show for it, the words 'Paid in Full' stamped on the top beside Karissa's name.

It's nearing dusk already when I make my way back to Brooklyn, parking in the driveway of the house. I head inside, the sound of loud music greeting me before I even open the door. I make it only a few steps into the foyer, calling out Karissa's name, when animated laughter cuts through the racket.

It's female, and familiar, but it's not Karissa.

Torture to her Soul

Melody.

My pulse quickens, my fingers twitching at the sudden swell of irritation. I clench my hands into fists to stop them, but it does little to help. I want to squeeze the life out of that laughter, smother the insufferable chatter to make it stop.

She gets under my skin and claws at me.

The noise is coming from the den, the one room I feel most at home. The only fucking place I ever feel *safe*.

Inviting someone into my house is like letting them touch my food or pour my drinks: for me, the trust is damn near impossible to come by. I've been bugged before, had my phones wiretapped, and it's all too easy for something to slip by, skating in right under my nose. I don't let people into my life, and she opens up my sanctuary to someone I hardly know.

Melody Carmichael. Her father works on Wall Street. Her mother is a homemaker and runs a book club. It's the picture perfect family, but it's an image I don't trust. Deeper, beneath the surface, there's always another story, buried secrets that a man like me knows how to unearth.

There's a downside to everything, a dark side to everyone, and those who willingly walk in the shadows are a hell of a lot more convincing than those who only acknowledge the sunshine.

My best friend shot me in the chest, but at least he had the decency to look me in the eyes when he did it.

I avoid the den and head to the kitchen instead, seeking out a strong drink to calm my nerves, but my footsteps falter right inside the doorway. It's an utter disaster. Dishes and trash are everywhere, pans still on the stove with leftover food stuck to them. It smells grotesquely burnt, another failed dinner, this one abandoned based on the half-filled pizza boxes on the counter beside the charred mess.

I can feel myself growing hot as I clench my jaw. Closing my eyes, I take a deep breath, trying to keep my anger at bay. *Relax. Don't worry about it.* I count to ten to calm down, but it's senseless.

Because the moment I reopen my eyes and see the mess again, my vision gets cloudy, and it takes every ounce of restraint I have to keep from losing my cool.

My patience is officially gone.

Grabbing pans from the stove, I knock them against the trashcan, dislodging the food before tossing them on the counter, not caring about the noise they make as they bang against the marble countertops.

I fill the sink, the bubbles nearly overflowing as steam rises from the scalding water. I toss the dishes in, my mind a flurry of dark thoughts as I tear off my coat and shove my sleeves up to my elbows.

I scrub, and scrub, and scrub, the blistering water scorching my skin. I grit my teeth, trying to distract myself with the pain from it, trying to focus on the sting to internalize it, but it's counterproductive. Every laugh, every sigh, every syllable that reaches my ears from the den is like hitting the reset button, my resentment escalating again and again.

She has a lot of nerve.

The world around me falls into a haze, my hands moving on their own. I scour everything within sight until my hands are raw, scrubbing so hard with a steel wool pad that my fingers bleed, cleaning in the darkness to try to purge the vindictive thoughts, but they're all that exist.

They eat me up when I get like this.

I'm so lost in the anger, so consumed by the rage, that I don't hear her footsteps, don't sense her presence, until the overhead light flicks on. The brightness momentarily stalls me. I clutch a glass so tightly that the knuckles of my reddened hand turn as white as cocaine.

I'm damn lucky the glass doesn't shatter.

I almost wish it would.

I'd take a shard and slash a fucking vein.

"Naz?"

Her voice, so close, uttering my name, is like throwing gasoline on already raging flames. I drop my head, feeling myself violently shaking.

A lot of fucking nerve.

"Turn around," I say, my voice low, so cold it's almost unrecognizable to my own ears. I need her to go back to where she was and give me time to calm down, to clean up this mess and bring order back to my world, before I take this out on her.

"What?"

"Turn around, Karissa. You don't want to do this right now."

"Don't want to do what?"

I don't answer her, and she doesn't go away.

No, instead she comes closer, her footsteps finally registering as she strolls through the kitchen toward me, her steps measured. She treads lightly, but her approach is an ominous roar to my ears. I breathe deeply to keep myself from reacting, standing as still as possible, closing my eyes when she speaks again.

"Ignazio?"

Her hand is on my back, her touch tentative, but it's enough to set me off. The glass slips from my hand, crashing into the sudsy water as I spin around. Karissa is caught off guard and starts to pull away, to back away, but I snatch ahold of her wrist and yank her to me instead.

She flinches, eyes wide, as I shove her back against the counter in the corner, pinning her there.

"Is this what you want? Huh?" I stare straight in her dark eyes as I lean closer. "You want to mock me? You want to provoke me?"

"What?" The word shakes as it spills from her lips. "What are you talking about?"

"I'm talking about what you're doing," I say. "What you're doing *to me*."

"I'm not doing anything to you."

Her eyes water. I have enough sense to loosen my hold on her

27

wrist, in case I'm hurting her, but it makes no difference. A tear streams down her cheek as she stares into my eyes, body tense like she's holding her breath having to be so close to me.

Me.

She can't fucking stand to be near me.

I split myself open for her, exposing the vulnerable parts of me, the parts nobody else gets to see, and she accepts it. She accepts it, and loves it, but she doesn't understand it. And when I finally explain it to her, explain how I'd be victimized, how I'd been hurt, how my life had been destroyed, she acts like I'm the one in the wrong.

"I give you space, Karissa. I give you space, even though everything in me tells me not to, because it's what you want. I give you space, and how do you repay me? By goading me. By inviting people into my home, into my space, without even consulting me. You want your space? Then give me mine, too, and stop disrespecting it!"

"I haven't—"

"You have," I say, cutting her off. "Your little innocent act isn't going to work on me... not anymore. You know what you're doing. You're not ignorant. You know how it affects me, and yet you keep on doing it. I let you, because you needed time, you needed my patience, but you're out of time now, Karissa, because I'm out of patience. You want to play this game? You want to fuck with me until you get a reaction? That's fine. I'll give you exactly what you want."

I press up against her, my nose brushing against hers as she struggles to break the hold I have on her. Tilting my head, leaning further down, I pause with my lips just a breath away from hers.

I want to kiss her.

I'd give anything to have her kiss me back again.

I can feel it as she whispers, "Let me go."

"Make me. I *dare* you."

She shoves me with her free hand, slipping around me so quickly

I hardly have time to react. I let go of her wrist a second too late, and she winces as her arm awkwardly twists. She grabs her wrist where I held her as she backs away, shaking her head, another stray tear flowing down her cheek.

"There's something wrong with you!" she shouts, loud enough that Melody hears, calling out from the den to see if Karissa's okay. "You're... you're fucking sick."

"Tell me something I don't know."

"I hate you!"

"Again, tell me something I *don't* know."

"Karissa?" Melody calls, stepping into the doorway of the kitchen, hesitating as she glances between us, her eyes laced with suspicion. "Is everything okay?"

I stare at Karissa, cocking an eyebrow, waiting on her to respond. She doesn't want me to address her friend, not right now, not when I'm in this mood.

Karissa slowly nods, still rubbing her wrist. "Yeah, it's fine, but uh... you should probably go. Naz and I... well..."

"I get it," Melody says quickly, waving us away. "Lover's quarrel and all that. I'll, uh... I'll see you later this week, okay? We still on for the café?"

"Of course," Karissa says, forcing a smile. "I'll see you then."

Melody waves before scurrying out of the house. It isn't until the front door opens and closes, signaling she's actually gone, that Karissa turns back to me again. The fear is gone from her eyes, as is the anger I've been accustomed to these past few weeks. All that greets me now is sadness.

Heartbreak.

She keeps rubbing her wrist, clutching onto it. My anger lessens as worry seeps in. I step toward her, reaching for her arm. "Are you okay?"

Before I can touch her, she yanks away, backing up to put some more space between us. "Like you care."

"I do," I say. "If I hurt you..."

She scoffs. "All you do is hurt me."

I want to say something, to refute that, but I can't.

Karissa's silent for a moment before looking at me, her voice a whisper. "You know what the worst day of my life was, Naz?"

I barely hesitate. "The day I killed your father."

She flinches at those words, but she shakes her head as she crosses her arms over her chest. "The worst day of my life was that day in my dorm room. You warned me to stay away from you... but I didn't listen. You said if you didn't walk away then, you never would... but I didn't listen to that, either. And I see now you meant it. You really meant it." Her voice cracks. "I made a mistake. I should've never asked you to stay."

She could pick up a knife from the counter and plunge it in my chest right now, and it wouldn't bother me—wouldn't hurt me—as much as those words do.

I'd rather be shot again than to hear what she just said.

But she knows that.

And maybe she means those words.

Maybe that was the worst day of her life.

But that offers little consolation to me.

It *stings*.

Wordlessly, I push away from the counter and take a few strained steps toward her. Karissa stands still as I slowly walk right by her, refusing to meet my eyes as I stare down at her.

I pause beside her, leaning closer, my lips near her ear. "But you did," I say quietly. "You asked me to stay, so get used to it, sweetheart, because I'm not going *anywhere*."

Her skin is soft. Pure. Rarely touched.

Although Karissa keeps her eyes closed, her body completely

still, I know she's awake. I can tell it from the catch in her throat, the soft shudder of a breath she lets out when I climb in bed beside her. She's wearing a flimsy black tank top and a pair of underwear.

She always wears very little to bed.

I wear even less.

I sleep naked. I have no qualms about it. I try to be a gentleman, try to be understanding and keep my hands to myself, but it's hard.

It's fucking hard.

Especially times like this.

Times when I know she's awake, when I know she knows I'm here, so close but so damn far away. It leaves an ache in my muscles that is hard to shake. I catch myself touching her, my fingertips trailing whatever sliver of skin is exposed. She remains still but I can feel her shiver, feel the goose bumps rising in the wake of my touch.

It's too much.

It's never enough.

I want more. I need more. I'm greedy and I want all of her. I want to love her, want to hold her, want to be inside of her again.

I want to fuck her mercilessly.

Last time I did, I hardly remember it.

I was drugged, and she was planning to leave. It's been a month... a long torturous month without her touch. I want to slip my hand beneath the fabric, strip her bare and hold her close.

But if I try, she'll use the word. *Red.*

I wanted to rip her fucking tongue out for using it on me the way she did.

Sighing, I roll away from her, facing the other way. I won't touch her tonight, as much as it pains me. She's upset, and I don't want to make things any worse than they already are.

I don't know how we're ever going to get over this.

One step forward, half a dozen back...

I'm a light sleeper, my body naturally attuned to my surroundings. Every time she shifts in the bed, rolling over or stretching her legs, curling up or clutching her pillow tighter, I'm startled back awake, jolted to a consciousness that isn't easy to shake.

Sleeping with someone—sharing a room with them, letting them into your most private places, seeing you in your most vulnerable moments—takes a lot of trust. I'm strong, and fast, but even a dim-witted asshole could slit someone's throat in their sleep, incapacitate them before they even woke up.

All it takes is a few seconds.

I know.

I drift off eventually, in and out of sleep. I can feel it when Karissa gets up in the morning, can hear her quiet footsteps as she leaves the room. I try to go back to sleep once she's gone, but it's impossible.

As hard as it is to sleep with her beside me, it's even harder having her gone.

Curiosity gets the best of me after a few minutes.

I climb out of bed and throw on some clothes, slowly making my way downstairs. Karissa is in the kitchen, standing by the counter, pouring herself a bowl of cereal. Coco Puffs. It's still weird, seeing this space used so much, utilized for breakfast, lunch, and dinner. Sometimes she just hangs out in here, just leaning against the counter for the fuck of it.

Strange.

Stepping past her, I grab a bottle of water from the fridge, opening it and taking a sip when she speaks.

"I'd kill for some coffee."

Her voice is light, the words coming out easy, like talking to me these days still comes naturally.

Huh.

Leaning back against the counter, I eye her peculiarly. "Literally?"

She turns her head my way, rolling her eyes. "It's an expression."

"I know it is," I say, screwing the lid back on my bottle. "If you want coffee, call the café down the block and have them bring you some."

"And what, order fifteen cups of coffee?" she asks. "They have a minimum delivery amount, you know. I'm better off just walking there, but that requires putting on pants, and well..."

And well, she's not wearing any.

My eyes slowly scan her at the mention, drinking in the sight of her creamy skin in the soft light from the window. Sometimes I think she does this just to tease me. She never used to show so much skin. It's tempting, that's for sure.

I want to caress every inch of her.

"Do you want me to go get you some?" I offer when I meet her eyes again. "I will."

"No, it's fine," she says right away. "I don't want anything from you."

I shrug, pushing away from the counter to stroll past her when I hear my phone ringing off in the den. Ray again. *Always Ray.* "Fair enough. If you change your mind—"

"I won't," she says. "I'm not going to change my mind."

It's quiet again, as I walk out of the kitchen, her voice barely a breath when I hear her amend, "Not when it comes to you, anyway."

Chapter Three

"So there's this guy..."

This is how a lot of conversations start with Ray. If I had a dollar for every time I've heard those four words...

Actually, I'm sure I have a few thousand for every time.

"What guy?" I ask needlessly, knowing he'll tell me whenever he's ready. Ray has a flair for the dramatic.

"This guy," he says, "who did some work for me. He's in the car business, you know... he owns a shop and stripped a few cars. He got in deep, though, and decided he wanted out, but you know as well as I do there is no *out*, so the jackass filed a report. For harassment! Can you believe it? He called the police and thought they would do something for him!"

Yes, I can believe it.

People seem to believe the police are actually there to help them.

I used to think it, too.

Before I learned the truth.

I glance at Ray as we sit in the back office of Cobalt, sipping drinks even though it's not even noon. Brandy is fast asleep in the corner, on a leather couch along the wall. I wonder if they spent the night here. I've never seen her at Cobalt so early in the morning before.

"And what, you want him taught a lesson?"

"Nah, we already took two knees," Ray says. "I'd rather he just be dealt with already."

"Yeah, okay," I say. "I'll handle it."

Ray rattles off the guy's name and some identifying details—Josh Donizetti, late forties, blond hair, walks with a limp because of the kneecap incident. The garage he owns is over in Brooklyn, not far from where I live. That's really all I need, but Ray reaches into his desk and pulls out the man's business card for me anyway.

I finish my beer as Ray switches topics, rambling on about something. I don't know. He's not talking to me. Not really. He's just talking. Unlike me, Ray doesn't like silence.

When my bottle is empty, I set it aside and stand up, slipping on my coat before reaching my hand toward Ray.

He shakes it, smiling genuinely. "I don't know what I'd do without you, Vitale."

Without me, he'd be poorer, and weaker, and probably would even be dead. He relies on me more than he likes to admit... more than the other guys know. They think their boss is the strongest man in the city, the most powerful, and on the surface it seems that way. He slaps his name on most of my deeds, taking credit.

I don't mind.

I don't do it for the glory.

I don't need any credit.

I don't want people kissing my ass every day.

"I'll call you," I say. "Just as soon as it's done."

I spend all afternoon finding the garage in Brooklyn, staking it out, watching the man of the hour as he limps around the workspace, struggling to bend down, straining as he works on cars. Bastard probably suffered enough, both of his knees wrecked. He's lucky to be walking at all.

But he made the grave mistake of going to the police. It's unforgivable in our world, something nobody is immune from. No matter who you are, or what you do, or who loves you... it's a deadly sin we don't forgive.

The first person I ever killed was a guy named Joseph Manchetti. I did it clean and simple, a shot through the back of the skull. My hands shook that day when I pulled the trigger, and I barely made it a block away before doubling over along the side of the road and losing everything in my stomach.

It wasn't because he was dead, wasn't because I took the life of a married man, the life of a father, the life of a man severely in debt to a mob that only wanted his mortality as payment.

It had nothing to do with him.

It was the adrenaline.

It had been the first spark of life I'd felt in my veins since the night it was all stolen from me, the first time I felt normal again. It was a high unlike any other, the high of controlling someone's last breath. My heart beat wildly in my chest, a heart I wasn't sure existed anymore.

The most inhumane moment of my life reminded me that I, too, had once been human.

I felt alive again.

I grew addicted to that feeling.

Eventually, I stopped getting sick afterward. The high didn't feel as high. The adrenaline didn't come on as strong. Like any true junkie, I needed more and more to gratify me. Clean and simple became messy and torturous, the sensations heightened by witnessing the aftermath. I perfected it, figuring out the best way to get the biggest thrill with the least amount of risk.

I didn't care how they felt as long as I got to feel again.

As I sit in my car across the street, watching the man move around the shop, my fingers start to tingle from anticipation. I toy with his business card, running my fingertips along the rough edges of it, biding my time, but the pull is strong. It's funny, in a way, that they call it a hit.

Because it is.

It's a hit.

A high.

And I crave it.

I wait until dusk, the neighborhood quiet, everyone from the garage gone except for the man I'm here to deal with. He's working on an old muscle car, lying beneath it.

Carefully, I get out, discarding the business card in the center console, and tug on my black gloves as I cross the street. I quietly step inside the garage, my footsteps hardly making a sound. The man doesn't hear me, or see me, doesn't know I'm here until it's too late.

I hit the old jack, the car abruptly lowering, so fast the gimp doesn't have a spare second to get out of the way. He can't move, can only scream, as two tons of metal come crashing down on his chest.

He kicks his legs as he silences, his body violently shaking.

I linger for a moment, watching.

There's something mesmerizing about death. It's the offering of peace, I think. No matter the pain of life, the torture, the struggle, it'll all end eventually.

We're born to die. That's just the way it is.

I'll die someday, somehow, and I'm not afraid. Death will be a release for me. Until then, I live vicariously through others, watching them reach the point of acceptance, watching as they fight for one more breath.

Life never grants them it, not when I'm around.

Just like it never gave her another chance.

Sometimes I think I'm cursed that way.

It's a self-imposed punishment that barely keeps my demons at bay. It's cathartic, but only temporarily.

The release leaves me unstable.

I walk away while he's still twitching, keeping my head down as

I cross the street again to where my car is parked. I drive away without giving the garage another look, pulling out my phone and calling Ray, merely saying "it's dealt with" when he answers before hanging up. I don't go home right away, instead navigating the streets for a while to clear my mind, to let the rush of adrenaline purge from my system.

Facing Karissa like this would be dangerous.

The silver and black machine takes up a quarter of the stretch of countertop, the pristine fixtures shining under the early morning sunshine streaming through the window. I lean against the counter on the opposite end of the kitchen, hearing Karissa move around above me, her footsteps making their way through the hall and down the stairs.

My eyes meet her as soon as she steps in the room. I squint when she flicks on the bright overhead light, watching as she hesitates, seeing me lurking in the darkness. The fear that greets me makes my insides coil, my skin taut. My chest feels heavy, like she punched me in the gut with that look.

No matter how many times I swear I'm not going to hurt her, she still forgets. And even if it's only for a moment, it's too much.

"Good morning," I say.

She stares at me, the panic dissolving to her usual shade of confliction. She doesn't respond, her gaze shifting away from me, her brow furrowing when she spots the machine on the counter.

"It's a countertop coffee system," I explain. Her eyes dart to me, surprised, and I shrug, snatching the user's manual off the counter beside me and holding it out to her. "You said you would kill for coffee."

"So you bought a machine?" she asks, taking the manual from me before looking back at it. "You couldn't just buy a normal little coffee pot? One that doesn't take reading a novel to learn how to operate?" I start to respond when she cuts me off, grumbling, "of course you couldn't."

She looks at the front of the manual for a moment before tossing it down and turning away from it. She snatches a bowl from the cabinet, slamming doors and drawers as she fixes herself her usual morning cereal. I watch in silence as she brushes right past me, grabbing the milk out of the fridge. She pours it into her bowl, some sloshing out that she doesn't bother to clean up.

Standing there, her back to me, she takes a bite and stares out the window.

Still so angry...

Slowly, I stroll over to her, pausing right behind her, so close my tie rests against her back. I'm still wearing yesterday's clothes. I don't know if she even notices, or cares, that I didn't sleep beside her, that I didn't come home until some godforsaken hour and then spent until sunrise putting together a goddamn machine to give her coffee. I don't know if she missed my presence then, but I know she feels it now.

I know, because she shivers when I lean forward, and in the reflection of the window I see her eyes briefly flutter closed. I bring my lips to her ear, my voice low as I say, "I think the words you're looking for are *thank you.*"

Chapter Four

Faith.

Trust.

Pixie Dust.

The words shine bold, written in gold, on the colorful old poster. I saw it a few times in the past, hanging in Karissa's dorm room, but I haven't seen it since she moved out of there.

Until now, anyway.

The big eyes of the little blonde fairy glare at me across the bedroom, from where she's now affixed to my wall, haphazardly tacked there. The poster is crinkled, and crooked, the bottom right corner torn.

It looks like it belongs in a trashcan, not hanging beside my bed.

The sight of it makes my skin crawl from anxiety. I want to tear it down... or, hell, at least hang it up straight, smooth out the wrinkles and make it presentable. But I don't. I do nothing but stand in the doorway, irritated, and stare at the goddamn thing in the dim lighting.

Shaking my head, I turn around and head downstairs. I'm too exhausted to deal with its sudden appearance right now. I spent all afternoon dealing with things for Ray, handling business, and I just want to be able to unwind for a bit, put that all behind me and relax.

The only light on in the house is the den, the sound of the television filtering out when I head that way. More cooking shows, I assume. Always the goddamn Food Network. Stepping in the doorway, I pause again from surprise when the same little blonde bitch from upstairs greets me on the screen.

Tinker Bell.

Huh.

Karissa's sitting on the couch, wearing pajamas, her feet tucked beneath her. I stroll over and plop down beside her, so close my thigh brushes against her leg.

She tenses, her body rigid, but she doesn't look at me. Instead, her eyes are fixed on the screen. I watch her for a moment as I loosen my tie before kicking my shoes off and turning to the television.

Peter Pan.

It puzzles me.

I know a lot about her, but one thing that confuses me is why she loves this movie so much. I've thought about it, considered it, and I know she's young, but it feels so juvenile for someone so mature.

"You know," I say, "some people think Peter Pan is actually a horror story."

From the corner of my eye, I see her forehead wrinkle with confusion. She casts a disbelieving look my way.

"I'm serious," I say, meeting her eyes. "There are theories that Peter Pan is the grim reaper and Neverland is purgatory. That's why they don't age there." She stares at me in silence, not yet turning away, so I take it as an opening to keep going. "But of course there are other theories, too, that the Lost Boys don't age because Peter kills them before they can. There's a line in the book, I don't know if you've read it, but it says: *When they seem to be growing up, which is against the rules, Peter thins them out.* Pretty self-explanatory, don't you think?"

42

I run two fingers across my neck, simulating slitting my throat. Karissa stares at me.

And stares at me.

And stares at me some more.

Her expression is blank, but her eyes shoot fire. If she could burn me with them, she would. After a moment she turns away, snatching up the remote and pressing the power button. The television cuts off as she stands, tossing the remote onto the cushion beside me.

"You have to ruin everything, don't you?" she grumbles, not giving me a chance to respond before she disappears from the den.

Once she's gone, I tilt my head back, resting it against the couch as I close my eyes.

It's a lost cause.

It's obvious, I think, but unacceptable. I can't seem to do anything right when it comes to her. I'm sure she thinks I have all the power, that she's at my mercy, but that's only because I fight day in and day out to maintain some semblance of control around here.

Because without that? I know I'll lose her completely.

And if I lose her?

We both might as well be dead.

Standing up again, I head out of the den, leaving my things lying where they are, too drained to maintain order today. Tomorrow I'll deal with it, deal with everything around me that seems to be falling to pieces, but tonight I only have enough energy to deal with her.

And I can't deal with her the way I deal with everyone else. They get a knife to the throat or a bullet to the back of the head. All I have for her are words, and they seem inadequate at best.

She wants nothing to do with my kindness.

Doesn't believe a word of my promises.

Machiavelli believed it was better to be feared than loved, because attachment is easily severed, but the terror of pain is ever present. I have her fear. I know I have her fear. I see it sometimes when she looks at me. But what I don't know is how to keep her love when it feels close to dissolving every time I talk to her, like she picks apart every syllable looking for something else to hold against me, something to prove to herself that I'm the monster she believes me to be.

And maybe there is a monster inside of me.

Scratch that, I know there is.

I feel it rear its ugly head sometimes. I feel it eating away at my body, poisoning my thoughts when the darkness takes over. My insides are black but my heart still beats.

It still beats.

And it fucking beats for her.

So there is a monster inside of me, yes, but it doesn't make up all of me.

Besides, isn't there a monster in everybody?

The lights are off upstairs, the bedroom obscured now that the sun has finally set outside. My eyes adjust to the darkness easily, used to adapting to the blackness after years of training them, and the first thing I notice is the poster.

It's not there.

I stare at the empty wall, seeing the tacks still forced into the plaster, corners of the paper stuck to them.

She ripped it down.

My eyes scan the room quickly, spotting it on the floor beside the bed, torn straight down the middle, both halves crumpled.

I stand in the doorway and stare at the destroyed poster for a moment before a quiet sound registers with my ears, the softest whimper that I almost hadn't caught.

I know that sound, know it intimately, a sound that haunts my existence.

Fuck.

It's a catch of breath, the faint gasp of air from a chest that desperately needs it.

I live every day tortured by the memory of that.

My gaze shifts right to the bed, to where Karissa lies, wrapped up in the blanket like she's trying to shield herself from the world outside of it. I can't see her face, can't make out much more than the shape of her body, but as the sound resonates through the room again, I know.

I know she's crying.

She's crying because of me.

It feels like my chest is caving in, the weight of her grief a heavy burden to carry. I don't place all the blame on myself, but I know, as much as I don't want to admit it, I had a hand in hurting her.

I tried not to.

I swore I wouldn't.

But I did.

We can't help it sometimes, I think. We regularly fuck up just as easily as we breathe. The only missteps I ever make are the ones I have no control over, the shoves by fate that are unavoidable, but even still I always manage to keep my balance.

But with her, I'm losing it.

I'm losing my footing.

She's going to bring me to my knees if she makes that sound again.

Slowly, I walk over to her side of the bed, my footsteps quiet. I can see her body tense as I pause beside her, my shadow blocking the little bit of moonlight streaming in through the window. I stare down at her, seeing her eyes are open, tears streaming down her flushed cheeks. Without saying a word, I reach for her, gently brushing a trail of tears away with my knuckles before pushing some hair back off her face, tucking it behind her ear.

She stares blankly at nothing, not meeting my eyes, not acknowledging my presence. Leaning down, I press a kiss to her cheek, tasting the salty wetness, reveling in her warmth. The moment my lips meet her skin, she does it again, makes that noise, the sharp inhale of desperation that runs through my body, settling in my rigid bones.

I kneel beside her and force her to look at me, to see me. There's no way I can possibly sleep tonight, no way I can relax, with her this way. "What can I do, Karissa?"

The question is quiet, but she flinches, like I shouted at her. Her lip curls into a sneer, hatred brewing in her eyes. "Go to Hell."

She chokes on the words, chokes on them like they're the bitterest things she's ever tasted. The passion makes my skin prickle. It's probably wrong, to get a thrill out of it, but fuck if her hostility doesn't make something stir inside of me, something primal and seedy. A twisting, a coiling, a brewing that makes my cock harden and my skin thicken.

The sensations are dangerous to evoke.

I run the back of my hand down her cheek again, wiping away more tears. "I've been heading that way for a long time, sweetheart."

The words are barely from my lips when I'm shoved, hard, nearly falling backward. I catch myself with my hands as she sits up, the blanket dropping from around her as she wraps her arms around her chest. She's not crying anymore, the resentment drying her tears.

The anger I can deal with… anything but the heartache.

Before she can speak, before she can react, I'm up again, my hands on either side of her on the bed as I lean forward, so close my nose brushes against hers.

She inhales sharply, this time from surprise.

"Careful," I whisper, my voice low and raw from the restrained emotion. "You know I like it when you fight."

"Fuck you."

I press my lips to hers, kissing her roughly.

She doesn't kiss me back.

It lasts only a few seconds before she pushes against my chest, shoving just enough space between us for her to hit me.

Hard.

She clocks me right in the mouth, her fist unexpected, catching me off guard. I grimace at the sharp stab of pain and grab ahold of her wrist before she can punch me again. She winces, flexing her fingers, glaring at me, her nostrils flaring as she shakes from anger.

The metallic tang of blood coats my tongue as I run it across my bottom lip, feeling the small gash where my teeth sliced into it. It burns, already pulsating to the rampant beat of my heart.

It isn't often someone has the guts to swing on me. Even more rare is my guard being down enough for them to actually connect.

The feelings I shoved down just a moment ago boil over, the fuse lit, everything I keep caged in all exploding out. I drag her back onto the bed as I climb on top of her, and she yells something, but her voice is barely a breath in the breeze, a dull murmur drowned out by the humming of electricity inside of me.

There's only one word that will break me out of this haze.

Red.

Red, the color of rage, the color of hate, the shade that takes over my life to the point I can barely think straight. Red, the color of blood, the thick ooze that seeps into hardwood floors and soaks fabric, rarely removable once its been spilled. Red, like the flush of her cheeks, and the curve of her mouth that just begs to meet my lips again. Red, like the claw marks she rakes down my arms, my chest, my neck, and my face. She's fighting, but she's pulling and not pushing, holding me to her as she annihilates my skin.

Red.

Red.

Red.

I kiss her hard again, the sting from my split lip absorbing deeper, seeping into my muscles, fueling me on. I bite her, not enough to draw blood, but enough for her to feel it like I do.

"Say it," I growl, pressing myself against her. I'm hard, so hard it hurts. "Say the word."

I want her to say it.

I *need* her to say it.

Because if she doesn't—if she doesn't scream it at the top of her

47

lungs, if she doesn't spit it at me like venom—I'm not going to be able to stop. Red tints my vision, a hazy coating over everything, and 'red' is the only thing that can take it away.

"Say it," I tell her again, my lips hovering just above hers, so close I can feel her quick breaths, "but don't say it unless you mean it."

She glowers at me with more fury than I've ever seen from her before. My little kitten transformed into a ferocious beast, a hungry lioness that's capable of tearing me apart. And she will. She'll shred me.

All she has to do is say that word, and I'll be in pieces.

"Say it," I taunt. "Fucking *say* it."

Her lips part, and I wait. Every muscle inside me tightens, straining, my chest constricting as I wait for that word to greet my ears, but all I get is a shaky exhale. It comes out like a growl, the sound lingering in the air around us for a fraction of a second before she lifts her head just enough to smash her lips to mine.

And I'm gone.

Clothes are tattered and bodies are battered as we strip away every stitch of fabric separating us. There's nothing gentle about it, nothing loving.

This isn't love.

This is hate.

Real hate.

She hates me, and I think it soothes her, pacifies her heartache, letting her unleash that rage on me.

I don't mind.

I welcome it.

She can hit me, beat me, torture me, and I'll take it all. I'll happily absorb the impact of her fists and the bitterness of her words. She can purge her aggression, lose herself with me, and I'll never begrudge her for it.

Because I know the feeling.

I know the anger, the hate, and the pain.

And looking at her, as she pulls from my lips for a fraction of a second to stare me in the eyes, is like looking in a mirror again… a broken, jagged sliver of glass reflecting my soul back at me.

This time, it's the dark half.

She's just as fucked up as I am.

And maybe I did that to her.

Maybe it's wrong of me.

But fuck if it doesn't feel right this way.

I kiss her cheek, chin, neck, chest, again, and again, and again, my teeth nipping at her flesh as I drag her further onto the bed, settling between her thighs. She's already wet, her skin flushed, every part of her heating in anticipation.

Grabbing her legs, I shove them apart, forcing her knees to her chest as my lips meet hers again. I push inside of her, hard, thrusting deep, and she cries into my mouth, growling a lone curse. "Fuck."

"I'm going to," I whisper against her lips. "I'm going to fuck it all out of you, every bit of it." I pull out and thrust right back in, eliciting another cry. "I'm going to fuck you until you beg me to stop." Another thrust. Another cry. "And then I'm still not going to stop, not until you say the word to make me." I pull back to look at her as I thrust again, deeper than before. Her breath hitches. "I'm not going to stop until you say it… until you *mean* it."

She stares at me, stubbornly, defiantly… silently. It's a battle of wills, one she'll never win.

I'll fuck her until my heart gives out.

Hell, without her, I don't need it, anyway.

She says nothing, and she doesn't have to, because I don't give her much of a chance. I'm pounding into her so hard each thrust forces her deeper into the bed. She tries her hardest to stay silent, her face contorted, her jaw clenched to keep from making noise, but I can hear her compulsive whimpers, feel her swallowing back the cries as I lick, and suck, and bite all around her throat, giving her every bit of myself.

I don't hold back.

I'm done holding back with her.

She knows who I am.

She knows what I'm capable of.

She doesn't get the kid gloves anymore.

Minutes pass. Ten. Fifteen. Twenty.

It might be half an hour.

It could be half a day.

The room is deathly dark but I can make out her strained expression as I refuse to let up, moving her and twisting her around, treating her like the ragdoll I learned she likes to be. She takes it all in stride for a while before it gets to be too much, her whimpers more agonizing, her muscles tenser, her orgasms coming on stronger and closer together, her entire body spent.

I can feel her legs twitching, her hands vicious against my skin. The claw marks on my back throb, burning from the sweat dripping along them. She's drawn more blood, a ripped fingernail tearing a slice across my cheek, but I don't bat an eyelash.

She can wound me.

She can scar me.

She can do whatever she wants to me.

I can feel her body taut beneath mine, the onset of another orgasm. She inhales sharply, the breath leaving her lungs in the form of words. "No more."

"What's that?" I ask. "I didn't hear you."

"No more," she says, pushing against my chest. "I... I can't take any—" Her breath hitches. "Anymore."

The word is strangled as she comes, convulsions gripping her body. She clings to me, a tear leaking from the corner of her eye. I don't stop. She knows I won't. She starts fighting, hitting me again, biting whatever she can reach, and drawing more blood as I restrain her.

"Say it," I tell her again, knowing I've found her limit, the place where she draws the line. "Say the word."

All I want is for her to admit defeat.

For her to break out of this rut again.

She stares into my eyes, breathless, as I pin her to the bed, her wrists clasped in my hands. Her lip quivers. I have to fight the urge to nibble on it. After a second she exhales sharply, and I close my eyes in anticipation. I can feel my orgasm brewing, straining my muscles.

I'm dangerously close.

Her voice is so low it's nearly drowned out by the sound of sweaty skin slapping, the lone word little more than a whisper. "Yellow."

My eyes open right away. It's instinctual. I rein myself in, moving slower, gentler, as I stare down at her.

"Yellow," she says again, chanting the word. I slow until I damn near stop, but still she says it, again and again.

Yellow.

Yellow.

Yellow.

She knows I won't ignore it.

A shiver rips down my spine as I come, but I get no pleasure from it. I pull out before I'm even finished, letting go of her wrists and moving away. I sit back on my knees, running my hands through my hair and gripping the locks tightly as I stare up at the ceiling in the darkness. My cock throbs as my skull pounds. I watch the ceiling fan spin around and around as I breathe deeply, counting to ten.

She fucking yellow'ed me.

Neither of us can win this way.

We're a disaster, a certifiable catastrophe, and there's nothing beautiful about the way we're going. She's trying to be unbreakable but I'm unshakeable. She's going crazy, and I'm already goddamn insane. I clipped my jailbird's wings so she couldn't fly away from me, and then I wonder why the fuck I can't make her soar.

That familiar sound echoes through the room again, like she's sucking in air but still can't breathe. I drop my head, eyes seeking her out just as she starts to cry. This time she doesn't hold back, doesn't try to bury it deep inside. It leaks out, a flood of emotion, the time bomb finally detonating.

I can feel the explosion.

There it is.

BOOM

She sobs so hard she's hyperventilating. I lay down beside her, wrapping my arms around her and pulling her toward me, her head on my chest. I expect her to shove away, to lash out, but she just lays there, her body limp and heavy against mine.

She didn't say the word, but she should've.

She meant it.

"Breathe," I whisper into her hair. "Just keep breathing, and it'll be okay."

Chapter Five

The man who greets me in the mirror the next morning is shattered.

Red welts and scratches rake down my chest, winding up my neck and running down my arms, a few stray ones slashed across my cheeks. My bottom lip is swollen, a small gash faintly visible, the skin discolored. Heavy bags line my eyes from no sleep, my muscles tense, and jaw clenched, as I absently grind my teeth together.

I run my fingertips along a bruise forming around the juncture of my neck and my shoulder, the slight imprint of teeth marks embedded in the skin.

I've killed men with nothing but my bare hands and walked away with fewer injuries.

Sighing, I turn on the bathroom faucet and splash cold water on my face, running my fingers through my hair, before turning the water off again and walking out. I tread lightly on the stairs, heading downstairs in nothing except a pair of sweat pants I grabbed from the drawer.

Karissa is awake now... or up, anyway. I don't think she slept much either, if at all, as we lay in bed all night, lost in the darkness.

Smothered by the silence.

Drowning in the bitter truth.

The scent of coffee clings to the air in the kitchen. It has been two weeks—fourteen long mornings—since I brought that machine home.

She finally touched it.

Karissa stands by the counter in a pair of underwear covered by one of my white t-shirts, her back to me. I pause in the doorway, taking a moment to appreciate the sight of her. I can make out the profile of her face, seeing her passive expression. She holds a small white cup, one I assume she dug out of the cabinet with the other china I've never used. Steam rises from the top as she lightly blows into it before taking a small sip.

And another.

And another.

"Good morning."

She turns at the sound of my voice. Her gaze flits my direction and she freezes, eyes scanning my face and down my chest, admiring her handiwork. I expect her to walk away, to blow me off like she usually does when I try to start a conversation, but instead she strolls my way.

Her feet stall after a few steps, and she lingers in front of me, a mere foot between us. I remain quiet, stoic, as she holds her cup out, wordlessly offering some.

My chest tightens.

It's an olive branch, I realize, but one I don't take.

She sipped it, so I don't think there's anything wrong with it, but I remember exactly what happened last time I thought that.

After a second, she sighs, realizing I'm not going to touch it, and pulls her cup back as she walks away.

"Thank you for the coffee machine, Naz," she says quietly. "I appreciate it."

Ray's trying not to laugh.

I'm trying not to punch him in the face.

I slouch in the black leather chair at Cobalt after nightfall, nursing a bottle of cold pale ale, hoping the alcohol can soothe my frayed nerves, but it's pointless, given the way Ray's gawking at me.

I turn my eyes toward him and raise an eyebrow in silent challenge, as the corners of his lips spastically twitch. He's shit at keeping a straight face, and he most definitely can't hide his amusement today.

It dances in his eyes.

He's enjoying this.

After a moment, he loses the battle entirely and a small chuckle echoes out as he full-blown grins. "How you feeling, Vitale?"

At least he's not drunk yet.

Because if he called me Naz with that look on his face?

I *would* punch him.

Potential consequences be damned.

"Fine," I respond, taking a sip of the beer. It tastes extra bitter, or maybe I'm just in one of those kinds of moods. Karissa has me flipped upside down. I don't know if we're coming or going.

"Fine," he repeats, swirling his glass of scotch around, the ice cubes clinking against the side as he waves his drink toward me. "If that's fine, I'd hate to see the other guy."

He's looking for information, information he knows I won't volunteer, but he isn't stupid, not in the least. He'd be worried if he truly believed some guy got the best of me like this. The scratches are the tale-tell sign of a woman scorned, and only one woman could leave these marks on me and still live afterward.

Ray knows this, but he doesn't get it.

He doesn't get why Karissa is still breathing.

Why I haven't... why I won't... why I *can't*... kill her.

He laughs again, this time a sharp edge to it, as he takes a sip of the dark liquor. "Such a waste."

I glare at him, hoping he's talking about the wasted opportunity and that it isn't an insult aimed at me.

Unlike the other guys he keeps around, I never took an oath to be here. I was never inducted into the organization he runs, never vowed my life to the things they do. I do them, all right. I do more than most of those other guys do. But I do it with an understanding, a mutual sort of respect, that it didn't take the prick of a trigger finger to forge.

I do it because he's like a father to me.

I do it because I want to.

I do it because long ago I decided this is exactly what I was meant to do.

So while I'm loyal, and Ray knows it, he can't treat me like he does those other guys. He can only push me so far. We wouldn't stab each other in the back, but there's nothing to keep us from someday stabbing in the front.

Nobody's truly safe.

My best friend proved that.

The thing is, I wasn't the only one who wanted Johnny dead.

Ray did, too.

He wanted the Rita bloodline destroyed.

He wanted them chewed up and spit out.

He wanted them to suffer like he did.

Like *we* did.

The only vow I ever took to him was that I would do just that.

That I would destroy them.

That I would get justice.

The only thing keeping Karissa alive—keeping Ray from outsourcing elsewhere, from putting a hit out on her life—is that he's not willing to cut ties with me. It's personal, and for the moment that outweighs any sort of business, but I'm not a fool.

It might not always be that way.

I'm sure Karissa thinks I'm a monster for forcing her to stay with me, and maybe I am. Maybe I'm a fucking despicable human being. I'm certainly not a good man. But she doesn't realize it's because of that she's still breathing. It's because of that she wakes up every morning to hate me another day.

She's alive because I couldn't bring myself to kill her, and nobody else is stupid enough to cross me by doing it.

"A waste, huh?" I take a sip of beer before gazing at the bottle, swirling what's left of the liquid around inside of it. "It's all a waste, if you ask me. None of it should've happened."

"But it did," he counters. "Only a fool would ignore that it did."

Now that *is* an insult, but I keep my cool, finishing the rest of my beer. "Yeah, well, good thing I'm not a fool. I don't ignore anything."

I set the empty bottle aside and stand, smoothing wrinkles from my suit coat. I don't bother saying goodbye, merely grasping Ray by the shoulder and squeezing it on my way past him to the door.

It's a sweltering night, the kind where the darkness feels thicker than usual and the air is heavier in my lungs, making my chest tighten when I try to breathe. I hate these nights. It's the kind of air that held Maria's last breath. The ominous sensation crawls across my skin, a chill in the heat, like I'm fighting a current that wants to take me under, but I won't let it.

Never let it.

My car is parked in the back private lot of Cobalt, down the alley that runs beside the social club. I stroll toward it, in no rush, not sure what to do or say when I face Karissa again.

I hit the lot, walking toward my car parked beneath a glowing streetlight, pressing the button on my keys to unlock the doors when I hear a noise behind me. It's quiet, and restrained, the kicking of loose gravel, a rustling in a non-existent breeze. The hair on my arms prickles in alarm, my back stiffening as every inch of me goes on high alert.

Somebody's there.

My heart pounds rapidly in anticipation, my mind working fast to strategize. I don't keep a gun on me unless I know I'll need it. I can't even carry a Swiss Army knife into the city without the NYPD calling it a deadly weapon. My eyes dart around in the darkness, looking for something I can use in defense, but nothing stands out.

Hands it is, I guess.

I was blessed with tough ones.

As long as I have my hands, I'm not defenseless.

The noise creeps closer—ten feet away at most. Steeling myself, I spin around, prepared to attack before they can make a move, when I catch sight of the face, familiar wide brown eyes catching me off guard for a few seconds, long enough for the barrel of a gun to be aimed right at my chest.

Carmela Rita.

She stands just beyond the reach of the light, her hands shaking the small caliber handgun, her finger on the trigger. I freeze in spot, making no sudden movements so not to set her off prematurely.

Because she'll shoot.

I know she will.

The look in her eyes tells me so.

"Hello, Carmela," I say calmly, keeping my voice steady as I greet her. "Nice to see you again."

"Don't even... don't you dare talk to me like that!" she grinds out, her voice shaking. "Don't talk to me like we're friends!"

She grips the gun tightly with both hands now, yet it still shakes, unsteady. She's crazed, more so than I've ever seen someone before. She's a feral cat backed into a corner, ready to claw my fucking face.

Pity for her, her daughter beat her to that.

Slowly, I raise my hands in the air to show her I mean no harm. Not now, anyway. I have no intention of hurting her today.

"Fair enough," I say. "Why don't you tell me why you're here?"

"You killed him!" she says. "You killed Johnny! You took everything from me, and I want it back! I need it, and you're going to give it to me!"

Karissa, I think. She wants Karissa.

She's not going to get her, though.

I won't let her.

I *can't.*

I can't let Karissa become collateral damage.

My mind works fast, trying to come up with something to say, some way to distract her, to throw her off for long enough to give me the upper hand. I don't think she knows where I live, not unless Karissa told her before they lost contact. Few people know where my house is for this reason. "You want—"

"I want my daughter," she interjects. "But I need money right now."

My brow furrows. "Money?"

"Johnny was keeping me afloat. I have nowhere to go without him. I have nothing left! I need money, I need a way out of this, and you're going to give it to me."

She takes a step closer, into the light. She's more of a mess than I originally thought—dirty and deranged. I wonder how she's sustained herself these past few weeks without Johnny, but it's clear whatever she had set aside has dried up if she's desperate enough to try to strong-arm *me.*

"I don't have money on me. I'll have to go get you some."

"Liar!" She waves the gun at my face. "Give me your wallet."

I hesitate before slowly lowering one of my hands, reaching into my back pocket for my wallet. I pull it out and open it, deciding to placate her by voluntarily handing over a bit of cash, but that's not good enough for her.

"Toss the whole thing to me," she demands. "And don't try anything funny, Vitale. I'll shoot you."

Shit.

I toss the wallet across the lot. It lands a few inches from her feet, and she carefully leans down to pick it up, making sure to keep the shaky gun aimed toward me, her finger still on the trigger. She struggles to keep it pointed my direction while she looks in the wallet, just a glance confirming I lied right to her face.

There's over a thousand bucks in there.

I'm hoping she'll swipe the cash and toss the wallet aside, but instead she pockets the whole thing before focusing on me again. "Now give me your keys."

"My keys."

"Yes."

"You're stealing my car, too, Carmela? I thought you were smarter than that. You know new cars are equipped with GPS. You won't get far."

"You're lying again," she says. "If anyone would have a car that couldn't be traced, it would be you. You'd never let anyone track your movements."

Smart.

I'm almost impressed.

"Besides, I don't want your car," she says. "I just have to be sure you can't follow me right away."

She's smart, all right.

Slowly, I start to take the Mercedes key off the ring when she shakes her head, taking another step toward me. "Give me *all* of them. You're not going to outwit me."

Too smart.

But she underestimates me.

I keep a spare key in my car.

I begrudgingly toss the keys, glaring at her as she picks them up. As she starts to back away, panic runs through me. I have to find a way to stop her, to stall her. I can't just let her leave.

I take a step forward, her name on my lips. "Car—"

The backdoor to the club opens and loud voices carry through into the lot. Their presence sets Carmela off, the lighting of the fuse. I can see it on her face, but it's too late for me to react, too late to diffuse this.

The explosion goes off unexpectedly, a gunshot lighting up the lot between us a fraction of a second before pain rips through me. A curse leaves my lips in a sharp exhale as my chest suddenly feels like it's engulfed in flames, the burning coating my left side, pinprick numbness radiating from it.

Fuck.

Fuck.

Fuck.

I can't breathe.

I grasp my side, wincing, and inhale sharply as a second gunshot cuts through the night, clinking as it slams into my car door, ricocheting and hitting the glass of the driver's side window. My knees buckle as I hit the ground beside the car, trying to shield myself as she unloads the gun, bullet after bullet striking metal around me. I can feel them as they tear past me, crashing into the car.

She pulls the trigger, over and over.

Click.

Click.

Click.

I raise my head, blood seeping through my shirt when I hear the distinct clicking sound. She's out of bullets. I'm breathing heavily, adrenaline spiking my system. The pain runs deep, like someone stabbed me with a hot iron poker. I'm hoping it's just a flesh wound, but it hurts like a son of a bitch.

Carmela frantically takes a few steps back. The gunshots scared away whoever had come outside, but there will be others soon, and she knows it. She knows they're coming, and she's defenseless, and I'm not dead. Either I'm a lucky son of a bitch, or she's a terrible shot. Our eyes meet for only a few seconds, a few seconds where I drink in her sheer terror.

And then she's gone.

In a blink, the time it takes to reopen my eyes after closing them, she's running, disappearing into the darkness. I force myself up, clenching my jaw from the pain, struggling to get my breathing under control. I'm steady on my feet for the moment, but I'm losing blood.

I can feel it.

I can't stay here.

The police are never far off, and there were way too many gunshots for nobody to report it. I hear people rush out the door of the club, yelling, but I don't stop to see who it is. Climbing in my car, I open the glove box, fishing out the spare key. It's hard, using only my right arm, my left hand clutching the wound, but I manage to get the car started before anyone reaches me.

Everything's a blur as I speed away.

My vision is skewed, my head fucking throbbing.

I'm not sure how the hell I get home.

But by the time I pull up in my driveway and throw the car in park, I feel like I'm already hanging by a thread. I don't bother cutting the engine, forcing myself toward the house, needing to get inside. I should go to the hospital, I know, but I can't.

They ask questions.

I don't have any answers.

The door's unlocked when I make it there. I usually get mad when Karissa leaves it latched, but I'm thanking God for it at the moment. I push against it as I shove it open, the blood coating my hand as I struggle. I slam the door closed behind me and lean back against it, wincing.

I hear footsteps coming down from upstairs as I push away and stagger through the foyer.

Karissa.

"Naz?" she says, her voice borderline panicked as she appears in front me, eyes wide with terror. Yanking her earbuds out, she rushes at me, grasping at my shirt. "Oh God, you're bleeding, Naz! You're fucking *bleeding!*"

I stare at her, mesmerized by the fright in her voice—not because of me, but *for* me. She scared for me?

"What happened to you?" she asks. "Jesus, there's blood everywhere!"

"Shot," I grind out. "Just once, I think."

"Shot? Somebody *shot* you?"

Her hands frantically paw at me, and I grimace, gritting my teeth to not cry out but a curse slips from my lips.

"Oh God, I'm sorry!" She pulls away quickly. Blood stains her palms, her hands shaking as she scrambles for her phone. She drops the damn thing once... twice... before she's steadied enough to even press a button on the cracked screen.

Her and that fucking phone...

"Just... hold on," she says. "Hold on, okay? I'll get you some help."

She starts dialing 9-1-1, but I stop her before she can press the last number, shaking my head as I reach for her phone. "No! No police."

"What?" She looks at me with shock. "Naz, you're hurt! Like really bad hurt! You need a fucking ambulance! You need to go to the hospital!"

"Carter," I mutter. "Call Carter."

"Who's Carter?"

"He's a doctor," I say. "His number is, uh... it's three four seven, uh... eight five three... uh... one..."

"One what?" she asks when I hesitate. "What's next?"

I shake my head. *Fuck.* Everything's hazy. I'm swaying. "My phone... it's in my phone. Look for Carter."

She drops her phone and digs into my pants pockets, grabbing mine. She calls the number as I stagger past her, ignoring her protests. The wound is bleeding badly, but I don't think it hit anything major.

Had it hit an artery, I would be dead by now.

I can hear Karissa, her voice sounding underwater. She speaks frantically into the phone before she calls out to me. "Naz, wait... he says not to move, to stay where you are!"

Before I can even respond, she's grabbing a hold of me, trying

63

her best to help me as I head into the den. I collapse on the couch right inside, trying to keep my eyes open. I need to get this bleeding stopped.

"Tell him to hurry," I mutter.

"He's on his way," she says, throwing my phone down before the words are completely from her lips. "What can I do? What do you need?"

"Put pressure on the wound," I say. I'm getting too weak to do it, the pain too much for me to inflict any more on myself. Self-preservation is a bitch.

"How?"

"Just... get a towel or something. Use anything."

She looks around for something to use before, in a snap decision, pulling off her shirt. It happens in a blink, one second she's just sitting there, the next she's practically on top of me in nothing but her bra, her white tank top balled up in her fist.

She couldn't just go get a towel?

Shoving my hand out of the way, she presses the fabric to my side hard. I grimace, groaning as the burning rips through my gut.

"Fuck, Karissa," I mutter. "I'm already wounded, and you start taking your clothes off. Are you trying to kill me?"

"Not funny," she says, a slight tremble in her voice, her tone dead serious. She doesn't find it funny at all. Forcing my eyes open, I peer at her, my vision blurry but clear enough to see tears silently streaming down her cheeks.

That sobers me up quickly.

"Hey," I say, my voice gritty as I reach for her, brushing her cheek with the back of my hand, ignoring the fact that I smear a streak blood on her face. "Don't cry. It's going to be okay."

She doesn't meet my eyes, keeping her gaze trained on my side as she presses against it with everything in her, the tears still falling. I'm not sure what to say. I don't know if it's the bloodshed or the realization that I'm hurting her again that makes me feel like

64

throwing up, the nausea so intense it burns my throat, everything fuzzy, my chest feeling like it wants to cave in.

My heart might really give out at this rate.

The dizziness is coming on hard, my vision fading as sweat forms along my brow, running down the side of my face as I try to focus on staying conscious. Every second gets harder, every breath more of a struggle.

"How do you know?" she asks quietly. "How do you know it's going to be okay?"

My eyes drift closed, my eyelids too heavy, the wooziness too strong for me to fight, the current sweeping me under. I struggle with every last bit of energy in me to respond, my words barely a whisper.

"Because you're not getting rid of me that easily."

"Naz! Oh God, Naz!"

I'm caught in that space between sleep and awake where the world is a slow-motion haze, an illusion I can't believe. It's not real. It can't be. It can't be happening. Her voice is a fiery scream of terror, a sound that rattles my bones and stops me from breathing.

"Naz!"

She screams again, my name morphing into an ear-splitting shriek. It's a blink of an eye, a split second where I stare in the thick darkness at a cold, calculated face that used to regard me warmly.

They say when this life takes you it's usually at the hands of a friend.

I never thought it would be him.

The gunshot lights up the room before the blast hits me straight in the chest, like a firecracker going off beneath my ribcage. I can't speak, can't react, as the pain ruptures inside of me, expanding, exploding.

Fuck, I'm dead.

I'm dying.

I fall back on the bed, my vision already blacking out from the blast, blood staining the white sheets surrounding me. It looks black in the darkness, shadowy oblivion threatening to take me away.

She's still screaming.

She's screaming my name.

Over and over again.

Naz.

Naz.

Naz.

The name dies on her lips as another gunshot echoes through the room, her voice swallowed up by a loud gasp. A gasp for air, for another breath, for another chance... a gasp that rocks me to the core, a pain I feel beneath my skin, gripping me harder than the buckshot in my chest, constricting my heart until it explodes.

A blink, and he's gone. There's nothing but darkness around me, the room completely still.

Another blink, and I force myself to move, defying the laws of nature as I struggle to pull her into my arms. She's still gasping, desperate, trying to speak, her lips moving as they sound out my name, but there's no sound to accompany it. I hold her tightly, fighting... and fighting... and fighting, but there isn't enough fight left in the world for her.

One more blink, and she's gone, too.

Chapter Six

Through the heavy blackness, the faint scent of antiseptics hits me, making my nose twitch. I shiver, the flimsy blanket covering me stiff and cold, like a sheet of thin ice, as air blows down on me from somewhere up above.

Before I even open my eyes, I know exactly where I am. I've been here before. This isn't the first time I've woken up this way.

Last time I thought I was in Hell.

The hospital.

The air is icy around me, deathly silent, but I can hear chaos in the distance: beeps from machines, the rush of footsteps, whispered chatter. Forcing my eyes open, I'm not surprised that darkness greets me.

It's still nighttime.

If it's even the same day...

My vision is blurry and my head is foggy. Medicine heavily runs through my system, a grogginess that comes only from being drugged, but it does little to ease the pain.

I don't want to move.

It hurts to fucking blink.

Ignoring it, I shift position anyway, clenching my jaw when I try—and fail—to sit up in the bed. My fingertips tingle, my mouth dry, as a sudden swell of nausea rushes through me.

My head feels like it's ready to explode.

Collapsing back with a resigned sigh, my hands explore what I can feel of myself. There's a big bandage on my left side, the source of most of the pain. An IV leads from my right arm to a machine, pumping something clear into my veins.

Whatever it is, I want nothing to do with it.

Grimacing, I yank the IV right out of my arm and throw it aside, ignoring the small stream of blood that runs from the tiny wound, dripping onto the floor. I yank out every wire running to me, pulling out needles, disconnecting myself from machines.

My blurry eyes scan the room in the darkness. I'm alone. I'm not surprised, but the nagging in my chest at the moment is about more than just my injuries. No matter how irrational it might be, part of me thought she'd be here, that she'd be at my side whenever I woke up.

But there's no sign of Karissa anywhere.

She found her opening, her chance to run when there's no way for you to chase her. She's free of you now.

It only takes a minute after regaining consciousness before the door to the room opens. My gaze shifts that way, instinctively looking for her, stupidly hoping it'll be her.

Instead it's a man I'm gravely familiar with.

Dr. Michael Carter.

Okay, so he's not *that* kind of doctor, per se.

He's a doctor of veterinary medicine.

Which means neither of us belong here.

Hospitals mean records, which mean mandatory reports, which means it's only a matter of time before the police come knocking. I go to Carter to stitch me up quickly and quietly, but this wasn't quick, nor is it going to be quiet.

68

The man at least has enough sense to keep the light in the room off, offering a nervous half-smile as he tentatively approaches.

I don't return the greeting.

There's nothing to smile about here.

My voice is scratchy as I ask, "Why am I here?"

He hesitates before cutting off the machines I just disconnected myself from before the alerts bring anyone else to the room. He sits down on the edge of the bed by my feet. "Didn't have a choice, Vitale. You lost quite a bit of blood."

"I don't care," I say. "You should've robbed the Red Cross before bringing me to this place."

He's quiet, contemplative, as he looks around, looking at everything except for me now. He knows he made a mistake. His gaze settles on the empty chair across the room, the one intended for visitors, but there are none of those for me.

Nobody cares *that* much, I think.

"I talked to the surgeon... he's a friend of mine, you know. Good man. He said the gunshot to your side was a through-and-through. Messy, but superficial. They stopped the bleeding and repaired the damage."

"So again," I say, "why the hell am I here?"

He shakes his head. "The woman who called? She was worried."

My gaze settles on the empty chair. "Couldn't have been too worried."

He lets out a strained laugh. "She was a mess when I got there. Out of her mind. The poor thing had more blood on her than you did. You were out like a light, but you were breathing fine, pulse weak but holding steady. Still though, she was trying to give you CPR, beating on you and blowing air into your lungs, doing more harm than good. Every time she pushed on your chest, you gushed more blood. Trying to keep you alive, and she damn near killed you doing it."

Despite myself, I smile at that. Sounds like Karissa—inadvertently fucking up my life, not even realizing what she's doing to me.

"So that's why I had you brought to the hospital," he says. "I know it's always a last resort, Vitale, but the condition you were in? The condition she was in? Felt like a last resort kind of situation to me."

"Did they report it?"

He sighs. "You know they had to."

I want to be furious at the man, for the obvious trouble bringing me here will cause, but I don't have it in me. I can't force myself to be pissed when my chest viciously aches and I can only seem to care about Karissa.

Her bitch of a mother shot me and I'm only worried about her. *Go figure.*

Shifting position, I grimace from the stab of pain as Carter stands up again.

"Just relax, okay?" He stares at the IV I threw to the floor and shakes his head. "I know I don't have any authority over you here... or anywhere... but I hope you trust my judgment. They're going to want to keep you here for 48 hours for observation."

"48 hours."

"Yeah, but I know you, Vitale, so I'm hoping you'll give them at least half of that. Just because it wasn't fatal doesn't mean it wasn't serious, you know."

I do know, but I say nothing, letting out a resigned sigh as I close my eyes, trying to lie still to ward off any more jolts of pain.

I fight sleep the rest of the night, too paranoid to let my guard down in a place like this, where it's too easy to get away with ending someone's life. All it takes is a slip of the wrong drug and everyone chalks it up to an accident. But there are no accidents, not where I'm concerned.

The nurse comes around, checking my vitals and trying to replace my IV, wanting to push morphine into me, but I send her scrambling away, refusing anything. The pain gets worse as whatever's in my system starts to fade, and with the agony comes the rush of bitter anger.

I'd rather end up in the morgue than the fucking hospital again.

By the time the sun rises outside, dawning a new day, I'm intolerable, unbearable, full of barely restrained fury that seeps into every word I speak, shining from my eyes at anyone who dares step foot in my vicinity.

I need the hell out of this bed.

The hell out of this place.

Out of this life, this fucking situation, this goddamn existence.

In a rash decision, I throw the blanket off and sit up, searing pain stabbing my stomach. I'm about to force myself to my feet when the door opens, voices immediately carrying through. I recognize one right away, a voice that makes the hair on my arm stand on end, every inch of me turning cold.

Blue. It's probably the only color that affects me more than red. Red is full of passion, but blue is what happens when the passion turns cold. I feel nothing—*nothing*—except for pure hatred, the kind that swells through the body and turns blood to ice, freezing everything inside of me when I'm doused with it. I'm a shell of a man filled with unadulterated indignation, and I make no apologies for it.

When coated in blue, I make no apologies for *anything*.

I look toward the doorway of the hospital room, catching sight of two men in blue uniforms with their shiny gold badges and tiny little pins bearing their names, the NYPD patches sewn on their scrawny arms. Dead center of the duo is a man wearing a drab gray suit, his voice the one chipping away at me like he's an ice pick and I'm a fucking glacier.

Detective Jameson.

The first time I met the man was in a room just like this, waking up with a broken chest and half a life left to piece together. He drilled me that day, drilled me for answers as to what happened, and I was honest.

I was too broken to keep it bottled in.

I told him Johnny Rita murdered my wife.

He told me he'd get justice.

He never did.

The man *lied* to me.

I can respect a murderer, and a thief, but I have no respect for someone who lies straight to my face. Say what you mean and mean what you say or don't say anything at all.

Life is too short to have the bullshit sugarcoated.

Detective Jameson strolls into the room, smiling a fake wide smile, his younger partner on his heels. I don't have much experience with Detective Andrews, personally, but he doesn't beat around the bush, doesn't force a smile or pretend to be somebody he's not. He's a real prick, and that almost makes me like him.

Almost.

"Mr. Vitale," Detective Jameson says, strolling toward the bed. "Sorry to hear what happened to you."

"I'm sure you are."

"I am. I'm happy to see you're moving around, though. Are you...?" He pauses, theatrically glancing around. "You aren't going somewhere already, are you?"

I don't humor that with a response, straining myself as I settle back into the bed. I can't get up now, not with all of them here. I'll probably fall flat on my face, and I won't give them that satisfaction.

Not to mention I'm wearing nothing but a backless hospital gown, and there's no sign of my clothes anywhere.

"Where would I go?" I ask.

"Good question," Jameson says, taking a seat in the black chair, not waiting for an invitation to hang around, while his partner leans against the wall nearby. The uniformed officers linger out in the hallway, not coming any closer. They're just here for back up.

For what? I don't know.

Not like I'd hurt any of them in the middle of a hospital in broad daylight.

No, I'd slip into their houses after nightfall instead.

"We just want to ask you a few questions in regards to the incident that happened last night," the detective continues, pulling a small notebook out of his jacket pocket, along with a pen. He flips it open to the first blank page, not looking at me as he asks, "Can you tell me who shot you?"

My response is immediate. "Yes."

Silence swallows the room for a few seconds before the man meets my eyes, raising an eyebrow. "Well?"

"Well what?"

"Are you going to tell me?"

"No."

His brow furrows. "No?"

"You asked if I could, not if I would," I clarify. "I have no intention of telling you anything."

Andrews chimes in, clearing his throat. "If you're afraid of retaliation—"

A sharp bark of laughter rocks my chest. I grimace, tears stinging my eyes, pain running through my body from the jolt like a bolt of electric striking my veins. I look away from the men, clenching my jaw and closing my eyes to push back the sensation.

When I reopen my eyes, my gaze hits the doorway and I stall, frozen at the unexpected sight. Karissa stands there, leaning quietly against the doorframe, wearing a too-big black t-shirt and a pair of flannel pants, looking like she just crawled out of bed. Her hair is piled wildly on top of her head, knotted and twisted, pieces falling down around her weary face. There are lines on her cheeks, a redness streaking the skin that only comes from an assault of recent tears.

She looks broken, but so goddamn beautiful.

I want to put her back together.

I want to break her down even more.

Her eyes meet mine, and my chest tightens at the distress I find lurking in the depths. There's sadness, yes, but even more I see the fear.

Is she still afraid of me?

73

Why is she even here?

Sighing, I drag my eyes from hers and look at the detectives again. I'm too exhausted and humiliated and in too much pain to keep up this charade. Jameson is speaking again, going on and on about the same nonsense, about keeping the streets safe, knowing good and damn well I'm one of the worst offenders in this godforsaken city. We both know it, but he can't prove it, so his half-hearted lecture falls on deaf ears, little more than the narcissistic wank of an ignorant man who craves power but can't even take down one measly murderous scumbag.

It burns him.

I'd like to set his house on fire and burn him for real some days.

"You want to know who shot me?" I ask, cutting him off. They both look at me, wide-eyed and hopeful, as Jameson clutches his notebook tightly. "Here, let me spell it for you, to make it easier. I want to make sure it doesn't get lost in translation."

Jameson waves his pen toward me. "I'm ready."

"It's, uh... F-U-C-K. Last name Y-O-U. You got that? Or do you need me to spell it again?"

Before the last word even leaves my lips, Jameson closes his notebook and stands up, shoving it back into his pocket. He knows it's pointless. He's getting not a damn thing from me. He motions toward the door, and Andrews heads that way as Jameson lingers, eyeing me peculiarly like he has something more to say.

Whatever it is, it's a waste of breath, breath he ought to save, because who knows when he might run out of those. He seems to think better of it after a moment and shakes his head, turning away.

Karissa's head is down, her eyes on the floor as she presses her back against the wall right inside the room, moving out of their way. Andrews walks right by her with little more than a scowl on his face, but Jameson pauses and smiles warmly. "Nice to see you again, Miss Reed."

"You, too."

Her voice is low, barely a whispers that cracks around those meager words. Jameson leaves, the uniformed officers trailing behind him, leaving the two of us alone.

I can't believe she's actually here.

It's dead silent, except for the noises out in the hallway. Karissa stands there for a moment before her eyes shift that way, like she's thinking of jetting out the door already. My stomach coils at the thought of her leaving, but I force the feeling back as I clear my throat, knowing she won't be the one to break this silence.

"You're here."

She doesn't respond right away, her eyes drifting along the scuffed linoleum floor again, before her gaze finally shifts my way. "Why wouldn't I be?"

Because you hate me.

Because I killed your father.

Because your mother's next, and based on that look in your eyes, I think you know it.

"Because you weren't here when I woke up this morning."

"Oh." She pushes away from the wall to trudge through the room, plopping down on the black chair that remained vacant all night long without her. She kicks off her flip flops and pulls her filthy feet up, tucking them beneath her as she settles in. "Well, we're not related, and they only let family stay overnight, so…"

"So they wouldn't let you back here."

"Yes."

Anger stirs inside of me. It's one thing for her not to come; it's another thing for them to turn her away. I can't fault her, as much as it stings, but I most certainly will hold it against them. "Did you tell them who you are to me?"

"No." Her voice is even smaller now. "You were out of it, so it wouldn't have mattered. I just stayed down in the waiting room until they told me you were awake."

"You stayed there all night?"

She nods slightly, tinkering with her hands, picking at her nails. My gaze shifts to them, the skin pink and scrubbed raw. I wonder how many times to washed her hands to rid them of my blood. Her engagement ring is visibly absent, a fact that doesn't surprise me. She never even put it back on.

Maybe it's an act of rebellion.

A way to assert some control in an out-of-control situation.

Or maybe she wants nothing to do with ever marrying me.

I don't ask her about it, though, and she's never brought it up. She sits there silently, attention focused on her lap, before she lets out a sigh. "I thought you were going to die."

I can't tell how she feels from her hollow voice, so I ask a question I dread. "Are you disappointed I *didn't?*"

It's like zero to sixty in a second flat, her head turning, narrowed eyes meeting mine. Tears swim in the corners, threatening to spill over as she glares at me with so much hostility, if I weren't so goddamn injured, I might move away from it. The woman tells me I'm a monster, but there's a little beast in her that she unleashes from time to time.

I probably shouldn't love it as much as I do.

"I should be," she says, her voice shaking as she fights to keep those tears from falling. "I should want you dead. God knows you probably deserve it. I should hate you... I *do* hate you. Some days I wake up and wish you'd disappear, so I'd never have to look at your face again... but then I thought you might. I thought you might actually die. I though you *were* dying." She pauses, a tear breaking free. She wipes it away with her fingertips as she looks away from me, laughing bitterly under her breath. "I thought I might never see your face again, might never hear your lying voice again, and that hurt more than I expected it to."

I watch her as she brushes away another tear... and another... before I respond. "I've never lied to you."

"You keep saying that," she says, her voice an octave higher than just a moment ago, stronger, like maybe admitting she might not like to see me dead lifted a weight off her chest. "And the sad part is, I think you actually believe it."

"I do," I say. "I've never lied to you."

"Well maybe that's true in whatever universe you live in, but here in the real world there's such a thing as lying by omission, and it hurts just as bad. You deceived me. You played me. Toyed with me. The whole time we were together I wondered 'why me?' And now I know why. You were manipulating me! So maybe you didn't lie to my face, but you certainly weren't being honest. You weren't being real. You can't smile and act like you love me one second then destroy my world the very next. You can't do that and expect me to still trust you, Naz."

You can't smile and act like you love me one second then destroy my world the very next. Those words hit me like a punch to the chest. Somebody did that to me once, and I certainly never forgave him for it.

"I never tried to be somebody I wasn't," I respond. "Maybe I didn't show you all my cards up front, but I never misled you about what game we were playing."

"It's not supposed to be a game!"

"That's where you're wrong," I say. "The world is a game, Karissa. There are winners and losers in life, and I did everything in my power—and I'll always do everything in my power—to make sure I never lose. Maybe I have to cheat sometimes, and I don't always play fair, but I can't. Not if I want to survive it. You can hate me for that, but it won't stop me from protecting you. It won't stop me from making sure you win, too."

"And what if you can't?" She finally meets my eyes again. She's putting it all out in front of me, her heart on her sleeve, airing her grievances instead of bottling them in. "What if we both can't win?"

"I've already told you what happens then."

"What?"

"I give you the plank, Karissa."

77

It takes a moment for her to understand. The Plank of
Carneades. If only one of us could survive, who would it be? Some
people believe murder is justified when it's vital to save yourself. And
while I'm not one to frown upon stealing another life, there are
certain people I could never bring myself to take from this world.

Certain people like her.

Just her.

Because a world without her in it, I'm not sure is a world worth
living in anyway. I've lived a life of darkness already, years where the
sun didn't shine on me, and now that I've seen daylight again, I don't
think I could ever turn my back to it.

She stares at me, not bothering to brush away a stray tear when
it breaks free. It falls from her chin into her lap as she shakes her
head, like she can't believe what I'm telling her.

She doesn't respond, doesn't press the issue, as she shifts around
in the chair and lays her head against the arm of it, using the hard
surface as a makeshift pillow. Silence smothers the room for a few
minutes, neither of us speaking or even moving. My eyes are glued to
Karissa as hers slowly drift closed.

Hours pass, each tick of the clock agonizing. I'm stiff and tired,
annoyed and in pain, wanting to be anywhere but in this goddamn bed.

People leave me alone, stepping into the doorway and glancing
in, but moving on without addressing me. It's late afternoon when
Karissa reawakens, stretching and yawning, clearly uncomfortable
sleeping in that chair.

She should be at home.

We should *both* be at home.

"You don't happen to know where the clothes I came here in
are, do you?"

Karissa's attention shifts my way. "They were ruined."

"And you didn't bring me any extra?"

"No," she says. "Why?"

"Because I'd like to get the hell out of this place."

"You want to leave? Already?"

"I shouldn't have even come here."

"You were hurt," she says incredulously, sitting up straighter. "Like, seriously hurt. This is exactly where you need to be."

"There's nothing they can do for me," I say. "I'm not going to eat their food or take their drugs, not going to sleep in this bed with people I don't know lurking around. The only thing that can help me at this point is rest, and I'm not going to get that here."

"But—"

"Look, I'll walk out of here like this if it comes down to it," I say, motioning toward myself, "but I'd rather not have to."

She looks at me with disbelief. "Like that?"

"Yes."

"Wearing that gown?"

"Yes."

Her expression cracks with a small smile, one she quickly wards off, but she isn't fast enough. I caught it, and that smile is all I need to lessen some of the pressure in my chest.

Shaking her head, she stretches her legs out in front of her before standing up. "Let me see what I can do."

She strolls out, leaving me in the room by myself. Once alone again, I grit my teeth and force myself to a sit, shifting my body so my legs hang off the side of the bed. I lightly grasp the bandage on my side, breathing deeply, steadily, to try to ward off the pain.

I expect her to be gone for a while, and I have to piss like a son of a bitch, so I force myself up, gripping ahold of the bed as I steady myself on my feet.

My vision blurs and my body burns as I shuffle across the room toward the small, adjoining bathroom, shutting myself inside.

I struggle to relieve myself, one hand gripping the sink, the other only vaguely aiming as I piss all over the toilet seat. I wash my hands before shuffling back away, startled by the sound of the voice as soon as I step into the room.

"Whoa," Karissa says, standing just inside the doorway. "You're up."

"You're back."

"I am," she says, stepping around me. Her face flushes, that smile touching her lips again. "Here, found these."

She hands me a ball of dark blue clothing—a pair of medical scrubs. "You get these from a doctor?"

"Got them from *someone*," she says. "Found them in the staff locker room on the first floor."

"You stole them?"

"Borrowed them."

Shaking my head, I eye them peculiarly. They're clean and look damn near a perfect fit. Making my way over to the bed, I grip on to the frame to steady myself as I pull off the gown, letting it drop to the floor.

Karissa gasps, shielding her face. "You're going to do that right here?"

I let out a small chuckle, the laughter only fueling the pain more. "Yeah, well, it's nothing you haven't seen before."

"Maybe so, but the whole world can see it right now."

"I'm not ashamed," I say, sitting on the edge of the bed to try to put on the pants, but it's damn near impossible. I can't bend over to pull them up my fucking legs. My eyes water from agony as I struggle in silence for a moment before Karissa grabs a hold of them, wordlessly helping to put them on.

I take over once they're within my reach, covering up, and grab her arm when she tries to move away. Her face is bright red, bashful, and she avoids looking me in the eyes when I pull her my way.

"Don't be embarrassed," I say. "I'm certainly not. Besides, I seem to remember you taking *your* clothes off last night."

"You were bleeding. I had to use something."

"You keep telling yourself that," I say, letting go of her. "I always knew there was a little bit of an exhibitionist in you."

She rolls her eyes, but she doesn't deny it.

The shirt is much easier to pull on than the pants. After I'm dressed, I survey myself, satisfied I'm no longer indecent. "Thanks for swiping the clothes for me."

"I borrowed them," she stresses again.

"Whatever you want to call it, jailbird," I say, glancing at her and raising an eyebrow. "You ready to get out of here?"

She doesn't answer right away, as if contemplating my question, but eventually offers a shrug as if to say, 'what the hell, let's go.' I follow her out of the room and into the busy hallway. I'm moving as slow as a tortoise, each step painful but I force myself to keep going, my bare feet slapping against the filthy fucking floor.

"How'd we get here, anyway?" I ask as we head toward the elevators.

"Ambulance."

"Do you have any money on you?"

"Uh, no, I don't think so."

I sigh as we pause in front of the elevator. "We're going to need to find a way home."

As soon as I say it, I glance up, my footsteps faltering when I see Ray standing at the nurse's station. Just as I spot him, the nurse on duty points my direction. Ray turns, eyeing me right away.

Karissa stalls beside me, stepping closer to my side as he approaches. I put my arm around her, instinctively, protectively, but more so to lean on her.

I'm unsteady on my feet.

Ray momentarily ignores her presence when he stops in front of us, focused fully on me. His eyes study me, picking me apart, like he's looking for weaknesses. "Leaving already, Vitale?"

"Yes," I say. "What are you doing here?"

"Just came to check in on you," he says. "You sped away last night, wasn't sure what happened, but I heard you'd been shot."

"Just a flesh wound," I say. "I've had worse."

"That you have," he says, nodding. "Well, come on, let me give you a ride home."

81

I start to argue, but I don't have a leg to stand on. What can I say? We have no other way to get anywhere. I stagger onto the elevator as Karissa stays at my side, the three of us heading to an awaiting limo, the driver still waiting behind the wheel.

It's strained, the whole way to Brooklyn, as I sit in the back of the extravagant vehicle beside Karissa, right across from Ray. Nobody speaks. Nobody knows what to say. My mind is a jumble of thoughts, my body in agony, my chest heavy from the implications.

When we pull up in front of my house, Ray clears his throat. "Can I have a moment of your time, Vitale?"

Hesitating, I relax back in the seat, motioning for Karissa to go ahead inside. She leaves, closing the door behind her, and we sit in silence for a moment. I stare out the window, my eyes drifting to my car in the driveway, the side of it ravished by bullet holes.

Ray looks apprehensive, his eyes shifting from me to my car in the driveway. "Who did this?"

A lie is on the tip of my tongue. I try to swallow it back, but it springs free. "I don't know."

I've never lied to Ray before.

"You don't know?"

"No," I say. "They blindsided me, stole my wallet and my keys, then panicked and shot me."

"And you don't know who it was?"

"No," I say. "I don't."

His eyes meet mine again, guarded, as he seems to consider all of it. He doesn't believe me, I see it in his eyes, but he, too, knows I've never lied to him. He doesn't want to think things have changed between us. I don't want to think it, either, but I feel it.

I feel the shift before he even addresses it.

"You're getting soft, Vitale. You let someone shoot you. You let them rob you and get away with it."

"Just because they got away last night doesn't mean they'll get away with it," I say. "I always get my revenge."

"Revenge," Ray echoes, letting out a dry laugh. "I'm starting to think we have different definitions of that. I thought revenge meant payback, justice, an eye for an eye... a family for a family... not taking the easy way out."

Easy. I shake my head. "That's where we differ, Ray. You seem to think what I did was easy for me, that letting go of a plan I spent almost two decades plotting was easy, but you're wrong, because there was nothing easy about it. I still feel like I failed, like I didn't get any justice for Maria."

"You didn't," he says, matter-of-fact, those words piercing me like a knife to the chest. "You pissed on my daughter's memory by letting Carmela live."

"Yeah, well, that's only temporary."

After last night, there's no way around it.

I can't let Carmela continue to walk the streets after what she just did. I tried to give her a pass, a chance to flee for Karissa's sake, but it's too late now.

She made a grave mistake.

"And their kid?" Ray asks, turning to look at me. I don't look his way, but from the corner of my eye I can see his serious expression. "Karissa?"

"What about her?"

"You're just going to let her live," he says. "You let her go on breathing, living in that house that should've been my daughter's, sleeping in your bed, sleeping with *you*, giving her the life my daughter should've had, the life my daughter could've had, would've had, and you're going to fucking give it to her? *Her*?"

Every word from his lips stabs at me, eating away at my insides like festering poison, tearing me apart one syllable at a time. He's not saying anything I haven't thought myself more than once, the sense of betrayal already existing inside of me, but the accusatory tone in which he spews it only stirs it up more.

I feel like I'm going to pass out.

"The daughter of my daughter's murderer," he mutters. "That's who you chose, who you let replace her."

"Nobody will ever replace her," I say, having to force the words out through the swell of emotion in my chest. "I'm not trying to replace anyone, but I can't help how I feel about Karissa."

"Guess we disagree there, too," Ray says. "You could've helped it. You could've avoiding all of this by slitting that bitch's throat like you were supposed to. Isn't that what you said, Vitale? *Make her choke on the filthy blood that created her.*"

I damn near flinch when he says it, the anger in his voice an echo of mine the first time I said those exact words. It was only months ago, weeks that somehow turned me into someone I don't know. I get Ray's confusion. How can he understand what I'm still coming to terms with? For damn near twenty years I dreamed of bleeding every single one of them dry, and now that it's within my reach, I hesitate.

No, I don't hesitate.

I change my mind.

I do a full reversal, a fucking one-eighty, practically overnight because of Karissa.

She's not just under my skin, she's in my organs, wrapped up in my cells, infecting me.

"I'm just trying to understand, Vitale," he says. "Just trying to understand how you can bear to breathe the same air as that girl and not spend every second of it thinking it should be my daughter breathing instead. That it should be your daughter, or your son, instead of Johnny's kid. How can you be with her, fuck her, do things with her you used to do with my daughter, and not still want to slit her fucking throat because of how unjust it is?"

I'm not sure what to say, how to respond to that. I sit there for a moment, not moving, still staring out the window. "She wasn't part of the original plan."

"Plans change."

Torture to her Soul

"Exactly," I say. "And they've changed again. Killing her would make me no better than Johnny, and that's not the kind of man your daughter loved in the first place. Killing Karissa won't do Maria's memory any justice. Killing Karissa will just make it all worse."

I climb out of the car then, not bothering to thank him for the ride. I start to close the door, hearing his voice just before it slams between us. "Another thing we'll have to disagree on."

Standing on the curb, I watch as the limo pulls away, disappearing down the street. Shaking my head, I turn to the house, staggering that direction.

The first thing I see when I step inside, the first thing my eyes are drawn to, are the smears of dried blood all over the floor around my bare feet. I glare at the streaks of dark red, sighing exasperatedly, as Karissa steps into the foyer in front of me.

I close my eyes.

Deep breaths.

Inhale.

Exhale.

I can't clean it up now.

I'll do it later.

Don't worry about it.

When I reopen my eyes, Karissa's right in front of me. She reaches around where I stand, securing the locks on the door, as I run my hands down my face.

It's probably senseless.

I'm not sure if Carmela knows where I live. It's not listed on my license, but if she knows, if she finds out, she now has a key to the place. I know she's smart, but she's also proven to be fearless, and that can be a deadly combination.

As if I weren't paranoid enough before...

Karissa helps me upstairs the best she can. I collapse on the bed on my back, legs hanging off the edge, as my eyes drift closed right away. I don't want to sleep, I shouldn't risk it, but I can't help it. She says something to me, her voice gentle, her fingers even gentler as they run through my chaotic hair, but I don't comprehend it.

The pull is too strong to fight.

Chapter Seven

Appear as you may wish to be.

I sleep deeply, long hours lost in the abyss, time slipping away, before I finally regain consciousness. I lay in the darkness and stare up at the ceiling as I blink rapidly, trying to come back around.

I'm alone in the room.

My head is pounding and my body feels like it's on fire. I don't dare move a muscle yet, eyes trailing the ceiling fan as it spins around and around, blowing a hint of cool air on my sweaty face.

I'm weak—so fucking weak it hurts to blink, taking every ounce of energy I have left to keep breathing. It would be too easy for someone to end my life today. I'm vulnerable, and susceptible, still alive for the moment but feeling like I've already got one foot in the grave.

I've felt that way for a long time, actually.

I wonder when the other foot will finally join it.

I'm still tired, but I need to stay awake, so I close my eyes to steel myself, gritting my teeth as I force myself out of the bed. Time waits for no man. The world won't just roll over and take it. I have to face it head on, pick myself up and trudge forward as long as I can.

I can't be weak.

I have to be strong.

My legs feel heavy but my footsteps are light, slow and measured, as I make my way downstairs. I head for the kitchen, the light on in that room, my mouth as dry as sand, my throat raw like scratched with sandpaper. Stepping in the doorway, I pause when I see Karissa standing at the counter beside the sink, haphazardly chopping some vegetables and throwing them in a pot on the stove.

She struggles with the knife as she massacres a carrot, the sections uneven, pieces flying all around. Shaking my head, I stroll into the kitchen, watching her with a morbid sort of amusement. "Nobody ever taught you how to use a knife?"

My voice seems magnified by the silence. Karissa jumps, the sound of it catching her off guard. The knife slips as she brings it down on the carrot, slicing right into her pointer finger. Cursing, she instantly lets go of the knife and it clatters to the floor.

"Shit, shit, shit!" she chants as she hops around. "Jesus, Naz! You scared me!"

I say nothing, pausing beside her, grabbing her wrist and pulling her hand toward me to see the cut. Before I can get a good look, she yanks away, plunging the wounded finger into her mouth, wrapping her lips around it with a scowl on her face.

Nausea swims through me. I can almost taste the blood myself.

Disgusting.

I brush by her to open up the drawer closest to the refrigerator. It's full of this and that, a little bit of everything, one of the only drawers in the kitchen that doesn't sit empty. I search around inside, pulling out a small first-aide kit. I set it on the counter and pop it open, grabbing a Band-Aid.

I take her hand again, pulling her finger out from between her lips. I stare at it for a moment as a bead of blood surfaces from the small wound. The cut isn't too deep, she doesn't need stitches, but it obviously stings by the look on her face.

For years I sought this blood—hunted it down so I could drain it, to stop the heart that beats it, to rid the world of that disgraceful bloodline. I never imagined one tiny drop would have such an affect, how her pain, no matter how trivial, would inflict that same sort of ache in me.

Karissa doesn't fight me, watching silently as I open the bandage. "You know, there should be some rule that says only one of us is allowed to bleed per day."

"It's after midnight," she whispers. "You haven't bled yet today."

Yet.

Laughing dryly, I wrap the bandage around her finger, covering the wound. Bringing her finger to my lips, I lightly kiss it before letting go of her hand. "It's kind of late to be cooking."

"Your, uh... that doctor stopped by and he dropped off some prescriptions, and gave some instructions... you know, rest and drink fluids and stuff like that. He said you should try to eat something but that you probably couldn't handle much yet, so I just thought..."

She trails off, still not answering my question. "You thought?"

"I thought I'd make you some broth."

"Broth?"

"Uh, yeah, I guess it's more like soup since it's got chicken and carrots and celery and—" Her voice stumbles as she turns away from me to stir whatever's in the pot. She cuts her eyes my way after a second and frowns at my expression. "It's just that stuff, and some water and seasonings. That's it. Nothing else."

I want to believe her.

I really do.

"We didn't have any broth in the cabinet? I thought I saw a carton of it somewhere."

She grimaces. "There are certain things you shouldn't *ever* drink out of a box, and chicken broth is one of them."

"I'm guessing wine is another?" I ask, leaning back against the counter.

"I like boxed wine," she says. "It's cheap and does the trick."

"Well, I don't mind chicken broth out of a carton," I say, shrugging as I push away from the counter. "It hasn't killed me yet."

I start to walk out when I hear her voice, quiet as she mutters, "*I won't kill you, either.*"

I don't hang around, shuffling my way to the den. The scent of bleach reaches my nose as soon as I step in the doorway. My eyes trail the floor and along the couch, surveying the area, before turning around and glancing toward the front door.

All of the blood is gone.

Everything looks back in order, scrubbed and sanitized, every reminder of what happened here completely wiped away while I slept upstairs. A feeling stirs in the pit of my stomach that I instinctively try to shove back, but I'm too exhausted for pretenses, too drained to put on a mask.

Gratitude.

She cleaned up the mess I made, wiped up the spilled blood caused by her mother's hands. She didn't have to do it, but she did.

Sighing, I step into the den and settle on the couch, leaning my head back and closing my eyes, trying to breathe through the twinges of pain. I should go back to bed but I feel disconnected up there, trapped in a void where time doesn't exist.

I haven't been sitting here for more than a few minutes, nearly dozing off already again, my body on the verge of shutting down as it tries to process, when I feel something cover me. The material rubs against my skin, soft but startling. My eyes open, instantly meeting Karissa's as she drapes a blanket over my body.

That gratitude swells up again, but I shove it back down. "Why are you doing this?"

She smoothes the blanket before sitting gently down on the small table right in front of the couch, so close her knees rub against mine. It's a startling change from just the last time we sat in this room together, when she did everything in her power not to have any part of her touch any part of me. Hours feel like weeks, days like an eternity, but I know it was less than forty-eight hours ago.

Two days, and such a drastic difference.

"You had goose bumps," she says quietly. "I figured you were cold."

"I'm not just talking about the blanket. Why are you doing *any* of it?"

"Because you're hurt. You were just shot, Naz. Just yesterday. You shouldn't even be out of the hospital yet, much less trying to walk around like you're fine."

"But I am," I say. "I'm fine, Karissa. It's not the first time this happened to me."

"I know."

"And it probably won't be the last, either," I continue. "I can take care of myself. I've been doing it for longer than you've been alive. I don't need you to pretend to give a shit about me now just because I'm injured, because I'll heal, sweetheart. I'll be just as good as new, with or without your pity."

She pulls her hands away, hurt flashing across her face that dissolves quickly in a barrage of anger. Narrowed eyes focus on me as she clenches her hands into fists on her lap. "Do you *have* to be such an asshole? I'm just trying to help."

"Why?"

"Because you're *hurt*," she says again. "And regardless of what you think, it's not pity, or whatever the hell else you want to call it. Maybe you think you don't need anyone, and maybe you don't... I don't know... but that doesn't mean you don't *deserve* someone. You shouldn't have to be alone or take care of yourself right now, not when someone else can do it for you."

"Why would *you* do it? Why would you help me?"

"Because it's the right thing to do."

I stare at her as I mull over those words. She stares back for a moment before cracking, looking away as she shakes her head. She

91

starts to stand up when I let out a resigned sigh. We're at an impasse, and we're never going to break it if one of us doesn't give.

One of us meaning *me*.

She's conceding as much as she can.

"It's not your fault," I say quietly, my words drawing her attention back to me. Her brow furrows as I continue. I haven't told her who shot me... I haven't told anybody. But I can feel the shame wafting off of her, regardless. "If you're doing this out of some twisted sense of guilt, if you think it's because you owe me..."

"It's not that," she says quickly, although the tone of her voice tells me it is, at least partially. "I thought I was watching you die, Naz. That's not something I want to go through again. And I know you don't trust me. I don't know if you'll ever trust me again, but I'm not trying to trick you. I'm not trying to hurt you, or do anything except help. I just want to help you. That's it. Can you just... give me the benefit of the doubt?"

I have half a dozen reasons not to trust her, not to believe a single word she says. History certainly is on my side when it comes to that family. But I just told her this wasn't her fault. Holding it against her now would make me less of a man than I try to be... less of a man than I *want* to be.

Leaning my head back again, I close my eyes, drawing on her words from just days ago about the coffee machine. "Thank you for the blanket, Karissa. I appreciate it."

Give and take, I remind myself. There has to be give and take.

"You're welcome." Her voice is quiet. I feel her legs brush against mine, get a whiff of her fragrant perfume as she shifts closer, seconds later feeling her soft lips against my cheek. "Sweet dreams."

Sweet dreams. It's a nice sentiment.

But my dreams are never sweet.

I only have nightmares.

Memories.

The same one, over and over, time and time again.

The pain.

The anguish.

The gunshots.

Bang.

BANG

I drift off to sleep again right there on the couch, in and out of consciousness the rest of the night, trying to shift position, trying to get comfortable, but there's no relief to be found. Something wakes me around dawn, early morning sunshine streaming through the windows and illuminating the wooden floor, casting everything around me in gold tones. I'm shivering, heart racing wildly, a cold sweat coating my body from head to toe.

I need a shower.

And a fucking shave.

Something.

I lay completely still, straining my ears to try to riddle out what disturbed me, swallowing back the swell of nausea when I realize it was the front door.

It opened, and closed, the locks jingling. Soft footsteps descend upon the house, restrained like someone is trying to sneak from the living room into the kitchen, things shifting around, drawers opening.

Forcing myself up, I grasp the bandaged wound on my side, holding it like I'm trying to hold myself together. I slowly make my way out of the den, on alert, vision fuzzy and head foggy.

I'm a fucking mess.

If someone tried to attack me right now, they'd take me down easily. My blinks are accentuated by blackness, my reactions slowed.

I quietly make my way toward the kitchen and pause in the doorway, a sense of relief calming the tension in my muscles when I see it's Karissa. *Just Karissa.* She's dressed in a pair of cut-off jean shorts, barely covering her curvy backside, and a white tank top that's downright sinful.

I lean against the doorframe, unable to sustain all my weight on my tired legs, as I watch her. I need some energy back, and I need it back quick. Just staggering here took it all out of me. A few grocery bags surround her on the floor that she digs through, pulling things out to put away. Her earbuds are in her ears, the faint sound of music reaching me.

I wonder what she's listening to, but I don't ever ask.

She takes a fresh box of Cocoa Puffs and reaches up on her tiptoes to shove it onto the top of a cabinet. Her shirt rides up as she does, my eyes drawn to the sliver of exposed skin. She can be self-conscious about her body sometimes, especially when she catches me watching her, tugging fabric to cover up places she doesn't want me to look. It's senseless, though, because I know every inch of her.

I memorized every curve and crevice, every scar and scratch marking her skin. It's unforgettable, the dimples on the small of her back, the ridges of her ribcage when she's stretched out straight, the strain of her fingers when they clutch onto me, the curl of her toes when pleasure overwhelms her. She's perfectly imperfect, down to the scattering of freckles along her back and dotting her flushed cheeks.

Everything about her is beautiful to me.

Even when she's scowling, when she's angry and full of hate. She's beautiful when she cries, when she's in the throes of grief. She's beautiful when she smiles, when she laughs at me. But she's the most beautiful when she's doing nothing. When she thinks nobody's looking, when she thinks she's alone. Her walls are down, her defenses off, and the real Karissa shines through. She's pensive and passive, a calm breeze in the middle of a storm that somehow pacifies me. She gets lost somewhere up in that head of hers, and as much as I hate when she overthinks things, she's goddamn beautiful when she does it.

If I were hard pressed to explain why I fell in love with her, that would be my answer. *Because she's beautiful.* And I don't mean it in a superficial way. You're not going to find her on the cover of a magazine. She's more the kind you find at a museum, on a painting or in a piece of literature. Her beauty is in her soul.

She has enough of that for both of us.

Karissa drops down flat on her feet and turns back to the bags, jumping when she catches me standing here. She yanks the earbuds out, the music growing a little louder, as she lets out a gasp. "Jesus, you're practically an invalid and you *still* sneak up on me!"

"An invalid?" I raise an eyebrow at her. "Are you calling me worthless?"

"Well..." She gives me a playful smile as she steps toward me. "If the shoe fits."

"I'm wounded."

"You are," she points out, motioning toward my side. Her expression shifts the closer she gets to me, worry lining her face. The tranquility fades as once more turmoil takes over. Pausing in front of me, she reaches up and cups my cheek. "You're sweating like crazy, Naz. What are you doing standing here?"

"Thinking about how beautiful you are."

It's the truth.

That's exactly what I was doing.

I don't think I've told her that enough.

She rolls her eyes, the flush on her cheeks deepening, as she reaches up to feel my forehead. "You've got to have a fever."

Grasping her wrist, I pull her hand away from me and shake my head. "I'm fine."

"So you keep saying." She steps back and hesitates before walking over to where her purse sits on the counter. She searches through it for a moment, pulling out two orange pill bottles, and turns back to me. "I went and got your prescriptions filled, grabbed some other stuff while I was waiting for them. I didn't know what kind of health insurance you had..."

"I don't have any."

She looks genuinely surprised. "None?"

"No."

"You should really have some."

"Do *you* have health insurance?"

She doesn't. I know she doesn't. Her shake of the head doesn't surprise me a bit. Insurance means records, which means a trail of paperwork that can lead someone straight to you.

"Well, I don't need any," I say. "My doctor takes cash payments instead."

"*Anyway,*" she says, disregarding my statement as she holds up the pill bottles. "I went ahead and just paid full price for them, you know, since I didn't know if you had any coverage, and I didn't want to wake you up to ask."

"I appreciate it, but you shouldn't have bothered," I say. "I have no plans to take them."

Her expression falls quickly as she looks between the pill and me. "If you're worried... I mean, if you think *I* messed with them, I swear I didn't. You can count the pills... check them. You'll see."

"It's not that."

"Then what is it?"

"I don't like being medicated."

"But you need them," she says, shaking the pill bottles at me. "Ones an antibiotic. You don't want to get any sicker. And the other's just for the pain. I know you *have* to be in pain."

"I'm fine."

"No, you're *not,*" she says, raising her voice, the last word cracking a bit as she forces it from her lips. I can see the gleam in her eyes from where I stand, unshed tears building around the edges. "You're being stubborn. You won't eat my soup, you won't take your medicine, you won't *rest*... I had to fight with you to get you to accept a damn blanket. You tell me *I* overthink things. Ha! Look at *you*! You're worse than I am!"

She's yelling at me.

Yelling.

She's beautiful when she yells, too.

A smile cracks my face, but it does nothing to calm her down. If anything, it gets her more riled up. She glares at the sight of it, cocking her head as she studies me. "What are you smiling at?"

"You," I admit. "You're still so beautiful."

"And you're goddamn delirious," she says, her voice dead serious as she steps toward me again, thrusting the pill bottles right at my chest. I wince as she hits me, nearly stumbling backward, letting out a low hiss as the jolt in my body makes the fire in the wound rage. Her expression shifts as if she's been doused with a bucket of ice water, eyes wide with regret. "I'm sorry, I—"

"Don't apologize," I say, clutching hold of the bottles. "I figured you'd like seeing me suffer."

"Yeah, well, you figured wrong," she says. "Believe it or not, I'm not that kind of person. I'm not a sadistic freak who gets off watching others struggle."

I stare at her as she takes a step back away from me. There's a fire in her today, stronger than it's ever been before, but I don't think she has it in her to be intentionally cruel. "Like me, you mean?"

"What?"

I palm both bottles in my left hand, reaching for her with my right. She startles as I run my fingertips down her neck, my hand coming to rest at the base of her throat. "A sadistic freak who gets off on others struggling."

"I didn't mean it that way. I wasn't calling you—"

Before she can finish, I pull my hand from her skin and turn away from her, shaking the pill bottles. "I'll consider taking the antibiotic."

"What about the pain killer?"

"I don't want to kill the pain," I say. "If I stop feeling it, I might forget."

"Forget you're wounded?"

"Forget *someone* wounded me."

97

She doesn't respond to that, standing silently as I toss the bottle of narcotics straight into the trashcan before setting the antibiotic on the counter. Shuffling over to the refrigerator, I grab a bottle of water and unscrew the cap, taking a sip.

"Masochistic," she mutters. "That's what you are."

"Those are some pretty powerful words for someone who just used her first safe words two months ago."

Rolling her eyes, she fishes the pain killers right back out from the top of the trash can and sets the bottle on the counter with the other. "Just think about taking them both, okay? I think you've suffered enough. No reason to torture yourself. God knows you torture *me* enough for the both of us."

She starts to walk out as I lean back against the counter beside the refrigerator. "Sounds like you're calling me sadistic again."

"Yeah, well, like I said earlier, if the shoe fits…"

I laugh to myself once she's gone, lingering there for a moment, sipping on the water. My thirst is unquenchable, my chest aching and stomach tearing up as wooziness continues to overwhelm me. After a moment, I push away from the counter and stroll out, slowly making my way upstairs.

I desperately need that shower.

I bypass the bedroom, where Karissa lays full dressed on her back on the bed, arm draped over her eyes. I think she slept less than me the past two days and don't want to disturb her when she's trying to rest. Instead I make my way straight to the bathroom, grimacing the second I glance in the mirror.

I took a shotgun blast to the chest and never looked this bad.

I was younger then, more resilient… or maybe I just didn't notice myself back then. The world revolved around everything I lost, when today what matters is that I'm still here. I'm falling apart, and I feel like shit, but I'm alive, and breathing.

And somebody's going to pay for it.

I struggle taking off the sweaty, stolen scrubs I'm still wearing, stripping out of them, leaving them in a pile on the floor. I start the shower, letting the water warm up, as my gaze surveys the white bandage on my side. I pick at the surgical tape, tearing it from my skin. I get it halfway off when there's a light tap on the bathroom door, my name softly called out before it opens.

From the corner of my eye, I see Karissa hesitate when she sees me standing here completely naked, but it only stalls her for a second. I'm still picking at the tape, hissing as I try to rip the bandage off, when she walks over and pushes my hands out of the way.

"Let me get that," she says, gently plucking it from my skin, making a face as she discards the bandage in the trashcan. I step over and survey the damage in the mirror. The wound in front is small, a perfect circle where the bullet sliced through the skin, but the back looks like it exploded out of me. The jagged, misshapen hole was haphazardly sutured closed.

"Oh God," Karissa whispers. "That's horrible."

"It's not so bad," I say. "It'll heal quickly. It'll *all* heal. A few days, and I won't feel it anymore. A week or two, and all I'll be left with are some new scars."

I turn away from her and climb into the shower, not bothering to close the curtain, not caring that I splash water all out on the floor. I'm too exhausted to care about anything today. I expect Karissa to leave me in peace, to walk back out the door, but instead she strolls closer to the shower. "Can I help you?"

"I don't know," I say. "Can you?"

She hesitates, wavering for a moment, before reaching for the hem of her tank top and pulling it off, tossing it to the floor with my clothes. I turn my head, closing my eyes, and let out a deep sigh as she undresses right beside me. I don't look—I can't. She steps into the shower behind me, her hands instantly running up my spine, sending a shiver through my body.

It's agony.

It's not in my nature to let anyone take care of me. I don't like relying on others for anything. But something inside of me breaks at the feel of her hands on my skin, her presence around me, as she tugs the shower curtain closed, casting the two of us in shadows.

She washes me as I stand there, gently cleaning the blood from around my wounds with a soft cloth, trying her damnedest not to hurt me any more. I stand under the spray letting the water rain down on me for a while, neither of us speaking, before the dizziness gets to be too much. Pulling away from her, I sit down on the edge of the tub, leaning my head against the tile wall.

She steps in front of me, under the spray of the water, and gazes down at me. No matter how hard I try not to look, my gaze rakes up her body, drinking in every inch of her frame, before meeting her eyes.

She says nothing.

I don't know what I'm supposed to say.

Instead, I wrap my arms around her, pulling her to me, my head resting against her stomach. She runs her hands through my hair, caressing it, as I close my eyes, letting myself, for the moment, feel it.

Feel it all.

Every bit of it.

Everything I avoid, and push back, and ignore.

I'm in love with the one woman I should never have fallen for.

We're a tragedy in the making. The game of tug-of-war we're playing will end up destroying us, because she doesn't have it in her to surrender, and I can't let go.

It's something else I love about her.

There's a fight in her.

But it's a fight that'll be our downfall.

Because I have that same fight in me.

We still don't speak. I hold her, until the water starts to run cold, a chill in the air making a shiver run through her. She pulls away from me, slips out of my arms, and climbs out of the shower. I sit there for a while longer, listening to her walk out of the bathroom, before reaching over and turning off the water.

Chapter Eight

I give myself one more day.

That's it.

Just one more, before the paranoia gets to be too much and I can't just lay around anymore.

I put on my brave face and force myself back on my feet. There's hell to pay with each small step I take, but I keep making steps despite it.

It feels like there's burning lava in my gut.

I grit my teeth and don't let it show, even when my vision gets hazy, even when my head feels dizzy, even when the pain makes my knees want to buckle beneath me.

Karissa isn't in the bedroom.

It's dusk, I think, or maybe it's nearing dawn. I'm not sure anymore. All I know is the house feels dark. Too dark. I lost hours, too many hours, hours that left me exposed and vulnerable. A nagging feeling continually hounds me, the silence deafening in her absence.

At first I think she's gone, but light streaming out from the bathroom pushes those thoughts back down inside of me. I find the bathroom door cracked open a bit and I push it open further, glancing inside.

She's in the bathtub.

I lean against the doorframe and watch her for a moment. The water teaming with bubbles shields the most intimate places of her body, but I can see enough for my imagination to take over.

Once again, I'm struck by how beautiful she is.

The relief of her presence is enough to dull some of the pain, at least temporarily. She's so ingrained in my life these days, burrowed so deep in my heart, that I think killing her now would really be the death of me.

I managed to survive last time love ripped me apart.

I don't know if I can survive that again.

And that's what Ray doesn't understand, I think.

Ray doesn't understand love anymore. He has a wife, and a mistress, hundreds of men at his beck and call, but I don't think he's ever loved anyone outside of his daughter. Love destroyed him that day, too, and he never recovered.

He doesn't understand how I can.

Karissa's reading, a familiar old book in her hands, one I recognize with just a glance. *The Prince*. I've read it so many times I can quote it verbatim. Based on the crease along her forehead, the puckering of her lips as she glowers, I'd say she doesn't find it nearly as fascinating as I do.

She's reading it, though.

I'll give her some credit.

"The Prince."

My voice sounds magnified in the silent bathroom. She jumps, startled, not noticing me until now. The book slips from her hands, hitting the water with a splash. Cursing, she snatches it back up before it fully submerges, shooting me a panicked look. "Shit, sorry, I didn't mean—"

I hold my hands up to stop her. "Don't apologize."

"But your book," she says, shaking the water off of it. "It's wet."

I stroll toward her, shrugging. "It's just a book."

"It's your favorite book," she says. "I'm guessing, anyway, considering half of it is underlined and highlighted and you scribbled all in the margins. Ugh, and I'm ruining it... I'm sorry, really. I didn't mean to, but you scared me. How the hell do you keep doing that? You'd think I'd be used to it by now."

"You'd think," I say, "but you lack intuition."

She rolls her eyes. "Oh no, I have it, it's just going haywire. I think my mother's getting to me."

Hesitating, I debate for a second before pushing away from the door and slowly strolling over to her. Gritting my teeth at the stabbing pain, I slowly sit down on the edge of the tub. It eases once I'm sitting. "Why do you say that?"

"She was always paranoid, you know, thinking people were watching her, and I guess in her case they sort of were..." She shoots me a pointed look. "But I don't know... I keep getting that feeling, too."

"The feeling that somebody's watching you?"

"Yes. I felt it yesterday, when I went to the store, and then today I went to the driveway, and I know it's only like ten feet but I just..." She trails off, frowning. "I guess I'm just jumpy after what happened to you."

It's not paranoia, I think, although I don't tell her.

It wouldn't surprise me a bit if she were being followed, if people were watching.

It puts me on edge.

"What are you doing, anyway?" she asks, changing the subject. "Why are you even out of bed?"

"I have things to do."

"Yeah," she says incredulously. "Like sleep, and rest, and recover."

"It's just a flesh wound," I say. "Barely even hurts."

She rolls her eyes but doesn't argue with me about it, her attention going to the book once again. "I really am sorry I got your book wet."

"It's fine," I say. "I can buy another copy."

Sighing, she closes the book, her cheeks tingeing pink. "But you'll lose all of your notes."

"Nonsense." I tap my temple. "It's all up here."

"I bet," she says, holding the book out to me, offering it up. I take it, feeling the soggy cover. It's old and vintage, definitely ruined. "It kind of did feel like I was getting a peek at your brain."

"And what was that like?"

"Complicated."

I laugh lightly, cringing. Shit, even *that* hurts. "Is that good or bad?"

She offers me a slight shrug, shifting in the water to pull her knees up further, wrapping her arms around them. The discomfort is creeping in as she tries to shield parts of herself from me, parts she doesn't want me to see.

She's needlessly self-conscious, considering I know every inch of her already.

"Huh." I glance down at the book in my hands as I consider that. "Men judge more by the eye than by the hand, for everyone can see but few ever come in touch with you."

"Are you...?" She twirls her fingers around in the water. "Are you saying you want to feel me up or something?"

I stand up again, shaking my head. "I'm saying you've touched me, Karissa. You've gotten a lot closer than the ones who can only see. That's why it's complicated."

I walk out, leaving her in peace, not wanting her to be any more uncomfortable than she already seems to be.

I drop the soaked book on the dresser in the bedroom before I head for my closet, pulling a suit off the rack. I hear Karissa pad down the hall, coming straight to the bedroom behind me. I cast a glance at her as she stalls right inside the room, clutching a stark white towel around herself as she regards me.

I pull the shirt off the hanger and slowly start putting it on as I look back away from her. It's a matter of seconds before she's in front of me, forcing my hands away to do it for me. "So, uh... are you saying you *don't* want to feel me up then?"

Her playfulness makes me smile. It's nice to hear it again. "I don't think you'll *ever* hear me say that."

Stepping back, I sit down on the edge of the bed to pull on the pants before looking at her again. My eyes trail the slivers of exposed skin in the dim moonlight before meeting her eyes. She's watching me curiously, brow slightly furrowed.

"Are you sure you're okay, Naz?" she asks quietly, stepping closer, wrapping her arms around herself. "I really wish you'd take it easy."

Looking up at her, I study her face, drinking in every drop of her expression. She sounds genuinely worried about me. Slowly, my hands reach for her, starting at her knees and running up her thighs, slipping beneath the towel and coming to rest on her bare hips. I pull her closer to me, between my legs, and rest my head against her stomach.

Again, she doesn't tense up or push me away.

Wordlessly, she runs her fingers through my hair.

"I'll be fine," I mumble as I close my eyes. "I'll relax when everything's taken care of."

"When *what's* taken care of?"

I sit there for a moment, not responding, just relishing touching her. I don't give her a chance to pull away from me again. This time, I let go.

"What time is it?" I ask, looking past her, seeking out my watch, but I have no idea where it could be, nor do I know where my phone is. I'm so out of touch. It's not like me.

"Uh, 7 o'clock, maybe."

"AM or PM?"

She looks at me incredulously. "PM."

"Do you know where my phone is?"

"Downstairs," she says. "On your desk in the den."

Nodding, I stand back up, fastening my pants before stepping past her to seek out some shoes.

"When what's taken care of?" she asks again. "Where are you going?"

Once more, I don't answer her.

She watches me for a moment before turning away, snatching up some clothes for herself and storming out of the room. I hear her as she stomps downstairs, hearing her banging things around and slamming doors.

She's angry.

What else is new?

Chapter Nine

Houses creak, shifting and settling when everyone's in bed at night. I bought this house when it was brand new, just after the last nail had been hammered into the woodwork. Until Karissa moved in months ago, I was the only one to ever occupy these rooms, the only one to walk these halls in the darkness or nap in the den in the daylight.

I started again from scratch.

No memories pad across these hard floors, no stories infuse themselves into these bare walls, but the house still makes noise at night, groaning like it's in mourning for what it never got to be.

Because walls and a roof? They don't make a house a home.

There was a small house on the other side of Brooklyn, within walking distance of my favorite pizzeria, that I used to think of as home. It had one floor, one bedroom, and the smallest kitchen I've ever seen, but it was the first place I ever got to call my own.

It was the first place I ever felt safe and secure.

The first place I found happiness.

The first place I felt love.

But it had nothing to do with the building that stood there. It was what existed inside those walls that made it that way.

I lived there for less than a year... less than a year before my home came under attack... but nineteen years in this house never came close to adding up to what I had there. I understood Karissa when she told me home wasn't a place to her, because it was never one to me, either.

Johnny took my home from me that day.

I burned the house down afterward.

"Guess it's true what they say."

The sound of Karissa's voice draws my attention. Turning around, I see her standing at the bottom of the steps, eyes trained past me at the front door. Early morning sunshine bathes the area around it in a soft orange glow, making the brand new locks lining the door shine brightly. I spent all night fortifying the house, doing everything in my power to make the place secure.

I can't stop Carmela from showing up here, but I'll keep her from getting inside if she does.

"And what, exactly, do they say?"

Karissa's eyes shift from the door to meet mine. Her hair is a mess, her pajamas disheveled. She clearly just woke up from sleeping hard, lost in tranquility, while I spent the past few hours drowning in paranoia. Every time the house creaked, I damn near clawed my way out of my own skin.

"History repeats itself," she says, "first as a tragedy, second as a farce."

Karl Marx. I recognize the quote.

Daniel Santino must've taught it to her.

Huh.

I wave toward the front door. "Something about this is funny to you?"

"Not really funny," she says, slowly stepping closer. "It's sort of curious, though, that I spent my entire life trapped behind locked doors and here it is, happening to me again. I always knew something was going on when my mother started buying extra locks and nailing down windows. It's just a bit of déjà vu seeing you doing the same thing."

Hesitating, I reach into my pocket and fish out a set of keys. I toss them to her without warning, and they hit the wooden floor by her feet with a clang. Bending down, she picks them up, eyeing me curiously.

"You're not trapped here, Karissa."

Her fist closes around the keys, her gaze burning through me as she arches an eyebrow, silent for a moment before asking, "Aren't I?"

"No, you're not. You can leave the house whenever you want."

"Can I?"

"Of course," I say. "Doesn't mean I won't follow you, though."

She glares at me for a moment before looking away, focusing back on the locks lining the door. "I take it back."

"Take what back?"

"It *is* funny," she says, although there's no humor in her voice. "The entire reason I was on lockdown growing up was because of you, and here I am, on lockdown once again, all because of you. Ironic, don't you think?"

"Does it make you feel like an Alanis Morissette song?"

Her brow furrows. "Who?"

Shaking my head, I stroll toward her. "Never mind. Sometimes I forget how young you are."

Her eyes meet mine once more. "I'm not young. You're just old."

"Huh." I pause right in front of her. "I remember once, not long ago, you were adamant I wasn't old. But then again, that's the same night you told me to stay, and you've been pretty vocal about how you regret that. Guess I shouldn't be surprise if you take back everything you've said."

She holds my gaze for a few seconds before closing her eyes and looking away. I don't linger, shuffling past her on my way to the den. I'm exhausted, and frustrated, wanting nothing more than to collapse in my bed and sleep for days on end, but there's still too much to do.

I've wasted enough time being unconscious.

I'm sitting at my desk, on the phone with American Express when Karissa appears. I expect her to take a seat on the couch, to turn on the television and do whatever it is she does, but she surprises me by approaching my desk instead. She perches herself on the corner of it while I lean back in the chair.

"I need to cancel my card and order a new one," I tell the person on the phone. "I also need to know if it's been used recently."

The lady gives me the usual spiel about timeframes and security as she looks up my history. Last swiped at a gas station north of the city limits the night it was stolen. *Huh.*

109

I hang up once it's settled and continue to watch Karissa as she stares out the vast window behind me. She's switching up her routine because of me, but not much has really changed. Not really. I don't want her to feel like a prisoner, but it's obvious she feels trapped.

She even said so herself.

"I have something for you," I say.

"I don't—"

"Want anything from me," I say, finishing her thought. "You don't want anything from me, I get it."

"Actually, I was going to say I didn't need anything."

"Well, good, because I think you'll want this."

Opening my top desk drawer, I pull out the receipt from NYU and hold it out to her. She takes it, slowly unfolding it as I close the drawer again. Her gaze goes to the receipt as she clutches onto it tightly. Her eyes flit across the paper as she reads. "You paid my tuition?"

"I did."

"But how did you know? I mean, how did you...?" She trails off, shaking her head. "Never mind, what *don't* you know when it comes to me."

Not much, I think, but I'll learn the rest eventually.

"You didn't have to do this," she continues, looking at me as she folds the receipt back up. "I wasn't going to ask you to do it."

"I know," I say. "But you risked a lot to come to NYU, so if school's important to you, you should keep going."

She seems at a loss for words, her mouth opening and closing a few times. After a few failed attempts at a response, she simply looks away, temporarily giving up on attempting conversation.

I know she's grateful, even if she doesn't say it.

Sighing, I shove my chair back and stand up again, swaying a bit. I grasp the desk beside her and close my eyes, taking a few deep breaths to steady myself. When I reopen my eyes, I see she's watching me, but I don't linger. I don't need her to worry.

I walk out of the den without another word.

I go upstairs to shower, standing under the frigid cold spray and hoping it'll jolt me awake, before heading into the bedroom to change. I'm dazed as I absent-mindedly pull on another one of my suits, only vaguely having to pay attention as I knot the dark tie. I sit down on the edge of the bed with my shoes when I glance toward the doorway, Karissa appearing yet again. She hesitates in front of me, leaning against the doorframe.

She still has something to say.

I think she finally found the words.

"You didn't go to sleep last night."

I cut my eyes at her. "I'm surprised you noticed."

"I always notice."

"Then I'm surprised you care."

"I always care, too."

"Yeah, maybe you do," I mutter, slipping on my shoes before letting out a light laugh. "Sometimes you care because you don't want me there."

She doesn't argue that, sighing dramatically when I carefully stand up again to grab my coat. "Are you going somewhere? *Again?*"

"I have to go sort out things with my car," I say. "I also need to get a new driver's license and deal with whatever else was in my wallet."

"It can't wait?"

"No," I say. "It can't."

"So you're going to be gone a while?"

The question makes me eye her peculiarly as I put on my coat. "Maybe."

"Oh."

"Planning to throw a party in my absence?"

Planning to run as soon as I'm not here?

"Of course not," she says quietly. "I just thought, you know, maybe I could go with you."

My fingers stall as I'm fastening the buttons. "You want to go with me?"

"If you don't mind... unless you're doing something, well, you know..."

"Illegal?" I guess, shaking my head when she nods in confirmation. "It'll all be boring and above board. No skirting any gray areas today, jailbird. Scouts honor."

She smiles slightly. "Were you a boy scout?"

"Yes," I admit, fixing my coat, smoothing the material. "All the way through Junior High."

111

"Really?"

"Yes."

"You must have a thing for joining organizations."

Despite myself, I laugh at that. I have a rule against talking about what I do for work, against even verbally acknowledging I play any role in the world of organized crime, but she's not an idiot, and I'm done hiding who I am.

She's seen me.

She knows.

"Yeah, well, I like to think it's mutually beneficial," I say. "They teach me what they want me to know, and I use what I learn to assist them however I can."

"What did the Boy Scouts teach you?"

"The basics," I say. "Tying knots, hunting, shooting targets, starting fires... *surviving*."

"And the, uh... other organization?"

I consider it. "Pretty much the same things."

She eyes me warily. "You must be good with so much training."

I step toward her, pausing right in front of her, so close the tips of my shoes graze her toes. She stares up at me, her expression earnest as she bites the inside of her cheek. Carefully, I reach out, running the back of my fingers along her jawline as her lips twitch. "What did I tell you about asking things like this?"

"That I should be careful what I ask," she says quietly. "That the answers aren't always pretty."

"Exactly."

"But I wasn't asking anything," she says. "It wasn't a question."

You must be good with so much training.

No, it wasn't a question.

"You ever hear the expression 'more is caught than taught'?" I ask. She shakes her head, and I lean closer, dropping my voice lower, whispering to her. "You can learn more watching the world around you than anyone could ever dream of teaching you. I'm good, all right, but it has nothing to do with any kind of training. I'm good, because the world showed me how to be. Very few have ever witnessed my greatest tricks, Karissa... even fewer lived to remember them."

Her muscles grow taut... I can see them straining as she tries to stay still, but my words send a shiver through her. I pull away, turning around to head for the door.

"I'll be downstairs," I say. "Get dressed if you want to come with me today. It's up to you."

I don't expect her to really come along, don't expect her to show her face again before I leave.

After retrieving some cash from a safe in the den, finding my spare car key and gathering my passport and social security card to use as identification, I head out the front door and stroll toward the driveway, surveying my car.

A few dings pepper the driver's side door, but a .22 caliber bullet is no match for the armored metal of the Mercedes S-Guard. I bought this car because it's arguably the safest on the market. Not bulletproof, per se, because nothing is bulletproof. A strong enough weapon can cut through even the toughest Kevlar, demolish even the sturdiest structure, but it's resistant to whatever might come my way. The side window took the worst of it, a spider web crack in the corner filtering out along the tempered glass.

I reach for the door handle, opening it, and freeze when I glance inside. Bloodstains streak the leather, but they're just that... *stains*.

The car has been wiped clean.

I hear a noise behind me as I'm staring at the interior and turn quickly—*too* quickly—nearly toppling over from the jolt of pain. I clutch onto the door, gripping it tightly, and close my eyes again to stop the world from spinning.

When I reopen my eyes, I see Karissa standing there.

She's wearing a pair of jeans and a tight black tank top, tall black boots and a pink scarf. Her hair is pulled along the side, loosely braided down her shoulder, just a touch of makeup on her face. She looks a lot like the woman I first encountered, the one who charmed me.

She proves me wrong yet again.

"I tried to get the blood out but it sat too long and I didn't know what to use," she says, motioning toward the interior of the car. "I thought... well, I figured you had more experience at that than me."

There's not an ounce of sarcasm to that statement.

It's the truth, anyway.

"You shouldn't have."

She shrugs. "It's the least I could do."

No, really, she shouldn't have...

Sighing, I turn back to the car, ignoring the stains as I climb in behind the wheel. I wait until she's buckled in the passenger seat before starting the engine and pulling away.

Karissa's quiet as I run errands all over town, spending an ungodly amount of time trying to get a new copy of my driver's license at the DMV. She sits beside me the entire time, following me from place to place, her presence loud even if she's low on words.

"Just one more stop," I tell her eventually. "I need to have the car dealt with."

Her eyes trail over the fractured side window. "Are we going to Donizetti's Body Shop?"

My brow furrows. "Where?"

"Donizetti's," she says again before looking at me. "I think that's what it's called. I found the business card..."

She starts to reach into the center console, and my stomach drops, realizing what she's talking about. *Shit*. Before she can pull out the business card, I stop her, shutting the console once again as I shake my head. "I get all my work done at the dealership."

"Oh." She settles back into the seat. "I figured he did your work for you."

I say nothing to that.

I'm grateful she drops the subject.

It's late afternoon when we make it to the Mercedes dealership in Midtown East. The lobby is quiet, only a few people hanging around, talking to salesmen or waiting for their cars. A strange blue glow surrounds the desk as I stand in front of it, leaning against it, waiting as the receptionist finds room in the schedule to squeeze me in.

"It should just be a few minutes, Mr. Vitale," she says, bright red lips smiling widely, flashing her inexplicably white teeth at me. It's forced, and fake, the kind of smile that's bought and paid for. I hate when people smile needlessly, like their faces are puppets and corruption pulls the strings. "Just take a seat and someone will be right with you."

She takes my only spare key and waltzes away as I let out as a sigh and turn away from the front desk. Karissa is sitting in a blue chair across the lobby, right in front of the television, fidgeting distractedly.

I stroll that way, and she glances up at me, but I step past her to the counter along the side, to the small Dean & DeLuca set up, grabbing two shots of espresso before strolling back toward Karissa. She watches me warily as I hold one of them out to her.

"Here," I say. "We might be here a while."

They say minutes when it's always more like hours.

"Thank you," she says quietly, taking the little paper cup from me, offering a small smile of gratitude. Unlike the one that greeted me just minutes ago, this one is genuine.

I like this smile.

I miss it.

"You're welcome," I say, sitting down in the chair beside hers, stretching my long legs out as I take a sip of the espresso. It's thicker than usual, a slight bitter edge to it. I grimace, the taste lingering in my mouth, and glance at Karissa to see her do the same.

She scrunches up her nose. "This coffee is terrible."

"It's espresso."

She scoffs, taking another sip. "Same difference."

"Same difference? Really?" I shake my head. "You're a disgrace to Italians everywhere."

She laughs. "Good thing I'm not really Italian."

"Oh, but you are," I tell her. "Your father was an Italian citizen, so by default you would be, too."

She hesitates, taking another sip. "Is my mother an Italian citizen, too?"

"Uh, no, she's not," I say, leaning back in my chair as I regard her. "Her parents... your grandparents, as it is... were second or third generation."

Karissa's eyes widen. "My *grandparents*?"

"Yes," I say. "You have some of those, you know... most people do."

I can tell looking at her that she never thought about it, never considered the fact that she'd have more family.

"They're dead, though, right?" Her voice is quiet. "Growing up, my mom always told me her parents passed away."

"Yeah, they died in a car accident."

"So she didn't lie to me about that, at least."

"I suppose there's that," I say, drumming my fingers against the arm of the chair. "Although, you know, Carmela isn't your only parent. Johnny's mother is still around."

"Really?"

"Yes, she lives over in Harlem. She's a bitter hag, kicked your father out on his ass when he was just sixteen, but she's still around. Her name's Janice."

"Janice," she mumbles. "Interesting."

As I'm sitting there, sipping the espresso, the lady from the front desk comes waltzing over, that fake smile still plastered to her face. "Mr. Vitale, do you have some identification on you? I need to use it to verify you're the owner so we can order the new key from headquarters."

"Yeah." Reaching into my coat pocket, I pull out the paper from the DMV, the temporary driving authorization until my new license comes in, and hand over my passport along with it, in case she needs a picture. She walks away with them both, returning a moment later and handing them back to me.

I start to slip them into my pocket when Karissa's voice cuts through the silence. "Can I see?"

I cut my eyes at her. "See what?"

"Your passport."

I hesitate, but figure there's no harm in letting her look. Anything she'd learn from it are just things I'd tell her if she asked, anyway. I hold it out, and she takes it, setting her espresso down.

I continue to sip my drink.

She flips the passport open and immediately bursts into laughter, the sound washing through me, easing some of the tension in my muscles. I know exactly what she's laughing at before she even says anything. "Michele? Your middle name is *Michele*?"

She pronounces it like most Americans, feminine and soft, her laughter escalating as she repeats it again and again. *Michele*.

"It's not Mah-shell," I say, correcting her. How many times did I say these words growing up? "It's Me-kale-ah. It's the Italian form of Michael."

"Are you Italian?"

"Clearly."

"No, I mean, are you a citizen like my, uh... Johnny? I figure you have to be, with a name like yours, but you have an American passport, so..."

"Oh, no," I say. "New Yorker, born and bred."

"So your parents just like, uh... traditional names?" she asks, tripping over the word traditional as she fights to keep her humor at bay. "Names like Michele?"

She laughs again, louder this time, as she intentionally mispronounces my middle name. Reaching over, I grab the passport to snatch it back but she grips it tightly, fighting for control. "No, wait, I'm not done."

Yanking from my grasp, she shifts her body so it's out of my reach. Shaking my head, I relax back into the chair, giving up. I don't have it in me to be annoyed, or angry, even as she snickers to herself. It takes a brave soul to mock me. She knows who I am, and what I'm capable of, but she's not afraid of my reaction.

Deep down, she's not afraid of me.

She's forgetting again, I think. Forgetting she's supposed to hate me. Forgetting what sort of monster I can be.

I can't be upset in the slightest over that.

It makes me smile, even if it's at my own expense.

"No, really, why the hardcore Italian name?"

"You'd have to ask my parents," I say. "I had nothing to do with it."

"What are their names?"

"My father's name is Giuseppe."

"And your mother?"

I hesitate, knowing she's going to laugh again, but I can feel her gaze as she awaits my response. I finish my espresso in silence as the dealer who always handles my car steps out into the lobby, his gaze scanning the area before settling on me.

"It's Michelle," I say, pronouncing it the feminine way. "Her name is Michelle."

Standing up, I throw my cup in the trash when Karissa snorts with laughter, just like I knew she would. My name might be the Italian equivalent of Michael, entirely masculine, but it's undeniable—I was named after my mother. She laughs long and hard as I step toward her, carefully leaning down, my hands on the arms of her chair on both sides of her. She looks at me, a hitch in her laughter as she inhales sharply.

I inch toward her, slowly, my expression dead serious.

"Laugh it up," I say, staring her in the eyes, the tip of my nose brushing hers as I move toward her ear, whispering, "we'll see how funny you find my name the next time I make you scream it."

Her eyes widen, her amusement quickly fading, a flush creeping up on her cheeks. I pull away from her, turning to the dealer. He grins at me—another fake, forced smile that I always get around this place, as he holds out some paperwork, including the bill, and my spare key.

"I ordered a replacement key, but it won't be in for a week or so," he says. "The one you have here will still work fine. I remotely deactivated the key that was stolen, so it can no longer start the car. It can, however, unlock the doors and the trunk, but in that case the alarm will sound, and nothing short of you cutting it off with your key will stop it. We can make an appointment to have the manual locks changed, if you'd like."

"I'll think about it," I say, nodding as I turn from him. "Thanks."

I start back toward Karissa when the dealer calls out to me. "Uh, Mr. Vitale, about the damage. The, uh... bullet holes."

Karissa's eyes drift to me when he says that. I turn away from her again to look at the man. "What about them?"

"Would you like us to fix it?" he asks. "There's no interior damage, of course, since it's an S-Guard... and thank God for that, right? But the body shop can take care of the cosmetic damage."

"Maybe some other time."

I head over to the main desk and pay the bill, pulling the cash straight from my pocket, mourning the loss of my wallet, before heading back to Karissa. Wordlessly, I motion for her to follow me, and the two of us head out of the dealership to where my car's parked near the garage service doors. I open the passenger side for her, and she pauses, regarding me warily. I can see the curiosity in her eyes, and I have all the answers in the world, but she never asks the right questions.

Without commenting, she slips into the passenger side, letting me shut the door. I climb behind the wheel and start the car, merging into Manhattan traffic right away.

She sits in the cool leather seat, still holding onto my passport. She opens it again as I drive, scanning through the pages, a contemplative look on her face. "No Italy."

"Excuse me?"

She holds up the passport. "There are no stamps from Italy in here."

"Oh, yeah, they never bother to stamp it."

"Why?"

"I don't know." I've never given it much thought, always grateful to be waved straight through whenever I've landed in Rome. "Why does it matter?"

"Because you told me you've been to Italy."

I turn to her as I pull up at a red light, surprised by her accusatory tone. "I have."

She looks torn as to whether or not to believe me, and I realize then why it matters so much. She's still looking for a reason to doubt me, looking for justification to hate me, grasping any smidgen of skepticism that comes along to try to convince herself that she shouldn't love me.

She doesn't want to love me.

I don't blame her.

But the fact remains that she does.

She loves me.

And she probably hates that fact more than she hates me most days.

I look away from her when the light turns green. She seems to, for the moment, decide to believe what I'm saying. She glances back at the passport, scanning over the few stamps I've collected before closing it.

She tosses it in the center console and slouches in her seat, shifting her body so she can lean against the door and stare out the window. "Do your parents still live in New York?"

"Yes."

"Here in the city?"

"Yes."

"And you don't see them?"

"No."

"Why not?"

I sigh as I pull up at yet another red light. Traffic is heavy today. It's going to take a while to get back to Brooklyn at this rate. I'm exhausted, and nauseated, and my body is really starting to ache.

I cut my eyes at her, seeing her inquisitive look. "You sure you're not writing a book about my life?"

She rolls her eyes. "I'm just trying to figure out who you are."

"You know who I am."

"No, I don't." Her voice has a hard edge to it, a slight hint of anger that makes my skin prickle. "You're like a caricature to me, Naz… you're an outline of a man, a vague sketch of a person, and I'm just trying to fill in the rest of the picture, add some color between all these black lines, and I don't know how to do that, how to figure out who you really are, without prying it out of you."

"What do you want to know?"

"Everything," she says. "I want to know everything about you. And I know you told me the answers might not be pretty, but I don't care. If we're going to have any chance in hell of doing whatever it is we're doing, of actually building something together, I'm going to have to understand what makes the answers so ugly in the first place."

I consider that for a moment, sitting in silence as I stare through the windshield at the bright red light, waiting for it to change. Once it turns green, I make an unexpected turn, cutting in front of other cars, ignoring the blare of their horns, as I hook a left down a nearby street.

It veers us away from Brooklyn when I take yet another left, setting us back in the direction we just came.

"Are you hungry?" I ask, glancing at Karissa.

She stares at me with disbelief. I can see the fury brewing in her eyes, anger at being disregarded, at having her questions ignored. Any walls I busted down are already being reconstructed, her guard going back up, her armor coming on.

I'm grateful for it, for the moment.

She's probably going to need it.

"You haven't eaten yet today," I say when she doesn't answer.

"Yeah, well, you haven't eaten in like a week."

She's exaggerating, but that doesn't matter, considering I have no intention of eating today, either.

"You must be hungry," I say. "Let's get you something."

She merely shakes her head as she looks back away. I don't talk anymore as I drive north through Manhattan. I sneak glances at the other side of the car whenever traffic stops us, seeing her expression hardening, the anger still there, growing along with her confusion.

She wants so badly to ask where we're going, to demand I tell her where I'm taking her right now.

The deli is in a faded brick building in Hell's Kitchen, wedged between a butcher shop and a little corner grocer, tucked in below a bunch of cluttered old apartments. Metal bars needlessly cover most of the tinted glass windows, a green awning running the length of the building above them, *Italian Delicatessen* written in block letters along the brick. The actual name of the place isn't on it anymore, hasn't been for decades although the spot it used to hang up top, front and center, is still discolored compared to the area around it.

It doesn't matter, though, not really.

Name or no name, the deli's iconic.

People drive in from upstate for one of their sandwiches, for just a taste of their fresh mozzarella, for a pound of their smoked ham. They can move it to a fucking alley and sell it out of the back of a truck and people will still make the trip.

Everyone thinks it's a sign of the owner's modesty, that he never gave a shit about recognition, that he never bothered to have the sign replaced after renovations years ago. *The food's what matters*, he tells people when they ask. *Who cares what you call it as long as you come eat.*

But I know it's not humility. It's regret.

He just doesn't care for the name anymore.

I park the car in the closest spot I can find, just down the street, and feed some change into the meter when I get out. Karissa sits in the car while I do it, like she doesn't plan to come with me, but after a moment she gets out, her expression unchanged.

"We don't have to be here if you don't want to be," I say. "I'll take you home right now."

Part of me hopes she'll agree to that.

I've endured enough shit this week to go through *this* on top of it.

But no such luck.

"No, we're already here," she says, waving all around her. She has no idea where *here* is. "We might as well stay."

"If you're certain."

"I am."

I wish like hell I was.

Pressing my hand to her back, I lead her down the street, slowing as I approach the familiar deli. My eyes studiously scan the outside, instinctively searching for anything that changed since I was last around, finding it just as I remember. I reach for the door, tugging it open, the obnoxious bell on top of it jingling as I motion for Karissa to go inside.

It grates on my nerves.

The inside is unassuming—checkered floor, a dozen wooden tables, dim lighting and tall, winding counters. Glass cases take up half the front beside the register, filled with meats and cheese, a cluttered handwritten menu board hanging above it all.

A young guy tends to the lone register, helping those waiting in line, while a man steadily cuts meat a few feet to the side, his back to the customers. He's sturdy, six-feet of solid mass covered in leathery skin, his dark chaotic mess of hair flecked with quite a bit gray.

He moves fluidly, despite his age.

Cool.

Confident.

He owns the place.

He whistles loudly as he works, like an oversize dwarf right out of Snow White, the off-key tune the only noise in the place above the chatter. There are no televisions, no music, no Wi-Fi.

Just a man whistling Johnnie Ray's 'Just Walking in the Rain'.

I haven't heard the song in ages...

Karissa strolls through the deli, taking the place at the back of the line. I join her, wordlessly waiting, the sound of the casual whistling clawing at me. Every second that passes makes my knees weaker, my vision hazier, my head a throbbing mass of pain.

I'm sweating.

Aching.

I shove my hands in my pockets.

This was a bad idea.

A fucking terrible idea.

Neither of us talks during the wait. She reads the menu, scanning the dozens of options as we slowly, steadily move closer to the front.

It only takes a few minutes.

Everyone's cleared out ahead of us, only two or three waiting behind us. The guy working the register looks up. He can't be much older than Karissa, and he seems to only have eyes for her. He grins the kind of grin that says he'd like to take her to dinner then have her for dessert afterward, as he says enthusiastically, "what can I do you for?"

I want to reach across the counter and grab him by the throat, rip his fucking voice box out for even talking to her.

In another place, I might.

At another time, I probably would.

I would gut the boy for having the balls to even think about flirting with her.

But in my state, the pesky little punk could probably take me out.

Pathetic.

Karissa returns his smile before glancing my way, expecting me to answer that question. I stare at the guy working, watching his expression change when he takes note of mine, and clear my throat when I turn to Karissa.

I wipe the sweat from my brow. *Here goes nothing.* "Order whatever you'd like, sweetheart."

The words aren't even entirely from my lips when silence falls over the deli, the meat slicer pausing mid-stroke, the whistling halting in the middle of a note. I can feel the abrupt shift in the air, coldness sweeping through, like the sun vanished behind some thick clouds, blanketing the world in the kind of shadows where men like me live.

I shiver.

I can feel eyes on me. I don't move from where I'm standing, merely shifting my gaze down the counter. Lips that whistled so exuberantly a second ago are now pressed into a thin line of contempt, like the man's forcing them together to keep from saying something.

His back's no longer to me.

I can only imagine what he's thinking. His eyes are harsh and critical, the recognition running deep but none of it is sentimental.

Karissa obliviously starts ordering—an Italian sub special for her—before she addresses me. "Naz, what are you getting?"

"Nothing," I say, staring at the man a moment longer before turning to the guy at the register. "Nothing for me, so just her Italian."

He rings it up and I quickly pay, not waiting for my change. I just slap a twenty down on the counter before turning my back and shuffling away, slipping into the chair at an empty table in the middle of the deli. Karissa joins me, not saying anything, until her sub is ready and it's set in front of her on the table.

Her gaze bounces between the food and me with confusion. "You didn't want anything?"

"No."

"Why not?" she asks, taking a bite of her sub, practically moaning as she chews. "Jesus, it's really good."

I believe her.

The food here always is.

But I can't eat right now and certainly not at this place.

"You know how you think I'm paranoid for believing people might try to poison me?"

"I wouldn't really say you're paranoid," she says, "but yeah..."

"Well if anyone were to ever actually do it, I'd put my money on him."

I motion with my head toward the counter. Her eyes widen, her gaze shifting from me to her food again with a hint of panic. She suddenly looks sick.

"Relax," I say, letting out a light laugh at her strong reaction. "Your food's fine. He wouldn't mess with it."

"How do you know?"

"He has no reason to," I say. "You haven't insulted him."

"And you have?"

"Yes."

"How?"

I stare at her, considering how to answer. "By existing, mostly."

She nods and goes back to eating, as if she understands, when she doesn't. Not really. Not yet, anyway. But she will, just as soon as the man starts unraveling, the shock of my appearance wearing off and undoing his carefully constructed happy-go-lucky, whistle-while-you-work façade.

Most people overlook men like me, or see us as a necessary evil, staying out of our way to keep from crossing our paths, but he's too strong willed, too wound tight with a misguided sense of righteousness, the stick up his ass hitting way too deep for him to just keep his mouth shut and mind his own business.

Coming here was definitely a bad idea.

I know better than to do it.

But Karissa wants to know things... things just telling her won't make her understand. I can shout that the sky is blue all afternoon but until you look at it yourself, you'll never understand what shade. It could be deep royal blue or a faintly tinted white.

And when it comes to this man's feelings toward me, it's as dark as midnight.

The whistling never starts up again, but there's more noise now, things rattling and drawers banging. It reminds me of Karissa trying to cook in the kitchen.

Karissa's food is nearly gone when I hear the voice ring through the deli, his words polite, but his tone is always brash, like just the sound of it can rub a person raw, grate the skin right from their body and expose them to the bone. This is nothing new—he greets customers every day, every chance he gets, making sure the food is good and they like being here.

Our table is in the center of it all, but he does a wide circle around it, saving us for last. Karissa watches the man curiously as others smile whenever he smiles, laughing along with him. His humor can be infectious with the right crowd, but I'm not his target audience.

Neither will she be, for that matter.

Finally, he comes to our table. Karissa glances up at him, her expression slipping. She turns to me, hesitant, and I can practically see her heart beating out of her chest in alarm.

There's no warm welcome here.

No smiles or laughs for us.

He looks *furious*.

He presses his palms flat against the table, leaning over until his face is a mere few inches from mine. I can feel the heat radiating from him, smell the sweat coating his skin, the tinge of salt mixing with a hint of tobacco, a scent I'd be ecstatic if I never inhaled again.

My gaze shifts to meet his for the second time in a day, trying to come off as relaxed and at ease, but the inside of me is taut, coiled like a spring.

"There isn't somewhere else you can be?" he asks, voice low. His breath reeks of hot cinnamon, like the flavored toothpicks he chews on to keep from smoking. "Somewhere else you can eat? There are thousands of restaurants in this city, Ignazio. Thousands. Why do you come here?"

"The food is good."

"*The food is good*," he mocks. "You didn't order anything."

"I was concerned about safety."

He narrows his angry eyes at my casual words, taking it offensively. "You think I would mess with your food, do you? Think I would try to make you sick? Poison you, like those other schmucks you deal with?"

"I think it's possible."

"You think so highly of yourself. You always have. But I would never. Never. This is my life... my food is everything... and you're not worth it. You're not worthy of eating my food, period. I would certainly never contaminate it for the likes of you."

The voice is slowly skinning me alive, pulling me apart piece by piece. I stare at him hard, seeing Karissa's stunned expression from my peripheral. I don't turn to her. I do nothing but drum my fingers on the table, absorbing every word he says, knowing she hears it, too.

Good.

Maybe she'll get what she wants from this.

Validation.

She's not the only one who hates me.

There are people out there who hate me even more than she ever could.

She's not capable of the kind of hatred this man brings.

126

"You're scum," he continues. "You think I'm a bad guy; you think I would taint my food for you, that I would hurt what I love, but that's you, Ignazio. You. Not me. You're the one who ruins everything."

The voice is his, but those words are hers... words Karissa said to me just a few days ago. *Do you have to ruin everything?*

Reaching into his pocket, he pulls out a twenty-dollar bill and slams it on the table in front of me, eyes still fixed on my face. "You aren't welcome here, and neither is your blood money. Take it and get out. As far as I'm concerned, you died a long time ago, and I'm glad for it. I won't let you haunt us anymore. I can't look at you, can't look at this demon you've become. You're better off staying dead. God knows you look it right now." He steps back, turning his focus to Karissa. "Run, little girl. Run far away from him."

My eyes follow him as he stalks through the deli, heading straight to the back, disappearing behind a swinging door. I stare at it in silence, taking deep, even breaths to steady myself, willing myself to remain calm, to stay in this seat. Dead silence overtook the deli while he berated me. I'm certain Karissa wasn't the only one who overheard everything he said.

"Naz?" Karissa whispers, her voice shaking. I stare at the still swinging door, contemplating following him back there as I continue to drum my fingers against the table. After a moment, she reaches over, placing her hand on top of mine to still my movements. "Ignazio?"

My gaze shifts from the door to my hand—to her hand, on top of mine, nails painted pale pink, a stark contrast to her soft tanned skin—before I meet her eyes. She looks shell-shocked, a look I've seen time and time again, the look of someone who knows they witnessed something they shouldn't have... the look of someone worried how I'm going to react because of it.

"I'm fine," I say, clearing my throat when my voice catches because I know I certainly don't sound fine. "Are you done eating?"

Her brow furrows as she looks at what's left of her food, like she can't believe I'm even talking about it at a time like this. "Uh, yeah..."

"Are you sure?"

She nods. "I'm not hungry anymore."

"Then let's get out of here."

I pull my hand away and push my chair back, standing up. I smooth my suit coat as I wait for her to get to her feet, not looking at any of the other customers as I lead her toward the exit, leaving the money lying on the table. He can toss it in the fucking trash for all I care. I open the door for her, stepping out behind her, closing my eyes and gritting my teeth at the sound of the bell jingling above me.

"What just happened?" Karissa stops on the sidewalk, right in front of the deli, not moving when I try to get her to. "Who the hell does that guy think he is? Why would he talk to you that way?"

She stares at me, eyebrows raised, awaiting an answer. I'm not sure what she expects me to say. It's pretty self-explanatory, I think.

"I'm not his favorite person."

"Obviously," she says, waving toward the building. "I mean, what's the point in us stopping for something to eat if you can't even eat? Why would we come here? Why would you bring me here, knowing that?"

She's speaking loudly, making just as big of a scene as we endured inside, people walking by glancing between us curiously, wondering why she's yelling like she is.

I step toward her. "You asked me a question."

"I asked you a lot of questions, none of which you ever seem to want to answer unless it's convenient for you."

"Convenient?" Her use of that word rubs me the wrong way. Easy… convenient… why do people think these things aren't a hassle for me? "Do you think that was *convenient* for me, Karissa? You think I enjoyed being berated in front of all those people, that I got a kick out of having him tear me apart in public like that? Do you think I did that for the fun of it, for the hell of it? Because I didn't. I didn't enjoy a second of it. But you asked a question, you said you want to know me, so I showed you."

"Showed me what?"

"Why I don't see my parents."

The anger in her expression melts as she gapes at me, the wheels in her mind turning fast as she puts together the pieces of why we came to this place. It's all there, it always is, if she'd just fucking open her eyes and pay attention. *More is caught than taught.* But I don't have it in me right now to stand here patiently, to hang out on this

128

dirty, cracked sidewalk while everyone in the goddamn neighborhood watches, waiting for her to get her shit together.

I wave down the street, toward where the car is parked.

"Can we go now, before I pass out?" I ask. "Or do you need to yell at me some more first?"

I see the flash of guilt as she lowers her head and starts walking. I sigh, shaking my head again, my eyes scanning the outside of the deli once more, lingering just a moment on the discoloration where the sign used to be, back when it meant something to the owner, before I single-handedly tarnished a name that used to make him proud.

Vitale's.

As soon as we're in the car, Karissa turns to me, rambling before I can even start the engine. "I'm sorry. I didn't realize..."

"Don't apologize."

"But I'm sorry. I really am. The things he said—"

"Are true," I say, cutting her off before she can dwell on it. "I'm not a good man, Karissa. I've told you that, your parents have told you that, and now you've heard it from mine, too. Don't apologize to me for it, because I'm not going to apologize to you. I'm not sorry for being who I am. You wanted to know, so I showed you, end of story. There's nothing left to say."

My words silence her. She turns away from me, shifting her body in the seat, and stares out the window the entire trip to Brooklyn. By the time we make it to the house, the sun is starting to set outside and I'm still not done with everything I need to do. I'm running on no sleep, exhausted mentally and physically, utterly emotionally spent.

I'm a mess.

Frustrated, I pull into the driveway and cut off the car, but I just sit there, not moving. My eyes flicker to the rearview mirror, to the vaguely familiar car parked along the curb. I spotted it as soon as I turned onto the street.

Detective Jameson.

Just great.

I climb out, pausing, as the doors to the lurking car open and the familiar men appear. Detective Jameson approaches as his partner lingers behind, watching.

"Detective," I say when Jameson pauses in the grass a few feet away. "Is there a reason you're here?"

"Just thought I'd check to see how you were doing," he says. "Heard you were already back on your feet. Guess the incident at Cobalt didn't knock you down for long."

I just stare at him. He sounds casual, conversational, but I'm not stupid.

The detective's attention shifts to Karissa when she steps out of the car. "Miss Reed, nice to see you again."

She looks panicked and says nothing.

"Well then," Jameson says, looking away from her to turn back to me, his gaze skimming along the side of my car as he does, looking at the damage. "Tough break about the car."

"It's not as bad as it looks."

"Still, I know a guy who could fix it for you. You might know him, actually. Name's Josh Donizetti."

The detective pauses, raising his eyebrows like he's waiting for some confirmation that I know who he's speaking of. I do, of course, and he knows I do.

I can see it in his eyes.

"Anyway, he has a shop not far from here. I'm sure he'd give you a good deal. He often works with guys like you." Jameson turns around like he's going to leave, but pauses, snapping his finger, theatrically sighing. He's a terrible actor. "Oh, right, never mind... totally slipped my mind that the man died recently. Tragic, really. Quite the accident. Car fell on him. You wouldn't know about that, though, would you?"

He glances back at me.

He knows.

Somehow, he knows.

Not good.

"Of course not," I say. "Wouldn't know a thing about it."

The detective nods, his gaze turning to Karissa. He tips his head, acknowledging her again. "Miss Reed."

I stand there, not moving, watching as the man leaves, the car disappearing down the street. Once they're gone, I head straight inside, not lingering downstairs, going right up to the bedroom. I pull off my coat and kick off my shoes, sitting down on the edge of the bed.

I can hear Karissa as she comes inside behind me, hear the clink and clank as she fastens all the new locks on the door, hear her footsteps as she carefully makes her way upstairs.

Unknotting my tie, I glance up in the doorway when she appears.

"You're wrong," she says right away.

I pull the tie off and toss it on the bed beside me. "I doubt it."

Her lips twitch ever so slightly, a hint of a smile at my retort. "But you are."

"Okay," I hedge, unbuttoning the cuffs of my shirt as I watch her, wondering where she's going with this. "What exactly am I wrong about?"

"Earlier you said there was nothing left to say, but there is. There always is."

Sighing exasperatedly, I start unbuttoning my shirt, not bothering with a response. If she has something more to get off her chest, I'm sure she'll say it without any coaxing.

"Maybe you're not a good man—"

"I'm not."

She stalls at my interruption before finishing her thought. "Okay, but that doesn't mean you're a *bad* man, Naz."

I pull my shirt off, tossing it aside before looking back at her. "What does that make me then?"

"A man," she says. "Just a man."

Her words make me wish I could believe them. It's nice, having her say it, though. "There is nothing either good or bad, but thinking makes it so."

The smile returns a bit. She realizes I'm quoting Hamlet. She's smart. She knows what I'm doing. "So you think you're a bad man?"

I gaze at her in silence for a moment. "I do."

"Well, I don't think a bad man would think that," she says. "A real bad man wouldn't see anything he did as bad. He'd feel justified. He'd have no regrets."

I open my mouth, words on the tip of my tongue, but her sincere expression makes me swallow them back. She's wrong—so very, very wrong. I do feel justified. I have no regrets. I make no apologies. It is what it is. But it's endearing, how much she believes what she's saying, how she truly wants to think I'm not a bad man. But I know I am, and enlightenment doesn't negate it.

I just accept it.

She can't, though, and I love her for it. Yet another reason I love this damn woman. Despite everything she knows I've done, despite most of the time hating me, she can't let go of that sliver of hope, that part of her that thought she saw some good in me somewhere. I told her she couldn't change me, but she didn't believe that shit for a second. I wish... I fucking wish... some part of me could let her be right about this.

Instead of arguing, I return her smile. So misguided, but I appreciate it, and I'll let her keep that wishful thinking, fight to protect the untainted part of her for as long as I can. "Thank you."

"For what?"

"For thinking that."

Her smile grows a bit more, her shoulders relaxed. She thinks I'm proving her right, but gratitude doesn't erase greed, just like water can't magically wash away all the blood on my hands. You might not see it, but it's there, and it always will be.

On a whim, I motion for her to come closer, expecting to be shot down, but instead she strolls right over to me. My arms snake around her waist, running along the curve of her ass before my hands slip beneath her shirt, resting on the small of her back.

Her skin is warm.

I love touching her.

"I love you, you know," I say quietly, gazing up at her. "No matter what. I meant that."

She hesitates, her mouth opening and closing as she tries to find words. Instead of saying it back, she merely whispers, "I know."

Chapter Ten

Sleep deprivation is a funny thing.

There reaches a point of exhaustion when you're just not tired anymore. Drowsiness ceases. You're awake. Alert. The blurriness of fatigue fades away with a strange attentiveness, head clear and eyes wide open.

They call it catching your second wind.

It's something that often accompanies death, too... natural death, anyway. When they reach the point where you think they can't take much more, something sparks inside of them, and the end, for the moment, feels much like a beginning.

Life dangles a bit of hope in front of the most desperate, only to snatch it away afterward.

I've never witnessed it happen, never been around someone that death took naturally, but I've employed the tactic before. I try to make it clean, and quick, an execution and not an experience, but sometimes the moment calls for a little more. It's fascinating, watching the surge inside of them manifesting physically, relief sparking in their eyes when they think maybe, just maybe, they'll make it.

Maybe they'll live.

Maybe they'll survive it.

They never do.

I wonder if it's wrong, teasing them that way, or if it's something they ought to be thankful for. I can only imagine how they must feel—the relief, the gratitude, the reverence for life. I wonder how many find God in those seconds, how many feel God for the first time in their mundane lives, as adrenaline and dopamine and all that feel good shit their body stores up releases in one big flood through their bloodstream.

Whoosh.

The highest high, brought on by the lowest low. Maybe they think it's a gift, a 'once-in-a-lifetime opportunity' you don't want to miss... or maybe it's nothing more than a cruel trick.

I'm not sure.

I don't know how I'd prefer it.

These are the things I think about when I lay in bed at night, staring at the ceiling in the darkness, past the point of exhaustion and well into my second wind. It has been, what? Two days? Forty-eight hours since I last closed my eyes and drifted off to sleep.

I'll sleep when I'm dead. That's something my father used to say, something he told my mother whenever she got on his case about working so much. The man never slept either, running on a perpetual second wind every day.

Life is short, barely a blink for some of us.

Why waste half of it with your eyes closed?

I'll sleep when I'm dead.

Maybe I'm already there...

Sighing, I turn my head, looking away from the ceiling, and glance at the bed beside me. Karissa is fast asleep on her stomach, facing me, her leg hitched against mine as I lay on my back. Her face is so close that even in the darkness I can make out the splattering of freckles along her nose, more prominent these days because of the sun. She looks so peaceful. I wonder if she's dreaming.

I wonder how often she thinks about dying.

Gritting my teeth from the pain, I shift onto my uninjured side, careful not to disturb her. I reach over and push some stray hair out of her face, tucking it behind her ear before running the back of my hand along her flushed cheek.

I think about her dying all the time.

Leaning over, I press a kiss to her forehead, giving myself just a second to linger, before climbing out of bed. I dress in silence, pulling my clothes on in the dark, and walk out of the bedroom without giving her another look. I head downstairs, grabbing a bottle of water in the kitchen, and stare at the pill bottles on the kitchen counter.

I still don't take them.

I leave the house, making sure to lock up, and glance at my watch under the glow of the outdoor lights.

Five in the morning.

I don't know where I'm going, or what I'm doing, but I can't stare at that ceiling, can't lay in that bed beside Karissa and dwell on dying anymore. I drive around for a while, letting the darkness consume me, letting the silence swarm me, before somehow ending up in Hell's Kitchen around dawn.

A hint of light touches the morning sky, the temperate already warm... it's going to be a sweltering day.

I park the car near the familiar deli for the second time in less than twenty-four hours, locking the doors before strolling toward it. It's empty inside, the chairs upside down on top of all the tables, but I can see a hint of light in the back, beyond the swinging door.

I know he's here.

He always is at this time.

The door is locked, not budging when I pull on it. Sometimes I wonder if he put the bars on the place because of me. I remember when he first opened it, when I was just a kid, when Vitale's hung prominently and the glass was exposed, open and friendly.

Everyone was welcome back then.

I was only eighteen the day my father told me to get out and never come back, the day he told me my kind wasn't welcome here anymore.

The bars went up a week later.

I've kept my distance ever since.

I round the corner, slipping down the small alley that runs behind the stretch of buildings. Dumpsters line the graffiti-riddled walls, the smell of trash and piss burning my nostrils as I pass. The back door of the deli is lit up from the inside, the door propped open a crack thanks to a cinder block.

My father stands just inside, in front of a long metal table, chopping vegetables with his back to the door. He stalls when he hears me step inside, his shoulders squaring, but he doesn't turn around.

Five. Ten. Fifteen seconds pass, as I stand just inside the kitchen, before he goes right back to what he was doing.

"Twice in one day, Ignazio," he says without even looking, the sound of the knife against the cutting board magnified as he expertly chops. I learned how to do that from him, how to use a knife gracefully like it's an extension of my limb.

I just use it differently.

"It's almost sunrise," I say, shoving my hands in my pockets as I lean back against the wall beside the door. "It's a brand new day."

He finishes that head of lettuce before moving on to another. "If you want to get technical, it's only been twelve hours since your last visit. That's *half* a day."

"Yeah, well, what can I say? You're always so hospitable. I can't seem to stay away."

He works in silence, easily shredding the second head of lettuce as I stand there, before he finally sets the knife down and turns around. He wipes his hands on his old, stained white apron before running his palms down his face, sighing exasperatedly.

Torture to her Soul

Tired eyes greet me, surveying me, judging, as he leans back against the metal worktable.

Giuseppe Vitale is the most fearless man I know. I've never seen him cower from anyone—not from the police, not from the wise guys who used to try to extort money from him, and certainly not from *me*. He has high standards and a low tolerance, and I never quite fit in with his expectations. I disappointed the man from the moment I started talking, and he drove me further away every day with his criticism.

We'll never see eye-to-eye. He wrote me off the day I started working for Ray, and Ray become the kind of father to me that Giuseppe would never be. But the fact remains—the man in front of me gave me life.

I'm grateful for it.

And I respect him.

Even if it isn't mutual.

"Who was she?" he asks, crossing his thick arms over his broad chest.

"Who?"

"That girl you brought here."

I regard him curiously. "She didn't look familiar to you?"

"She did," he says, "that's why I'm asking. She's got one of those faces, you know, and you don't forget a face like that, ever. Used to walk in the front door of the deli after school every day, looking for one of your mother's cookies. Such a sweet face... haven't seen it in a long time because of you."

He blames me, naturally.

I started it all, set up the dominos to eventually fall.

Had I not stolen from Ray's shop that day, he wouldn't have offered me that job, and Johnny and Carmela probably would've never even crossed his path. I met Maria the first time I walked into her father's house at sixteen years old, and it was through me that she met the rest of them.

I was the center of it all, and my father knows it.

I was a damaged nucleus.

He always believed I was too weak to hold anyone else together.

The day of my wife's funeral, my father walked up to me, grasped my hands tightly, looked me dead in the eyes, and said, "rats will always desert a sinking ship, Ignazio."

I thought, at first, it was compassion. I thought he was sympathizing that my friend turned on me. It wasn't until later that I realized it was a swipe at the person I'd become instead.

I was a sinking ship.

He didn't blame Johnny for running for his life.

He didn't blame them for jumping overboard.

He blamed *me* for going under.

"She's their daughter," I say. "Johnny and Carmela's."

"Does she know who you are?"

"Yes."

"Then why's she with you?"

It's a damn good question. I don't know how to answer. I could list a dozen reasons she might be with me but it would amount to nothing in the way of explanation. At the end of the day, she's with me because she has to be. Compared to that, the rest means nothing.

If she could've left long ago, she would've, and I think she still might if she ever gets an opening.

Shaking his head at my silence, he turns away from me and picks up the knife again as he sets back to work. "I wish I could say I'm surprised, surprised you'd drag that girl into your mess, but I'm not. Your mother, though... your mother would be devastated. Disappointed. *Disgusted*. You can destroy yourself all you want. I don't care. I'm done caring. You want to be one of those schmucks who calls himself a man but lives like a thug, you do that, but you do that away from me, and away from your mother, and you especially do that away from innocent little girls."

I'm glad he's not looking at me, because his choice of words makes me grimace. "She's not a *little girl.*"

"Yeah? How old is she?"

"Nineteen."

He laughs. *Laughs.* "I remember you at that age. Running the streets, thinking you were a man... a big man... but you were no man. You were a little boy with a gun and a grudge, thinking you had it all figured out. But I'll tell you—you didn't. You still don't. You never grew up, and look at you. Look at you!" He doesn't look at me, but I can only imagine what he'd see if he did, the wall holding me up as I clutch my wounded side. It's throbbing. "I heard you got shot again. One of the neighbors heard about it, told your mother. I thought she was going to have a stroke!"

"It was nothing," I say. "I'm fine."

I feel like I've said that a hundred times this past week.

"You look like death," he says. "You're taking yourself down again, you're going under, and you're going to take that girl with you if you're not careful. And that certainly doesn't make you a *man,* Ignazio."

It's nothing he hasn't said before, but I caught him early enough in the morning that the harshness hasn't taken over. What I hear now is exhaustion with a hint of concern.

The concern is for Karissa.

He's just plain tired of me.

"You know, I didn't come here for a lecture."

"You shouldn't have come here at all," he says. "I told you you're not welcome. You're trespassing right now."

"You gonna call the police? On your son?"

"My son's dead," he says, matter-of-fact. "He died on the streets when he was just a kid. I don't know why you come around, why you're even here right now."

"Yeah," I mutter. "I don't know either."

I consider leaving when he turns around, pointing the knife at me. There's no threat to it. He's just trying to make a point, trying to get my attention. "You care about that girl?"

"Yes."

"Remember what happened the last time you cared about one."

He turns back away from me, and I know he's said all he's going to say. If I don't walk back out the door right now, he'll call the police. He will.

And I can't let it get that far.

I can't do that to my mother.

My father gave up on me long ago.

My mother's the lingering hope that maybe I'm not all hopeless.

"It's infected."

I move my forearm from across my eyes and glare at the man standing over me. Dr. Carter. I don't like people in my house. I don't invite people in my house. But yet here the man is, standing in my den again.

My gaze moves from him down to my chest, as I lay shirtless on the couch. The skin on my side is enflamed, the wound oozing. It's throbbing, every inch of me burning up, raw and painful to the touch.

Infected. No shit.

I can even *smell* it.

My eyes turn back to him, but I don't say anything. He was the compromise, a forced concession. Karissa insisted I needed to go back to the hospital but I said I was fine, so she called him instead.

I'm ten seconds from removing him from the vicinity.

Carter clears his throat, surveying my injury as he holds his medical bag. "Did you take the medicine you were prescribed?"

"No," a voice calls from the doorway. "He didn't."

Karissa.

Sighing, I cover my eyes with my arm again, not in the mood for this.

Carter has dealt with me enough to know his line of questioning is pointless, so he doesn't bother asking anything else. I keep my eyes closed and clench my jaw when he puts on a pair of latex gloves and starts poking around at my skin. He flushes out the wound,

TORTURE TO HER SOUL

sterilizing it, before covering my side with a fresh bandage.

I feel it, as he sits near me, perching on the table right in front of the couch.

"I get it, Vitale," he says quietly. "If you wanna suffer through this, go right ahead. We both know the pain won't kill you. But this infection? If you're not careful, it will. Take the antibiotics, keep the wound clean, and for God's sake, stay off your feet."

"For how long?" Karissa asks, listening to our conversation. "How long will he be down for?"

I want to make a snipe about why it even matters but the truth is, I couldn't get up and move around if I wanted to right now. I pushed myself too fast, too far, and I hit bottom before I could even really start.

"Until he's better," Carter says. "He needs to relax and sleep."

"I'll sleep when I'm dead," I mutter.

"Yeah, well, at the rate you're going, that might be soon."

The man walks away. I listen to his footsteps as he heads for the front door, Karissa behind him, showing him out. I can hear their voices in the living room, whispered words I can't make out, before the front door open and closes. Relief eases the tension in my muscles once he's gone and I hear the locks jingling, Karissa securing them.

I don't hear her footsteps.

No, she's deathly quiet.

I don't know she's there until the couch shifts, starling me when she sits down on the edge. I move my arm again, peeking at her as she holds out the orange prescription bottle and shakes it in my face.

"Antibiotics," she says. "You heard the man."

Words are on the tip of my tongue.

I don't take orders from anybody.

I nearly say the words but swallow them back at the last second as I force myself up into a sit. I grimace, one hand clutching the bandage on my side, as I snatch the pill bottle from her with my other hand. I glance at the label, reading the instructions:

Take four times daily for seven days.

Wordlessly, I open the bottle and take out a pill, popping it in my mouth and swallowing it dry. I toss the bottle down on the table in front of me before lying back down and closing my eyes.

"You're supposed to take it with food."

141

"I'm not hungry."

"Then at least let me get you some water."

"I'm fine, Karissa," I tell her. "Good as new."

"You're delusional."

"You mispronounced *handsome.*"

She scoffs. "Not today. You look like shit."

I move my arm when she says that. The moment I meet her gaze, she rolls her eyes and turns away. "Whatever, so maybe you're still handsome, even when you look like you've been fucked by the grim reaper."

Those words make a laugh echo from my chest. It hurts like hell, but it's worth it, I think, based on the smile that touches her lips. Reaching toward her, my fingertips touch her cheek before grazing her lips. "You're getting awfully brave with your words lately."

"It's because you're infuriating," she says when I drop my hand. "You're so stubborn. I know you probably don't need anybody in life, but I'm here, you know, so I might as well..."

"Help me," I say when she trails off.

"Yes."

I consider it for a moment before letting out a resigned sigh. Appearing weak is against my rules, showing vulnerability too dangerous outside of these walls, but when it's just the two of us, when we're right here, maybe there's no harm in it.

"Fine," I say. "You want to help me?"

"Yes."

"Make sure nobody else steps foot in this house."

She smiles slightly. "That I can do."

One week.

I give myself a week this time, seven days to rest and recuperate. I take the antibiotics when I'm supposed to and give Karissa some leeway. By the seventh day, I'm feeling much more like myself, my strength coming back, the infection cleared. The wound still hurts a bit when I move, but it's healing. Before long, I'll barely notice it's even there.

But for now, I still remember.

For now, I won't forget.

I won't forget how it got there.

Won't forget what I have to do about it...

Chapter Eleven

You can only make one first impression.

My father stressed that when I was a kid. Stand up straight. Don't slouch. Hold your head high. Don't scowl. It takes less than a second for someone to make up their mind about you. Just a glance. The blink of an eye.

It's something I grew up remembering. People see me how I want them to. But as important as it is, making a good first impression, it's the last impression that matters most, I think. They might not remember what they first thought about you. Feelings evolve. People change their minds. But they'll never forget the last moments. They're eternal.

Last words.

They say when Al Capone was on his deathbed, he begged the ghost of Jimmy Clark to leave him in peace. Capone was a troubled man, haunted by the past, tortured by the memory of a man he ordered slaughtered in a garage years before.

I wonder if that'll be me.

I wonder if it'll all catch up to me someday.

Will my carefully controlled world be ripped apart because

something finally broke me at the end?

I hope I'll be more like Frank Gusenberg, as he lay in a hospital bed, fourteen bullets pumped into him from Capone's men.

"Who shot you?" the officer asked.

"Nobody shot me," the man said before taking his last breath.

I think about it a lot.

I choose my words carefully.

Don't say it unless you mean it.

You never know when it might be the last thing you ever say.

The old meatpacking plant is abandoned, deep in a rundown neighborhood in Queens. Slaughterhouse Number Five, Ray jokingly calls the place. It's seen more death than a soldier in war. Although the outside of the structure is still sound, the bricks all in tact, the inside is demolished.

Back to work I go.

A man hangs from a meat hook on a rafter by chains around his wrists, dangling so low to the ground that his shoes scrape the concrete. He's battered and bloodied, a fucked up, snot-sobbing mess. I don't know his name. I don't even know what he did to end up in this place. But he's here, and when you end up in his position, there's only one way out of it.

In a body bag.

"Any last words?" I ask.

The man blinks slowly as if drugged, but I know there's nothing in his system. No, his body is just shutting down on him. Who knows how long he's been here. I got a call from Ray this morning, asking me to end the suffering.

So there's this guy...

He stares at me like he's seeing an angel of death, and I guess in a way that's what I am.

I'll take his life as payment for his sins.

With a gloved hand, I reach into my coat and pull out the cheap .22 caliber pistol, already loaded, definitely not registered in my name.

The great state of New York will tell you I don't own any weapons.

I point it at him, giving him time to come up with something to say.

His silence is deafening.

"Last chance," I tell him. "Make it profound."

He spits on the ground, a mixture of blood and saliva, before muttering, "Fuck you."

Admirable last words, although a bit cliché. Not the first time someone's said them to me in this place. I aim the gun and pull the trigger, the gunshot echoing loud as the bullet rips through his skull, ending him right away. His feet drag the cruddy ground as his body sways from the impact.

I drop the gun and walk out, discarding it there. It can't be traced back to me. Nobody will ever know I was even here.

I've said it before.

I'll say it again.

I'm not a good man.

I never will be.

I drive around for a while afterward to purge the adrenaline before making my way back to Brooklyn. It's still early, so I'm surprised to find Karissa moving around already, showered and dressed.

She's in the kitchen, wearing a pair of cutoff jeans shorts and one of my white undershirts overtop of a bright pink bikini top, the strings tied around the back of her neck. Her hair is pulled back into a loose ponytail, her skin free of makeup as she stands beside the refrigerator and shoves some bottles of water into a little foam cooler.

"Going somewhere?" I ask.

She swings toward me, smiling widely.

The sight of her smile makes my chest ache.

She's in an awfully good mood this morning for some reason, but whatever it is, I'll take it. Whatever makes her happy, I'm on board.

"Well, yeah... it's the fourth."

"The fourth?"

"Yeah, you know... the Fourth of July. Let freedom ring and all that jazz."

Ah. I didn't notice, but I usually never do. Holidays are just more days to me. A title and a national declaration don't give them meaning. She looks excited about it, though. "Huh."

Her expression falls at my reaction. "That's okay, isn't it? I mean, you've been feeling better, so I didn't think you'd need me, especially since you were gone this morning, and Melody called, so I thought..."

She's rambling.

Nervous.

"It's fine," I say, although I'm not entirely sure how I feel about it, personally, her slipping into a large crowd somewhere in the city, possibly disappearing forever. More than once these past few weeks she's mentioned feeling like someone's watching her. It's only a matter of time before her observer decides to make a move. "Just... be careful out there."

She eyes me warily for a moment. "I will."

"Good, because you tend to find trouble when you're off on your own."

I'm only half-joking, but she smiles, amused. "What can I say? It's a talent."

I nod, my eyes lingering on her for just a moment, before I turn away, letting her finish what she's doing.

"Naz?" she calls out. "You don't want to go along, do you?"

The invitation surprises me. "I'll pass."

I stroll toward the doorway when her voice rings out again. "Are you going to follow me today?"

The question stalls me yet again. She's calling me out for keeping an eye on her, matter-of-factly, like she's truly curious about the answer. It's been a while since I've done it... since she's gone somewhere for me to do it... but I can't deny the thought crossed my mind.

Pausing, I turn back to her. "And if I am?"

"Then you might as well just come along," she says, shrugging as she uses the icemaker on the refrigerator to send a swarm of crushed ice down into the little cooler. "The whole watching me from afar thing is kind of creepy, you know. I get that you don't trust me, but stalking is only cool when Edward Cullen does it."

Edward Cullen... I can't place the name. "Edward Cullen?"

"Yeah, you know, the vampire? From Twilight?" She looks at me like she expects me to get it, but shrugs it off after a second and continues. "It doesn't matter. It's kind of creepy when he does it, too. The point is, if you're going to keep an eye on me, to make sure I'm being good or whatever, you should just come along."

It's peculiar to me, how casual she talks about the situation, but something she said rubs me the wrong way. "It's not that I don't trust you."

"Do you, then?" she asks. "Do you trust me?"

"No."

The response makes her laugh.

"But that has nothing to do with it," I say. "I do it so I know you're safe."

"I'm fully capable of keeping myself safe."

"You really think that, Karissa?"

"Yes."

"Well, you think wrong," I say. "You can't recognize danger when it stares you right in the face, sweetheart."

Real danger doesn't come with a gun; it doesn't come at you with violence or anger. When someone sees red, they get careless, emotional, and it's a hell of a lot easier to diffuse a ticking bomb with all the wires exposed than one that's quiet and hidden. The biggest dangers have smiles on their faces and sweet words on their lips. They don't threaten or coerce... they entice. They have the power to make you believe whatever they want you to believe, and they do it with manipulation, through seduction.

And Karissa has absolutely no idea when it's happening to her.

I know, because I did it, and she easily fell for me.

She crosses her arms over her chest. She's feeling defensive because of what I just said. Her eyes regard me for a moment in silence before she shakes her head, deciding not to engage in that argument. "Whatever. I just think if you're going to be out there anyway, you ought to just come along."

"I'm not going to interfere with your plans."

"It's not interfering if I invited you."

"Why would you invite me?"

"Because I want you to come."

I raise an eyebrow. "You *want* me to come?"

"Uh, yeah." She shrugs. "Otherwise, I'll just be paranoid all day, thinking someone's watching me again."

"What do you have planned?"

"We're going to the park near the bridge to cook out and hang out and swim before the fireworks. Melody will be there with her boyfriend, and some other people… friends of hers. It would be nice to have someone else there… someone to talk to. Besides, who knows? You might even have some fun."

Highly unlikely, I think, but I don't say that, letting her believe what she wants. I would turn her down, decline the invitation, but her words nag at me, making a denial nearly impossible to force from my lips.

"Fine," I say. "Okay."

A flicker of surprise passes her face that she wipes away quickly with another smile. "You sound so enthusiastic."

"Cooking out and hanging out aren't really my things," I admit. "I prefer delivery and solitude."

"I've noticed," she says, going back to what she was doing when I got home, tossing a few sodas in on top of the ice. "What about swimming, though? You said nothing about swimming."

"That's because I can't swim."

She nearly drops a soda, swinging around fast. She doesn't bother trying to hide her surprise this time. "You're kidding."

"Do I look like I'm kidding?"

Her eyes survey my face as she shakes her head. "That gives a whole new meaning to you giving me the plank, you know."

"Not really," I say, casually leaning against the doorframe. "Either way, I end up drowning, whether I can swim or not."

"Yeah, but at least if you can swim, you have hope of maybe surviving."

"Sometimes it's better to not have hope."

She scoffs. "That's nuts. If I'm going into the water, I'd like to know I at least have a chance."

"Even if it's false hope?"

"Absolutely." She sticks the top on the cooler, closing it up when she's done packing it full. "I'd rather have a reason to fight than to just give up right from the start. I don't care if the hope is a lie and I'm just delaying the inevitable... at least give me something to cling to. Something's always better than nothing."

She leans back against the counter beside the refrigerator and crosses her arms over her chest, a peculiar look passing across her face as she regards me. I know her well enough to know she's thinking about her mother, about the deceit, about the glimmer of hope her mother tried to instill in her in life, twisting the ugly truth into a semi-decent lie... a lie I shattered, a hope I took away. I destroyed the fantasy with reality.

She'd be happy living in the clouds, but I grabbed her by the feet and dragged her back down to the ground.

Karissa would prefer the second wind, I realize. Even with death knocking at the door, inevitably coming to take her away, she'd want nothing more than to believe there was a chance for her to stay.

"You'll really come?" she asks after a moment.

"Yes."

"I'll call Melody," she says. "Her and Paul were going to pick me up, but since you're going they don't have to."

"Okay."

She pulls out her phone but doesn't use it yet, still looking at me, studying me, like maybe there's something else she wants to say. Her eyes trail me from head to toe before meeting my gaze again. "You *are* going to change, right?"

Instinctively, I glance down at my suit. "I wasn't planning to."

"It's the Fourth of July," she stresses. "It's a cookout, not a board room meeting or, you know, whatever it is you do in those suits."

The way she words it makes me laugh. "I do everything in these suits... socialize, eat, work... I've even been known to fuck in them before."

The flush of her cheeks and the sly grin she tries to repress tells me she very clearly remembers that happening. "I'm just saying, you know... you might be more comfortable in something like I'm wearing."

She motions to herself to stress her point, and my eyes instinctively scan her body, all too happy to have an excuse to openly ogle her. "Something tells me I wouldn't look nearly as good in that outfit as you do."

She rolls her eyes, the blush only deepening. "You know what I mean."

"Yeah, I do," I say. "If it'll make you happy, I'll change."

"Thank you."

I end up changing into some of my workout clothes—a pair of black gym shorts and a plain white tee, digging a pair of black sneakers out of the bottom of my closet. I haven't worked out in a while, with Karissa keeping me preoccupied and my injury making it hard to even walk around for too long some afternoons.

After I'm out of the suit, I head back downstairs, hearing Karissa's voice as she talks into her phone.

"Yeah, I'm sure," she says. "We'll meet you guys there."

She hangs up, slipping the phone into her back pocket, before turning toward the doorway when I step back in. Her eyes widen, jaw dropping, as she gapes at me so hard it damn near makes me hesitate.

"What now?" I ask, glancing down at myself.

"Uh, nothing," she says, shaking it off as she averts her eyes. *Huh.* "I've just never seen you wear anything like that before. It looks good... I mean, I'm just saying, you look good."

The flush is back on her cheeks.

"Are you hitting on me, Karissa?"

"What? No! Of course not! I'm just saying..."

"You're saying I look good."

"Yes."

I let out a laugh, shaking my head, waiting for her to finish whatever she needs to do. It only takes her a few minutes before she turns to me and smiles, a large canvas tote bag on her shoulder, stuffed full of her things. I take her expression to mean she's ready and grab the foam cooler, motioning with my head for her to start for the door.

I stick the cooler in the trunk of the car, and she drops her bag beside it, huffing as she does so. "Jesus, it's hot out here today."

"You sure you want to go?" I ask, slamming the trunk closed. "It's only going to get hotter."

She scoffs. "I can handle the heat."

Brooklyn Bridge Park is on the upper eastside of the borough, located along the waterfront of the East River. I park the car in a garage a quarter mile away, knowing I'm never going to find a spot on the street, and grab the cooler from the trunk as Karissa once again slings her bag on her shoulder.

The fifth pier is packed, most of the picnic tables occupied, a few of the charcoal grills already heating. The grass is unnaturally green, the air briny, permeated with the scent of salt this close to the water. Karissa tilts her head back as we get closer, inhaling deeply as a smile plays on her lips. "I love that smell."

She loves it.

Go figure.

It makes my nose twitch.

I notice the group as soon as we arrive, half a dozen people surrounding one of the tables. I don't know most of them, and from the way Karissa's footsteps slow, her approach tentative, I know she doesn't really know them, either. Melody Carmichael is dead center of the crowd, standing behind her boyfriend, as he sits at the table with two other guys. The others are female, pretty little blondes with deep tans, just like Melody.

They're paired up, I realize. Three couples.

No wonder Karissa didn't want to come alone...

My eyes survey the group before shifting to Karissa when she approaches, immediately hugging Melody. I linger behind quietly, setting the cooler down at my feet, and watch as greetings are made and introductions are done. Mandy and Monica—Melody's best friends from high school—along with their boyfriends, Scott and Jackson.

Melody comes to Paul last, wrapping her arms around him from behind and planting a kiss on his cheek that he wipes away the second she turns around. "And of course you know Paul."

"Yeah," Karissa says, her voice tentative as she only briefly glances his way. "Of course."

No one else seems to notice the change in her voice, the less than enthusiastic way she reacts to Paul's presence, but it screams loudly to me, waving a big red flag. I stare at the boy, assessing him. I've seen him before when I watched Karissa from afar, saw him the night at Timbers when Melody left the bar... the night Karissa was drugged and collapsed in the street.

Huh.

That's a strike.

I'm so wrapped up in that fact, caught up in riddling out the mystery, that I don't realize anyone addressed me until the hand presses against my chest. My eyes dart to it, seeing the bright red polish on the unnaturally long nails, before following the arm to the body of someone who shouldn't be touching me.

I meet Melody's eyes.

"Looking good, Naz," she says playfully, the soft blue twinkling with amusement. "I haven't seen you out of a suit before. I like it."

I look back down, staring at her intrusive hand until she removes it. *Finally.* "It's nice to see you again, Miss Carmichael."

She blushes at my tone like she thinks I'm flirting, but I'm just trying to keep from upsetting Karissa's friend. I smile so I won't scowl, offering kind words so I won't offend. As much as I despise deception, I know how to play the game when I have to.

And much to my dismay, I have to play it often.

I know their type. They smile too easily, welcome too warmly, their words as fake as the moans they make when they let their little boyfriends play around between their thighs. They come from well-to-do families and never want for anything. They don't know what it's like to feel pain. They don't know what it's like to struggle. They don't know what it's like to wake up one day and realize everything you thought you knew about life was a fucking lie.

They don't know, but I do, and Karissa does, too.

She's too good for them.

Despite being out of her element, Karissa seems relaxed, like she belongs with these people, and maybe she thinks she does... maybe she wants to... but I know better.

She's fought through life and managed to survive.

She hasn't had anything handed to her.

Paul and the other boys vacate the table quickly to start grilling. Karissa scoops up one of their seats while Melody sits beside her, the two falling into easy conversation. I listen for a moment before zoning out, switching my attention back to Paul. They're fumbling with charcoal, scattering heaps of it around inside the grill, before Paul pulls a small lighter from his pocket and flicks it, igniting the tiny flame.

He holds it straight up to one of the dry coals, expecting it to take off without any accelerant.

Despite myself, I laugh, loud enough that Karissa's voice temporarily wavers, but she doesn't stop to question me. I don't know shit about grilling, but starting fires? *Piece of cake.* It's just as much an art as it is a science, and it's clear, watching them, they don't have a resourceful bone anywhere in their bodies.

I let them fuck around for a minute, listening to them argue about how to go about it, the two others berating Paul for buying the wrong charcoal, for forgetting lighter fluid, for not knowing how to do anything. They're close to getting into a full-blown fistfight when I sigh exasperatedly, interrupting them before they throw any punches.

I don't say a word, merely slipping between the bickering boys and glancing around at their supplies, not finding much to work with, but it's enough to do the trick. A few napkins and a spray from a can of PAM grilling spray are all I need. I arrange the napkins so they're evenly distributed before turning to Paul.

He's gaping at me.

"Lighter?" I hold my hand out and he slips it in my palm with no question. I quickly flick it, lighting the edges of the napkins, ignoring the feel of the flame as it laps at my fingers. I stare at the paper as it ignites before turning away and tossing the lighter back to him. "You're welcome."

He doesn't thank me.

The idiot just gapes some more.

I stroll back over toward Karissa. She's watching me, her conversation with Melody forgotten as the girl moves on to talking to her other friends. I stall right in front of Karissa as she leans back against the picnic table, facing the water. You can see the Manhattan skyline clearly from here, the bustle of the city right across the river. Her eyes scan me before she tilts her head back. She arches an eyebrow as I stare down at her.

"You're good at that," she says.

"Good at what?"

"What you just did."

I briefly glance over at the grill. The flames flicker, burning away at the coals so intensely that the boys took a few steps away from it.

I turn back to Karissa, offering a slight shrug. "We all have our talents."

She's quiet, her eyes narrowing suspiciously as she studies my face, like she's trying to riddle something out from my expression, but I keep it blank. After a moment she leans forward, craning her neck more to look up at me. "Playing with fire," she says, her voice barely a whisper. "It's your specialty, right?"

My brow furrows.

"I heard you say that once," she says. "You were on the phone in the den."

She swallows thickly, like what she just said makes her nervous. My eyes are drawn to the contours of her neck. It's a beautiful thing, watching her throat muscles flex. It reminds me of how it felt that time she sucked my cock, the heat that engulfed me, the tingles, the tickles, when I felt myself slide down her slick throat.

As much as I loved it, I couldn't tolerate it for long. Fucking her is one thing—I own her, body and soul, when I'm inside of her, claiming every inch of her as my own. But when she took me in her mouth, when she peeked up at me from between my legs, the honesty in her eyes was too much to take.

That was when she owned me.

I'm scum, compared to this woman.

I should be the one on my knees.

That thought makes me laugh, and her expression shifts with confusion, as I reach over and trace my fingers along the length of her larynx, down to the dip in her throat, the notch where her necklace sits. She's wearing the one I bought her. She doesn't wear her engagement ring, but she never takes *that* off.

I pick up the pendant, rolling the round ornament between my fingertips, reading the words engraved on it. *Carpe Diem*. It's a funny feeling, I think, treasuring something you used to want to destroy. Not funny, ha-ha... funny as in what-a-fucking-joke.

I meet her eyes again. "Are you always going to be suspicious of everything I do?"

"Yes."

Her voice is barely a breath.

I laugh again, but there's no humor in it. I appreciate the honesty, but I hate the fucking answer.

"Just like you'll always be suspicious of me," she continues. "Maybe when you start trusting me again, I'll give you the benefit of the doubt, too."

"Maybe," I say, bending down, my lips near her ear as I whisper, "but you probably shouldn't."

I let go of her necklace and stand back up straight just as Melody turns, once again striking up conversation with Karissa. Melody's eyes are wide, pleading, her voice matching that look as she says, "so, did you think about it any more?"

Karissa glances at her. "Think about what?"

"Taking that class with me," Melody says. "Ethics & Society."

Karissa's expression shifts as she scrunches up her nose. "Hell no."

"Oh, come on!" Melody says, grabbing her arm and pulling on it, like a toddler throwing a tantrum. "Please? I can't take a philosophy class without you. That's all kinds of wrong. Jesus Christ, it's like, blasphemous."

"Then don't take it."

"But I want to, and I don't get why you don't."

"Don't what?" Paul's voice cuts through the conversation as he strolls over to the table. "What's going on?"

"Karissa doesn't want to take that class with me."

Paul laughs. "The philosophy class? Didn't she fail the first one?"

"I didn't *fail*," Karissa says. "I just didn't do as well as I hoped."

"That's because Santino was an asshole," Melody says. "You should've gotten an A in the class. You were great at it! That *to be or not to be, if there's a tree in the forest does it shit on a bear* kind of crazy is you all day long, Kissimmee."

The others laugh, and I'll hand it to Melody... she's certainly amusing... but all that really registers with me is the flinch Karissa makes at that nickname. *Kissimmee*. I wonder if she knows the deeper meaning behind it, the history her parents and I have in Kissimmee.

I wonder if I should tell her.

If I should tell her that's where her parents ran off to after destroying my life. If I should tell her they thought it would be their salvation. If I should tell her I tracked them there, found them living in that small house in Kissimmee, Florida, like they were the picture perfect family. It was the last place the two of them were together before Johnny sent Carmela on the run on her own and he came home, to face my judgment. *We'll always have Kissimmee*, I heard him once say.

He thought I'd leave her alone if he offered himself up on a platter, but I wasn't looking for an easy meal.

I wanted *equal justice*.

Paul walks away when one of his friends calls his name, wandering over to check the grill. The flames have died down a bit so I can barely see them from where I stand.

"Ethics and Society," I say, joining the conversation. "I'm assuming that deals with controversial social issues. Sounds fascinating."

"See!" Melody waves my direction. "He gets it! And remember that murder paper we wrote? You got an A on that one! This is right up your alley. Murder's totally your thing!"

I stifle a laugh at that.

I read Karissa's essay on murder. I saw it lying on Daniel's desk the first time I confronted him for how he was treating her in class.

It was horrendous.

She deserved to fail it.

But of course I made him pass her anyway.

"And come on," Melody continues, really laying it on thick. "There's a whole section on sexual morality. You have to take it. Everyone else is all *blah blah blah*, but this is the business! Nowadays everybody wants to talk like they got something to say, you know? But nothing comes out when they move their lips. It's *ridiculous*. Where else are you going to get such titillating conversation?"

I have no idea what the hell the girl is rambling about, but it somehow cracks Karissa, the corner of her lips flickering with the hint of a smile. "From Eminem."

Melody clutches her chest dramatically, throwing her head back. "God, I wish. That man could titillate me all night long. But he's not here, and you are, so I think you should totally take this class with me."

"Besides," Paul shouts as he slaps the metal grate on top of the grill, "it's not like you have to worry about Santino this year. Someone already took care of that for you."

Karissa's eyes immediately shift in my direction as Melody's attention is diverted. She chastises her boyfriend for making light of their professor's death, while the gaze that's pointed at me is full of nothing but suspicion. She knows. I know she does. She hasn't come out and asked me, hasn't brought it up beyond the initial conversation the night she was questioned by the police, but I can see in her eyes that she's thought about it.

She wants to ask me.

I hope she never does.

Because if she's looking for remorse or some sort of rational explanation, she's never going to find what she wants from me. I don't regret for a second what I did. The man had it coming.

I jabbed that fucking pointer stick of his right through his heart.

I'd never stabbed someone in the heart before. It's callous, and personal, and I prefer to keep it strictly business. But he crossed me, and offended me, and I wanted him to look at me when death took him away. I expected it to be quick but he struggled. He fought, and he tried to run, the goddamn stick still sticking out of his chest when he got to his feet.

I learned a lesson that day.

I'll never do that again.

That's why I slit Johnny's throat before I put the knife in his chest.

I curve an eyebrow at Karissa, waiting for her to turn away from me again, but she doesn't.

She stares.

And stares.

And stares.

I feel like she grating at my soul when she stares at me that way.

Like she's scraping away some of the blackness, trying to salvage what might still be beneath. I wonder if she'll be disappointed to find every part of me is tainted, that even my good isn't as good as it should be.

After a moment, Melody turns back to her, refocusing, and drawing Karissa's attention away from me. "So? Will you at least consider it?"

Karissa sighs exasperatedly. "Fine."

"You'll think about it?"

"I'll take the damn class."

Melody squeals, once more grabbing her arm, this time excitedly. It doesn't take much to distract her as she switches subjects, inviting her other friends into the conversation when one of them chimes in and asks the million dollar question: "Who's the Santino guy?"

Melody launches into the whole tale, starting from the beginning, the first day Karissa walked into his classroom.

"He took one look at her and turned his nose up," Melody says, matter-of-fact. "He hated her for no reason. It was crazy."

Crazy, maybe, but there was a reason, and it certainly wasn't because he hated her. He never saw Karissa that day. I don't think he *ever* really saw her. He laid his eyes on a young girl who looked so very much like the one he fawned over as a teenager, the only girl Daniel Santino ever gave his heart to, and she crushed it, obliterated it. He always had a hard-on for Carmela, following her around like a puppy dog, lapping up every tiny speck of attention she gave him, devouring every bone she threw his way. Carmela humored his pesky crush, even went on a few dates with him.

She said it was compassion.

Said it was right to give him a fair shake.

But in the end she dropped him like a bad habit and picked up a worse one instead: Johnny.

He looked at Karissa that day when she walked in, and he didn't see his new student. He saw his old love. He saw the one who got away. And he wasn't angry to see her face again.

No, what Karissa sensed from him was *terror*.

Because he knew that was a face I'd been looking for.

And he knew, when I found it, exactly what I planned to do.

Melody is somewhere in the middle of the semester in her story, about when I seemed to have come in. I can tell Karissa's uncomfortable, with the way she's fidgeting, the way her eyes won't quite meet anybody's. I'm grateful when Paul interrupts, barging into the conversation with talk about the food as he slaps it on the grill, and I see Karissa breathe a sigh of relief, too.

I don't know why she puts herself through this.

I don't spend time around people unless I have to.

The day drags on into the late afternoon. Despite the 'no alcohol on the premises' sign we passed on the way in, they break out a cooler full of beer and crack open cans. I sip on a bottle of water Karissa brought while she gives in and drinks along with the others.

It's hot as fuck.

The company is boring.

I'm sweating, downright miserable, but I say nothing, picking apart an over-cooked burger I have no interest in ingesting. I'm sitting on the edge of the bench beside Karissa, so close ours arms brush together whenever one of us moves. Nobody notices or pays much attention to what I'm doing, except for Karissa, as her eyes routinely seek me out. She's trying to be coy about it, her gaze curious. After a few times, I catch her eyes and she freezes, knowing she's been caught.

I take a small bite, straining as I chew, fighting the urge to gag on the dry meat as she watches me.

After a moment, she leans closer, close enough that only I can hear, as she whispers, "what if it's poisoned?"

I grab a napkin from the table, spitting out everything that's in my mouth. *Disgusting.* I toss the napkin down on top of my plate and shove it aside.

I'm done with that shit.

Her eyes widen. "I didn't mean for you to do that."

"It wasn't you," I say, grabbing my bottle of water and taking a swig. "I couldn't choke that down if I had to."

She looks from me to her plate, to her untouched burger, then back to me again. She says nothing, standing up and grabbing her plate, hesitating before grabbing mine, too. After throwing them away, she chugs what's left in her can of beer and tosses it in the trash before grabbing another from the cooler.

Late afternoon morphs into early evening. Everything is cleaned up, most of it discarded, abandoned besides the coolers, as they decide to make their way down the waterfront to go swimming.

I sit along the side of the in-ground pool, at a round little table with a gigantic blue umbrella over my head. People pack the small area, at least a hundred sets of eyes that could easily wander Karissa's way, but she seems to not care as she sheds her clothes, discarding them at the table beside me, leaving her standing there in a slinky pink bikini that makes her tanned skin glow.

The metallic material covers her most intimate places—places I'd kill a man if he ever dared to look—but otherwise leaves little to the imagination. Her curves are proudly displayed, every dimple and dip, cleft and crevice, every inch of her flesh that beckons to me at night when she lays beside me in the dark.

It's sinful.

It's unbearable.

It takes every ounce of strength I have to let her walk away from me looking like that.

She strolls over toward the edge of the pool as she pulls her hair up, securing it on the top of her head in a sloppy sort of bun. I tear my eyes away from her, sighing exasperatedly as I run my hands down my sweaty face and close my eyes. When I reopen them, the first thing I see is Paul standing on the opposite side of the pool, directly across from Karissa, his eyes slinking down her body, going dangerously close to those places they ought not go.

Strike two.

My skin prickles, a coiling inside of me that I quickly try to unwind, to pull back apart before it wraps me up too tight to fight it. Karissa slips into the water, immediately disappearing beneath the surface.

Only then does the boy look away from her.

He jumps it, swimming over to his girlfriend, immediately picking Melody up and dunking her as she squeals loudly with laughter.

They joke around, playing in the water, swimming and splashing. It's strange, seeing Karissa that way, so at ease around people, so relaxed and happy, like the reality that I slapped her with two months ago faded away, taking a backseat to the life she created here. I haven't seen her smile this much since… well, since before she got hurt.

TORTURE TO HER SOUL

The evening starts to slip away, growing later as the sun shifts position in the sky, edging closer toward the west. Karissa eventually pulls herself out of the pool, dripping water as she strolls over to me, her arms crossing over her chest as she approaches.

She digs a towel out of her bag to dry her hair. When she realizes I'm watching, she wraps the towel around her, covering her body as she smiles sheepishly.

"Why do you do that?" I ask.

She raises an eyebrow. "Do what?"

"Shield yourself from me," I say. "All those people in the pool didn't bother you, like you weren't at all uncomfortable with *them* looking."

"They weren't looking."

"They could've been."

"They weren't," she insists. "I mean, maybe they looked, but they didn't pay me much mind. But you..."

"But me?" I ask when she doesn't finish.

"You *look* at me."

"And that's a problem?"

She sighs, clutching the towel tighter around her as she turns, like she's about to walk away. I sound defensive, I know, and hell, maybe I am, but I'm not trying to frustrate her.

I can see those walls going up between us, though.

Before she can leave, I reach out and grasp her arm, stopping her. Her muscles tense as I pull her back toward the table.

"I'm not trying to be a pain in the ass," I say, tugging her down onto the chair beside me. "I'm just trying to understand."

"You know," she says, shifting her body toward me but still keeping her skin covered. "For someone who knows everything about me, you don't seem to really understand anything."

Her voice is firm, borderline antagonistic.

I got under her skin.

"Those people?" she continues, waving over toward the pool.

"They can look all they want. I don't notice when they do, because I don't care what they think. Not anymore. I used to... I used to want to fit in, to be normal, and sometimes I still feel that way, like I could be that way if I tried, but I'm not. I know I'm not. My parents are murderers and liars, and you..." She laughs dryly. "You are what you are. So yeah, those people can look if they want, but they don't see me, and I don't care what they think they see. But you look at me. You look at me hard. And I know you see me. And maybe, Naz... maybe I care what you think."

The others are out of the pool, making their way toward us before I can respond. I let go of Karissa, and she stands back up, dropping her towel only long enough to slip her shorts back on and pull on her top.

"I need a drink," she mutters.

"Hell yeah!" Melody says, throwing her arm over Karissa's shoulder. "That's the spirit. Let's fill up my cup and get fucked up!"

Chapter Twelve

We make our way toward the front of the park, to the grassy area around the first pier. The area's busy, but they find a vacant spot in the middle of the gathering crowd. They spread out blankets, making themselves at home, as I take a seat along the edge of one alone.

They drink some more.

I mull over Karissa's words in silence.

They joke around, laughing and playing, acting like the teenagers they are.

I get lost in my own head.

By the time the sun finally sets, darkness creeping over the area, Karissa is wasted. Between the heat and her empty stomach, she never stood a chance. I'm gazing across the river at the Manhattan skyline in the night, admiring the lights in a city that never sleeps, keeping an eye on Karissa the best I can. She eventually breaks away from her friends and strolls over to where I'm sitting, pausing right in front of me. "What are you doing over here?"

My eyes shift to her, scanning her in the darkness. "I'm admiring the view."

"Oh." She glances behind her. "Am I blocking it?"

"No," I say. "You *are* it."

She rolls her eyes and starts to step aside when I grab ahold of her, catching her off guard. Her reflexes are stunted, her strength diminished from the alcohol sloshing through her veins. I pull her down onto the blanket with me, and she lets out a startled squeal before laughing when she loses her balance, falling right into me. I grunt when her knee grazes my crotch, just barely missing landing right on my cock. My side stings, but she's giggling... fucking *giggling*. I can't be mad. "You're drunk, jailbird."

"Just a little," she says, holding up her fingers half an inch apart, nearly pinching me in the fucking nose with them.

"You should've eaten something earlier."

"Yeah, right," she slurs. "I wouldn't eat *anything* that guy touched."

"Who?"

"Paul."

Huh.

Strike three.

"I could've bought you something. It's not good to drink on an empty stomach."

She blows out a dismissive breath. "Puh-lease. What's good anymore?"

"You," I say, brushing her wild hair from her face. It came down sometime after swimming, now a tangled mess, waves falling everywhere. "You're still good."

She laughs again, laughs like that's the funniest thing she's ever heard. I expect her to try to get to her feet, to stagger away, but instead she shifts around in front of me, settling between my legs. She leans against me, her back flush against my chest, her head coming to rest just below my chin. She smells like chlorine and sweat, her skin slick and glowing, more freckles dotting her shoulders and her cheeks.

The sun did a number on her today.

Even her nose is pink.

"Tell me something," she says. "Would somebody good love somebody like you?"

It's a valid question, maybe a bit spiteful, but it's the closest she's coming to admitting she *loves* me in a while. I rest my cheek against the top of her head as I consider it. "Probably not."

She's quiet for a bit, just lounging there. I snake my arms around her, feeling her warmth as I hold her close. It isn't until the fireworks start up, blasting off from the bridge and filling the night sky, that Karissa finally speaks again.

"Beautiful," she whispers as her friends loudly cheer, raising a ruckus nearby. I smile at the amazement in her voice, listening to the bangs as they detonate back to back, watching as the blasts bathe her skin in flashes of different colors.

"I've always liked fireworks," I say. "The gunpowder, the chemicals and fuel carefully calibrated, making something so powerful, something so deadly, seem so harmless. Knowing how much control, how much heat, how much energy it takes to set off the explosions at the perfect time... fascinating."

She tilts her head, shifting slightly and sitting up more to look back at me. Sensing her gaze, I meet her eyes. They look black in the night.

"You light up when you talk like that," she says.

I shrug a shoulder as I study her face, light igniting parts of it, casting the rest in shadows. "You make something beautiful enough and people forget just how much it can hurt you."

She stares at me again.

That stare.

The one that makes it feel like she's clawing at my skin, ripping apart my outsides to find her way deeper in. I think I get it now, what she was saying earlier.

Because nobody looks at me like she does.

I stare back, holding my ground, waiting for her to turn around. Waiting for her to back down, to be the first to look away, but I don't intimidate her, not the way I intimidate everyone else. I never have.

I don't know if she was born this goddamn fearless, if it's encoded in her DNA, gifted to her by her flawed bloodline, or if it's something life taught her, something molded into her all those years she was unknowingly on the run. I wonder if she got that from her father, or if it was *me* who caused her bravery.

She inches forward ever so slightly and hesitates, contemplating, her eyes flickering to my mouth so faintly I almost don't catch it. She takes a deep breath, exhaling with resolve, before closing her eyes and coming the rest of the way.

My brave, brave woman kisses me.

It's soft. Tentative. Sweet. Her breath is shaky and her lips barely part, but it's a kiss, none-the-less, and I fucking savor it. It's not the first time we've kissed since everything turned ugly, not even the first time she's initiated it, but this kiss is different. This kiss feels less like hunger and more like heartache, like she's quenching a thirst by trying to remember how to drink.

Tiny sips.

That's all she takes.

Little pecks against my lips before she pulls back away.

She stares at me again.

Five... ten... fifteen seconds.

And then she turns around.

She settles back into my arms, lounging on the blanket between my legs as she stares up at the sky in silence, watching the fireworks with the same fearlessness she looked at me with.

I'm not the only one of us who knows how to play with fire, I think... and I'm not the only one who enjoys it, either.

"You want to know what I think about when I look at you, Karissa?"

"What?"

"I think there's nobody else like you in the world."

The fireworks seem to go on forever.

Karissa says nothing else to me.

Not at the park, not on the walk to the car, and not on the way home.

The silence isn't strained like it usually is when she doesn't talk. She's right here beside me, completely at ease. I don't know if it's because she's too damn drunk to remember or if she just finally forgot she hates me.

I lead Karissa to the front door of the house when we get there, my hand pressed against the small of her back. She steps up onto the small porch, waiting, as I dig for the right key. It takes a moment as I fumble with the new locks, a strange sensation creeping up my back, prickling my spine.

The hair at the nape of my neck stands on end.

Key halfway into the lock, I freeze as the feeling consumes me, my muscles taut as I strain my ears. There's somebody there. Carefully, I turn my head, slowly surveying the dark neighborhood around us, looking and listening, but I see nothing.

Nothing but blackness.

I'm not a fool, though. The darkness can't trick me. Just because I don't see it doesn't mean it's not there. I sense it, feel it crawling across my skin.

Somebody's watching us.

Somebody's watching me.

Somebody's watching *her*.

I scan the area again, waiting for something to happen, for someone to appear out of the shadows, and damn near jump when someone touches me. My eyes dart to the hand on my arm before I look at Karissa, seeing her eyeing me peculiarly. "Is something wrong, Naz?"

Yes, I think.

Something is definitely wrong.

Somebody is here.

I glance behind me again, giving one last look at the street, before turning back to her, offering a small smile so not to alarm her. She's too drunk to feel it right now, I think. "It's nothing."

I turn the key, finishing the last lock, and push open the front door. I motion for her to go ahead of me inside, trying to shove down those feelings of being watched as they nag at me. Karissa doesn't listen, though, wavering on the porch, before she steps closer until she's almost flush up against me. I stare down at her, watching as she slowly licks her lips.

She reaches up on her tiptoes but I stop her, palming her cheeks, cradling her face in my hands. I hold her there, her lips a few inches from mine, as I stare into her dark eyes, looking for some sign of uncertainty.

"You're drunk," I say seriously. "You don't know what you're doing."

"I know exactly what I'm doing," she whispers. "I'm just a little drunk. I'm not an idiot. I know who you are... what you are... I know what you've done. And I know what I'm doing, too. I know what I want."

"And what's that?" I ask. "What do you want?"

She reaches up and grabs my wrists, pulling my hands away from her face. She's not strong enough to force me to move them, but I don't resist. She pushes back up on her tiptoes, pressing her lips to mine as her eyelids flutter closed.

I kiss her back, but I keep my eyes open.

That feeling won't stop, won't go away, building and building inside of me. I'm paranoid and starved, too damn exhausted to deal with it. As soon as I try to pull away from Karissa's lips, she wraps her arms around my neck and pushes me toward the open doorway, into the foyer. I step backward, finally breaking the kiss, and look out at the street again suspiciously.

A shadow moves in my peripheral.

Maybe it's my imagination.

Maybe I just need some fucking sleep.

My head turns that way, but I see nothing in the darkness, nothing but trees and grass, cars and mailboxes. Fireworks pop off in the distance, filling the air with loud cracks like far away gunshots, causing wounds that Karissa soothes when she kisses me again.

Fuck it.

I slam the door closed, tinkering with the locks, making sure every one of them is secure before giving her my undivided attention. Whatever's out there, be it friend or foe, the shadows or the wind, isn't going to get inside and hurt what I have right here.

We make our way upstairs, not rushing but not hesitating, her lips glued to mine, her arms wrapped around my neck. I kiss her deeply, each second more passionate, as my hands settle on her hips, fingertips brushing the bare skin beneath the hem of her shirt.

I break the kiss long enough to pull her top off. She raises her arms straight up in the air, surrendering to me as I strip her. Her clothes are discarded fast but I intend to take it slow, to savor every moment.

I pull her onto the bed, climbing on top of her fully clothed, my lips moving from her mouth and down her cheek, to her chin and neck, working my way along her jawline. I kiss and nip at the skin, my tongue grazing her salty flesh, as her hands run along my back, beneath my shirt.

Sitting up, I tug it off and toss it aside before my mouth finds her chest. I circle a nipple with my tongue before wrapping my lips around it, sucking on the sensitive flesh. She moans, arching her back, as she fists my hair.

"Please," she pleads when I move to the other nipple, giving it the same attention as I awkwardly kick off my shoes, discarding them at the end of the bed. "Please, Naz."

I kiss along her collarbones before finding her mouth again, smothering her begging with my lips. I shove my shorts down, fumbling to get them off without breaking the kiss, and settle between her legs. The warmth radiating from her makes me shiver. I can still smell the sun on her skin, the scent intoxicating me when I inhale sharply as I push inside of her.

Fuck, she feels so good wrapped around me. So good, that it's hard to believe something like this could ever be bad. That I could ever be wrong for her. And I know I am... I'm the last person she should give herself to... but moments like this, when she gasps, that first sudden exhale, like she's surprised by how perfect we fit together, like she's finally whole again after missing a part of her, gives me hope.

Hope that maybe, even though it's wrong, somehow I can find a way to make it all right.

"Tell me," I whisper, running my tongue along the shell of her ear. "Tell me how you want it to be. Tell me what you need from me."

I'll give her anything.

I'll tear my fucking chest open with my bare hands, rip out my heart and hand it to her, if that's what she needs.

All she has to do is tell me.

All she has to do is ask.

She could bark out a million demands, and I would work myself to the death making them all happen, but instead she merely whispers, "I want you to love me."

So I do.

I love her.

I take my time inside of her, my lips never leaving her skin as I thrust deep, filling her with every inch of me that I can. I make love to her until her skin is flushed, coated in another layer of sweat, until she starts pleading with me again, this time to give her more.

Harder.

Deeper.

More.

More.

More.

Her breasts are flush against my chest, her nipples hard as she presses them into me like she's desperate for more friction. Her hands rake down my spine, not digging into the skin, not drawing blood, but I can feel the mark they leave behind, a trail of tingles I can't shake. My face is nuzzled into her neck as I breathe heavily, panting, my tongue lapping at the sweaty skin before I press my lips to the spot just below her ear and suck. She squeals, fisting my hair again.

I can feel her body tensing beneath me as I slide in and out of her, holding her so close I graze her clit with each stroke. I increase the pace, just enough to thrust a bit deeper, to hit it a bit harder.

She lets out a strangled noise, throwing her head back. I bite down on her shoulder as she comes, listening to her cries of pleasure as the tiny convulsions rock her body. I can feel mine getting close, building inside of me. I don't have the energy to hold it back, to delay it any longer.

I shiver, grunting into her neck as I come inside of her just as her own orgasm starts to fade. I thrust a few times, riding through the waves of pleasure, before stilling on top of her.

I don't move away, don't let go of her, staying deep inside of her as I hold her against me, listening to her raspy breaths, feeling her pulse as her heart frantically beats.

Don't regret it, I think, closing my eyes. *Don't tell me you regret giving yourself to me.*

She lies still, not moving an inch, like she's trying to get her thoughts in order, like she's trying to pull herself together.

Don't fucking regret it.

Whatever you do.

"Naz, I—"

Before she can get out whatever it is she wants to say, a sudden noise interrupts us, the obnoxious blaring loud even upstairs in the bedroom.

It only takes a second for it to hit me.

My car.

I quickly pull away from Karissa and jump to my feet, grabbing my shorts from the floor and pulling them on.

"Stay here," I tell her, running out before she can question me. I sprint downstairs and head toward the front door, grabbing my keys from where I discarded them when we got home.

I head into the den and walk along the bookshelves, my fingers quickly skimming the spines of books until I come upon my copy of War & Peace, still in the right spot.

Luckily Karissa hasn't ever tried to read it.

I pull it off the shelf and open it up. The pages are cut out, leaving a gaping hole right in the center, a silver revolver tucked into it. I pull the gun out, tossing the book on the desk, and make sure it's still loaded as I head for the front door.

The alarm is blaring so loudly it's practically vibrating the ground. I hit the button on my spare key, relieved when it shuts off through the wall. I strain my ears, listening to the silence, before unlocking the door and slowly opening it. My heart furiously pounds against my ribcage as my eyes scan the yard, the gun gripped tightly in my hand, prepared for anything.

It's quiet, and still. There's nobody around, nothing except my car, the driver's side door hanging wide open, a familiar set of lost keys dangling from the lock. I eye them for a moment before stepping over to the driveway and pulling them out, giving a quick glance inside the car before slamming the driver's side door closed.

I'm staring out into the darkness when I hear a squeak behind me. Everything inside of me seizes momentarily before kicking into high gear, fueled by adrenaline. Spinning around, I raise the gun at whatever's moving, my finger slipping right off the trigger as soon as I see her.

Karissa.

I'm aiming right at her face.

She freezes in the doorway to the house, whimpering. I move the gun away at once, raising my hands to show her I mean no harm.

"Fuck, Karissa, don't sneak up on people. You're going to get yourself hurt. I told you to stay where you were."

Her frantic gaze darts all around me, trying to make sense of things as I flick on the safety and stick the gun in my waistband.

"What's happening?" she asks. "I mean, what was...?"

"It was just the car alarm."

The answer calms her a bit, although her gaze keeps flickering to my gun. "What set it off?"

"Don't worry about it," I say. "I handled it."

She wants to ask more but the racket of the garage door raising interrupts her when I push the button so I can move the car out of the driveway. It gives me a moment to collect myself as I run my hands down my face, taking a deep breath.

"Relax," I say when it's quiet again. "It could've just been a raccoon."

"A raccoon?"

"Yes."

She shakes her head. "I thought you didn't lie to me?"

"I don't."

Her eyes are skeptical, borderline angry as she steps closer, coming outside. She doesn't believe it.

"I said it *could've* been a raccoon, which is true. It could've been."

"But it wasn't."

"No," I admit, "it wasn't."

"Who was it?"

"If I had to guess, I'd say it was the same person who robbed me."

She gapes at me. "How do you know? Did you see them?"

"No, I didn't see anybody," I say, holding up the returned keys, jingling them in the air. "Just an educated guess."

She stares at the keys before meeting my eyes. "Do you know who it is?"

I nod.

She pauses. "Do I know them?"

Another nod. This one's hesitant.

I stare at her, waiting for the question I dread.

175

Don't ask me if it's your mother.

Don't ask me that...

"Is it, uh...?" She frowns, looking away from me as she gathers her thoughts. "Is it safe?"

Reaching out, I graze my fingers along her jawline before cupping her chin. I tilt her face, making her look at me again. She looks worried, so I offer her a smile, just a small one, to try to ease her concerns. Is it safe? Absolutely not. It never is in my world, and it never will be.

Death lurks around every corner, watching and waiting, and someday, it'll come for me again.

"Nothing will happen to you," I tell her, running my thumb along her soft bottom lip. "I'll make sure of it."

She returns my smile. I don't know if she believes me, but I can tell she wants to. Slowly, little by little, she's putting her trust in me again.

Chapter Thirteen

"Happy Birthday."

I'm sitting on the couch in the den, my plain white shirt lifted up, tucked beneath my chin as I survey my left side, when those two words ring out.

Happy Birthday.

My eyes dart to Karissa as she stands in front of me. "Excuse me?"

"Happy Birthday," she says again, smiling tentatively as she holds out a small container of chocolate pudding and a spoon. "For you."

I drop my shirt, letting it cover my chest again as I eye her warily. I hesitate so long her smile falls, worry casting shadows over her face. Slowly, I reach for the pudding cup and take it as she sits down beside me with her own. She already has hers open and is taking a bite before I can even think of what to say.

"How do you know?" I ask, peeling the top off the pudding. I'm not even hungry, so I'm not sure why she gave me this.

"It was listed on your passport."

"Ah."

"I would've made you a cake," she says. "Or, well, had you one made, but I didn't think you'd eat it, you know, in case it got doped with cyanide." She casts me a sideways look as she takes another bite. "I guess I could've bought like a honey bun or something, but we had pudding in the fridge, so..."

"So pudding it is," I mutter, taking a small bite before I wave at her with my spoon. "I didn't expect anything."

"I figured," she says, "considering you never even mentioned it."

She devours her pudding, practically licking the plastic clean of chocolate, as I set mine down on the table without taking another bite. I pull my shirt back up as she watches me.

"It looks better," she says, setting her empty container down beside mine. Reaching over, she runs her fingertips along the skin around my wound, her touch so light it sends a tingle through me. The forming scar is nasty but it's healing, barely even sore anymore.

Sighing, I relax back against the couch, relishing the sensation of her touch. "It feels better."

Her hand moves, shifting away from my injury, and runs along my stomach, caressing the skin. She traces the ridges of my abs, following the trail of hair up to my chest as she slowly edges toward me.

I close my eyes when she leans my way, feeling her lips as they press against my stomach, trailing kisses up toward my chest. Her hand brushes against my lap, rubbing my cock through my pants. It stirs beneath her palm, just the simple touch enough to make it harden.

Reaching beneath the fabric, she grasps a hold of me, stroking a few times as she releases me from my pants. I open my eyes just as she shifts position and drops her head toward my lap.

"Karissa..."

Her eyes dart to mine, but she doesn't stop, doesn't waver, as she takes my cock into her mouth. The wet warmth soothes me, and I want to protest, I should protest, but it feels too good.

Too fucking good.

My hands settle on top of her head, lightly running through her hair. She sucks... and sucks... and *sucks*, teeth grazing and tongue stroking until my head starts spinning and I feel like I'm going to explode.

I should warn her.

I should stop her.

I should end this, but I'm weak.

I'm fucking weak.

I'm regaining my strength, but the woman still has the power to destroy me.

I come hard, my body tensing, pain running through me. It hurts. It *hurts*. But this pain feels better than anything I've felt in years. I grip on to her hair as she swallows, not letting go until she releases me from her mouth. I close my eyes, breathing deeply. "I told you never to do that..."

"No, you told me I don't belong on my knees, and I wasn't on them," she counters, sitting up, her gaze on my face. There's a twinkle in her eye when I look at her. *Amusement*. "You know you should always say what you mean."

She tries to move away them but I grab a hold of her, pulling her onto my lap. I grunt when she straddles me, pain stabbing my side from my injury as her knee hits it.

"Shit, sorry," she says, panicked when I wince, but I grip tightly to her hips to keep her there, shaking off her apology.

"It was my fault," I say, clenching my jaw. "I should've known better."

I stare at her, hands shifting from her hips, running up her back. I grip the back of her neck, pulling her to me, and kiss her as ringing echoes through the room. My phone. I try to deepen the kiss, but Karissa pulls back. "Do you need to get that?"

I shake my head, kissing her again and again, as she whispers against my mouth, "don't you... need to... at least see... who it is?"

"I know who it is."

"Who?"

179

"My mother."

She pulls away completely as the ringing stops, her gaze briefly darting across the room toward my phone. "How do you know?"

"Because it's my birthday."

I try to kiss her again, but she resists, her palms flat against my chest.

"Your mother," she says. "Is she as pleasant as your father?"

"Few people are as pleasant as Giuseppe Vitale." I shake my head. "My mother's a good woman. You'll never meet a nicer person."

"So why don't you ever see her?" she asks. "Why didn't you take her call?"

"Because she's better off without me," I say. "When you love people, you want what's best for them, and sometimes what's best for them isn't you."

"You said that about me once," she says. "You said you loved me, and you wanted what was best for me, even though you thought what was best for me wasn't you."

"I meant it," I say. "But I'm also *in* love with you, and I'm a selfish son of a bitch. It was wrong, but I wanted you... I want you. So I'm keeping you."

She laughs dryly. "You're keeping me."

"Yes."

"You ever consider maybe your mother wants to keep you, too?" she asks. "I don't mean that in a creepy kind of way, you know... I mean, like, just because someone's bad for us doesn't mean we don't want them in our lives, anyway. I was still willing to give up everything for you."

"You were."

"Yes."

"Past tense."

Her brow furrows. "What?"

"You said you *were* willing," I say, "not that you *are* willing."

She considers that as she climbs off of me, getting to her feet.

"Yeah, well, I guess I'm still deciding."

"Deciding what?"

"Whether or not I want to keep *you*."

My phone starts making noise again as Karissa grabs our discarded pudding containers to throw them away.

"You should answer that," she says. "Talk to your mother."

I don't correct her as she walks out, but it's not my mother this time. The ring is different. It's vague, barely noticeable, but it's a different tone. Ray.

Sighing, I get to my feet and shuffle across the room, snatching my phone off of my desk. I stare at the screen for a moment before pressing the button to silence the ringing.

Unlike my mother, he's not calling to wish me a happy birthday. He probably doesn't even realize it's today.

"Let's do something," I call out to Karissa when I hear her move around the kitchen. "Grab some lunch or something."

She appears in the doorway. "Yeah?"

"Yeah."

My phone starts ringing again right away, once again blaring Ray's tone. Karissa eyes it curiously. "You don't have anything else you'd rather do?"

I send the call to voicemail and turn off the phone as I shake my head. "No. Nothing."

⤜⤛

"What's Cobalt?"

My eyes turn to Karissa when she speaks. I'm not even off our street and she's already asking questions out of nowhere. "Cobalt?"

"Yeah, Cobalt."

"Where'd you hear that?"

"That detective," she says. "I heard him mention Cobalt, that it's where the shooting happened. I know it was weeks ago, but I was just thinking, and well... what is it?"

181

"It's a chemical element," I say, "and a shade of blue."

"Yeah, and it's also the name of a Chevy car," she counters, "but that doesn't tell me where you were shot."

I fight a smile at her brusque tone. "You didn't ask where I was shot."

"Fine," she says. "Where were you shot?"

"In my side."

"Naz..."

"In Greenwich Village," I say, knowing she's not going to drop it. "Cobalt Social Club."

She curves an eyebrow at me. "A social club?"

"Yes."

"You're a member of a social club."

"Yes."

"Is that a euphemism? Like a gentleman's club?"

"No, no strippers. No women at all, generally, although sometimes they bend the rules. It's more of an exclusive hangout that you need membership to get into."

"And what do you do there?"

"Socialize," I say. "Drink."

Conduct business.

Plot schemes.

"So it's a special kind of club," she reiterates. "Where you drink and hang out with other men like you."

"Essentially."

"You know that sounds a lot like a gay bar, right?"

Laughing, I cut my eyes at her. "I suppose, when you put it that way, but it doesn't really matter what it sounds like. It is what it is."

She shrugs, looking away from me to gaze out the window. "Can I see it?"

"See what?"

"Cobalt."

"Uh, like I said, women aren't generally allowed..."

"I don't want to go in," she says. "I just... I want to see where you were... where it happened."

I don't have a response for that.

I'm not sure why it matters.

Neither of us says much else on the ride into the city. She

eventually pulls out her phone, swiping her finger across the cracked screen to send colorful birds flying through the air at little green pigs.

She needs a new phone. I'm not sure how much longer that one's going to survive. As much as she drops it, I'm surprised the thing still even works.

I don't know why I'm doing it, but I drive straight to Cobalt to satisfy her curiosity. I pull through the alley, into the back lot, and swing the car around, idling there. There's no sign outside, nothing to indicate what the building is. "Cobalt."

Karissa's brow furrows, and I can see she has more questions as she turns from the building to look out the side window. "So it happened here?"

"What?"

"This is where you were shot."

"Oh." I glance around. "Yeah, over by the light."

She nods, looking at the light for a moment before turning back to me, offering a small smile. "Thanks."

I don't dawdle, putting the car into drive again to leave. I pull out of the lot and hit the breaks when I reach the end of the alley. I'm about to merge into traffic when a sleek black limo swerves like it's going to pull in beside me, instead coming to a stop near the entrance, blocking my exit.

My stomach sinks, my insides coiling as I grip the steering wheel tighter at the sight of it.

Ray.

He gets out from the back of the limo, holding the door open after him for Brandy, apparently trailing along yet again. Ray shuts the door after she steps out, his gaze shifting my way, eyes meeting mine. He looks as if he's going to walk away, to let the fact that I've avoided him slide, until he takes a look at my passenger seat and his expression shifts.

Shit.

Ray hesitates, his arm around Brandy, his focus going from Karissa back to me. Leaning over, he whispers something into his girlfriend's ear, her face perking up when she looks at my car. She starts waving frantically, excitedly. I just sit there. From the corner of my eye, I see Karissa offering them a slight wave.

That's the only invitation the blonde needs.

Brandy rushes over to the car, motioning for Karissa to put down the window, but she doesn't move. Begrudgingly, I lower it for her, my eyes fixed on Ray as the man slowly strolls over to join his girlfriend.

Brandy starts rambling, endless, pointless chatter. *Hey! What are you doing? How are you doing? Where are you going?* Karissa stammers through answers, offering what little she can, what little she knows, as Ray stiffly nods to me. "Vitale."

I return his nod, not saying anything.

"Ray and I were just going to grab something to eat," Brandy says. "You guys should have lunch with us. What do you say?" Before either of us can respond, she turns to Ray, grasping his arm, a hopeful look on her face. "What do you think, Ray?"

"I don't know, Baby Doll." He lets out a deep sigh, eyes fixed squarely on my face. "I'm sure Vitale has better things to do today."

I still say nothing.

It's a test; I'm sure of it. A test as to whether or not I'll prioritize him, if I'll put the man who's like a father to me, the organization that made me a wealthy man, a family that saved my skin time and time again, above everything else going on in my life.

I want to.

I should.

Even when I had nothing, when everything good had been torn away, leaving a gaping void of blackness, one thing persevered: my loyalty. I dedicated what was left of me, every last fiber of my being, to the man in front of me, to honor his bloodline, to make right how they were wronged.

I should park the car right now, get out and go have lunch with the man who picked me up when I hit bottom, who gave me purpose to keep on living. I don't go to church, I don't even know if I believe in a just God, but I always believed in Raymond Angelo.

He was my savior.

But now I'm starting to lose faith in him, too.

Tempted by the evil beside me, the original sin... my forbidden fruit. I took a bite of her on a whim and realized, despite what the world led me to believe, she wasn't rotten to the core. He wants me to toss her aside, throw her away, let her decay into the ground where he thinks she's meant to be, but I'm not sure anything else could ever sustain me.

I drank from the Holy Grail.

He's not taking that away.

My gaze shifts from Ray to Karissa, who sits quietly beside me, hands folded in her lap. As deep as my loyalty runs to the Angelo family, something brews even deeper, something so strong it momentarily startles me.

The love I have for this woman.

A woman who's finally giving me the time of day again.

I look back at Ray, and I still say nothing, but I don't have to. He sees it in my eyes. I know he does, because I see it in his, too. I see the sense of betrayal he's starting to feel, chipping away at our allegiance.

"Another time then," Ray says, taking a step back, pulling Brandy with him before she can object. "Do what you gotta do, Vitale."

I watch as he backs up, serious eyes fixed on me for a moment, before he finally turns around. Sighing deeply, I close my eyes as I shake my head, before brushing it off. I can feel the tension in my muscles, tension him retreating won't ease.

I should've gone with him.

I should've picked loyalty.

But I couldn't, not this time.

I failed his test.

"Where to now?" I ask Karissa, reopening my eyes. "Anymore suggestions?"

She sighs, slowing putting up her window. "How about somewhere where nobody knows either of us?"

"I think we'll be hard pressed to find a place like that in New York."

The stock ticker scrolls by along the top of the laptop screen as I jot down a few ideas on a scrap piece of paper. I'm trying to pay attention, to riddle out a potential new scheme to get Ray off my ass, to try to placate the man, but movement in my peripheral keeps distracting me.

Karissa has abandoned her usual seat in the den, opting to scour the shelves near me instead. She pulls books off, glancing at their covers, flipping through the pages before shoving them back on. Sometimes in the same spot, other times wherever they'll fit.

I had them alphabetically ordered.

I'm trying not to be irritated by it.

My gaze flickers toward her, breathing a sigh of relief when she bypasses *War & Peace* without even hesitating. She ultimately settles on something further down the room, clutching it to her chest as she turns away from the bookshelves. Catching my eye, she smiles before strolling past me, her gaze flitting to the computer screen.

She tends to mind her own business, but what little she sees is clearly not what she expected.

Her footsteps falter as she looks back at me. "Do you have a portfolio?"

"A portfolio?"

"Yeah, you know, an investment portfolio. That's what it's called, right? When you buy stocks and stuff?"

"Uh, yeah, it is. You learn about that from Melody?"

"Pfft, no, what would she know about that stuff?"

"Well, her father's an investment banker, isn't he?"

She stares at me, blinking a few times as she considers my question, but she doesn't answer it. She doesn't have to.

Rhetorical question.

"You know, it freaks me out how much you know about people," she says, retreating to the other side of the den. "And for the record, I learned about portfolios from that talking E-Trade baby."

She's dead serious as she says it. I let out a laugh, shaking my head, as I turn back to the screen and try to focus again.

It's pointless, though.

Even across the fucking room she still distracts me.

Sighing, I close the laptop and stand up, strolling over to where she sits. She has the book she snatched from the shelf open in her lap. I sit down beside her, curious about what she settled on.

J.M. Barrie's *Peter Pan*

Huh. "Ever read that before?"

"Nope," she says. "I figured you had a copy around here somewhere, though, since you could quote it."

"Yeah, it's a good one. I have most of the classics."

"I noticed." She stares down at the page for a moment before glancing at me. "Can I ask you something?"

"If you really must."

She laughs. "Yes, I must."

"Then I'm listening."

"You have all these books and all these movies, this massive entertainment set-up, but you don't have any music."

She grows silent, eyes regarding me like she's waiting for an explanation about what she just said.

"That was an observation," I point out. "That wasn't a question."

She rolls her eyes. "Why is that, Naz?"

"Why don't I own any music?"

"Yes," she says. "I mean, you don't have a radio or anything. You don't even listen to music in the car when you drive. No Mp3s or CDs or eight-tracks or whatever kind of wind-up phonograph shit they had when you were a kid."

"Phonograph? How old do you think I am?"

She rolls her eyes. "Practically ancient. I'm already starting to see some gray in that hair of yours."

She's being playful, but it wouldn't surprise me with the stress I'm under. I'm aging every fucking minute dealing with her. "First of all, if I'm going gray, it's because of you. You make me crazy. And secondly, I don't have any music because I find it pointless."

She gapes at me.

Gapes at me like I just confessed to being a murderer.

Scratch that, she didn't seem this damn distressed when she actually realized I was one of those.

"How the hell can you find music pointless?"

"Because it's just noise," I say. "It serves no purpose except to fill the silence, but I happen to enjoy the silence, personally."

The more I talk, the more horrified she looks. "Are you fucking with me?"

"No," I say. "But I'd like to be—"

"Fucking me," she interjects, cutting me off. She's finishing my thoughts. I'm getting predictable. "I know you would. But I just... wow. Really, Naz? My mind is blown right now. How can someone seriously not like music?"

"Why do *you* listen to it?" I ask, raising an eyebrow as I motion toward the tangled earbuds she has lying on the arm of the couch. "Why do you walk around here with those always in? Other than the fact that it keeps me from trying to talk to you, of course."

Her cheeks tinge pink as she rolls her eyes, like it's the most absurd accusation she's ever heard, but the blushing tells me I'm right. "Whatever, I listen to music because there's so much emotion in it. It feels like I'm tapping into another part of my soul, like some part of the universe actually understands me. It makes me feel alive. Like, I can literally feel the music when I listen to it. It doesn't do that to you?"

I shake my head. "I feel nothing."

Except for annoyance because I can't think straight.

And sometimes a raging headache to accompany it.

She stares at me with what feels eerily like pity.

Karissa Reed... Karissa *Rita*... pities me.

Unbelievable.

"But, wait... you understood my Tupac reference when we talked about Machiavelli, didn't you? I could've sworn you did."

"Just because I don't enjoy it doesn't mean I know nothing about it. Tupac was around back in my wind-up phonograph days, you know." I cast her a sardonic look, which makes her laugh and shrug, as if to say 'hey, not my fault you're an old ass man.' "I'm surprised you know anything about him, actually. He died around the time you were born."

"Yeah, well, music never really goes out of style, especially Tupac," she says with a smile. "Now *that* I did learn from Melody. She knows the lyrics to every 90s rap song, but I don't think the girl would know what the hell an investment portfolio is, regardless of what her father does for a living."

Karissa goes back to reading then, focusing on the old book. I watch her as she flips a few pages before curiosity gets the best of me. "Why do you like it so much?"

"Music?"

"No, Peter Pan."

"Oh, uh... it's just sort of always been my favorite. Since we moved around all the time, I never really had many friends, never had anyone to talk to. Whenever I got close to someone, my mother would freak out… guess she thought I'd spill who we really were, even though I didn't even know… but she was so afraid of you catching up to us, I guess."

She doesn't say it with anger. Doesn't say it with sadness. She speaks matter-of-fact like it's just a truth she's come to accept.

"And there's something magical about the idea of escaping, of never growing up or having any responsibilities," she continues. "When I was young, I thought it was all real, that there was a whole world out there my mother kept me from. I used to open my bedroom window at night, leave it wide open, just in case." She smiles wistfully, her gaze still fixed to the book, although she's not reading anymore. "My mother caught me, though, and told me to stop, but of course I didn't listen."

"Of course."

"So yeah, that's when she started nailing all the windows shut," she says. "I always pried the nails back out, though, but I remember getting mad and yelling about how much I hated her for locking Peter Pan out, and she just told me I was being ridiculous. She said if anything were to come in my window, it wouldn't be something from a fairy tale."

She turns her head to look at me. "Now that we've gone all Freud on my life, why's *Twelve Angry Men* your favorite movie?"

"Ah, well, I'm afraid it's not nearly as fascinating of an explanation. It just intrigues me how if you plant a seed, people will cultivate it. It's not hard to get them to believe whatever you want them to believe."

"You mean like you convincing me you were Prince Charming?"

"I did no such thing. I told you point blank I wasn't a good man. And I've told you the same thing multiple times since."

"Reverse psychology," she says. "What did you expect me to think?"

"I expected you to believe what I said."

"Yeah, well, actions speak louder than words," she replies. "You say one thing and then do another, and I guess I trusted what you did instead of what you said. I fell in love with the man who swept me off my feet, who acted like I was special to him."

"You were," I say. "You *are* special to me."

"I know." Her voice is flat. "I'm a Rita."

189

I stare at her, surprised that she'd say that. She is a Rita, there's no denying that fact, but she's so much more than that to me. You'd think after all this time she'd grasp that fact, considering I tell her every time it comes up, but I get it now, I think. Nothing I say will ever mean more than what I do for her. She watches, like me. She touches, like me. She learns from seeing and not from listening.

Reaching over, I cup her chin, tilting her head until her eyes meet mine. "Let's go somewhere, get out of this house... out of this city."

She looks skeptical. "Go where?"

I shrug. "Wherever you want to go."

She seems not nearly as confident as I feel about that idea. "I don't know."

"Come on." I brush my thumb across her bottom lip. "We'll spend some time together, no distractions, no worries... just you and me. I'll show you how special you are."

"I'll think about it."

With that, she looks away from me again, pulling from my touch to focus on the book in her lap, conversation over.

Finished.

Done.

Karissa concedes.

It doesn't take much coaxing.

All I had to say was the magic word: *Italy.*

Two days later we're in the back of the town car, bags in the trunk, on our way to the airport. It's early in the morning, the sky outside still dark. Karissa stares out the side window, laughing dryly to herself when we pass the sign welcoming us into New Jersey. "Did you know?"

I glance at her, raising an eyebrow in question. "Did I know what?"

"The last time we went to this airport, when I asked you what was in New Jersey and you gave me all those bullshit answers," she explains. "Did you know that's where my parents were? Did you know what was *really* in New Jersey then?"

"Ah, no," I say. "I had no idea."

"Really?" she asks. "Because when I told you where I'd been that day, you seemed to know exactly where the house was... exactly where to find them."

"I recognized the address."

"How?"

"Because I'd been there before," I say, hesitating, not sure if I should go on, but I can tell from her expression she's going to ask more questions if I don't just put it out there. "I tracked your father there years ago."

"What happened? When you found him, I mean..."

"Nothing much," I say. "Your mother had already left him, and I wasn't ready to kill him yet. I wanted him to suffer like I had. He ended up settling into his little suburban life while your mother jumped from city to city."

"Did you ever find her again? Did you find *us*?"

"Yes," I say, "but I was always too late. I'd show up after you were already gone, find a few things that your mother left behind, tracks she forgot to cover, but she got better over time. *Smarter*. I lost her trail about three years ago, after Syracuse, and didn't pick it up again until you showed up in the city."

Karissa stares at me the entire time I'm speaking, looking me dead in the eyes without flinching.

It's quiet for a few minutes as she stares at me in contemplation, before she asks, "When did you change your mind?"

She's looking for an explanation, some sort of revelation that will justify this trust she's giving me. She wants to believe I'm a changed man, that the person she loves isn't the same monster she fears, but I've got not such admissions for her. I am who I am, and I do what I do, and I can't apologize for it.

But goddamn if that look in her eyes doesn't make me wish I could.

I wish I could be a better man.

I wish I could do that for her.

But I'm not, and I can't, because she's damn stubborn and I'm too fucked up to ever make a difference.

Wishing is for fools.

It doesn't change anything.

"When did I change my mind about what, Karissa?"

"About killing my mother," she whispers. "About killing me."

Although her voice is low, it doesn't tremble. My instinct is to ask, 'what makes you think I've changed my mind?' But she speaks like she's fearless and I don't want to make her afraid of me.

I won't kill her.

I can't.

Her mother, on the other hand, is an entirely different story.

"I'm not sure," I answer. "I don't know when it happened."

"Bullshit."

I admire her bluntness and fight off a smile, knowing laughing at the moment will only cause her hurt. There's nothing funny about this situation. "It wasn't what I'd call a conscious decision. I saw you, I talked to you, I took you home with me... took you into my bed... and somewhere along the way I fell in love with you. And when the time came to actually see my plan through, I realized I couldn't do it. I realized I didn't *want* to. Maybe it happened later; maybe it happened the first time I laid eyes on you. I don't know, Karissa. All I know is it happened, and that's the truth."

She holds my gaze for a few seconds before breaking eye contact, ducking her head as she turns away to look out the window again. We ride in silence after that, neither of us saying a word the rest of the trip to the airport. She doesn't talk to me when we get out of the car, doesn't talk to me when our bags are unloaded, and doesn't even talk to me as we board the plane. It's smaller than the one Ray chartered during our trip to Vegas, but it's just the two of us now, so we don't need anything too fancy.

Karissa veers as soon as she's inside, plopping down in a single seat off to the side by herself. I pause, wondering if I've upset her, before taking a seat across from her, putting some space between us.

She doesn't look at me. Her eyes are fixed out the window, her elbow propped on the arm of the chair, her chin resting in her palm. I hate it when she drifts away. She looks lost, and I wish I could find her, bring her back where she belongs.

I exchange words with the pilot, and within a few minutes we're up in the air. I relax back in my seat, stretching my legs out. It's going to be a long flight... a *very* long flight.

Over eight hours from gate to gate.

TORTURE TO HER SOUL

I watch Karissa as she watches the morning sky. It's starting to lighten outside, but the lights in the cabin are dim, casting her in soft shadows.

Ten minutes.

Twenty.

Half an hour.

Time drifts away slowly.

It's an hour or so into the flight before I hear her voice again.

"Do you regret it?" she asks quietly. "Do you regret loving me?"

I don't answer. Not right away. I stare at her until she finally turns her head to look at me, until she breaks and can't keep her gaze away a second longer. In her eyes I see apprehension, the kind that tells me my answer might break her the way she once ripped me apart with the word *red*.

"I have no regrets," I say finally.

Her brow furrows. "None at all?"

"None."

"After everything you've done, you regret none of it?" she asks. "How can that be?"

"Because you can't go back and change things once they're done. You can't rewrite history. Dwelling on it, wondering what could've been different, wondering how things might be in a perfect world, is a waste of time. Because this world isn't perfect, life isn't perfect, and it never will be. I'm only one man, and I only have one life, and I'm not going to waste it regretting my decisions and wishing I could change things that can never be changed. Wishing gets you nowhere, sweetheart. Believe me—I know. I wish and I wish and I wish and it doesn't make a goddamn difference. I lost my life in a single moment that a hundred years of regret wouldn't ever give me back. So no, Karissa, I don't regret anything."

There's something in her eyes, something I don't expect to see: sadness. I don't know if she believes a word that just came from my lips, but it's clear what I said got to her. Her mouth opens, and she hesitates, before whispering, "Did you ever even grieve?"

"Of course I grieved. I've spent two decades grieving."

"No," she says, shaking her head. "You spent two decades plotting revenge. That's not the same thing. Anger's just a small part of grief. You can't just get angry and be done with it. You have to

193

really feel it, Naz, or you'll never accept it."

I can feel my arm hair bristling. She's clawing at me, getting under my skin.

"You say you don't feel regret about anything, and maybe that's true. But if it is? I feel sorry for you."

Those words are a punch in the gut. My expression hardens, my muscles taut. "I don't need your pity."

"It's not pity," she says. "It's understanding. You don't like to hurt, so instead you inflict the pain on others. I get that now. But grief isn't something you can finish; it isn't something with a beginning and an end. Grief is something you absorb, something you accept. But in order to learn to live with it, you still have to live."

"I am living."

"You're avoiding," she says. "You're deflecting."

The more she talks, the more pissed off I get. If I wanted to be psychoanalyzed, I'd pay a fucking shrink.

She drops the subject, once again turning to look out the window.

One hour down, seven more to endure.

It takes the entire rest of the flight for me to push back my anger, for me to calm down enough to unclench my fists. She sleeps. I just stare at her, mulling over her words.

As soon as the wheels are on the ground and we come to a stop, I'm out of my seat. Karissa doesn't hesitate. She follows me off the plane, clutching hold of her brand new passport.

I had to call in a bunch of favors to get it for her.

We head through customs, flashing our passports, and are waved right through.

But Karissa hesitates.

Her feet root into the ground, blocking the line. She stares at the worker in silence, eyebrow raised, her passport still extended.

The man looks like he wants to strangle her.

She's an infuriatingly stubborn woman, I know it, but she's *my* stubborn woman, and my hands are the only ones that will ever wrap around her throat.

"*Timbrare il passaporto*," I say sharply, capturing the worker's attention. *Stamp her passport.* He scowls, digging in his drawer, and pulls out the small ink stamper. He pounds it against the first page in her passport before sliding it back to her.

"Thank you," Karissa whispers, smiling with satisfaction as she starts to walk away. I nod my appreciation, and he returns the gesture before moving on to the others behind us.

He just waves everyone else through.

There's a car waiting in front of the airport, a driver holding a sign with Vitale printed on it. We're staying at a hotel deep in the middle of Rome, just a few floors tall with a handful of rooms, small but luxurious, the kind of place where you get privacy but all the amenities you'd ever want.

Home away from home.

As soon as we step inside the hotel, I'm greeted with warm smiles and kind Italian words. I catch most of what they say even though I'm distracted, my attention continually drifting to Karissa.

She seems awestruck.

Eyes wide, curious and cautious, as they drink in our surroundings. We're led up to our suite on the top floor, and I'm trying to shove back my hostility so not to put off their hospitality, but I'm aggravated and exhausted and I'd much rather be left alone right now.

As politely as I can, I tell the workers to go the fuck away, shutting and locking the door behind them.

The suite is fairly big, given the modesty of the place: an open sitting room with couches and chairs, a fireplace and a television opposite a small kitchen, a large marble bathroom, and a bedroom with a king sized bed and access to a private outdoor terrace.

Karissa explores while I head straight to the bedroom and unpack my things in the small walk-in closet, feeling a bit better once I've found some order, some sense of control in my surroundings. I'm putting my last suit on a hanger when Karissa comes in.

She pauses near the doorway, leaning against the wall as she gazes into the closet, looking at me. I cut my eyes at her, meeting her stare.

"I didn't mean to upset you," she says.

I scoff, smoothing the dark material before hanging up the suit. "Yes, you did."

"But—"

"You meant every word of it," I say, stepping out of the closet toward her. "Never take back something you meant. I'd rather you offend me intentionally if it's something you believe than lie to my face just to placate me. I might not like what you say, but you're one of the few I respect to say it. Don't ruin that by taking back your words. Own them. Respect me that much."

"Okay."

That's it.

That's all she says about it.

Okay.

She's still looking at me.

My anger still hasn't waned.

I turn, prepared to walk away, when she lets out an exasperated sigh. "How long are you going to stay pissed?"

"Who says I'm pissed?"

"Me," she says. "I say you're pissed."

I turn back to her, surprised she's pushing this issue, that she's pressing these buttons she knows better than to press. "You sure you want to do this right now? You sure you want to have this conversation?"

"Yes."

No hesitation.

No second-guessing.

She stares at me, awaiting an explanation.

Fair enough. I'll give her what she wants.

"I'm going to stay pissed for as long as I am pissed," I tell her. "And I'm going to keep getting pissed as long as life keeps pissing me off."

"Maybe when you're done being pissed about it all, you'll finally let yourself start grieving what you lost."

"I *have* grieved."

"You're not supposed to lie to me."

Her accusatory tone sets me off. She thinks I'm a liar? That I lie to her? That's what she thinks of me? I've been teetering on a knife-edge all damn day and she just pushed me too much, too far, too fast.

Before she can react, I grab ahold of her, pinning her against the wall, my body flush against hers, my hand around her throat. She gasps loudly, startled, the sharp inhale sending shivers through me, gunning straight for my cock.

I'm hard. *Instantly.*

I don't squeeze, my fingers resting at her jugular, forcing her to look up at me. I can feel her pulse. Her heart beats wildly. I restrain her there, staring down at her, tip of her nose to the tip of my nose. Her breaths are unsteady, her hands shaking as they grasp my forearms.

I wonder if she's terrified or turned on...

She could get away if she wanted, weasel from my grasp without much effort, but she doesn't move. Her eyes shine brightly, wide and alert, regarding me with anticipation.

Staring at me with expectation.

It's not a rebuff, as she shoves against me, her chest hitting mine. No, it's an invitation.

No way will I decline.

I shove her roughly against the wall again, pulling her head up further, forcing her onto her tiptoes. I smash my lips to hers, kissing her hard. Her hands claw at my forearm, nails raking against the skin, but it's just for show. She fights my presence but keeps me there, gripping tightly so I can't break away, as she kisses me back.

The chills roll through me like waves, tingling from the top of my head to the bottom of my feet, making my cock throb in between. I'm pulsating to the rhythm of her heart as it pounds against my fingertips.

Thump.

Thump.

Thump.

Fuck.

I tear at her clothes with my free hand, teeth nipping at her skin, biting and licking along her jawline. Frustration mounts inside of me. It's probably twenty seconds. It feels like twenty minutes. It's a goddamn eternity not being inside of her.

I let go of her neck, yanking away from her clutch. She grabs ahold of my shirt to stop me from moving away, but I have no intention of leaving. My hands grasp her shorts, yanking them down along with her underwear. She kicks them off as I unbuckle my pants, not bothering to do any more.

It'll take too many seconds.

Grasping her hips, I pull her up. She wraps her legs around my waist and kisses me again. A gasp echoes from her lips when I thrust inside of her, filling her deeply, slamming her back against the wall.

"Fuck," I growl as she wraps her arms around my neck, gripping handfuls of hair and yanking as I do just that.

Fuck.

I fuck her.

I fuck her hard, fuck her with everything in me, fuck her until my skin is sweaty and my knees are weak, until my skull throbs and my body feels like it's going to detonate. I fuck her until my side feels like I've been shot all over again. She presses against the wall as I pound into her, again and again, the light switch digging into her back. The force moves it, the lights flickering, but she doesn't seem to notice and I don't give a shit.

Her eyes are squeezed shut, her bottom lip clamped between her teeth as she tries to restrain her cries.

Shifting position, I try to slide a hand between us, but we're too close and she's relying on me to hold her up. Grunting, she nearly slips from my grip as I grasp her hips tightly and pull her away from the wall. I stagger across the room, her body colliding with the crisp sheets of the still made bed in the dim lighting. Her eyes open as I climb between her legs, hovering over top of her. A sliver of blood slices her bottom lip from where her teeth pierced the fragile skin. Her tongue darts out, slowly licking it away as she stares at me.

Watching her ignites a fire in my veins.

A fire that can't be tamed.

I push inside of her again, driving her thighs apart from the force of the thrust. My fingertips find her clit, rubbing firm circles around it, as I fuck her so deep I can practically pierce her soul. She can't stop her cries this time, can't swallow them down like she did before, the strangled noises bouncing off the walls so loudly I'm surprised they don't quake the ground.

It doesn't take long before her body tenses, muscles growing taut from her impending orgasm.

As soon as I feel it building, clawing at her from the inside, I pull from her lips. She inhales sharply, filling her lungs with a deep breath, before my hand wraps around her throat once more.

She exhales with surprise.

This time, I squeeze.

The tan drains from her face, her eyes widening as I press against her jugular, constricting blood flow and obstructing her air. Sheer terror courses through her veins. I know, because I see it in her eyes, even more intense now than the first time I did this. Last time she was confused, and rightfully so, but this time she knows what I almost did to her.

What I *wanted* to do to her.

She knows, and she feels it. Her hands try to pry mine away, nails clawing at my wrist as she struggles, battling my hold and my weight, bucking her hips. Color seeps into her cheeks again, this time redness coating her skin, as she gives up trying to stop me and fights back instead. Her hands rip at my clothes before she grasps ahold of my tie and yanks it, trying to choke me back. It's futile, her fighting. I don't even budge.

It's only a few seconds. A few seconds before her eyes start to glaze over, her mouth moving but no sound coming out. Her legs quiver around me, every inch of her rigid as she arches her back, again squeezing her eyes shut. Her body explodes in pleasure the second I release my hold. She gasps loudly, her lungs hungrily devouring a breath.

A breath I granted her.

A breath she almost didn't get.

She screams, an ear-splitting shriek that rattles my bones as it batters me. Her body convulses, my name the only coherent word rupturing from her lips. "Naz!"

The sound of it is a punch to the chest. I lose it. My body shudders as I come hard, the force of it momentarily paralyzing me. I can't fucking move. I fist the sheets on both sides of her curvy frame, gritting my teeth as a curse slips through again. "Fuck."

I pull away the moment I can control myself and look down at Karissa. She has her eyes squeezed shut, and she's panting, her body desperate, greedy for all the air it can get. She doesn't move an inch, lying flat like her limbs stopped working, the only sign of life the rise and fall of her chest.

After her breathing slows down, she peeks open her eyes, instantly meeting mine. The terror is gone, instead replaced with relief. The sight of it sends a chill down my spine. It's like a rebirth, waking up to a new world, a reverence for life and an appreciation for each breath that didn't exist before. No one is more grateful to be alive than someone who thought they were going to die.

Second wind.

Second chances don't come easily. Most people don't get them. Most people don't know what it's like to come back from the brink of death.

It changes people.

It certainly changed me.

Chapter Fourteen

Rome's quiet at night.

The city is bathed in a burning glow from the lights of the buildings, the only thing visible in the stark blackness. From my chair on the balcony, I can see for miles, but there's not much to look at this late.

Three, I think, maybe four in the morning. I've been out here for hours, ever since Karissa fell asleep. Insomnia is a bitch that stalks me in the darkness, making my surroundings more haunting than serene.

I feel dead most nights. The walking dead, except I still have a pulse, a faint heartbeat. It's hard to feel alive when you've been obliterated inside, hard to feel real when you no longer remember how to dream.

It's probably fitting.

The only people that seem to be out at this hour are the Italian police, the military force called the *Carabinieri*, wielding their machine guns, monitoring the streets. You'd think it would unnerve me, but I feel more at ease here than back in New York.

Nobody here is gunning for me.

The doors to the room are open behind me, a breeze wafting through, ghosting across my sweaty skin. I'm still dressed, my sleeves shoved up to my elbows, shirt halfway unbuttoned, and tie discarded. I stretch my legs out, crossing them at the ankles, when I hear movement in the room.

Her footsteps are subdued, like she's purposely tiptoeing, as she makes her way out onto the balcony. Her presence looms right behind me, shadows falling over me. She walks right around me, approaching the edge of the balcony to look out. She's wearing only a t-shirt and underwear, the white fabric illuminated in the darkness.

She gazes out at the city, taking in the view. "It's so... orange."

The peculiar description makes me smile.

"It is," I say. "The glow reminds me of flames, like the city's on fire."

She turns around to look at me, leaning back against the wall lining the balcony as she crosses her arms over her chest. "Rome burned once."

"It did."

"I heard the Emperor did it... that he burned it down so he could rebuild it like he wanted it. They say the jackass played the fiddle while it burned."

"Is that what they say?"

"Yep."

"Huh."

Her eyes narrow. "Is that wrong?"

"Yes."

"How do you know?" she asks. "You weren't there."

"Neither was the fiddle," I point out. "It wasn't even invented then. And while I'm sure he could've had his own city destroyed, it's not really logical, since he lost his palace in the fire, too."

"He built another."

"But he salvaged what he could from the old," I say. "A man desperate enough to burn his home to the ground wants a clean slate... he wouldn't carry anything over."

"Maybe it just got out of hand," she says. "Maybe he lost control of it."

"Unlikely."

"You sound like you know a lot about this."

I contemplate how to respond to that, or if I should even humor it, since it wasn't a question.

"I know enough," I say. "I was once that desperate."

She stares at me for a moment before uncrossing her arms and pushing away from the wall. She wordlessly strolls over to me, surprising me as she slips into the chair, draping herself across my lap and settling into my arms. I pull her to me, shifting to give her more room, and press a kiss to the top of her head.

She smells like me.

The scent of sweat and cologne is all over her.

She's staring out at the city lights again, completely at ease. I brush her hair back off her shoulder as I gaze down at her, seeing the faint fingertip shaped marks on her neck. They're barely visible and will probably fade by morning, but they call to me like flashing neon signs. I graze my thumb along one, making her tense.

"Does it hurt?" I ask.

"Not anymore," she whispers.

"But it hurt when I did it?"

She hesitates. "I'm not sure."

My brow furrows. How can she not be sure?

Almost like she can read my mind, she sighs and shrugs. "I mean, yeah, it hurt, but it's hard to remember if it was more pain or fear, so I don't know if you actually hurt me or if I was just terrified you might."

"I don't do it to hurt you."

She tilts her head, looking back at me. "Why do you do it?"

Heavy question.

I'm not entirely sure how to answer.

"You like it, don't you?" I ask. "The high's like nothing else."

I've seen the way her body convulses, the pleasure so overwhelming she sometimes starts to cry. I can only imagine the intensity.

"For me, maybe, but what about you?" she asks. "What do you get out of it?"

An even heavier question.

I don't want to answer this one.

But she's looking at me, so vulnerable and open, it all laid out for me to see. She may hate me sometimes, but it hasn't stopped her from letting me back in. I owe her that much in return, even if the reality of what she'll see isn't pretty.

It's ugly.

Fucking wretched.

Just like me.

"My wife died."

"I know she did."

"So you know," I continue, "that I watched her die. That I held her, and stared down at her, watching as she took her last breath."

"Yes."

"There was nothing I could do for her... no way to save her... no way to make her breathe again. I was dying myself, but I didn't care, didn't care if I bled out right there just as long as I could keep her breathing. Nothing worked, though."

She says nothing as I look at her, thumb still gently stroking the discolored spot on her neck.

"So what do I get out of it, Karissa? I get to watch you inhale. I get to make you breathe. It's like you're coming back from death, and it's a goddamn beautiful thing to see. And maybe that's sick. Hell, I know I'm sick. But it gives me a high, too."

"It's not sick," she says, looking away to settle in my arms again. "It makes more sense than most things you do."

I laugh. "Everything I do makes sense."

"Yeah? So why are you with me?"

"Why—?"

"Not," she cuts me off before I can finish. "Why not? That's your answer every time, you know. Every single time. But it's not an answer, and it doesn't make any damn sense."

I have no other answer.

She doesn't press for one.

Instead she sighs, closing her eyes, and drifts off to sleep in my arms. I rest my cheek against her head, staring out at the glowing city as she starts to snore.

I get no sleep myself.

Why am I with her? I don't know. I really don't.

I'm with her simply because I want to be. Because I need to be. Because she needs me, I think, and if I'm being honest, I need her just as much.

∽∾

"Italy." Her voice is a stunned exhale, the word accompanied by an edge of laughter. "Fucking *Italy*."

At first, I think she's on the phone, that she called somebody back home, but I see her cracked iPhone with the pink case lying on the center of the bed, while she stands out on the balcony. Water drips down my chest, my hair still soaked from the shower, as I stand in the room and pull on a pair of boxers.

Quietly, I step toward the doors leading outside, catching sight of her leaning against the wall and staring down at the city. It's just after dawn. Rome's coming alive again as tourists start to swam the area, cars packing the streets. She's in her pajamas, hair a tangled mess. She just crawled out of bed.

"I can't believe it," she says quietly, and I realize she's talking to herself. "I'm really in fucking Italy."

"You are."

She jumps, startled by my voice, and clutches her chest as she swings around. Her face is flushed, a smile flickering the corner of her lips as she gazes at me. It doesn't escape my notice that her eyes trail the length of me, lingering on my bare stomach leading down into my boxers.

"I didn't hear you."

She never seems to.

I step out onto the balcony with her, running my hands through my wet hair. "Yeah, you were in the middle of what sounded like an interesting conversation."

Her flush grows as she averts her eyes, biting her bottom lip before turning back away from me to look at the city once more. "It's just... unbelievable. I never thought I'd actually be standing in Italy. I've always wanted to come here." She cuts her eyes at me as I pause beside her. "Which, somehow, you already knew."

I offer her a smile in place of a response. Before that afternoon in Vegas, I wasn't aware she wanted to come here. I had no way of knowing. As much as I know about the woman—her mannerisms, her past—her deepest desires are still secret from me.

I'd been lost in my head, sitting at that table in the courtyard, the ring box heavy in the breast pocket of my coat, mulling over whether or not I was making the right choice proposing to her. Years ago, I had everything figured out, my entire future drawn before me, a picture-perfect life that went up in flames, a story ending in the middle of a book, the rest of the pages left blank, wiped clean by the harsh reality that I was all alone now and I always would be.

Or I *thought* I would be...

I kept going through it again and again. I loved her, I wanted to keep her, but I knew doing so would be an injustice. Something I wanted to make right was so fucking wrong; something that made me feel whole would fracture her. I'm not an idiot. I'm not a fool. I knew what the truth would do to Karissa, and proposing to her would only make that worse.

I almost didn't do it. Almost backed out. *Don't tie her to you*, I thought. *Don't lock her in a cage*. Thoughts of Maria kept infiltrating the moment, memories of what happened to her, thoughts of the woman she'd never get to be, the life she'd never get to live with me. I couldn't do that to Karissa, could strap her to someone she didn't even know, drag her deeper into a world she didn't realize wanted to swallow her whole. Maria never got to be a mother. She barely got to be my wife. I never took her on our honeymoon.

'I've always dreamed about going to Italy.'

'I know.'

I answered quietly, absent-mindedly, not even realizing what I was doing until I turned my head and looked at Karissa, drawing me back into the moment, out of a past that ended prematurely.

At the end, I ultimately pulled out the ring, ignoring everything that stood against me because of something Karissa said: *'I don't want to walk away from you. I'm never going to.'*

She swore she meant it.

I'm still trying to take her at her word.

Looking away from Karissa, I glance down at her hand, eyes lingering on her bare ring finger for a moment before turning to face the Rome skyline.

"Why don't we get dressed and go explore?" I suggest.

"Yeah?"

"Yes."

"I wish I had a camera," she says, looking around. "It's so beautiful. I never want to forget it."

"Go shower," I say, motioning back toward the room. "I got you covered."

The water is just starting up in the bathroom when I pull on some clothes—jeans and a white t-shirt—and head for the door. I slip out without saying anything to Karissa and am back within twenty minutes, holding a shopping bag from the store down the street. When I step back into the room, Karissa is standing there in nothing but a towel, hoards of clothes dumped out from her bags and covering the bed.

"For you," I say, hesitating before dropping the shopping bag right on top of her things. Brow furrowed, she looks inside the bag and gasps. I don't know much about cameras... it's black and made by Canon. The man at the shop said it was the top of the line and the price tag certainly reflected that notion.

"Jesus, Naz, you didn't have to do that!" she says, pulling it out and holding it up. "We could've grabbed one of those disposable ones, you know... they're like five bucks. This is..."

"Worthy of Rome," I say as my phone in my pocket starts vibrating, the familiar beeps ringing out. "Charge the battery and we'll head out."

I pull the phone from my pocket as I step out onto the balcony again for some privacy. *Ray*. My signal is decent here in Rome, good enough that I know I can carry on a conversation with the man, but I'm hesitant to answer.

The ringing stops within seconds and I stare at the blank screen, not at all surprised when it starts up again almost immediately. I press the answer button as I sit down on the edge of a lounge chair. "Yeah."

"You're alive."

There's no humor in his voice.

No sarcasm.

It makes my insides coil.

Genuine question.

"Why wouldn't I be?" I ask.

"Well, I haven't seen you around. Figured something must've happened to you. It's not like you to stay away so much."

"I've just been busy."

"Is that right?"

"Yes."

"If I didn't know any better, I'd say you were avoiding me," Ray says. "You aren't avoiding me, are you?"

"Of course not."

"Good to know," he says. "I'm down at Cobalt. Come have a drink with me. We'll chat."

"I would if I could," I reply. "I'm out of town."

"Yeah? Where you at?"

"Rome."

"Rome," he echoes. "That's a little more than out of town, Vitale. That's a whole different country. Something come up?"

"No, it's not business," I say. "It's personal."

He's quiet, so quiet I'd think he hung up if I couldn't hear the clatter of the club in the background. I wait him out, sitting in silence. It takes nearly a full minute before he speaks again. "You took the Rita girl to Italy?"

"I did."

He's quiet, again, but not as long this time. "The misses is having a dinner party next weekend. Saturday. I know you've been *busy*, but I'd like it if you found the time to come."

"I'll be there."

"Good," he says. "And bring the girl with you."

The line goes dead before I can conjure up a response to that. Sighing, I just sit there, reveling in the silence for a moment, taking a moment of peace for myself. I clutch the phone in both hands, my elbows resting on my legs, as I stare at nothing, trying to clear my head.

The glass door from the room slides open after a while. I glance that way as Karissa stalls in the doorway, wearing a sleeveless flowered dress that falls just above her knees.

"We just have to wait on the thingy to turn green," she says, holding a user's manual in her hand, her eyes scanning it. It's bigger than the one for the coffee machine I bought her, but she didn't hesitate to utilize this one.

"Waiting on the thingy," I repeat, "to turn green."

"Yep." She glances at me. "It shouldn't take too long, right?"

"Your guess is as good as mine."

209

Two hours later, the light on the charger is still yellow. Karissa runs around, fixing her hair, putting on makeup, changing shoes half a dozen times, all the while telling me how sorry she is for holding us up. I can only take it for so long before I step in the room and grasp ahold of her hips when she tries to walk past me, locking her in place. "Stop apologizing."

"But—"

As soon as she tries to speak, the light on the charger flickers, turning green. I motion toward it. "See? It's ready."

Ten minutes later, we're finally out the door, camera in her hand, the first shoes she tried on back on her feet. It's still early, barely ten o'clock in the morning as we set off through the streets.

"Where are we going?" she asks.

"Where do you want to go?"

"Anywhere," she says, shrugging.

"Huh."

"What?"

"For someone who dreamed of coming to Italy, you're awfully indecisive."

She rolls her eyes. "Okay, fine. The right answer would've been everywhere. I want to see everything, so I'll go anywhere, really, wherever you take me, because I want to do it all. Better?"

"Better."

We hit the usual tourist spots, museums and churches, taking in the Pantheon, the *Piazza Navona*, and the Spanish Steps. She snaps picture after picture excitedly, and I just watch her, admiring her enthusiasm. We grab a light lunch at a small café before making our way to the Colosseum. The lines are ridiculously long, but I see Karissa's expression light up as she eyes it, so there's no way we can skip it.

We get in the back of the line to wait. Karissa snaps a few pictures from the outside, taking in the scenery, the picture-perfect little tourist with the camera glued to her face. It's almost like I'm not even around, and that's okay for the moment, I think. Her guard's down, defenses lowered.

It's the whole point in coming here. If it means me being ignored, so be it.

As long as she's happy…

After nearly thirty minutes we're finally to the front. I buy two tickets and we make our way around the winding paths into the Colosseum. Her eyes light up as she takes it the sight of the interior, parts of the ancient amphitheater crumbling and withering away, but even I have to admit it's a magnificent beast of concrete and stone.

Karissa snaps more pictures as we walk around before she lowers the camera and approaches a free railing, giving her a better view all around.

"It's beautiful," she says quietly, staring down at the exposed underground tunnels. "I wish I could've been here back then and seen it all in tact."

I can't help myself. I laugh at the reverence in her voice. It's not mocking, although the look she casts me makes me think it sounds that way. "Yeah, that would be nice, I guess, if you like that sort of thing."

"What sort of thing?"

"Mass slaughtering."

Her eyes widen.

I laugh again.

So innocent.

"What did you think the Romans used this place for, Karissa?"

"I don't know," she says. "Plays, and shows, or sports, or like, festivals."

"Oh, they were festivals, all right," I say. "Just the kind that involved a lot of gore."

"I mean, I knew there were gladiators," she says as I step closer, pausing beside her at the railing. "I knew people watched them fight to the death sometimes. But they were warriors."

So naïve.

"Back then, they'd execute thousands of people in one day," I say. "And they certainly weren't humane about it. There would be so much blood they'd have to put down a layer of sand on the floor to soak it up. They'd unleash lions on unarmed men, and fifty thousand people would sit in this place and watch them be ripped apart, piece-by-piece. You wouldn't have lasted a minute in one of those seats, Karissa. You couldn't even watch the boxing match in Vegas without shielding your eyes when somebody got hit."

She looks torn between fascination and revulsion. "We just waited in line for half an hour to stand inside what's practically an execution chamber? Why?"

"Because, like you said, it's beautiful."

"Death?"

"I meant the Colosseum, but sure." I casually lean against the railing, eyeing her peculiarly. "Death can be. It's a part of life. Some of us are lucky to live longer than others, but everything that's born will eventually die. None of us are immortal."

"That's depressing," she says, looking around again. "Can we go somewhere else now... somewhere preferably where people weren't murdered for sport?"

"How about the Trevi Fountain?" I suggest. "You can throw a coin in and make a wish."

"Can I wish for immortality?"

"Sure," I say, "but I think you'd have better luck going to the Vatican for that. That's where miracles happen."

"Oh, can we go there?" she asks excitedly. "Can you, like, go to the Vatican?"

"Yes," I say with a laugh, unsure if she means *me* specifically. "I'm pretty sure I won't burst into flames. It's a far walk, though, and the lines will be long, so we might want to save it for another day."

"Okay," she says, smiling. "Trevi Fountain it is, then. Nobody died there, right?"

"Some guys probably died while building it, but otherwise, I don't think so."

She laughs, like I'm joking, but I'm not.

People die everywhere.

Every step you take—everywhere you stand—the ground beneath your feet is tainted by some kind of casualty. It's an inescapable fact. Nothing is untouched by death. Nothing.

The area around the fountain is packed. It's late afternoon, melding into early evening, the tourists out in droves. I fish a coin out of my pocket and hand it to Karissa as I stand back, watching as she squeezes in the crowd. She forces her way up front with ease, standing there for a moment before closing her eyes and tossing the coin in. She reopens her eyes then, staring down at the water for a few seconds, before slipping back out of the crowd to rejoin me.

"Did you wish for your immortality?"

She laughs. "Nope."

"What did you wish for?"

She shakes her head, her hair swishing back and forth. "Not telling."

"Why?"

"Because then it won't come true."

"Says who?"

"Says everyone. Those are the rules."

"Ah, come on," I say, reaching for her, pulling her to me. "You can tell me. I'm an exception."

"What makes you so special?"

"Because I just am," I say, grinning when she rolls her eyes. I reach up, cupping her chin, brushing my thumb across her lips. "And because I'll make your every wish come true. So you can tell me, because I'll do it for you. Whatever it is. It's yours."

She stares at me in contemplation. "I'll think about it."

Leaning down, I kiss her softly. "That's a start."

She takes some more pictures before we stroll away, just

walking through the streets with no real destination in mind. We stop inside a few shops and I buy her some gelato, watching with amusement as she takes the first bite. Her eyes roll in the back of her head as she sticks the spoon back in the small bowl, getting a scoop of the messy tan-colored gelato.

"Here," she says, holding the spoon out to me. "Try some."

Hesitating, I shake my head. *Chocolate Hazelnut*. "No thanks."

Shrugging, she takes another bite.

And another.

And another.

We walk for a while longer as the day wears on and end up at the Villa Borghese, a large park in the center of the city. We head down a path, near the lake. Karissa's footsteps slow then, her eyes darting around, before she nudges me. "Can we sit down for a bit?"

I motion toward her. "Whatever you want. I'm following you."

She veers off the path right away, tromping through the lush grass. She plops right down beneath the shade of an old tree, away from everyone else, and I join her, sitting down carefully nearby. Her shoes are kicked off swiftly as she lounges back in the cool grass. "Uh, that's so much better."

"I bet."

"So how does it feel?" she asks, propped up on her elbows to look at me.

"How does what feel?"

"To be one of us regular folk," she says. "You went all day with no special treatment... had to wait for a table to open up, had to stand in line, weren't catered to or shuttled around wherever you wanted to go. Must've been torture for you, you know, being treated normal."

I stretch my legs out as I shake my head. "I like the anonymity. It's nice not having to worry about whose eyes are watching and whose hands are in my food, if a gun's pointed at me or if there's an ambush waiting around the next corner. Back in New York, I live with a target on my back. Sure, they treat me well when I'm in front of them, but when I turn around, well, there's no telling what they're planning. It's different here, though. Nobody's out to get me here."

"What about me?" she asks. "You're not worried about what I might do to you?"

"Not at all."

She seems genuinely surprised, like she expects me to perceive her as a threat. If it weren't so ridiculous, I'd laugh again.

"You have it all twisted, Jailbird," I say. "You seem to think I was upset because you drugged me, but that's not the case... I was upset that you put yourself in danger. I'm *still* upset about that. You put me out of commission and then ran off in the middle of the night where I couldn't protect you."

"I was fine."

"And thank God you were, but you might not have been. I'm not the only dangerous thing out there, you know. I'm not even the *most* dangerous."

Karissa's quiet for a moment, her eyes everywhere except for on me, as she absently plucks the grass around her. Eventually, she lets out a sigh, her voice low when she finally speaks. "It's weird, isn't it?"

"What?"

"My mother was so afraid of you, but never once did she mention you. She never showed me a picture, never even uttered your name."

"I wouldn't call that weird. It's easy to justify your fears when they're out in the open. Even Ray's visible—everybody knows his name. But it's different with me. I think your mother thought it was more dangerous to acknowledge me, to put my name in your head. Besides, we used to be friends, your mother and I, and as much as she worried about me coming for revenge, I don't think she ever really believed *you* were in danger. She didn't think I'd kill an innocent." Sighing, I reach for her legs, grabbing and tugging on them. She yelps, laughing, as I pull her feet into my lap. "She thought me a better man than that."

I start rubbing her feet as she lets out a low rumble, curling her toes. "Oh God, you are," she says, relaxing back in the grass with a smile. "You're a *great* man."

I pause what I'm doing and look at her incredulously.

"Oh, no, no, don't stop," she says, peeking an eye open at me. Shaking my head, I focus back on her feet as she lets out a laugh. "And really, don't look at me that way. I've seen a side of you today that I've never seen before. You're patient, and genuinely nice."

"And what, I wasn't nice before? I wasn't patient?" I ask. "I distinctly remember eating cheap, bland noodles in the smallest, messiest room I've ever stepped foot into. I think I deserve at least a little credit for that."

"You do," she agrees. "But it's just... I don't know. It's strange. I'm never sure what to make of you, what to think anymore, especially when you look at me. You get this expression on your face sometimes, and I'm not sure whether you want to kiss me or kill me."

"That's probably because I'm not sure either."

Once more, she opens her eyes to peek at me. I offer her a smile and she tentatively returns it, holding my stare for a moment. "You're a peculiar one, Ignazio Michele Vitale."

She does it again, pronounces my middle name like my mother's feminine version. I run a single finger lightly down her sole and she laughs, squirming, trying to kick away from me but I hold her foot there, tickling.

"Naz!" She sits up, trying to yank her leg away as she shoves me, laughing wildly. "Stop!"

"Stop," I mimic, stilling my hand, but I don't let go of her leg. "What happened to 'don't stop'?"

"I changed my mind."

"Sounds like you."

She shoves me again, removing her feet from my reach when I finally loosen my hold. Instead of moving away, she shifts around so her head is on my lap. I stare down at her, running my fingers through her hair as it fans out. Her eyes drift closed as I do it, a smile playing on her lips.

We don't talk much.

What else is there to say?

I laid it all out for her, and she took it in stride.

Maybe there's a chance for us, after all.

"Come on," I say after a while. "It'll be getting dark soon."

Sighing, she climbs to her feet. "How far away is the hotel?"

"About a mile."

"Ugh." She grimaces, grabbing her shoes from the grass. "That's too far."

Turning around, I pat my back. "Hop on. I'll carry you."

Her eyes widen. "A piggyback ride?"

"Yes, why?"

"I'm way too big for that."

"You weigh, what, ninety pounds? A hundred?"

She laughs with disbelief as she puts on her shoes. Instead of climbing on my back, she slips her hand into mine, linking our fingers before tugging on my arm. "You just proved it again, Naz."

"Proved what?"

"There's good in you, after all."

Chapter Fifteen

"Do you wanna play around?"

I speak quietly, the words low and gruff as I force them from my lips. My conscience tells me not to ask, to not push her tonight, but my cock is hard and my heart is wide open, and I want every bit of this woman I can get.

Karissa is gazing out the balcony door, hands pressed against the glass. She turns her head at the sound of my question, regarding me warily.

I think she might say no.

Fuck, please don't say no...

After a moment, she turns around to face me, relaxing back against the cool glass. Her lips part, and I wait for the rejection, wait for her to shoot me down, but instead she whispers, "yeah."

"Yes?"

She nods, saying it again a little louder. "Yeah."

I regard her for a moment before casually strolling toward her, my hands in my pockets. It takes everything in me not to snatch a hold of her, shove her dress up, bend her over the closest surface and fuck the daylights out of her.

All night.

Until morning.

Fuck her until she can't stand anymore.

But I've taken enough from her, and I'll continue to take until death does us part. Tonight is about her, though, about making her remember how much she once loved me. She's under my skin and I want to make myself at home inside of her body.

Because I need her to get something out of this also, something that makes her feel good. I need her to know that she's special to me, that it's about more than just her blood.

My eyes rake down her body.

She's beautiful in that dress.

She'll look even better out of it.

"Tell me," I say, pausing right in front of her. "What's your biggest fantasy?"

Her eyes widen. "What?"

"Your fantasy," I say again, the back of my hand lightly skimming down her arm, barely touching her, but the contact makes her shiver. "It doesn't matter what it is. No matter how small or strange it may seem."

"I, uh... I don't know."

"Come on, we all have our kinks," I say, going toe-to-toe with her, putting no space between our bodies. I have her pressed back against the glass, my cheek resting against hers as I whisper in her ear. "I want to know what turns you on, what you think about when you're all alone, touching yourself."

She inhales sharply as I run a hand up her body between us, caressing her stomach and fondling her breasts in that dress. My tongue runs along the shell of her ear as I give her a moment to think about an answer.

"I, uh..." Her voice shakes. "I'm not sure."

She's nervous.

I want to put her at ease, but another part of me would rather shove her over the edge, pull out of her everything she buries deep. But I need her to open up willingly, and she's not volunteering that part of her.

Stubborn woman.

Fucking beautiful, stubborn ass woman.

She's going to be the end of me.

"You want me to tell you a secret?" I ask when she comes up with nothing. "Want to know what turns me on?"

She nods.

"There's nothing sexier than hearing you sigh," I confess. "Especially that first thrust... your breath hitches, and you gasp, like you can't believe how good it feels to have my cock inside of you."

"I can't," she admits as she ducks her head shyly, staring up at me through her thick lashes. "It's my guilty pleasure."

Guilty pleasure.

"Are you ashamed you love it?"

"Always."

"Are you ashamed you love me?"

She hesitates for a second before whispering, "sometimes."

She says it like she's afraid for me to hear it, like she's afraid of my reaction.

But the thing is, I know how she feels.

I know the shame and the turmoil.

I know how it feels to love someone you shouldn't.

I fell in love with her.

It was my worst nightmare.

But sometimes nightmares are simply fueled by fear... fear of something we don't understand. A clown isn't scary when it takes off its makeup. A monster isn't so terrifying when you turn on the light. My enemy was my enemy until I looked inside of her and realized we weren't so different, after all.

She talks to me about regret, but what she doesn't realize is that even if she destroys me in the end, I'll never want to erase what we have. I'd never want to take back a single moment of this.

I'm not heartless—my heart is just hardened, while the rest of me is hollow. But she breathes life into what long ago stopped trying to live.

She's oxygen, and without her, I'm dead.

Her eyes dart to the floor as her head lowers even more. My hand trails further up, cupping her chin so she'll meet my gaze. "I know how you feel."

"Do you?"

"I told you before—I like you, and that's a problem for me."

"Have you found a solution to that problem yet?"

I smile, my thumb gently caressing her face. "I have."

She's silent for a few beats before she whispers, "What is it?"

"Marrying you."

All at once her expression shifts as she rolls her eyes. "How is that a solution?"

"Well, you won't be a Rita anymore."

As soon as I say it, she pushes against my chest, catching me off guard as she slips around me. I reach out and catch her wrist, holding her there before she can walk away.

She spins back in my direction, sighing exasperatedly.

I can't help it.

My cock twitches as the sound comes from her lips.

"I'll always be who I am, Ignazio," she says seriously. I hate when she calls me that name but once again my cock twitches. She's furious. And *that*? I fucking love it. "You could drain every drop of blood from my body and it wouldn't change anything. It's in my cells. My body. It's in me, every single part of me."

She yanks her arm from my grasp, but she stands there, not walking away.

"I'm not going to marry you because I'm a Rita. That's not a solution. I'd rather you just kill me now if that's all this is to you... if it's just some stupid alternative to ending my life. When I marry you, it'll be despite that fact, just like I'm here with you right now despite it."

She's upset, ranting, and continues to go on and on, but I'm caught on something she said seconds ago.

When I marry you...

Not an *if*.

A *when*.

I catch myself smiling, and she catches it, too. Eyes narrowed, scowling, she spits venom at me in the form of scathing words. "What the hell do you find so amusing?"

"You," I admit, laughing and stopping her when she tries to walk away from me again. "Ah, don't be that way. It's your fault, really, for being so beautiful when you get angry."

"You're crazy."

"I am," I say. "You make me that way."

There's no arguing that fact.

She merely glares at me.

"Come on," I say pulling her closer. "I want to know what turns you on. Is it role playing?"

She slowly shakes her head.

"Threesomes?"

She scrunches up her nose. *Thank God*. I'm not sure I could share this woman with anyone.

"Dirty talk?"

She lifts a shoulder in a half shrug as her cheeks flush. I take that as a 'yes'.

"Being watched?"

There's the reaction I've been waiting on, the flush extending down her neck, her lips twitching as she averts her eyes.

Ding.

Ding.

Ding.

I pull on her, and she doesn't resist, letting me slip my hand into hers and lead her outside, onto the balcony. It's near dusk, the sky a vibrant pink and orange swirl that's slowly fading into darkness. I pause on the balcony and gaze at her, eyes raking down her body.

This is going to be fun.

Letting go of her, I take a step back, holding my hands up to stop her before she follows me. Her brow furrows, but she listens, watching me warily as I take another step and sit down on an oversize lounge chair, long and wide enough that I can stretch my legs out and still have plenty of room.

I settle in, relaxing back, and kick my shoes off before looking at her again.

She's fidgeting nervously. *Good.*

"Strip."

The word sets her face on fire, cheeks bright red, eyes widened with shock. "What?"

"Strip," I say again. "Take your clothes off."

She doesn't move an inch. "I thought you wanted to play around, that we would..." Her eyes dart toward the glass doors leading back into the room. "That you'd, you know..."

"Playing around isn't always about me. I was rough on you last night. Tonight we'll try something different."

"Oh."

That's all she says, like she never considered we could play around any other way that didn't involve violence.

I nod toward her as I say the word for the third time. "Strip."

This time she doesn't question it.

Reaching down, she grasps the bottom of her dress and quickly pulls it over her head before letting it drop to the floor, leaving her in a strapless black bra and a matching thong. She kicks off her shoes before hesitating, eyeing me questioningly.

I nod, encouraging her to go on.

The bra hits the patio floor within seconds before she hooks her thumbs on the sides of her thong, taking a deep breath and closing her eyes as she yanks them down. She stands there afterward, completely naked, but positions her arms in front of her in an attempt to shield her body.

I just stare at her, taking in every curve that she'll let me see.

She fidgets more from the unabashed attention.

"Well?" she says, a bite to her words. "Are you happy now?"

Huh. Defensive.

I like it.

"Very," I confess. "Although, your stripping skills could use a bit of work."

"Yeah, well, excuse the fuck out of me. You just said take them off... wasn't aware I was supposed to put on some Def Leppard and make a show of it."

"Now you know for next time."

She rolls her eyes, and I can't help but laugh.

"So is this how we're playing around today? Humiliating me?"

"No, but I'm intrigued by the fact that you're humiliated. I was under the impression being watched turned you on."

"This is different."

"How so?"

She groans with frustration. "It just is. You're looking at me, and you're not saying anything."

"What do you want me to say?"

"I don't know." She throws her hands up in exasperation, forgetting she was trying to cover herself. "Anything!"

I motion for her to come closer and she obliges, stepping right over to me. As soon as she's close enough, I grasp her hips, pulling her down onto the lounge chair with me. She straddles my lap, her hands resting between her legs.

"I love every inch of you," I tell her. "Every part of your body that makes you nervous gives me pleasure. I see no flaws, nothing for you to be ashamed of or humiliated over... nothing you should hide from me. I've seen it all, and I love it. You're beautiful, baby."

Her expression softens, shoulders relaxing. "That's the first time

225

you've ever called me that."

"Called you what?"

"Baby," she says quietly. "You never call me that."

"Does it bother you?"

"What? No, of course not." She looks at me like she's legitimately confused. "Why would it?"

"Some women find it degrading."

"Not me. It makes me feel..." She smiles softly as she trails off. "Well, you know."

"Makes you feel what?" I ask curiously.

"Like I'm special," she says. "Like you cherish me. Like you love me."

"I do," I say, my hands drifting from her hips up to her chest, my fingertips grazing her breasts, thumbs brushing against her erect nipples. "I'm in love with you, baby."

She smiles when I say it again, biting down on her bottom lip to fight off a full-blown grin. Had I known the word would have such an impact on her, I'd have said it long ago.

And I would've said it over... and over... and over again.

I kiss her softly, tweaking her nipples as she squirms against me. My lips move from hers, tracing her jawline, before I whisper in her ear. "Touch yourself."

Her eyes widen as I pull away, relaxing back in the chair. "Seriously?"

I nod, my hands moving back to her hips. "I want to watch."

"I, uh..." She's nervous again. "I don't know."

"Just lay back and close your eyes," I say. "Show me how you pleasure yourself."

It doesn't take much more coaxing before she lies back on the lounge chair between my legs, her head at the end near my feet. She shifts around, inching closer. Her hands cup her pussy, just covering it for a moment, before she slowly starts touching herself. It's stiff at first, her movements rigid as anxiety eats at her, but the more she rubs, the more her body loosens up. She traces circles around her clit, my eyes drawn to her red nail polish against the glistening pink as she spreads her legs wider, giving me a better view.

My cock is so hard it hurts, straining my pants as it throbs. I'm desperate to pull it out, to stroke it fast for some much-needed relief, but I'm frozen, awestruck, watching her. I caress her skin, my hands gently running from her knees up her thighs and back again.

She writhes, rubbing faster, harder, as she starts to whimper. She's getting close already. The sound, I'm convinced, is going to fucking kill me.

Death by orgasm... and it's not even my own.

I was wrong. I thought she was most beautiful doing nothing, but no other moment touches this one. She trusts me, I realize. Trusts me enough to let go, to show me the her no one else ever sees, the her she is when she's all alone.

The *her* that only Karissa really knows.

Her whimpers turn to cries. Her back arches. I feel the muscles in her legs clench, her knees locking and toes curling as orgasm tears through her.

"Oh God," she moans. "Uhhh, Naz!"

Eyes closed, giving this to herself, and she cries out for me. *Me.* I nearly come in my fucking pants. A groan vibrates my chest as my hands settle on her inner thighs, gripping hold as she trembles from pleasure. It only lasts a few seconds until she stops rubbing, until she collapses back onto the lounge chair.

She doesn't look at me. She just lays there, her breathing strained as she cups her pussy again. I loosen my grip on her thighs, my hands coming to rest on her knees. My thumbs lightly stroke her kneecaps and it only takes a few seconds before she giggles.

She's ticklish.

Her eyes peek open and meet mine. I can tell she's still nervous, but she's smiling like she's relieved.

"I'm glad that's over," she says.

"Oh, but you're wrong," I reply. "That was only beginning."

I slip off the lounge chair and grab her hand, tugging her to her feet. Her legs are wobbly as I pull her across the balcony.

"Wait, where are we going? What are we doing? Wait!"

I don't respond. Answering is senseless. She knows exactly what I'm doing as I tug her over to the wall surrounding the balcony. It's only a few feet tall, stopping in the middle of her torso as I pull her in front of me, her back to my chest, and press her up against it.

Her hands immediately come to rest on her breasts. We're too far up for anyone on the ground to get a good look at her. She'd be nothing but a vague shadow in the impending darkness at that distance. But tall buildings surround us, wide-open windows facing us.

Plenty of opportunity for the overly curious to appreciate the gorgeous view she's giving the city of Rome.

"Naz," she hisses as I unbuckle my belt, doing just enough to grasp my cock and pull it out. "What do you think you're doing?"

Stroking a few times, I press up against her, having to bend my knees. I push her legs further apart with my own, rubbing the head of my cock along her entrance. She repeatedly says my name, trying to get me to answer her, resisting with words but her body buckles to my every whim. She seems to instinctively arch her back, sticking her ass further out, as she rises up on her tiptoes for me.

"Naz, dammit," she says. "You're crazy."

"You already said that," I groan as I slowly push inside of her. "Now you're just repeating yourself."

She's always been tight, but it's even more constricting at this angle. Her body hugs mine as I slide right in home. She says my name again—Naz—but this time it's not a sign of protest. It's a sigh of surrender, a moan of pleasure, as she sags against the cold concrete and welcomes me inside of her.

One arm snakes around her waist, holding her there, pulling her back into me, as my other hand slips up her chest, between her breasts, coming to rest at the base of her throat as I force her upright so she can't try to hide anymore. She grasps my forearms tightly but doesn't fight me, holding on like I'm stabilizing her.

I move slowly. I have to. The angle is shit, our heights mismatched, the universe working against us, but it's enough to do the trick. It's not about fucking—it's about feeling. About giving her what I know will get her off. And I can tell, the way she lets her weight rest against me, succumbing to my hold, that I got her right where I want her.

She's practically waving a white flag.

She's mine.

"Baby," I whisper into her hair. "Baby, baby, baby..."

She shivers. I can feel her body tremble in my arms, like her insides are melting from the word as she thaws for me. My hand around her waist shifts down, just low enough for me stroke her clit to the rhythm of my thrusts. She squirms, her breathing labored, as she relaxes even more, growing comfortable. Goose bumps coat her skin. I can see them crawling up her arms, making their way to her neck as I lean down and trail kisses along her shoulder. Her hold on me tightens, nails lightly digging into the skin, body nearly dropping as the orgasm sweeps through her. I keep her upright, bearing her weight, as I ride her through it, loving the sounds of her cries as she tries to swallow back my name.

It's Heaven and Hell, hearing it. Beautiful torture, fueling an ugly need.

As soon as I'm sure she can stand on her own, I let go of her, pulling out. She tenses, surprised, words halfway from her lips when I spin her around, grasping her hips and lifting her up, planting her ass right on the edge of the wall. She gasps, clinging to me as she lets out a startled cry.

"Relax," I say, laughing. "You're not afraid of heights, are you?"

"No, but—"

"I got you," I say, meeting her eyes, cocking an eyebrow at her terrified expression. "Trust me, Karissa. I'm not going to let anything happen to you."

The terror turns to confliction, like she's torn between believing my words and fighting to get away, leaving her stagnant in the middle with tears building in the corner of her eyes. I'm not sure why she's about to cry, but it sure as hell looks like she is.

"I swear to God, Ignazio," she grounds out between clenched teeth as she loosens her hold just a bit, giving me room to breathe. "If you let me die, I will haunt your every waking moment and find a way to kill you personally."

The sheer ferocity in her words makes me smile. I keep one arm securely around her but move the other, running the back of my hand along her flushed cheek. "I know you will."

"I mean it."

"I know you do."

"I die, you die."

"I don't doubt that for a moment."

"Good," she says with a sigh, her arms resting on my shoulders as her fingers run through the hair at the nape of my neck. "Now fuck me, before I change my mind about this."

A light laugh leaves me as I push inside of her again, filling her deeper at this angle. I have to lift up some, but it's easier than bending down. I pull her closer to the edge, closer to me, giving me better access as I thrust harder than before, increasing my pace.

She's tense at first but gives in fully after a moment, her restrained moans becoming full blown shouts as darkness falls around us, the only light nearby coming from behind us in the room. We're nothing more than shadows dancing along the wall, the obscurity making her brave.

Oh so brave.

Closing her eyes, she tilts her head back, trusting me to hold her there, to keep her from falling off as I fuck her now, harder and harder, faster and faster. The melodic skin slapping echoes through the silence, mixing with her whimpers and cries.

"You like it, don't you?" I ask, my free hand running through her hair before fisting a handful of it, making her yelp as I pull on it, exposing her neck to me. I kiss her throat, running my tongue along it, tasting her sweat, before digging my teeth in near her chin. "You like it when I'm rough with you."

"I love it," she says breathlessly.

"Because you still trust me to take care of you," I say. "You trust me to be careful with you."

"I trust you."

"Because you still care about me," I say, my lips near her ear. "You love me."

"I do," she whispers. "God help me, I love you."

Before it's even fully from her lips, I force her head back down. Her eyes open, startled, before I smash my lips to hers, kissing her hard. It takes her a second to kiss me back as I let go of her hair and grab her hips, pulling her toward me on the balcony. She slips off the edge of the wall, right against me, my body pinning her there to the concrete. I thrust hard, fucking her with everything in me, grunting as my muscles grow taunt, tension building inside of me.

Fuck, I'm going to come.

I pull from her lips to take a deep breath, my eyes darting over her shoulder, drawn to the building right across the street. A figure stands on an adjacent balcony facing us, close enough to see exactly what we're doing. My lips curve involuntarily, a laugh escaping my lips. "We've got an audience, sweetheart."

She tenses. "You're joking."

"Nope," I say. "A man came out to watch the show."

"Oh, God." As soon as she says that, I pin her against the wall to free my hand again, slipping it between us to stroke her clit. She barely has time to inhale before the words come out yet again in the form of a moan. "Oh God."

It doesn't take long for her to come again, her legs shaking, body quaking around me, as a loud cry vibrates her chest that she can't restrain. It's an agonizing shriek of pleasure that rocks me to the core,

231

exploding somewhere deep inside of me so I can't hold back my own anymore. I grunt, slamming her against the concrete as I thrust hard, coming inside of her.

After a few thrusts, I can't take anymore and have to pull back, slipping out of her. I quickly tuck my cock away and grasp her hips to make sure she's stable as she drops to her feet, wobbling. Instead of slipping past me, rushing inside or dodging for her clothes just feet away, she collapses into me, wrapping her arms around me as her head comes to rest against my chest. I hug her back, engulfing her in my arms, and press a kiss to the top of her head.

A catcall cuts through the night air, a loud whistle echoing across the street. My eyes dart that way as the man claps. "*Bravo!*"

"Oh my God," Karissa groans. "I can't even..."

She slips out of my grasp, darting away, leaving her clothes discarded right where she took them off as I call out "Can't even what?" but she's gone before I even get out the first word. The man across the street shouts out something else, the fast and fluent Italian lost on me as I watch Karissa's shadow move around.

Laughing, I wave at the man and head inside. "*Ciao.*"

Chapter Sixteen

"Do you want to—?"

"Nope."

I stall, standing in the middle of the hotel room, a cold sense of dread sweeping through me when Karissa cuts me off mid-question, not letting me finish what I was going to ask.

Déjà vu.

I thought we were past this nonsense. Yesterday had been better than ever. I've never felt as close to her as I did laying in bed last night, holding her, no clothing between our bodies, no secrets separating us anymore.

I expected to wake up to a new day, a fresh start, but instead she does *this*?

Karissa's stretched out on the bed, wearing only one of the big white robes supplied by the hotel, her hair still damp from her shower. She's flipping through channels. There are only a few, mostly in Italian. She doesn't know a damn thing that's happening on any of them, but they're stealing her attention.

I don't like it.

The urge to punch the television nearly overwhelms me.

My hands clench into fists involuntarily. Almost like she can sense it, Karissa stops on one of the channels and tosses the remote down, her attention turning to me. Her brow furrows as she takes in my stance before she smiles. "If it requires walking, abso-freaking-lutely not. After yesterday, I am beat. The only way I'm going anywhere is if you carry me."

"I offered to carry you yesterday and you refused."

"Yeah, well, not today," she says, relaxing back against the pillows as she gazes at the television again. "The only way you're getting me to move from this bed is if you pick me up and physically move me."

"Ah, well, lucky for you, I can think of plenty of ways we can pass the day without leaving the bed," I say, sitting down beside her. "And I was going to ask if you wanted breakfast. I was going to order room service."

"Uh, yes, I take it back... that would be *amazing*. Do they have bacon and eggs? Oh, and French toast, or does France have a monopoly on that in Europe?"

"Actually, the French didn't invent French toast," I reply. "That was probably the Ancient Romans."

"So I can get it here?"

"No."

She pouts dramatically as I grab the bedside phone and press the button for the main desk. I ask that some espresso and cornettos be sent up. It only takes a few minutes before there's a knock on the door. I answer it, letting the man wheel the tray in, and wait until he's gone again before bringing it over to Karissa. I hand her an espresso and set the tray near her feet.

"Seriously? A croissant?" she says, picking one up and eyeing me as I sit down beside her. "Now this I know is from France."

"I think they originated in Austria, actually."

"Jesus, Naz, next you're going to tell me pizza isn't Italian."

"Oh, no, pizza is certainly Italian, just not pepperoni pizza. You order that on your pizza here, and you'll get *peperoni*, with one 'p', instead."

"What's the difference?"

"They're sweet peppers."

She scrunches up her nose. "Way to kill the fantasy."

"It's what I'm good at. One of the many things, anyway."

Before she can respond, I reach over and run my hand up her inner thigh. She squirms, taking a sip of her espresso, and moans just as my hand reaches her bare pussy. I graze her clit, lightly stroking it, as she continues to sip from her cup, throat muscles flexing as she swallows. Her moans grow louder, throaty groans of pleasure, as I rub circles a little harder, caressing her beneath the robe. I can't see what I'm doing, but I know her body better than my own.

Even blind, I could rock her world.

I set my own drink aside, moving the tray of food out of the way, and shift in the bed to settle between her legs. She doesn't move an inch as I shove her robe up, starting at her knees and trailing kisses up her thighs, my hands settling on her hips.

Bringing my mouth to her pussy, I slide my tongue along her center before licking her clit, lightly sucking on it. She cries out, the sound muffled as she still sips on that goddamn drink. She guzzles what's left of it, throwing it back like it's nothing, before flinging her hand. The small cup goes flying across the room, slamming into something before hitting the floor.

"Oh God," she groans, her hands resting on the top of my head. "That's it."

I lick and suck, nibbling on her inner thighs, pumping two fingers inside of her, curving them to hit her g-spot. She comes apart, easily, quickly, her legs shaking as she grips my hair tightly. Her back arches as an orgasm sweeps through her. I can feel her pussy contracting from the pleasure, squeezing my fingers, her body practically begging for more of me.

Before it even subsides, I'm on top of her, my knees pushing her legs apart wider as I pull my cock out of my boxers, shoving my pants down just enough to thrust inside of her. She wraps her arms around me, her cheeks flushed, her lips curved in a sly smile. I kiss her, my tongue meeting hers, and grin against her mouth.

I know she can taste herself on my lips, but she tastes like espresso.

"Was it good?" I whisper.

"Best fucking coffee ever," she mumbles.

Karissa's running around again.

Dodging from room to room, tugging on her curled hair, slathering on lotion, putting on jewelry, and changing her shoes a dozen times.

I stand out on the balcony, holding my phone, and watch her curiously. I wonder if this is how she acted in the past every time I invited her to dinner or told her I was coming over.

It amuses me.

She seems so nervous.

Like I make her nervous.

Not in the way I'm used to with people. It's the kind of nervous energy that radiates off of her and soaks straight through to me, the kind that makes my chest tight at the sight of her. She doesn't have to try to be beautiful. It comes naturally.

But she tries, anyway.

She tries because of me.

The glass door to the balcony slides open. She appears there, wringing her hands together.

"It's ridiculous, isn't it?" she asks. "The dress is too much. I shouldn't have picked it."

I sent her out on her own earlier--with an escort, of course, a translator provided as a courtesy by the hotel. I told her to pick a dress for tonight, that I'd made us plans, and acted as if I couldn't care less about what she did. I cared, though, and I would've rather gone with her, but I had business to attend to.

Business forced onto me by Ray.

One of his Sicilian contacts was in Rome for the afternoon, and Ray wanted me to meet him to get some files. I don't know what it's for, nor do I care.

Not my business.

It never is.

As much as I didn't want to leave Karissa alone, I preferred it to bringing her around those guys. We can be brutal in America, but the kind over here are savages.

I tried to call Ray, to tell him it was handled, but he didn't answer.

"You look beautiful," I tell Karissa. "It's not too much."

"Really? You like it?"

"I like you."

She smiles, looking down at herself. "But what about the dress?"

Sighing, I slip my phone in my pocket. "Let me tell you a secret, sweetheart."

She glances at me, her interest piqued. "What?"

"Most men, myself included, don't notice the clothes. We just notice how you look in them. The wrapping paper is nothing compared to the toy inside. So the dress matters not to me. It's pink..."

"Purple."

"And it's some sort of satin."

"Silk."

"Proves my point," I say. "It's just a dress. But you? You're beautiful. Dressed up, dressed down, not dressed at all. You're beautiful every way you come... especially when you come."

Her cheeks flush. "Thank you."

"No need to thank me. I'm just speaking the truth."

She twirls a bit, eyes down on her dress, before she looks at me. For the first time since arriving in Rome nearly a week ago, I'm wearing a black suit. I almost feel out of practice, like a different person pulled it on this afternoon.

I don't know how to feel being this man again.

"You look handsome," she says.

"I look like I always do."

"I know. Handsome."

I smile, stepping toward her, grasping her hip as I motion for her to go ahead of me.

There's a car waiting downstairs, a sleek black Mercedes limousine. Karissa eyes it peculiarly before sliding in the back when the driver opens the door for us. He greets her in Italian, and she smiles sweetly, avoiding responding. I return his greeting, climbing in after her, settling back into the leather seat as we get on the road.

"Are you going to tell me where we're going?" she asks.

"*La Bohème,*" I respond. "*Teatro dell'Opera di Roma.*"

"Say what?"

"To see *La Bohème* the Rome Opera House."

"An Italian opera?"

"Yes."

Her eyes light up excitedly. "What's it about?"

"It's a tragic love story, as most of them are."

"Is it good?"

"It's supposed to be. I haven't seen it, though, so I guess we'll find out."

The car takes us to the Baths of Caracalla, to the outdoor theater where they put on the shows in the summertime. It's a fair night, not a cloud in the darkened sky, the stars twinkling high above us. The ancient ruins tower high around the stage. Karissa stays right beside me, slipping her hand into mine as soon as we're out of the car. I glance at her, seeing her shy smile as she tucks in at my side.

Our seats are front and center, the best possible at the flat outdoor venue. We slip into them, and Karissa resists when I try to let go of her hand. I put my arm around her shoulder, pulling her toward me, as I relax in the seat as much as I can.

The opera's sung entirely in Italian, but it doesn't seem to inhibit Karissa in any way. She's enraptured, staring at the stage in awe from the very first note. Chills dance along her skin—I see them creeping up her arms as she absently fiddles with the material of her dress.

Halfway through, I feel my phone vibrating in my pocket.

It stops periodically before starting up again, over and over. I can't hear it, the ringer off, but feeling it is driving me up the wall. I'm on the verge of losing my cool when it finally stops.

I breathe a sigh of relief.

I'm only vaguely paying attention to the show, my thoughts drifting, when Karissa slouches against me, sniffling. I glance down at her, confused when I see tears in her eyes.

"Are you okay?" I whisper, concerned.

"No."

I shift in my seat, grasping her chin. "What's wrong?"

Her brow furrows before something seems to strike her. She laughs, despite the tears streaming down her cheeks. "It's sad, Naz. She's dying."

I look from her to the stage, to the woman on her deathbed, the music haunting. *Huh.*

Karissa rolls her eyes, looking back away.

The opera is over not long after. The crowd erupts in applause. Karissa is on her feet, excitedly cheering, louder than the rest. Her enthusiasm makes me smile. I stand up, clapping a few times, before grabbing her elbow and motioning for us to leave. She doesn't seem to want to go, too caught up in the moment, but obliges, taking my hand once more as we head out into the aisle.

I pull out my phone, calling for the car service on our way out. The man tells me it'll be thirty minutes. Hanging up, I shift through my missed messages, seeing Ray called me twelve times.

"It'll be a half hour," I say, slipping my phone away before looking at Karissa.

I'll deal with Ray later.

"We can walk, can't we?" she asks, looking around.

"I thought you were done with walking."

"That was days ago," she says. "I'm good as new."

"It's two miles."

"That's fine. It's a beautiful night."

Shrugging, I tug on her hand, and we stroll away from the theater. The streets are fairly quiet at this hour, most tourists gone inside for the night.

"You didn't think that story was sad?" she asks.

"I wasn't really paying it attention," I admit.

She's quiet for a moment before asking, "Are you okay?" Her eyes are on me. I can feel them, but I don't look her way. "You seem... off."

"In what way?"

"I don't know," she says. "It's hard to put my finger on it. I'd say you were depressed, but that's not really it. You're not sad. You're just... not really there."

"I'm thinking."

"Thinking?" She gasps, grabbing her chest in mock horror. "You? Mr. Less Thinking, More Feeling?"

I smile at her humor. It's nice to have her so at ease, but it unnerves me that she caught the change in my demeanor. I've been feeling off all day. I let myself be me again, let myself slip back into old habits, succumbing to old desires, and lost sight of the here-and-now, and the reality is our little bubble can't last forever, can't remain in tact once we step foot back on American soil. I can't be this man there, can't be this man and still survive the life I've chosen to live. I've made promises to Karissa, whispers when we were alone in the dark that are going to be hard to keep come daylight.

We walk in silence for a while, just strolling along.

I expect her to ask me what I'm thinking about, but she lets it drop.

We're still a mile from the hotel when her footsteps slow. I can tell she's tired, her feet hurting from the shoes she's wearing. I stop, offering her another piggyback ride.

This time, she accepts.

She squeals as she hops on, her arms tightly around my neck, hands clasps together at my chest, and her legs around my waist. Her hip is right on my wound but it's barely noticeable, nothing more than some soreness. She rests her head against the side of mine as I carry her. She's light, and feels so right clinging to me.

I think I could carry the woman forever.

Her breath is warm against my ear as she laughs, whispering after a moment, "Do you think we could get married here?"

I damn near drop her.

My grip slips, her legs sliding, but her hold is so tight she keeps herself from falling. I clutch ahold of her again, pulling her up, steadying her. Before I can even think of what to say to that, she continues.

"I don't mean, like, right now, but someday."

My words are tentative. "If that's what you want."

I carry her the rest of the way to the hotel, not putting her down until we reach the front door. She drops back to her feet, laughing.

I haven't ever heard her laugh so much as she has this past week. She's happy, happier than I've ever seen her. Despite it all, despite knowing the man I am, the man I have the potential to be, she finds it in her heart to be happy with me.

That's something I never want to lose.

Something I never want to destroy.

But I have a feeling, when we get back home, her happiness may not last as long as I hope.

And later, after she's asleep, when I stroll out onto the balcony and dial Ray's number, hearing his voice when he picks up on the first ring, I'm sure of it.

"I don't like what that girl's turned you into, Vitale."

No hello.

No warm greeting.

He's unhappy.

Maybe rightfully so.

But I know now, no matter what I do, I'm going to lose one of them. I'm going to disappoint either the woman who loves me, who breathed life into me, or the only man who ever really gave me a chance.

Either way, I fear, will be the end of me.

Chapter Seventeen

Custom made and tailored to my frame, my suits all fit me like a glove.

I have fifty of them, every single one a similar shade of black. Most people, looking in my closet, would think they're all the same, but I can tell the differences. Different weights and different fabrics, some for winter and some for summer, a couple with vests, most with three-button jackets and the rest of them with two. I rotate them, rarely wearing the same suit more than once a month.

They've survived years.

Some have lasted decades.

I bought my first black suit nearly twenty years ago. Until then, I dressed like an average kid from Hell's Kitchen—jeans, t-shirts, sneakers. You couldn't have paid me back then to put on a tie.

But I had a funeral to attend.

I needed a suit.

The fabric was heavy, or maybe that was just my heart. I felt constricted, weighed down like my body was made of concrete, my insides a block of stone that the world was steadily chipping away at. I was suffocating, but there was something strangely reassuring about the sensation, something soothing about wearing the dark, heavy suit, like a coat of armor, keeping the world from stealing any more pieces of my soul.

I put it on that day, and I never really took it back off.

Not for a long time, anyway.

I'm wearing it again, the first suit I bought. The chest is a little snug, but it still fits me almost like it did back then. It's strange, thinking I haven't physically changed much, but I feel like a vastly different man. Instead of wearing it like armor, it feels like it's rubbing me raw, exposing parts of me that I've kept locked away.

Kelvin is working the door at Cobalt. He nods at me when I step inside, averting his eyes right away. I stroll past him, into the main bar area.

Ray is sitting by himself in his usual chair, swirling scotch around in his glass.

Wordlessly, I step toward the man, sitting carefully in the seat beside him. The waitress glances over, not even bothering to ask before bringing a bottle of pale ale over, still sealed.

"Alone today?" I ask. It's a rare occurrence, Ray without someone to keep him company.

"Not anymore," he says, looking at me. "The guys are, well... and Baby Doll had something she wanted to do."

Reaching into my pocket, I pull out my keys and pop the bottle cap off, tossing it aside.

Ray watches me, raising an eyebrow. "I see you've found your keys."

"Yeah, they showed back up."

"Funny how that happens," he mutters, sipping his drink. "Just when you think something's gone..."

I shrug casually, taking a swig of beer when he trails off. "They're just keys."

He's not talking about the keys anymore and we both know it. We sit in silence, drinking, the air around us tenser than I remember it ever being between us. I'm not sure how to diffuse it. I don't know what he wants. An apology? An explanation? He'll get neither, but I don't think he really expects either one.

It's not in my nature.

He wouldn't accept it, anyway.

"So now that you're back home," he says, "where are you on our little problem?"

"Which problem?"

"The fact that Carmela's still breathing."

No bullshitting.

Straight to the point.

"I'm working on it."

"You've been working on it for a long time, Vitale. Too much longer and I might have to look elsewhere for a solution."

My stomach coils.

It's a thinly veiled threat.

He's saying he doesn't need me.

This job became mine because I had a personal vendetta, a reason to see it through. At the end of the day, any one of us could do it.

It would probably be better, logically. She expects me, and these days I'd be grateful to have that burden lifted from my shoulders. But backing out now is the equivalent of *bowing* out, and you don't bow out when it comes to Ray.

He takes you out instead.

I'm already walking a fine line with Karissa.

Maybe he'll let that slide.

Maybe, if I can convince him she's innocent.

But Carmela's non-negotiable.

"Nonsense," I say. "I got it handled."

"You sure about that?"

"Positive."

"And the girl?"

I hesitate. "What about her?"

"How's she going to accept what you have planned?"

That's a different question than he usually asks.

Maybe he's coming around.

Maybe.

"I don't see why she ever has to know."

"You keep secrets from her?"

I shrug a shoulder. "Some things are better left unsaid."

Ray throws back the rest of his scotch before standing up. He discards the glass and strolls over to me, pausing beside my chair. His thick hand clamps down on my shoulder, squeezing.

"You're like a son to me," he says. "I cut you slack because of it, because my daughter loved you, because she saw something in you, something I saw the day we met. You didn't cower, Vitale. You never cowered. Don't do it now. Don't cower."

He doesn't sound angry.

He sounds exasperated.

Reaching up, I clasp my hand overtop his for a moment, silently letting him know I understand. I return to my beer as he walks away, leaving me alone.

I finish my drink before standing up and strolling toward the exit. Kelvin is gone from the door, a guy whose name I don't know in his place. His gaze flickers to me only briefly before he bows his head.

I walk out, into the late afternoon sunshine, and make my way around the building when I hear a car pull into the alley behind me. They drive slow, the sound of gravel crunching an agonizing groan. I slow my footsteps, an ominous tingle creeping up my spine, my fingers twitching at my sides.

My heart beats wildly, but it's soothed right away when colored lights bounce off of the buildings, a high-pitched squeal echoing behind me.

Police.

Who thought I'd ever be relieved to encounter them? But on the hierarchy of people who could potentially sneak up on me, the police are currently the least of my problem.

I stop where I am, slowly raising my hands without turning around. I hear doors open, footsteps approaching hastily before hands are all over me, patting me down from behind. They're checking for weapons we all know they won't find as others stroll around in front of me. The familiar face of Detective Jameson greets me with a smile that has all the warmth of dry ice. "Mr. Vitale."

"Detective," I say, nodding at him as his partner joins his side. "To what do I owe this honor?"

Just as I say it, the officer patting me down roughly grabs my crotch. I close my eyes, groaning, willing myself not to react. *Jackass*.

"Just in the neighborhood," Jameson says casually as the officer grabs the back of my coat and yanks. I stumble, clenching my hands into fists, as Jameson's smile freezes, his eyes darting over my shoulder. "I think that's enough. He's clean."

"As always," I say, lowering my arms.

"Can never be too sure," Jameson says. "By the way, I heard you were out of the country last week... Italy, was it? Vacation looks good on you. You look... *refreshed*. Better than you looked a few months ago after your little trip to Vegas. Could be worse, though, right? Heard you lost a friend on that vacation."

I curve an eyebrow at him. "How about you cut the bullshit and tell me what you want? I'd like to be on my way."

"Ah, I thought maybe we could chat."

"Chat."

"Yes."

"Man to man? Or detective to witness?"

An officer behind me laughs. "More like suspect."

Detective Jameson shoots him a look that silences the man. Tension escalates. *Suspect*.

"If you have any questions for me, refer them to my attorney," I tell them. "Otherwise, I have nothing to say."

I try to walk away when Jameson steps directly in my path,

blocking me from leaving. Scathing words are on the tip of my tongue from impatience, but they're stolen from my lips when he motions toward the uniformed officers. All at once someone grabs a hold of me, forcing my hands behind my back. I struggle as they yank me backward, slamming me against the hood of the police cruiser as they put handcuffs on my wrists.

Pain rips through my side as I grimace.

"Uh-uh," Andrews says, strolling over and bending down so he's eyelevel with me. "You know not to resist."

I'm yanked back upright once I'm handcuffed.

"You have the right to remain silent," Jameson says, his voice monotone as he mutters the words. "Anything you say can and will be used against you in a court of law. You have the right to an attorney. If you cannot afford an attorney, one will be provided for you. Do you understand your rights?

He doesn't wait for my answer.

I'm shoved in the back of the police cruiser and hauled down to the police station, taken right to an interrogation room and left there.

An hour passes, maybe two.

It feels like forever until the door opens again and the detectives walk in with my lawyer on their heels. The man doesn't greet me. It's pointless. He's here to do business and he gets right down to it.

"What's my client charged with?"

"He's not charged with anything yet," Jameson says casually, taking a seat across from me. "He's being detained under suspicion of murder."

"Which murder?"

I nearly laugh at the way my lawyer words that, unable to stop the small smile from tugging my lips, as Jameson stares at him incredulously. It wasn't a "what" murder; it was a "which" murder, like maybe it could be more than one.

It could be...

"The murder of Daniel Santino, of course," Jameson says,

looking between us. "Is there another we should be looking into?"

"Of course not," the lawyer says. "And as far as Daniel Santino goes, we have humored your questions numerous times, and the answers have always remained the same. Mr. Vitale had no reason to want to harm the man. There was no bad blood between the two of them. With no motive, and no evidence, it's clear you're just grasping at straws, and you have been for quite some time."

"Oh, but we have a motive," Andrews chimes in, sitting up in his chair attentively. "Now, correct me if I'm wrong, Vitale, but your fiancée was one of Santino's students at the time of his death."

"So?"

"So our sources tell us she had a bit of trouble in his class, so you did something about it."

"Sources?" I chime in curiously. I hate that word. *Sources*. They're *rats*. "And who, exactly, would your sources be?"

"Now that we can't tell you," Jameson says. "But the informant is credible."

Informant. Yet another synonym for rat.

"Let me get this straight," the lawyer says. "A nameless source told you Mr. Vitale murdered a lifelong acquaintance because of conflict in a college class? Your motive is a bad grade?"

"It goes a bit deeper than a bad grade," Jameson says. "Santino was giving her a hard time."

"Is there any record of this?" the lawyer asks. "Complaints to administration? Grievances filed? Requests to transfer out of his class? Any proof she struggled? No, of course not. Instead you're relying on secondhand stories from anonymous sources. I have to tell you, detective, you're probably better off trusting the testimony of Pinocchio if you're looking for a grain of truth."

Neither detective is amused by the declaration, but I find it quite humorous. I would laugh if I weren't so uneasy by what he just said. I have suspected it for a while, but they all but confirmed it for me this afternoon.

Someone has loose lips that I'm going to have to seal shut again.

"Speaking of lifelong acquaintances," the detective says. "I want to talk about John Rita."

"Then talk about him," I say, "but I can't promise I'll listen."

My lawyer shoots me another look that tells me to be quiet. This time I listen.

Jameson glares at me. "It's curious that tragedy befalls everyone around you. Do you have any childhood friends left, Mr. Vitale?"

I shrug as the lawyer interjects, threatening to end this conversation if he doesn't get to the point.

"The point is he seems to be the only one left standing. Maria Angelo... Daniel Santino... John Rita..." He pauses, eyeing me. "You haven't seen Carmela Rita recently, have you?"

I say nothing.

It goes on and on, the same inane questions tossed at me, none of which I answer. It's after nightfall when I walk back out of the police station, a free man as usual. For as many times as they've dragged me down to this place in handcuffs, they've never once booked me into the system or paraded me in front of a judge. Suspicion alone can't make a charge stick, but this time they have something they never had before, something that gets them closer to making a case.

Information.

It takes me about an hour to collect my car and get on the road home. The house is lit up when I make it to Brooklyn, loud voices carrying through outside, feminine laughter that does nothing to ease my nerves.

Karissa has friends over again.

Unlocking the door, I step inside, immediately seeing the three of them. Karissa is sitting on the living room couch with Melody on one side of her, a surprising face on the other. I stare at the blonde visitor for a moment, stunned by her presence. *Brandy.*

Ray's girlfriend.

Guess befriending Karissa took precedence over Ray today.

"Hey," Karissa greets me, her voice tentative. "Look who we ran into today."

I'm not sure if she's nervous about my reaction, or if she's just not at ease with her company, but her apprehension is clear. Instead of questioning it, I offer a strained smile. "Hello."

"Vitale," Brandy says as she glances around. "Nice house."

Before I can respond, Melody chimes in, jumping to her feet. "Well, it's getting late, so I ought to get to getting, you know." She strolls my way, pausing in front of me. "Looking good, Ignazio. Can't wait to see what you look like in a penguin suit."

I regard her warily as she pats my chest, running her hand along the folds of my suit coat. Karissa grumbles, telling her friend to stop it, but Melody laughs it off.

"I should go, too," Brandy says, standing up. She avoids looking at me as she brushes past, heading for the door behind Melody. "We should share a cab back to Manhattan, Mel."

"Absolutely," Melody says, flashing a smile back at us. "You be good, kids. Drugs are bad, m'kay?"

I stare at them, watching as they leave the house. Karissa stands up once they're gone and strolls over, relocking the front door behind them.

"Sometimes I'm not sure if I even speak the same language as that girl," I say, pulling off my coat. "It feels like she's speaking in code."

Karissa smiles sheepishly. "I don't think even Melody knows what she's saying most of the time."

I unbutton my cuffs. "Penguin suit? Is that what I think it is?"

"Yeah, we were, uh..." Her cheeks flush. "They asked about the wedding."

"Did you set a date for it yet?"

"No."

Nodding, I walk past her, into the den, and kick off my shoes right in the doorway. I drop my coat down on the arm of the couch before plopping down on the cushion, stretching my legs out as I lay my head back. A slight pain knocks at my temples, the onset of a headache from hours of stressful interrogation.

"Are you okay?" Karissa asks, following me.

"Just a bit of a headache," I respond, watching her as she sits down beside me. "Long day."

"I bet," she says, tucking her feet up on the couch beneath her as she shifts her body to face me. "I thought you'd be home early, but I figured... well, I just assumed you were... working."

Working. She says the word tentatively, barely a whisper from her lips. Her eyes are peeled to my face, narrowed contemplatively, like there are questions she wants to ask but might not want to hear the answers to.

"I had a drink with Ray this afternoon," I offer, hoping she won't ever ask me the tough questions about how exactly I fill my hours. "I would've been home hours ago, but I ran into a little predicament."

"What sort of predicament?"

"The law enforcement kind."

Her eyes widen slightly, but she doesn't push for more of an explanation. Instead, she shifts around on the couch, positioning herself to lie on me, settling under my arm with her head against my chest. Sighing, I pull her tighter to me, kissing the top of her head before closing my eyes.

"I hope you don't mind I had company," she says quietly. "I made sure they didn't go in the den... or anywhere, really, except for where they were."

"It's fine," I say. "I was just surprised to see Brandy here. I wasn't aware she was a friend of yours."

"She's not... not really. Melody and I ran into her at the café. Turns out her and Melody know a lot of the same people. She actually knows Melody's dad, oddly enough, met him through work ages ago. I guess she worked with the Wall Street crowd or something. I don't even know what she does for a living."

"Ray."

I feel her lift her head up. Peeking an eye open, I see she's looking at me incredulously.

"Ray?"

"She does Ray for a living."

A moment of silence passes before it seems to strike her what I'm saying. She gasps, shoving against me. "Really?"

Laughing, I shrug a shoulder. "He pays her bills and gives her an allowance in exchange for being at his beck and call. She doesn't have to work, since Ray takes care of her. And before Ray, there were other men... one, I assume, being Mr. Carmichael."

"You mean she, uh... that she's a..."

She can't even say the word.

"She's a *professional girlfriend*," I say, choosing the nicest of the terms. I'd usually call her a whore, but I'm not in the business of offending Karissa's potential friends. I have nothing against Brandy, per se. I barely know her, have no interest in knowing her, but Ray trusts the girl for some inexplicable reason, so she can't be too terrible. After all, it might help Karissa to befriend someone connected to the life, and maybe it'll help Ray come around to my side of things. Ray's a sucker for his Baby Doll. If she likes Karissa, Ray will be more likely to warm up to her himself.

"But she seems so... sweet," Karissa says incredulously. "I mean, I knew she was with Ray and all, and that he's, well... and she's his, you know... but I thought what they had was genuine."

"It is," I reply. "We do what we have to do to survive, Karissa. Ray won't marry her, but it doesn't mean he won't give her a good life. And they're not alone. Men like Ray view wives as obligations. They're possessions. They treat them like work, like it's their job to care for them. Ray probably fucks his wife once a month, if that, but he's with Brandy almost every night. Because Brandy is where he wants to be. She's not an obligation. She's his happiness."

"He can't find happiness with his wife?"

"Ray? No. I'm sure it was possible at the beginning, but not anymore. They don't even *like* each other."

"But you're not like that, right? You wouldn't..."

"No, I wouldn't. I've told you before—I'm not interested in anyone else."

"But you might be someday," she says. "What if you wake up one day and don't *like* me anymore?"

"I don't know, Karissa. You tell me." I cock an eyebrow at her. "How does it feel to be stuck with somebody you don't like?"

She glares at me. "I wouldn't know."

"You wouldn't?"

"I like you," she says, hesitating before adding, "most days, anyway."

"Good to know." I pull her to me again. "And me not liking you is improbable, Karissa. Sure, sometimes you can be frustrating, but you keep life interesting, that's for certain."

She relaxes against me, sighing. "It's so weird to me. Like, even Melody's dad is like that? He's a freaking businessman. She said her parents are *perfect* together."

"Perfection doesn't exist," I reply. "It's a mask people wear to conceal their ugly truths. Never trust someone who only ever smiles at you."

She's quiet for a beat. "Ray only ever smiles at me."

I kiss the top of her head. "Exactly."

♾

"Next customer down here!"

The voice is loud and impatient, not the sort of friendly customer service one would want in a place like this. I step up to the counter, seeing the boy's annoyed expression as he glares down at the register, wearing a puke-green colored apron. He senses my presence and grumbles, "what do you want?"

"Depends on what you can get me."

He glances up, his annoyed expression growing, but he freezes when he catches my eye. I wondered if he would recognize me, considering we've only met once, but his wide eyes tell me he does. "Uh, hey... Ignazio, right?"

"Right."

Paul stares at me, contemplating, before clearing his throat and looking back down at the register. "So what can I get for you?"

"I want what you gave my fiancée."

He hesitates, eyes flickering to me again. I can see his concern, the expression all I need to give me my answers. I'm here on a hunch, little hints of suspicion that had been dropped around me the past few months, but what I lacked was information... information that his eyes just gave me.

Karissa drugged me once, not long ago, using a tiny vial of powder that she got somewhere. I've watched her meticulously since she came into my life. I know her habits. I know everyone she talks to, everyone she deals with. There are only so many ways she could've come upon such a potent drug, only a handful of people capable of getting it for her.

The list whittled down to just one... just one, who so easily gave himself away with a look. *Strike three.* He's out.

"I didn't, uh... I'm not sure what you mean. I don't know what she told you, but I didn't give her anything."

I can practically see him sweating, his voice low and cracking at his denial. People are easy to read, especially untrained liars.

"You've never waited on her before?" I ask, cocking at eyebrow. "She comes here all the time with your girlfriend."

"Oh, uh, yeah, sure." He wipes his forehead absently before offering a smile that's full of relief. "Chocolate Mint Tea."

"Yes," I say. "I'll take one of those."

Paul rings it up and I pay with a twenty-dollar bill, telling him to keep the change. I linger off to the side while they make my drink, keeping my eyes on Paul as I wait.

He's passive now, his voice quiet and his words polite.

I rattled him.

When my drink is ready, I nod to Paul in greeting before

walking outside. I stroll around the corner, to where my car is parked in the alley, and take a sip of the drink. *Disgusting.*

I throw it right in the Dumpster.

Paul gets off a few minutes later. I'm standing in the alleyway behind the café, leaning against the brick building beside Paul's car. He's too cheap to pay for street parking so he leaves it parked cockeyed not far from the Dumpster. He steps out, not paying any attention, phone glued to his ear as he rambles on to someone. He turns to head for his car, keys in hand, and gasps loudly, startled by my presence. The phone slips, crashing to the alley.

Before he can reach for it, I push away from the wall, stepping right on the phone, smashing it beneath my shoe. His eyes widen, horror flashing in their depths.

He doesn't have time to react before I grab a hold of him. Arms around him, my gloved hands grasp his throat, fingers going right for the jugular.

Ten seconds.

That's it.

Ten measly seconds and his body goes limp, falling unconscious in my arms. Karissa fights me in bed more than he just did. I drag him around the side of the Dumpster, where my car awaits, trunk already open. Picking him up, I shove him inside, grabbing a roll of duct tape. I unwind it, securing his wrists and ankles together before wrapping it around his head, covering his mouth and nose.

He'll be dead within minutes from oxygen deprivation.

Slamming the trunk closed, I toss the rest of the duct tape in the dumpster and climb back in my car, driving away from the alley.

Easy and clean, relatively painless, but that matters little to me. I won't watch him die, won't bask in the afterglow, but I would if I could. If I had my way, I'd make it slow and excruciating, but I'm short on time.

I have somewhere to be.

Glancing at my watch, I sigh.

I'm already going to be late.

It takes nearly an hour for me to make it back to Brooklyn with traffic. I park the car in the driveway and head right inside, opening the front door and stalling. Karissa stands in the living room, wearing a red dress and a pair of high heels, her hair down and slightly curled.

She's wearing make-up... *a lot* of make-up, her lips the same blood red shade as her dress. She's holding her phone to her ear and turns to me just as mine starts ringing in my pocket.

I don't bother looking. The moment she lowers her phone and touches the screen, mine silences.

She was calling me.

"I was wondering where you were," she says.

"I had something to take care of," I say, shutting the door behind me as my eyes scan her. "You look beautiful."

She fidgets with her clothing a bit. "It's your favorite dress."

I raise my eyebrows with surprise. "Is it?"

"Yes." She looks at me incredulously. "You said it was, anyway. It's the one I wore in Vegas."

"Ah, then definitely my favorite." I don't pay attention to what she wears, but that day was certainly one of my favorites. "So are you ready?"

"No." Her voice is firm, the word accompanied by the adamant shake of her head.

"No?"

"No," she says again. "I'm not going."

"You're not going?"

"No, I'm not," she says. "This isn't *my* thing, anyway. I don't see why I have to go."

"You don't see why you have to go?"

"Yes, so I refuse. Tell him I decline his invitation."

I stare at her for a moment. I can tell she's uneasy. I'm anxious enough at the moment without having to absorb her nerves also. "You want me to tell Raymond Angelo that you're refusing his request to attend?"

"Yes," she says, wavering for a second before continuing, "well, no... you couldn't put it another way?"

"What other way?"

"I don't know." She throws her hands up in exasperation. "Tell him I'm sick. I have the flu or something. I'm puking all over the place."

I wish I could, and I *would* if I could, but Ray is no fool. Her not showing up would be viewed as a personal snub, and I'm just now getting him to where he'll consider her existence as more than temporary.

I glance at my watch again. The dinner party starts in fifteen minutes.

"We won't stay long," I reassure her. "Let's just make an appearance to humor the man."

She scrunches up her nose but doesn't argue, heading right past me out the door. I follow her, locking up the house, and give a glance toward the trunk as I head for the car. She's already in the passenger seat when I slip inside, and I don't hesitate, starting the car up and pulling away.

I'm distracted during the drive, frequently glancing in the rear view mirror, listening intently for any sounds from the trunk. All is silent and still around me, except for Karissa's mindless chatter.

She's talkative today.

Nerves, I gather, but it does nothing to soothe my own. I drum my gloved fingers against the steering wheel as I wait at red lights, continuing to watch all around me, when her voice grows louder, practically growling. "Ignazio!"

I turn to her, alarmed. "What's wrong?"

"That's what *I'm* wondering," she says. "I've been talking to you for the past twenty minutes and I don't think you've heard a word I've said."

"That's because I haven't."

Her brow furrows, the frustration melting away to genuine concern. "What's wrong?"

"Nothing," I say, giving another glance in the rear view mirror just as the light turns green. "I'm listening now. What were you saying?"

"I asked if your hands were cold."

"No. Why?"

The response is from my lips before I give it any thought. My eyes drift to my hands clutching the steering wheel, to the leather gloves I'm still wearing.

She doesn't answer, knowing she doesn't need to.

She sees me look at them.

I have no explanation for her.

I wait until I hit the next red light to pull them off, reaching over to toss them in the center console.

Karissa watches me, shaking her head. "It concerns me when

you're like this. Last time you picked me up this distracted, I thought you were mad at me. You didn't look at me the entire drive, cancelled our plans and went straight to your house."

I know exactly what day she's talking about.

I had a body in the trunk then, too.

"I'm not mad at you," I say in place of an actual response.

"Good to know, but *something* has you on edge."

She doesn't say another word the rest of the drive. When I get to Ray's, we're already fifteen minutes late. Cars pack his driveway and the area around his house. I find a place to park across the street and cut the engine, remaining in my seat for a moment to try to clear my head. Karissa is staring straight ahead out of the windshield, anxiously biting on the inside of her cheek.

"Here," I say, reaching into my pocket and pulling out a peppermint, holding it out to her. "Take it."

She hesitates before snatching it up. "Are you suggesting my breath stinks?"

"Not at all." I pull out a piece for myself and slip it in my mouth. I tuck it along my cheek to suck on it. "It's a little trick I learned. Whenever a situation makes you nervous, suck on a piece of hard candy. It's psychological. Your brain thinks if you were in any real danger, you wouldn't be eating something, so it reasons that you're perfectly fine."

Also, it'll keep her from talking so damn much.

She pops the mint in her mouth. "I've never seen you eat one of these before."

"Very little makes me nervous."

"But you're nervous now."

Not a question.

I hope that doesn't mean my anxiety is obvious.

"Yeah, well, I don't want to be here any more than you do, sweetheart."

I lock up the car once we get out, my eyes skimming along the trunk involuntarily before I turn away. I offer Karissa a smile when I see she's fidgeting, reaching over to take her hand.

Linking our fingers together, I squeeze lightly, running my tongue along the peppermint in my mouth.

She stays in step with me, fingernails digging into the back of my hand when we reach the porch. I ring the doorbell, the front door opening instantly, animated voices streaming out from inside. Kelvin stands in front of us. I wonder how much Ray paid him to go from working the door at Cobalt to watching the door at his house.

"Vitale," he greets me, his gaze dropping right away as he steps aside. "They're waiting for you."

I say nothing, pulling Karissa inside as Kelvin shuts the door behind us. She stares at him briefly, wide eyed, before pushing herself closer to me.

"I *know* him," she hisses under her breath.

"He's the bouncer at the club you frequented," I say, filling in any blanks for her. "He also works at Cobalt."

She looks between us in shock before her eyes ultimately settle on me. "You have him watch me?"

"No, he just happened to recognize you that first night."

She doesn't look as if she believes me, but I don't have a chance to convince her otherwise. Before either of us can speak again, Ray's voice calls out from his den where everyone has gathered. "Vitale!"

Taking a deep breath, I squeeze Karissa's hand reassuringly before pulling her that direction. There are about two-dozen people hanging around, chatting and drinking, waiting on dinner to start. I stroll right over to Ray, Karissa in tow, and nod politely. "Ray."

"Glad you could make it," he says. "I started to worry when eight o'clock rolled around and there was no sign of you."

"I got a little caught up with business," I explain. "I wouldn't miss tonight for anything."

"Good, good." Ray slaps my shoulder, patting me on the back, before turning his focus on Karissa. Before she can react, he grabs her free hand. "I'm happy you could join us, Miss Rita."

I tense at his intentional use of that name—*Rita*. Karissa doesn't acknowledge it. He smiles at her silence, bringing her hand to his lips and kissing the back of it.

"Thank you," she says quietly, "for inviting me."

"Of course." He lets go and stares at her for a moment before turning to me. "Vitale, come... say hello to the men while the women chit-chat."

Karissa shoots me a panicked look, but Ray's waltzing away before I can refuse him. I lean toward Karissa, kissing the corner of her mouth, before whispering, "You'll be okay. I'll only be a few minutes."

I have to pry my hand away, seeing Ray watching me from his office door, waiting for me to join him. I walk past him, inside, and he slips in after me, shutting the door. A few men lurk in here, some of the top guys in the organization, sitting around, sipping scotch and discussing business.

Ray doesn't bother offering me a drink. He knows I won't accept it. He slips into his chair behind his desk while I perch along the side of the room, surveying them. They talk about this and that... schemes and plots... while I stay quiet, Ray watching for my reaction to it all.

He's putting me under a fucking microscope.

Ten minutes pass... twenty... thirty... I frequently glance at my watch, wanting this to be over. Forty-five minutes later, and I've had about as much as I can take. I stand up, trying to slip out undetected, but Ray won't let me go without a fight.

"Somewhere you need to be, Vitale?"

"Just going to check on Karissa."

"She's fine," Ray says.

"I'm sure you're right, but still, I'd like to check."

He hesitates before waving dismissively.

I head out of the office, back into the den. The crowd is thinner as people scattered throughout the house. A quick glance around tells me Karissa isn't here. My chest tightens, and I excuse myself just as someone tries to speak to me, making my way through the house, looking for her. I head past the living room, my footsteps faltering when I glance inside, catching sight of the vibrant red dress.

I stall in the doorway. She's alone, the room quiet and dimly lit, as she gazes up at the mantle above the fireplace. I watch her for a moment before slowly strolling toward her. I don't even have to look. I know what it is she sees.

I know, because I see it every time I come to this place.

"Karissa."

She jumps at the sound of my voice, glancing my way, a panicked look on her face. "I, uh... I was just heading to the bathroom, and well..."

"I get it."

I pause right behind her as she turns back around, her gaze going right back to the picture frame on the mantle. The photo is nearly two decades old but well preserved in the glass, like it was just taken yesterday.

Yesterday... it feels like yesterday. Feels like yesterday I stood in front of that photographer, an arm around Maria, wearing that godforsaken tuxedo while she nearly drowned in that poufy white dress. It was pretentious, everything neither of us were, but it had been her dream to have a wedding just like her parents.

So I'd given it to her.

"You look so happy," Karissa whispers.

"I was happy," I confess, my chest tightening as I gaze at the old photograph. "Very happy."

"Are you...?" She pauses for a moment. "Are you happy now?"

I can feel her gaze on me. My eyes shift to meet hers. I drink in her apprehension as she once more bites on her cheek nervously.

I'm not sure how to answer that question. A part of me yearns to just say 'yes', to ease all of her worries because I think it's what she wants to hear. What she *needs* to hear. But another part of me just can't lie to her.

"Not like I was then," I say, watching as the trepidation morphs to dejection. "I was naïve, Karissa. I thought perfection existed, and I thought I'd found it. I thought I was untouchable, that nothing and nobody could ever take away what I had. I was happy, because I was a fool. I've learned a lesson since then, a hard lesson, and I can't be that person anymore. I can never be that happy again."

She ducks her head, averting her eyes. I reach out and cup her chin, pulling her face up so she'll look at me again. I don't want her to misconstrue this, or walk away thinking I'm saying something I'm not.

"I'm not naïve anymore," I tell her. "But that doesn't mean you don't make me happy, because you do... in your own way. What I have with you isn't blissfully ignorant. It's real, and it isn't always pretty, but when it's good, it's good. So yeah, I'm happy, Karissa. A different kind of happy. The kind of happy that says even if this all destroys me, and it might, it'll all be worth it."

She smiles, a small smile, as she slips into my arms, nuzzling into my chest. I press my cheek to the top of her head, rubbing her back, when a throat clears from the doorway. Glancing over, I meet a set of beady dark eyes that pierce through us.

Martina Angelo.

"Mrs. Angelo," I say politely. "Nice to see you."

She says nothing, turning from me to look at Karissa. She curves an eyebrow judgmentally, her eyes scanning her slowly, picking her apart with a gaze. After a moment, the woman looks at me again. "Dinner's ready. Ray was looking for you. Figured you were off with your..." She waves toward Karissa dismissively. "*Her.*"

Martina walks away, leaving us alone again. Karissa looks up at me questioningly. "Ray's wife?"

"Yes."

She shakes her head. "I like Brandy so much better."

Their dining room table is massive, packed to the brim on both sides with chairs. The two closest to the head of the table adjacent to Ray remain empty. I pause as I give the room a glance, surveying the others, before leading Karissa to the empty chairs. I pull one out, whispering for her to take a seat.

She does so hesitantly.

I push it back in, offering Ray a polite nod as I sit down, taking my place between them.

Caught in the middle...

Dinner is strained. I can feel the tension all around me, wrapping its hands around my throat and squeezing. The others eat heartedly, laughing and drinking, happy to be here. A few months ago, I would've felt the same way.

But something changed.

I changed.

I'm not sure if it's in a good way.

I cut my eyes toward Karissa, watching as she stirs her food around with a fork. I don't think she's eaten any of it.

Neither have I.

Leaning over, I whisper in her ear. "Not hungry?"

She edges closer, her voice only loud enough for me to hear. "You weren't eating, so I figured it might not be safe for me, either."

Her lips curve into a small smile as I laugh, shrugging when she cuts her eyes at me. Her smile turns to laughter before Ray clears his throat beside us, garnering our attention. "Got

263

something funny you'd like to share?"

Karissa silences immediately, as I turn to Ray. "Private joke."

He doesn't look amused.

His gaze burns through me for a moment before his focus turns to Karissa. "So, Miss Rita—"

"Reed," she interjects. "My name is Karissa Reed... not Rita."

The entire room grows silent, the sound of clanking forks so loud I see Karissa flinch at the unexpected noise. People don't correct the boss, nor do they talk back to him. He could call you fucking Benedict Arnold and the rest of these guys would tolerate it so not to rock the boat.

But boat rocking is in Karissa's nature.

It's a side effect of her mother's smothering.

"Reed," Ray says, his voice terse. He's not sure how to react to her declaration. "Correct me if I'm wrong, but your father's Johnny **Rita**."

There's a sharp exhale through the room. That name is like poison—nobody wants to breathe it. Karissa glances around before clearing her throat and looking at Ray. "As far as I'm concerned, I have no father. My name has always been Karissa Reed."

Ray looks to me and lets out a laugh. It's cold, sending a chill through the air. "She certainly doesn't have a father *now*, does she, Vitale?"

He's usually not one to discuss these sorts of things in public, but he's trying to prove a point—a point that's clearly made when I see Karissa tense from my peripheral. Shaking my head, I look down at my plate. "No, she doesn't."

"Good thing, too," Ray says. "One less Rita means one less traitor in the world. Isn't that right?"

He's staring right at me. I can feel his eyes burning through my skull. My fingertips tingle, itching to wrap around his throat for him asking me these questions in front of her. But I have no choice but to respond, and to give him the answer he wants to hear.

"Right," I say. "One less traitor."

Ray laughs again, his voice barely loud enough for us to hear. "So many more to go."

As if dinner weren't strained before, it's practically torture now. They all go back to acting as if the exchange hadn't happened, and

Ray drops the subject like he hadn't been about to address Karissa in the first place. His work here is done, his goal accomplished. He wanted to put me in my place, wanted to show her who called the shots, and she saw it. She's feeling it. I can tell from the way she's not looking at me, the way she's not looking at *anything*.

She's still here, but she's gone.

Dessert is on the table, Double Chocolate Biscotti being served with coffee. I know Karissa would love it, but she doesn't even acknowledge it's there. The others are laughing, but she's on the cusp of tears. I can see her hands shaking in her lap as she fights to hold her emotion in, but it's getting to be too much.

Grabbing my napkin from my lap, I toss it on the table and stand. Leaning toward Ray, I whisper, "We're heading out now."

He looks at me. "So soon?"

I don't have to respond. He doesn't give me a chance, anyway. He stands up the same time Karissa does and reaches for her. His hands clasp a hold of hers before she can pull them away.

"I'm glad you could join us," he says, pressing yet another kiss to the back of her hand. "Always a pleasure, Miss Rita. Always a pleasure."

She pulls away without responding and jets from the room. Ray turns to me, slapping a hand on my shoulder and squeezing before sitting back down.

"Thanks for dinner," I say, although he knows I didn't eat a bite of it.

"You're welcome any time, Vitale," he says. "Be in touch about that thing we talked about. After it's handled, you and I will talk about the girl."

Karissa is standing at the car when I step outside, resting on the back bumper, leaning against the trunk. My footsteps waver, my muscles tensing. I unlock the doors, and she pushes away from the car, walking the rest of the way to get in the passenger seat.

She says nothing to me on the drive home.

Says nothing to me once we get there.

I pull the car into the garage and cut the engine, sitting there for a moment in silence. Karissa gets out, wordlessly using her keys to go inside without me. I give it a few minutes before following, finding her upstairs, already in bed, blanket pulled up over her head.

J.M. Darhower

I don't disturb her, staring at her for a moment before I walk back out. I go down to the den and sit there for a while in the darkness, my mind a flurry of thoughts, before I grab my keys again and head back out.

I have things to take care of.

I'm not sure what to say to her.

I drive through the boroughs, out of the city, to a small rural town to the north, heading down familiar roads I've driven dozens of times before. I pull up in front of the cabin situated on the edge of a span of woods. It's nighttime, and the windows are obscured with darkness, but the familiar Chevy Suburban parked out front tells me the one I need to see is home.

I bang on the door, impatiently, and listen as there's rustling inside. A moment later, locks jingle, the front door pulled open. The man is wearing a pair of pretentious silk pajamas, barefoot, his graying hair wayward, like I'd just wrangled Einstein from sleep. He rubs his eyes as he looks out, his expression falling serious when he sees me standing there.

Dr. Carter.

"Vitale," he says, his voice grave. "Uh, I wasn't expecting you."

"I have another," I say, foregoing greeting. "I need to use the facilities."

Him and I came to a sort of understanding years ago. I pay him handsomely and he hands over the keys to the small crematory out back. It's intended for animals, for the sentimental pet owners, but it works for what I need it for. The doctor's hands stay clean, relatively speaking... all he has to do is look the other way.

He hesitates before turning around and walking away. I step inside the open door, glancing around, as he retrieves the keys. I thank him with a nod and step out, getting in my car to pull around back.

Three hours.

That's all it takes for the incinerator to warm up and for Paul to disappear from the face of the earth. By the time I'm finished, he's little more than dust that's unleashed out my window on the drive back into the city, making the scumbag fade into the wind.

It's around five in the morning when I make it back home, pulling the car back into the garage, shutting the door behind me. I

266

flick on the light and pop the trunk, doing a thorough sweep of it, spraying every inch and vacuuming it out, removing every stitch of DNA left behind.

I look up when I'm finished, freezing when my gaze hits the side door leading into the house. Karissa is standing in the doorway wearing only a long t-shirt. My eyes trail up her bare legs before I meet her curious stare. Her eyes are bloodshot, her face lined with exhaustion. It doesn't look like she's been to sleep.

"What are you doing?" she asks, crossing her arms over her chest.

"Couldn't sleep," I say. "Decided to clean out the car."

"It wasn't already clean?"

"Not clean enough."

She regards me for a moment before stepping closer, peering around the side of the car, into the open trunk. There's nothing in here. Nothing at all.

After she looks, I close the trunk and offer her a smile as I lean up against the car. My eyes trail her again, unable to help myself. The shirt is loose, the neck stretched out. I can see her collarbones as it drapes along her shoulders. Reaching over, I trace fingertips along her skin around the neckline before grazing my hand along her throat and cupping her chin. I stare into her eyes, drinking in the alarm I find.

"Where'd you go tonight?"

"Out."

"What did you do?"

"Don't worry about it," I say quietly, running my thumb across her lips before leaning down and kissing her. "You have no reason to be afraid. I'm not going to hurt you... nobody is."

She stares at me for a moment before reaching up, covering my hand with her own. "How can you be sure?"

"Because I won't let them," I say. "It's as simple as that."

Chapter Eighteen

The first day of classes at NYU.

I sit in my car outside the building in Greenwich Village, gazing across the street at the entrance, watching as Karissa strolls inside, clutching a brand new textbook to her chest. She was adamant about taking the subway, but I assured her I had business in the neighborhood to get her to let me drive her today.

She agreed, begrudgingly, but insisted on taking the subway home. It was a tentative agreement, one I don't plan on following.

I'll be here when she gets out this afternoon.

I had her schedule memorized before even she did. Her first class of the day is the one she'd been hesitant to take: Ethics & Society, in the very same classroom she'd taken with Daniel. They'd remodeled it over the summer.

Apparently I left quite a mess and the floors needed replaced.

After that is English, and Math, before her day ends at exactly two o'clock.

I glance at my watch. Nine o'clock in the morning. That gives me exactly five hours to get some work done.

I wait until she's out of sight to pull away, cruising the few blocks through the neighborhood to Cobalt, parking my car in the back lot before heading inside. Kelvin is once more at the door and eyes me curiously when I step inside. He doesn't look down this time, doesn't look away, until I cast him a curious look.

"Vitale," he mutters.

I walk away, strolling right inside as I head for the bar, but I only make it a few steps when Ray's voice cuts through the air. "Hey! Look who it is!"

I turn his way, pausing when I see Brandy is draped over his lap in the chair. She's starting to become a permanent fixture in the place, like the ugly useless lamps they keep on all the end tables. There aren't even any bulbs in the fucking things.

"Ray." I nod in greeting. "Good to see you."

"You, too," Ray says, shifting around, practically throwing the girl to the floor as he gets to his feet. He reaches for my hand, grasping it and pulling me to him to give me a sort of half-hug. "You're up and around awfully early today. What is it, four in the morning? Five?"

"Nine," I tell him, waving for the waitress to bring me a drink as she strolls past. It's early, hell, but never too early for a cold beer.

"Nine?" He sounds incredulous as he glances at his watch, squinting. He's drunk. *Real* drunk. I can smell it on him as he sways slightly. They must've been here all night. "Shit, my wife's going to kill me. We have an appointment this morning for that, uh... that, you know..." He waves his hand as if I'm supposed to know what he means. "Hell, I don't even know. Guess it wasn't that important."

"Guess not," I respond. "I'm sure Martina would call if it were important."

"Yeah, or try to show up here," Ray says with a laugh. "Good thing she knows women aren't allowed inside."

My gaze darts to Brandy as she smiles, clearly listening, obviously the exception to the rules.

We all have those, I think.

Exceptions.

I used to be one of his.

"So what are you doing here?" Ray asks when the waitress brings my beer. I pop the top off with the bottle opener on my keys and take a long pull, letting it soothe my nerves. He retakes his seat, Brandy draping herself once more over his lap, as he motions to the chair beside him for me to sit.

I hadn't come here to socialize, or even to see Ray, but denying him isn't smart at the moment, so I sit.

"Just handling some business," I reply, taking another drink.

"Same business you were handling the other night before the dinner party?" he asks, raising an eyebrow curiously. "It's not like you to be late for things. Makes me wonder what was so important."

"Had to take care of a guy," I say. "No big deal."

"What guy? What did he do?"

"Endangered Karissa."

He smiles, letting out a little laugh. "Endangered Karissa."

"Yes."

"Funny, how you can go from wanting to kill her yourself to wanting to kill anyone who hurts her," Ray says. "Who was the guy, anyway? Anyone I know?"

"No," I say. "Just the boyfriend of one of her friends."

"So you took care of her friend's boyfriend because he endangered her?"

"Yes."

"How chivalrous," he mutters. "Something my daughter loved in you, might I add. Maria always went on and on about your manners, how you'd open doors and pull out chairs and offer her your coat when she was cold. She always said she found a hero in you."

I shake my head as I guzzle the rest of the beer, setting the empty bottle down on the table beside me. No amount of alcohol will dilute the bitterness of this conversation. "I'm nobody's hero."

"You're trying to be Karissa's."

"No, I just don't want to be her villain."

"Ah, hero, villain... what's the difference anymore? These days, killing kids in the name of love is more honorable than putting someone out of their misery. The world's gone backward."

"Maybe you're just looking at it the wrong way."

"Maybe," Ray agrees, "or maybe you aren't looking at it at all. Maybe you're blind to it."

"Maybe you are."

Ray shrugs. "One of us certainly is."

We're at an impasse, one we'll probably never get past. My gaze shifts from Ray to his girlfriend as she eyes me curiously. She hasn't said a word, but she's still listening.

"Maybe we should talk about this in private," I suggest.

"No need," Ray says flippantly as he motions around the scarce bar. "We're all friends here."

I don't have friends. I have family. And I don't trust half of them these days. But Ray believes what he wants to believe, and no amount of coaxing will change that with him.

Sighing, I stand up and walk away, heading toward the administrative office beside Ray's. I've put this off way too long as it is, but I can't delay it any longer. Ray is growing impatient, especially after that display at his house, and I need to put an end to this so we can all move on and salvage whatever is left.

I need to find Carmela.

The manager is in, sitting at his desk. It takes him a moment to recognize me, and he rises to his feet. "Mr. Vitale. What can I do for you?"

"I need to see the outside security footage from a few weeks ago," I say. "Around the beginning of June. There was an incident in the back lot."

"Ah, yes, that."

"You know what I'm referring to?"

He sits back down and shifts through some things on his desk.

"The same incident Mr. Angelo inquired about? Your shooting?"

I tense. "Ray asked about it?"

"Of course," he says. "The night it happened. He watched the footage."

My stomach sinks. Ray saw. He knows who fired the shot that night. He knows I lied to him, he's known since the beginning, but he hasn't called me out on it.

Why?

"I need copies of the footage made for me," I say. "All outside angles for the week leading up to the incident and the next day."

He raises his eyebrows as he gazes at me. "That's hundreds of hours. If you're looking for something specific, I can—"

"Don't worry about what I'm looking for," I say, cutting him off. "Just get me what I need, and make it quick."

"Yes, sir. I can have it for you this afternoon."

When I walk back out of his office, the bar is deserted. Ray and his girlfriend are both gone and the door is unmanned, as Kelvin likely made an exit with them. Strolling over, I plop back down in the leather chair, motioning for the waitress to bring me another beer.

Maybe I can enjoy this one...

A few hours later, the footage is ready. I grab the disks from the manager, nodding my thanks, and head out of Cobalt. I have just enough time to stop by the small café nearby and order a Chocolate Mint Tea before Karissa's school day ends. The café is in chaos. Seems one of their workers hasn't shown up for a few days, leaving them short staffed.

Go figure.

I'm in my car, parked in front of the math classroom, when two o'clock rolls around. I sit there, watching the building as the students stream out, looking for her, scanning the crowd for a hint of the pink sweater she wore today, but it's nowhere to be seen. The crowd thins, minutes ticking away.

She's not here.

My insides coil as I pull out my phone to call her. It goes straight to voicemail. I scan the neighborhood once more, double-checking I have the right place, and start up the car. I speed away, trying her phone again on the drive home with no luck.

She's not answering.

It's not even ringing.

I pull the car in the driveway when I get to the house and head straight for the front door. The knob turns as soon as I grasp it. *Unlocked.* I shove the door open, a shuddering breath hitting me right away, the sound of crying in the distance. My feet root into the ground, coldness running through me. "Karissa?"

The crying continues, a hiccupping sob, but above it I hear Karissa's calm voice call out. "In here."

The den.

I walk that way, pausing in the doorway. Karissa is sitting on the couch, her arm around Melody as the girl cries on her shoulder. My apprehension lessens just a bit with the swell of relief, but it doesn't completely fade away.

"What happened?" I ask, glancing between them uneasily. I hate crying, no matter who's doing it.

"It's Paul," Karissa says carefully, shooting her friend a sympathetic look when the name makes her cry harder.

"Ah." *Paul.* "Something happen to him?"

"Yes," she says, hesitating before sighing. "Well, we don't know. He sort of just… disappeared."

That he did.

Poof.

Gone.

Carried away by the wind.

"Disappeared," I repeat.

"Yeah," she says. "Nobody's seen or heard from him in days. The police say there's no sign of foul play, but his car was left at his work and his phone was all smashed up in the alley, so I don't know how they can say that. Clearly he didn't run away."

"He wouldn't," Melody chimes in, sniffling as she tries to control her sobs. "He wouldn't just run away. He had work… and school… he had me. Something happened to him, somebody did something to him. God! Why would somebody want to hurt him?"

Why? The million-dollar question.

I could answer it, but it wouldn't be what she wanted to hear.

Melody starts crying again. I take it as my cue to excuse myself. I pull the discs from my coat pocket and walk over to my desk, sitting down across the room, giving the two of them their space.

I pop the first disc in the drive and wait for it to load. Six cameras are positioned around the outside of Cobalt, two in the front and two in the back, with two more along the alley, giving a complete view of the building and the streets around it. The screen is split into squares, the feed from all angles playing simultaneously. I'm not exactly sure what I'm looking for, or if it'll even help, but I know Carmela. She wouldn't have just attacked me that night on a whim. She would've scoped the building out, put a plan in place and gone over it again and again.

Desperation doesn't completely erase a built-in knack for survival, which she clearly has.

I watch the feeds for a while, fast forwarding through hours of nothingness, watching the comings and goings around Cobalt, and waiting for something to spark my interest. I breeze through two days of footage as Karissa and Melody talk amongst themselves across the room. The crying grates on my nerves as I drum my fingers on the arm of my chair, growing more and more on edge.

I want silence, and peace.

I want this over and done with.

I need to put an end to it.

Move on with my life.

I'm on day three of the footage already when Melody finally pulls herself together and climbs to her feet. "I should go. It's getting late."

It is.

It's nearing dusk.

She's been here for hours.

"Are you sure?" Karissa asks. "You don't have to go. You can stay as long as you want. We have guest rooms."

My eyes dart over top of the laptop screen, meeting Karissa's right away. She shoots me a 'no nonsense' kind of look that silences me before I even say anything. She'll fight me on it. She will. And it'll get ugly if I interfere.

"I'm sure," Melody says, hugging Karissa. "Thanks for being there for me today. Sorry you missed your classes because of this."

"Not a problem," Karissa says right away. "Anything you need, you just let me know. I'm here."

"I'll remember that." Melody gives her a watery smile before turning to me. "Thanks for letting me cry on your couch, Ignazio."

"Thank Karissa for that," I say. "She extended the invitation, not me."

Karissa groans. "What he means to say is 'you're welcome' and 'come over anytime'."

Karissa walks her friend out as my gaze settles back on the laptop, the afternoon streaming away on the screen. After Melody is gone, Karissa strolls back in, pausing in the doorway. I can sense her gaze burning through me.

"You skipped school," I say without looking up, "on the first day."

"She needed me."

"For what? It's not as if you could do anything."

She says nothing.

I can still feel her gaze.

Glancing up, I meet her eyes. She's staring at me hard.

"Could you?" she asks. "Could *you* do something?"

"Like what?"

"I don't know... whatever it is you do. Dealing with people and finding things are your specialties, right? That's what you told me. So you can find people, too, right? I mean, you found me."

"Actually, you found me," I say, hitting pause on the feeds to look at her. "You stumbled right into my path."

"But you would've found me, eventually," she says. "You were looking for my mother... maybe you still *are* looking for my mother. I don't know."

She pauses, staring at me. She formed it as a statement, but I see the questions in her eyes. I'm not going to answer, though, and I don't think she expects me to, because she moves on quickly.

"I'm just saying, you do things... those kinds of things... so I thought maybe you could find him. For Melody. For me."

"For you."

"Yes," she says. "As a favor."

I lean back in my chair, eyeing her warily. She's opening a door I'm not sure she's ready to walk through. "Tell me something, Karissa."

She hesitates at my serious tone. "What?"

"When you poisoned my food, where did you get the drugs from?"

Her cheeks grow red, a hint of alarm in her eyes as she averts her gaze. "I didn't *poison* your food. I didn't want to hurt you."

"You're avoiding the question."

"It doesn't matter."

"It does," I say, "to me."

Shaking her head, she stares at the floor near my desk. "What does this have to do with anything? I'm sorry, okay? Is that what you want to hear? I'm sorry I drugged your food. I'm sorry I ran off in the middle of the night. I'm sorry I led you to my parents. I'm sorry I got my father killed."

"I thought you didn't have a father."

"I don't." Her voice has a hard edge to it. "I'm just saying..."

"You're saying you're sorry," I chime in when she doesn't finish. "But what you're not saying... what you're avoiding saying... is that

Paul gave you the drugs that sparked all of it."

She has no argument for that.

She just glares at me.

"Bad things happen to bad people, Karissa."

"Paul wasn't bad."

"He endangered you, didn't he?"

"Yeah, well, you were going to *kill* me!"

"I was," I admit, "but I never pretended to be good."

"What are you trying to say, Naz? Huh?"

"Exactly what I'm saying: if you want me to look for him, I will, but I'm not going to find him. Nobody will."

"How do you know?"

"Because if he was meant to be found, he would've been found already."

Karissa leans against the doorframe, mulling over my words. Shutting the laptop, I stand up and smooth my suit coat.

"Look," I say, "why don't we go out and grab some dinner, celebrate the first day of classes."

"I skipped them, remember? There's not much to celebrate."

"Nonsense. Regardless of if you were there or not, the day happened. There's a lesson to be learned there, you know. Life goes on without you."

"I hear you, Plato."

I smile at her sarcasm as I stroll across the room, pausing in front of her. "I prefer the words of Plautus." I cup her cheek, stroking her warm skin with my thumb. *"Let us celebrate with wine and sweet words."*

"I don't know Plautus."

"Huh." Leaning down, I kiss the corner of her mouth. "He also said the chap that endures hard knocks like a man enjoys a soft time later on."

She smiles softly when I kiss her again. "What does that mean?"

"Whatever you want it to mean."

"What do *you* want it to mean?"

I kiss her a third time, nipping at her bottom lip as I pull away. "Maybe I'll show you when we get home."

I forgot all about the goddamn Chocolate Mint Tea.

The full cup is still sitting in the car, perched in the cup holder between the seats, exactly where I set it when heading to pick her up from class. A peculiar odor clings to the interior from the hours old drink.

It makes my nose twitch.

Karissa stares at the cup during the drive into the city. I wait for her to ask me about it, but she doesn't say a word. I can feel the tension mounting, though, the theories forming in the back of her mind.

"I bought it for you," I explain before she even mentions the thing. "I tried to pick you up from class this afternoon."

Her voice wavers when she responds. "I told you I didn't need a ride home."

"That's never stopped me before," I say. "You weren't at the school, though, so I tried to call you."

"Oh, yeah." She finally looks away from the drink to glance at me. "My phone's not working."

"What did you do to it?"

She narrows her eyes. "What makes you think I did something?"

I smile at her defensive tone. "Because I know you. You're hell on that phone."

She rolls her eyes. "So, okay, I dropped it, and like the screen went black and now it won't turn on, but that doesn't mean I broke it. It could be unrelated, you know. Maybe it just died."

"Unlikely."

"Whatever."

"Regardless, we'll get you a new one. With a new number. I'll put you on my plan."

"How very... domestic."

"Well, you're going to be my wife, aren't you?"

She hesitates.

Hesitates.

"You're going to be my wife," I say, not phrasing it as a question this time for my own sanity. "What's mine is yours. Which, for the record, is also a Plautus quote: *for what is yours is mine, and mine is all yours.*"

She's quiet for a few minutes before clearing her throat. "I am"

"Are what?"

"Going to be your wife," she says, "someday."

"Someday soon," I amend.

"Not that soon."

"Soon enough."

"Whatever."

"*Whatever,*" I mimic. She's starting to love that damn word. "Speaking of, have you chosen a date? Have you thought about any of it?"

"No."

This time there's no hesitation.

Infuriating woman.

"No," I echo.

"It's not that I don't want to," she says. "I think I do."

"You think you do."

She groans loudly. "Can you not do that right now?"

"Can I not do what?"

"That! Repeating everything I say in that tone you use."

"Repeating everything," I say, "in the tone I use?"

"Naz!"

I breathe deeply, trying to combat the swell of frustration when she yells that name. I don't even realize when I do what she's complaining about. It helps me keep things straight to repeat her, to take her at her word and not misinterpret what she says.

"You think you want to," I say, picking up her train of thought. "Continue. I'm listening."

"I think I want to. I still feel how I felt the day you asked me, even though you never really asked me."

"I never asked you?"

She cuts her eyes at me, glaring, but doesn't complain that I repeated her words. "You didn't ask. You said 'marry me'. It wasn't a question."

"Huh."

She looks at me like she wants me to say more, but I'm not sure how to respond to that.

"Anyway," she says after a moment, stressing the word. "The point is, yeah, I think I want to, but the whole wedding thing is daunting. I just, I don't know... what's the point? It's not like I have anyone to give me away. Hell, I don't even have anyone to invite. Melody, I guess... I'd invite my mother, but I'd rather it not turn into murder, Game of Thrones style. She wouldn't come, anyway. And now Melody has her own stuff to deal with. I guess we could invite your former in-laws. I'm sure they'd be about as thrilled to attend as the rest of your family, who clearly all hate me. Maybe your father can cater the event."

Her words have a bitter bite to them.

I can't help but laugh.

"My father doesn't hate you."

"He clearly didn't *like* me."

"He just felt bad for you for having to deal with me."

"I don't need pity."

I smile at that. "Welcome to my world."

∽∾

"Killer."

The lone word echoes through the den. I glance up from my work, eyes darting to where Karissa sits on the couch with her notebook. A strange sense of déjà vu hits me. She's back to taking notes while watching cooking shows.

It's quiet as I stare at her.

She's frowning, looking right at me.

"Killer," I repeat.

Killer.

"Yes," she says. "Killer."

I have no idea what she's talking about. Is she calling me a killer? Does she know something she ought not know?

After a moment, her expression softens, a slight smile touching

281

her lips. "You have no idea what I said, do you?"

"Killer."

"Yes," she says. "I said I miss Killer."

It takes me just as long to comprehend those words, to realize she's talking about a damn dog. I remember her mentioning him when we visited the house in Watertown and then encountering the mutt in her father's house months ago.

"Ah," I say. "Your dog."

"Yes, I miss him." Her brow furrows contemplatively. "Is that weird? Everything going on, everything that happened, and I think the dog worries me most."

"That's a little weird, yes."

She laughs to herself, turning back to her notebook, and absently scribbles along the edge of the paper. I can tell she's distracted and paying no attention to anything. "I just... I don't know. I sometimes think he's the only innocent one in all of this."

"The dog," I say, wanting to clarify to make sure we're still on the same page.

Another laugh. "Yes."

"You don't think *you're* innocent?"

"Me?" she asks incredulously. "Not anymore. You screwed the innocence right out of me. *Literally*."

"I'm serious, Karissa."

"So am I. Maybe I used to be innocent, I don't know, but I'm not anymore."

"You really believe that?"

"Yes."

"Why?"

"Because I'm with you."

She means that. I can tell from the tone of her voice. She thinks she's one of the guilty parties, that she played a hand in what's going on.

"How innocent can I really be to sleep with the man who wants to murder my family?" she asks. "When you first told me about... about Maria, and the baby, and what happened to them... when you told me you wanted justice, I knew what you meant. I knew you were out for blood. And that night you told me, I loved you more for it. I respected you. The bloodlust didn't bother me. It wasn't until I realized you were gunning for me... for my family... that I was bothered by it."

"I'm not going to hurt you," I say for what feels like the millionth time.

"I know," she says quietly. "I believe that now. Maybe I always believed it. But you *do* hurt others. I'm not an idiot. I know what you're capable of. I've seen it. And still, here I am, worrying about a dog and what happened to *him*. My mother, she's resilient. I worry about her, too, but I just... I don't know. How could I even begin to defend her? I'm not even sure what she's capable of. But the dog... he's done nothing wrong, and I worry about what's going to come of him in this all."

If I were a shrink, I'd say something about projection, about how's she's channeling her fears for herself into another living thing because she's too scared to face them, but I know she doesn't want to hear that.

I know, because the hospital made me talk to one of them years ago. I almost ripped his fucking spine out when he tried to diagnose me.

Personality disorder, my ass.

No, Karissa wants to talk about the goddamn dog, so I'll talk about it.

"Don't worry," I say. "Killer will be fine."

"You mean that?"

"Sure."

She smiles, like my words set her at ease, even though it makes no sense. How the hell could I know anything? She goes back to scribbling in her notebook, her eyes bouncing between it and the television as she takes notes.

My gaze turns back to my laptop, every muscle in my body seizing the moment I look at the screen. There it is, in the top right hand corner, the camera view of the alley beside Cobalt.

An old Jeep Waggoner.

I almost missed it, distracted by Karissa. But I know that car. I recognize it. Carmela drove one the entire time she was on the run, the plates fictitious, completely untraceable. I hit pause, isolating the frame and enlarging it. *Bingo*. I hit play again, running the feed at half the speed. One person in the car, but something else moves around in the backseat.

Killer.

"You know, he used to sleep with me at night," Karissa says across the room, still going on about it. "He was kind of my best friend. He could always tell when I was upset or lonely and made a point to keep me company. And yeah, I know it's ridiculous, but he's kind of the only one who's never lied to me."

"I've never lied to you."

"That's a damn lie if I've ever heard one," she grumbles. "You're the freaking king of deception."

"There's a difference between lying and misleading."

"Maybe to you there is, but not to me."

I jot down the plate number, not sure how much help it will be, before letting the feed run at regular speed. I go back to all the camera angles, watching as the car circles the club before she speeds away. She hits the end of the alley and takes a right, heading south through the city.

Sitting back in the chair, my gaze shifts once more to where Karissa sits, tapping her pen against the notebook. She's not watching the television anymore. She's looking at nothing, staring into space.

Yet again, I'm overcome with how beautiful she is. Physically, she's a combination of her parents, but I don't see them anymore when I look at her. I don't see Johnny's freckles or Carmela's face. I see what's inside. I see the innocence, even if she doesn't feel like it's there anymore… I see it, burning so strong that even sleeping with a man like me could never dim it.

Sighing, I close the laptop and grab my phone from where it lays on the desk. "I have to make a few calls."

She glances at me when I speak. "Do you want me to step out?"

"No," I say, standing up. "You keep doing whatever it is you're doing. I'll be back in a few minutes."

I use the side door and head out into the empty garage, making sure to shut the door behind me. I pace the cement, toeing a small oil stain in the middle of the garage, pondering what could remove it as I call a few connections. I put the word out that I'm looking for a Jeep Waggoner, giving them the license plate number in case it will help with verification.

"Fifty grand," I tell them, nearly cringing at my own offer. It's a hefty amount to pay as a reward, but I'm hoping it'll entice them to scrutinize every car they pass. "Nobody confronts her. Nobody touches her. Fifty grand for an address, and I'll handle the rest myself."

I put the word out to about a dozen heavy-hitters, people I've trusted in the past to keep things quiet while getting the job done. I hang up for the last time thirty minutes later and slip my phone in my pocket as I head inside, going straight for the laundry room to get some detergent.

Tide.

I scrub the stain in the garage for damn near an hour, on my hands and knees. I don't stop until every spec of it has faded, my hands scraped and bleeding from the concrete rubbing them raw. Afterward, I head back inside, going upstairs to shower, to wash away the remnants of the day.

Once I'm clean, I make my way back downstairs wearing only a pair of gray sweats. I hear noise in the kitchen, the banging of pots and pans.

Karissa's cooking.

I step in the doorway, pausing, and lean against the doorframe to watch her. She seems more confident now than before, moving around fluidly, those earbuds in her ears. The counter is covered with supplies, a pot of something boiling on the stove, a cast iron skillet sitting beside it.

She turns, her gaze briefly flickering my way as she heads for the fridge. She pulls out a stick of butter and sets it on the counter, turning my way once more, offering a small smile. It's cautious, wavering as she pulls the earbuds out and drapes them around her neck.

Her mouth opens, and closes, before opening yet again.

I know what she's going to ask before she can even find the words to say anything.

"Are you, uh...?" She pauses, her expression hopeful as she motions toward the stove. "You wouldn't happen to be hungry, would you?"

"I might be," I say tentatively.

"Well, I thought I would... that I could... you know... make something."

My gaze shifts from her to the mess she already made. "I see that."

She doesn't come out and ask me.

She says nothing else, matter of fact.

She turns away, going back to what she was doing, but leaves the earbuds out so she can hear me, in case I have something to say. I watch her for a few minutes as she tosses cubes of potatoes into the boiling water, watching as she pours some oil into the frying pan. After she has going whatever it is she needs on the stove, she grabs some iceberg lettuce from the fridge and slaps it down on the counter, on top of a chopping board.

She grabs a small, serrated steak knife and jams it down the center of the head of the lettuce. She yanks it back out, and I cringe, shaking my head as I push away from the doorframe. She tries another tactic, going at it from the side, and barely misses stabbing herself with the knife.

"What are you doing with that lettuce?" I ask, strolling over to her, plucking the knife right out of her hand before she severs a finger. "Other than massacring it, obviously."

She glares at me, trying to grab the knife back, but I move it out of her reach and toss it in the sink.

"I'm making a salad," she says, grabbing the large bowl from the counter and waving it toward me as if to make her point. "Or I'm trying to, anyway."

"Trying is right," I reply, reaching past her and grabbing a 10-inch straight edge Chef's knife. I wave it toward her, taking a page from her book. "This is the knife you should use."

I flip the head of lettuce over, cutting off the end, and remove the outward layer, tossing it in the trashcan. I cut what's left straight down the center before sectioning it into quarters, quickly cutting it into smaller pieces and tossing them into her bowl. It's finished in under a minute and I turn to her, raising an eyebrow. "What else you got?"

She's still just standing there, gaping at me. It takes her a moment to respond. "Uh, um... here."

She grabs some tomatoes and sets them in front of me.

I dice them quickly, getting rid of the excess juice and seeds, and toss the tomatoes into the bowl. Before I can say a word, Karissa drops some cucumbers in front of me. I stare at them before cutting my eyes at her, seeing the smile playing on her lips as she turns her focus on the pot on the stove. She keeps shoving vegetables my way, even after the salad is done. Onions and green peppers, fresh thyme and oregano, things she needs for whatever she's cooking.

When all that is done, she sets a block of cheese on the counter. I eye it peculiarly before cutting it into perfect cubes. "What's the cheese for?"

"Dunno," she says, reaching past me and grabbing a cheese cube, popping it in her mouth. "I just like watching you do that."

Laughing, I toss the knife in the sink, stopping before she invents something else for me to cut up. "My father showed me how to use a knife when I was a kid. I spent my summers in the back of the deli with him."

"That's sweet," she says.

"It's only because I was free labor. He was too cheap to ever hire anybody."

"Still, I'm sure it was nice getting to spend time with him."

"Yeah, it was," I concede, wiping down a section of counter, cleaning up my mess. "It was the only time he ever recognized me for something good. Usually it was 'Ignazio, you disappoint me' or 'Ignazio, be a man', but those days he'd look at me and say, 'Ignazio, my son, you did good today'. It was nice to hear that."

"So he taught you how to cook?"

"He did."

"So why don't you?" she asks. "If you're worried about everyone poisoning your food, why don't you just cook for yourself?"

"Good question," I say. "Maybe I've got a death wish."

Before she can respond, I give her a smile and walk away. "I'll be in the den if you need anything, Karissa."

She doesn't stop me.

I'm thankful for it.

A few minutes pass—five, maybe ten—before I hear her cursing. Seconds later, I faintly smell smoke. Sighing, I lean back in my chair, hands clasped on the back of my head, my eyes closed.

I don't know what's happening, but I'm sure she can handle it. If not, she knows where I am.

Eventually, her cursing tapers off, and all goes quiet. I get lost in the peace for a moment until I hear her voice. "Naz?"

Opening my eyes, I look at her in the doorway. The tentative expression is back. "Yes?"

"If you're hungry, the food is finished."

She fidgets like a nervous child awaiting punishment. I nod in acknowledgement. "I'll be there in a minute."

It's a small concession on my behalf, but to her it's everything. Her face lights up, eyes sparkling. I get a glimpse of her radiant smile as she leaves the room, easing my worries.

I'm offering her my trust again.

When I walk into the dining room, she's already seated at the table, in the same chair she always sits in with or without me. I take the seat across from her, eyeing our plates warily. Steak with loaded mashed potatoes and a bowl of salad.

"We can switch plates, if you want," she says quickly. "Or not, either way. We could even go halfsies, you know... like, *share*."

"It's fine," I say, pushing back my natural paranoia. "So you made steak."

"It's your favorite," she says. "I remember you telling me that."

"It is."

I pick up my fork and knife and immediately cut into it. The outside is seared nicely while the inside is dark pink, borderline rare.

. "I wasn't sure how you like it, and well, honestly, I don't think I could cook it a specific way. I had all these notes but when it came down to it, I kind of just threw it on and hoped for the best."

I cut off a small piece and pop it in my mouth.

I don't think she could ever look happier than she does at the moment. She takes a bite of her own, chewing as she tries to contain her smile. There's nothing sinister about the pull of her lips.

We eat and chat, like a normal couple doing normal things. I've eaten meals personally prepared by world-renowned chefs, but none ever meant quite as much as what's on my plate. She poured her soul out and offered it up, and it isn't perfect, but it was made for me.

I don't waste any of it.

I crack open a bottle of wine afterward and we drink heartily, the alcohol loosening her lips as she relaxes, talking about any and everything. By the time the bottle is empty, she's pretty well lit. I can see it in her eyes as they glisten under the lights of the dining room.

She gets up to take care of our plates but I reach out and grab her wrist, stopping her before she can take them away. Prying the dirty plates from her fingers, I shove them down the table, ignoring her feeble protests as I pull her onto my lap. She straddles me, her skirt riding up, her arms wrapping around my neck. My hands graze her knees before slowly running up her thighs, settling just beneath the material of her skirt as I lean forward, softly kissing her.

Her lips taste bitter, like the wine she drank.

But her words are sweet as she whispers to me.

"I love you, Naz," she says, the declaration barely a breath that I greedily inhale. "God help me, but I do. I love you."

It's the first time she's said that to me in months.

My left hand finds home on her hip, holding her there, while my right grazes the spot between her thighs, slipping beneath the fabric to stroke her clit. She moans into my mouth, kissing me hungrily, her fingers running through my hair. She's warm, and slick, my fingers caressing her before sliding right in. Her hips shift as she grinds in my lap, seeking more friction. I happily give it to her.

"That's it," I tell her as she fucks my fingers, my thumb stroking her clit every time she moves. "Take what you want from me."

She whimpers, her eyes closed, her pace increasing. "More."

"More what?" I ask, my lips finding her neck. "Tell me what you want."

"You," she whispers, her voice strained. "I want you."

"What part of me?"

"All of you."

I smile against her skin, nipping at her throat when she tilts her head back. "I'm right here, baby, and I'll give you anything you want. All you have to do is tell me what it is."

Her breath hitches when my thumb presses harder, rubbing her clit faster. She's getting close already. The woman has buttons I'm an expert at pushing, my hands tuned to every inch of her body. Just a few more strokes send her barreling right over the edge. Her body tenses, her face contorting with pleasure as she stutters out my name.

Standing, I lift her up and plant her right on the table, pushing her back onto it. She doesn't resist, her eyes opening and meeting mine as I grip the sides of her panties and pull them down her legs. I toss them on the floor and drop to my knees, knocking the chair away. My mouth meets her pussy, my tongue sweeping along her entrance before plunging in, tasting every bit of her.

It's Heaven.

She grinds her hips as her hands drift to her breasts, clutching them like she's holding on for dear life. I touch and caress, licking and sucking, fucking her with my tongue, driving her right back over the edge.

Once she relaxes from her second orgasm, I rise to my feet and stare down at her, splayed out on the table. Leaning down, I kiss her mouth, unable to stop my grin when her tongue sweeps along my lips.

"Thank you for dinner," I tell her, my hand stroking her outer thigh. "But I especially love dessert."

She grabs ahold of me when I try to pull away, wrapping her arms around me tightly. "I want you."

"I heard you before."

"I want you inside of me," she says, a flush overcoming her cheeks. "I want all of you, yeah, but right now I want you to fuck me."

Smirking, I pull her hands from around my neck as I peck small kisses on her mouth. "Whatever the lady wants."

I fuck her, right there, on the table. Fuck her on her back, on her side, on her stomach. I fuck her so hard her squeals turn to screams, then I fuck her slow and deep, moving agonizingly. She falls apart all around me, under me, over me, the tiny little threads that hold her together unweaving, leaving her stripped down to the core. She's uninhibited, intoxicated, and she's vulnerable to my touch.

I fuck her like I've never fucked her before.

And then I take her upstairs and I fuck her some more.

Afterward, we lay in bed, her body draped around mine, not a stitch of clothing covering either of us. Our skin glows from sweat and satisfaction under the gleam of moonlight streaming through the window. My fingertips absently trail her bare back, blindly drawing shapes around her scattering of freckles, as she sleeps soundly, her head on my chest. She doesn't even stir when my phone starts beeping on the nightstand beside me, somebody calling.

Carefully, I reach over and pick up the phone, glancing at the screen. *Unknown Caller*. I hesitate before answering on a whim. "Yeah?"

There's a moment of silence before a vaguely familiar voice comes on, one of the guys who runs point in upstate New York. "You know that call you put out earlier?"

"Yes."

"Well, I found her," the man says. "I'm looking at the car right now."

I hesitate, glancing down at Karissa, ensuring she's still fast asleep. Just a few hours. That's all it took for her to be found. She evaded me for years, but she's not running anymore.

I killed her husband.

I took her daughter.

I knocked her feet out from under her.

"Text me the address."

"Sure thing," he says. "And, uh, about that reward..."

"The minute I get what I need, you'll get what you want. Got it?"

"Got it."

I hang up, slipping the phone back on the nightstand. I don't look at it when it beeps with a text message. I don't want to know right now. Not today. Just one more night is all I need. One more night where I can pretend I don't have to do what it is I have to do. One more night of a clear conscience. Because come sun up, when I have to face reality again, I know I'm going to have to do the one thing I promised I wouldn't do.

I have to intentionally hurt Karissa.

I have to kill her mother.

Gathering her hair, I push it away, out of her face, as I rouse her from sleep. "Karissa," I whisper, shaking her slightly as I shift around in the bed. "Wake up, sweetheart."

She stirs, opening her eyes, and blinks a few times as she looks up at me. A sleepy smile overcomes her lips, that happiness coating her face. Blissfully ignorant. I remember how that felt. I envy it, for the moment.

I want it for myself again.

"What's wrong?" she asks, her voice thick with sleep.

"Nothing," I tell her, shifting her beneath me so I can hover over her beautiful frame. "There's absolutely nothing wrong. How could there be? I have you."

I didn't think it was possible, but her radiance grows. She wraps her arms around me, pulling me to her for a kiss, as I settle between her legs. I'm hard already. *Again*.

I push inside of her slowly, holding her tightly as I do, listening for the sound of her breath. The gasp of pleasure washes through me and I shiver, nuzzling into her warm neck.

I don't fuck her this time.

I can't.

I don't want to.

I make love to her, pouring my soul out to her like she did for me this afternoon. I trail light kisses everywhere I can reach, whispering how much I love her, the words ghosting across her skin. My nose brushes against hers as I stare into her eyes, drinking in the innocence.

"There's something about you," I say quietly. "Something I've sought for a very long time."

Her smile wavers, her expression sobering. "I've heard those words before."

"I know you have." I'd told her this exact thing the night in her dorm room. "And now that I've found it, Karissa, I'm not sure I can let it go."

She reaches up, brushing her hands through the hair that wisps across the forehead, before she cradles my face. "Then don't."

Chapter Nineteen

The injury therefore that you do to a man should be such that you need not fear his revenge.

The quote from *The Prince* has always been one of my favorites. I've lived my life by it for as long as I can remember. It's a lesson I learned through experience, through bloodlust and bloodshed. It's a lesson that has kept me alive and led to many other deaths.

If you're going to hurt someone, make it fatal.

Don't wound. *Kill.*

Don't let them walk away.

It's a code those in the old country live by—you don't just kill a man, you kill his whole family. Orphaned sons grow up to be vengeful men. Widowed husbands come looking for blood eventually.

I sit in my car, once more in the small town of Dexter, just a few miles to the west of Watertown. My vintage copy of Machiavelli's book lies open in my lap as I thumb through the warped, water damaged pages in the darkness. I couldn't believe it, when I looked at my phone this morning and the familiar address of the flower shop in Watertown greeted me.

Carmela went back home, it seems.

I'm curious why, and I have a few theories: maybe because it's the only place Karissa would know to look for her mother, or maybe it's because Carmela has nowhere else to go. But I think it's more complex, like maybe she knows what's coming, and when it happens, she wants it to be on her terms.

She has the upper hand here.

Or so she thinks.

Through the woods, I can see the house. The Jeep Wagoneer was abandoned at the shop in town, the doors all locked up. I'm not sure if she went back here or not, but she's in the area somewhere, and I don't know where else she'd go at night.

She has no money.

She had no friends.

She probably wouldn't expect me to bother looking here, since I'd already cleared her out of the place.

I linger for a while, just biding my time, watching the house as my hands stroke the cover of the book. It's all quiet, and dark, appearing abandoned, and I'm close to second-guessing myself when there's movement in the yard. Shadows move, the grass disturbed, seconds before a faint bark cuts through the silence.

Killer.

I watch attentively as the front door of the house just barely cracks open and the small dog darts straight inside. I continue to stare at it, even after all is still again, contemplating where to go from here.

Reaching into the center console, I pull out the small caliber handgun, carefully double-checking to make sure it's still loaded.

It's nearing midnight when I get out of my car and slowly make my way through the woods, watching my surroundings. No motion lights outside, I imagine, since the dog didn't trigger them. I'm thinking there isn't even any electricity.

That makes it tricky.

People take for granted the sounds that surround them. We tune them out naturally, but when they're gone, we miss them. They mask the unknown, and without that buffer, every creak and groan sounds grave and unnatural.

I approach the house, heading around the side of it. I remember the layout from the visit with Karissa. I head to where her old bedroom window would be, recalling her story not long ago about the windows. Her mother made a habit of nailing them shut, but Karissa rejected it and jimmied hers back open.

I try the widow, praying Carmela didn't catch it. It moves easily, barely making a creak. I haul myself up, careful to pull myself inside. My feet hit the wooden floor and I pause there for a moment, letting myself get used to the stuffy darkness.

It's deathly silent.

Once I've adjusted, I stand up, gripping the gun firmly as I stroll toward the door. It isn't latched. I remember. Karissa's bedroom door had always been broken.

I make my way toward Carmela's bedroom, my footsteps so light they don't make a sound. Her door is shut. I grasp the knob, testing it.

Unlocked.

I take a deep breath to steady myself, wondering if this is how Johnny did it, if this is how he felt when he broke into my house, when he killed my wife in the middle of the night. Did he hesitate outside the bedroom door? Did he even for a moment consider backing out?

Or was it easy for him, stepping inside, cocking that shotgun and destroying my life?

Shaking those thoughts away, I turn the knob and push the door open. It lets out an awful groan. The world around me seems to fall into slow motion while I still move at the speed of light. The noise echoes, everything around me crystal clear.

A dog growls nearby as the bed shifts.

Carmela sits straight up.

A second passes.

I stare at that familiar face, into those terror-filled eyes. A lifetime plays out around us, a world of memories and all those missed chances, the flood of what-could-have-been.

Could've been, but never will, because it's too late.

The chance is gone.

I raise my gun.

Another second.

I pull the trigger.

BANG

A single bullet rips right through Carmela's skull, dropping her instantly. I hesitated longer than she even felt it.

The growling turns to frantic barking. I turn the gun, pointing it at the mutt. His ears are laid back as he viciously bears his teeth, coming right toward me defensively. My gloved finger rests on the trigger.

I try.

I try.

I fucking *try* to do it, to pull the goddamn trigger, but I can't.

I can't do it.

"Fuck," I curse to myself, dropping the gun, abandoning it. The clank of metal against the floor makes the dog cower briefly. He whimpers before growling once more, terrified but protective, following me through the house as I head for the front door. I unlock it, opening it, holding it open for the dog to run out, but he backs away, staying in the foyer.

I consider leaving him there.

I almost do.

But I can't.

Again, I can't do it.

Karissa's voice echoes in the back of my head.

She loves him.

He's innocent.

On a whim I reach down and snatch ahold of the dog, lugging it outside with me. He barks and wiggles, frantic to escape my grasp. The second my grip loosens, he rears back, bearing his teeth as he clamps down on my forearm.

Pain shoots through arm and I instinctively let go. Shit. The dog hits the ground and I expect him to run, to escape, but he just stands there, growling some more.

Shaking it off, I do what I need to, improvising to ignite a spark, sending the porch of the house up in flames. I watch the fire spread, my thoughts drifting, a strange numbness running through me.

The affects of watching death used to linger for hours, making my fingertips tingle and my heart race, my body twitching as I tried to come down from it, but there's nothing today.

No euphoria.

No adrenaline.

Nothing.

My heart isn't racing. There's no life inside of me.

I'm a monster.

Karissa was right about me.

The only thing I feel at the moment is the throbbing of my arm and the stream of blood from the fresh wound running along my skin.

I can't believe the mutt bit me.

I save his life and this is the thanks I get?

I wait until the flames start sweeping through the house before I walk away. The dog follows me to my car, growling, trying to intimidate me. I have no time to dawdle, no time to waste. Someone will see the fire and call it in, and I can't be here when they come.

Nobody around here can know I exist.

Opening the back door, I snatch a hold of the dog and throw him in the backseat before he can bite me again.

Dr. Carter's once again half-asleep. He stands at his front door, blinking rapidly as he gapes at me under his dim porch light. "Another?"

His voice is gritty, full of disbelief.

He didn't expect to see me again so soon.

He thinks my body count has risen again.

It has, sure, but I don't need him for this one, just as I hadn't needed him when I killed Johnny. Ray would want evidence, tangible proof that justice was served.

He'd want Carmela found.

Shaking my head, I yank my shirtsleeve up, showing him the bite. Blood streams down my arm. I can feel it seeping into my button down shirt, staining the pristine white a dark shade of red.

"Come in," he says, waving for me to step inside, his eyes frantically darting all around before he shuts the door behind me. I follow him down the hallway, to the kitchen, trying not to drip blood on his floor.

Not because I care about his things.

More like I don't want to leave more of myself behind than I have to.

This isn't the first time he's sewn me up, and it won't be the last. I take a seat at his kitchen table as he flicks on the overhead light and gets down to business. His supplies are gathered, the bare minimum needed: just a needle and some thread.

I'd do it myself, but I can't sew for shit.

I know.

I've tried.

"I just need to grab the anesthetic," he grumbles, heading for the doorway, but I reach out and grab his arm, stopping him. His panicked gaze darts down to where my hand clutches him before he meets my eyes.

"Don't bother," I say, letting go of him. "Just get on with it."

"Are you sure?"

"I wouldn't say it if I wasn't."

Nodding, he proceeds to clean up the blood and disinfect the wound. It burns as the peroxide seeps into the small gashes lining the circular injury. I can make out the imprint of teeth, the skin already bruising in the familiar pattern.

The veterinarian eyes it warily before getting to work.

I hardly feel the needle when it goes in.

"Run in with an animal tonight?" he asks, making the first stitch.

"I don't think that's any of your business."

"No, you're right," he mutters. "It isn't."

Just a few stitches to close the biggest gash and he's done, pushing away from the table to clean up the mess. "When was your last tetanus shot, Vitale?"

"You'd know better than I would."

He pauses, contemplating. "You should probably get a booster, just to be safe."

"I'm not worried about it."

"You should be. Tetanus is—"

"The least of my problems right now."

"Well, at least let me get you some antibiotics."

"Don't bother," I say. "I'm not going to take them."

He shakes his head, turning to me. He's wide-awake now. He knows his chance for peaceful slumber is over. "It's amazing you're still alive, you know."

"I know," I admit, standing up. "I'll get going now."

I leave before he can offer any more sort of inane care, heading back out to my car. I pause beside it, seeing the dog in the backseat, still growling at me.

My gaze turns to the doorway, to where Carter stands, watching me. I motion with my head toward the backseat. "You think you can do something with this for me?"

His eyes widen. "The dog?"

"Yes."

"You don't mean..." He turns his head toward the back yard. "You don't want me to... do you?"

His stammering makes me laugh.

"I'm not telling you to kill it," I say. "I'm just asking you to do something with it. Tie it up out back, just temporarily, until I can make other arrangements."

Opening the back door, I let the dog run out. I don't wait for

Carter to say anything else, to even confirm he'll take care of the thing. Without another look, I get in the car to leave right away.

It's nearing sun up when I reach my neighborhood in Brooklyn, a touch of light spanning along the horizon. I'm exhausted, and frustrated, wishing I felt something more.

I pull the car into the garage, knowing I'm going to clean it out first thing, and head inside to get what I need. A towel, bleach, something to get rid of the dog hair. *Something to wipe away the memory.*

I always expected to feel relief.

I expected to feel a burden lifted.

But as I step into the house and come face-to-face with a concerned Karissa in the kitchen, what I really feel is a heavier weight pressing upon me. My chest constricts when I see the worry in her eyes... worry about where I've been, worry about what I might've done last night.

She can't even begin to imagine...

"You're home," she says, her voice low like maybe she's really saying it to herself.

I respond anyway. "And you're awake early."

"I couldn't sleep."

"Me, either."

I quickly kiss her cheek, making sure not to linger too long, before I head straight upstairs. I strip off my clothes, tossing them with the dirty, making a mental note to discard the button down before Karissa finds it. I head into the bathroom and wash up before pulling on a fresh suit and heading back downstairs.

It only took a few minutes.

She's still in the kitchen.

The scent of coffee clings to the air as she brews a fresh cup in the machine. I walk right past it, opting for a bottle of water from the fridge.

"If you need me," I say, "I'll be in the garage."

"Doing what?"

"Cleaning out the car."

"You just did that not long ago."

I don't bother to respond, not knowing what to say, as I head back out. I half expect her to follow me, but she doesn't. My own relief startles me. As much as I love having her around, I felt an inkling of something when I looked in her eyes, something I haven't felt in a long time.

Regret.

I've never regretted anything.

I certainly don't want to start now.

Chapter Twenty

There hasn't been a murder in Dexter, New York in over a decade. Not a single arson. Not even an assault. The only crime the small community sees is thievery, but one night in town, I destroy it all.

It's front-page news of the Watertown Daily Times.

Community Shocked by Violence

I stroll into Cobalt two days later, clutching a copy of the newspaper. Kelvin watches me curiously, not bothering to bow his head as I walk right past. I hear Ray's voice echoing through the club, loud and angry. Something has him in a bad mood.

He's about to get much, much happier, I think.

The yelling is coming from the office in the back. I stop by the bar, grabbing a beer to soothe my nerves, and head toward his office after taking a swig. I knock on the door, his grumbling cutting off at the sound, before he snaps, "Somebody's interrupting. I'll call you back after I deal with them."

My insides instinctively tense at his obvious anger, but outwardly I show no sign of distress. I hear him stomp across the room, the door yanked open, his voice calling out. "This better be good."

He sees me standing there, his expression shifting with surprise. He wasn't expecting it to be me.

"Vitale," he says. "Do you need something from me?"

"No," I respond, holding the paper out, tapping it against his broad chest, "but you needed something from me."

I can tell he's annoyed, but he reins it in, grabbing the paper and glancing at the front page. I stroll past him, not waiting for an invitation, and take a seat in one of the chairs on the opposite side of his desk.

"Perdio!" he exclaims, shutting the door as he lingers behind me. "You did it, didn't you?"

I read the article while sitting in traffic. I know exactly what it says. Police are working to identify the female body found shot and burned in the old house in Dexter. Nowhere in the article lists her name, but it's only a matter of time before they figure it out.

"You did it," he says again, sounding awestruck as he walks over and plops in his chair. He scans the paper for a moment before his eyes meet mine. "You fucking did it."

I don't respond.

I don't have to.

His elated laughter tells me no words are necessary. He slaps the paper down on top of the desk as he leans back in his chair, eyeing me.

"I gotta be honest, Vitale," he says. "I didn't think you'd do it. I really thought you'd gone soft, that you'd gotten too weak to handle business. That girl got under your skin, and I thought she broke you... I thought you forgot who you were, that you forgot why we were here... that you forgot what that family did. What they stole from you. I thought she made you forget, but now I'm thinking maybe you didn't forget at all."

"I'll never forget."

Ray glances down at the paper once more. "And you didn't forgive, either."

"Of course I didn't," I say. "There's no forgiveness for what happened. They paid for their betrayal, so it's over now. I took care of it. It's done."

He stares at me, not responding to my declaration. It makes my stomach clench from anxiety. After a moment, his eyes drift back to the newspaper on his desk as he drums his fingers against the old wood.

"You know, I had a run in with that detective not long ago," he says. "That Jameson prick."

"So did I. He always has questions."

"Yeah, but this time he knew things, things he shouldn't know. He connected dots he shouldn't be able to connect. Maybe you aren't getting sloppy, but someone's getting mouthy, and I don't like it. I don't like being harassed. One reason I've always relied on you, Vitale, is because you kept them at bay. But that isn't working anymore. It isn't working, because there's a rat in our midst."

"Any idea who?"

He eyes me hard. "A few months ago, the picked up your girl, didn't they? She went down to the station with them."

It's like he's doused my body in gasoline and lit a match right in front of me. The cold tension that seizes me makes my heart ache in my chest. Anger brews in my gut. I stare back at him, those words repeatedly rolling through my head. I can't believe he'd say that.

Can't believe he'd suggest it.

Sitting up straight, I point my beer at him, not liking where this is going. "Don't say it unless you mean it." I take a swig, having to force it down my throat. "Some things can't be taken back, Ray, so I'm warning you..."

"You're warning me?"

"I'm warning you," I say again. "Don't say it unless you mean it."

He hesitates.

Strained silence chokes the room.

After a moment, he looks away, opening a drawer in his desk and grabbing a large manila envelope. He pauses as he holds it before opening the top flap. He glances inside, pulling out the contents, and holds it out so I can see. My gaze drifts from him to it, and I tense at the photograph... a photograph of Karissa, standing outside the police station, Detective Jameson right beside her.

No.

No fucking way.

She wouldn't do that.

She wouldn't talk to them.

Not about anything.

Not about me.

No way.

Ray drops that photograph to the desk before pulling out another... and another... and another... dropping each one on top of the last. A dozen, maybe more. I stop counting. I stop looking. My eyes meet Ray's. He doesn't look smug at all. I sense no satisfaction.

No, I see pity.

Pity.

Fuck his pity.

"She wouldn't do it," I say. "It's a misunderstanding."

Ray says nothing to me before grabbing his phone and dialing a number. As soon as the line picks up, he mumbles, "Come in here for a second, will you?"

Moments later, there's a knock at the door. It opens, and in walks Kelvin. He glances between us nervously before focusing on his boss. "Sir?"

Ray motions toward the photographs. "Is this a misunderstanding?"

"No, sir," he says right away. "I followed her straight from the house in Brooklyn... she was inside the police station thirty, maybe forty minutes, before that detective walked her out. They stood out front for a few minutes, maybe five. I couldn't hear a lot of what they were saying, but he told her to come back if she had any more information."

As soon as he finishes, Ray motions toward the door, and out Kelvin goes again, leaving us alone.

"You had her followed," I say. "You had him tail her."

"I'm surprised you didn't," Ray counters, not an ounce of remorse in his words. "So unlike you to be so trusting. It's a good thing I wasn't snowed. That girl has Rita blood pumping through her veins. You think you can believe a word she says to you? The apple doesn't fall far from the tree, Vitale."

I shake my head. I don't believe it. I can't. Karissa wouldn't double-cross me. She wouldn't rat me out.

She wouldn't do that.

She loves me.

Ray gathers up the pictures, shoving them back in the envelope before pushing it toward me. "Here, you keep them. Call it a souvenir. I don't need them anymore."

I ignore them, not breaking eye contact. "What do you expect me to do?"

"Nothing," he says as he relaxes back in his chair. "Love her or leave her—I don't care. It doesn't matter anymore. You say it's done? Then it's done. I'm not going to tell you to kill her. What happens now is up to you. It's your skin. You do whatever you have to do."

I snatch the envelope from the desk and stand up, walking out without saying another word to him. I pass the waitress, dropping my bottle right on her tray. Kelvin stands at the entrance to Cobalt, looking at me curiously as I approach. He expects me to go right by without acknowledging him and is caught off guard when I grab his collar and slam him against the wall. It knocks the breath from him, and he inhales sharply, fear shining from his eyes.

"Don't go near her," I tell him, my voice a low growl. "I don't want to catch you ever following her again."

"But I was… I mean… he ordered me to!"

"I don't care," I tell him. "He might kill you for not following orders, but if I catch you within a mile of her, I will kill you. Got it?"

"Yes, sir." His voice trembles. "Got it."

∾

She's in the kitchen.

I stand in the doorway, still, stoic. She's cooking, again. The scent of the food is strong and makes my stomach churn.

It's not hunger.

It's sickness.

She didn't hear me come inside, hasn't noticed me standing here yet, giving me a moment to collect myself as I watch her. She seems at ease. Happy, even. She flits around in front of the stove, wielding a spatula, a smile on her face. I wonder if she's proud of what we have, of what we're building, or if she's only happy right now because she thinks I'm not around.

I clutch the envelope in my hand at my side, not wanting to believe the evidence it contains. Looking at her, I feel myself ripped in half, my loyalty skewed. Rats die. That's just how it is. Loose lips get sewn shut before they're tossed right off the ship.

There aren't any exceptions this time.

There can't be.

Why do I always have to make her mine?

I've killed men for less than what these photographs show. I've cut their throats in their sleep for even *thinking* of talking to the police. But the thought of killing her, of even hurting her, guts me. I may as well stick the knife through my own chest, rip out my heart with my bare hands and watch its last beat. It's been a long time since I invested in someone the way I've invested in her. Last time, it killed me emotionally. This time, it might finally be physically.

Because failing Ray's test doesn't mean bad marks.

It means certain death.

Johnny Rita couldn't kill me, but Ray, I think, could.

Ray could bring the whole world down upon me.

And he would.

It's her life or my own.

It's crueler than an order.

He's forcing *me* to choose.

Her death would be my fault, my choice, solely on my hands, and I'd have to live with it every day. It would be there in the morning when I awoke and still be there at night when I tried to sleep. I'm a murderer. I won't sugarcoat the label. I wear it with pride. But *this*?

This is suicide.

Karissa turns, startling when she spots me standing there. Gasping, she grasps her chest, dropping the spatula in surprise. She gapes at me, and I see the flicker of fear in her eyes, fear she tries to shove away as she put that smile back on her face. It's forced now, though. There's no more happiness.

"Naz?" she says. "Are you okay?"

"Why wouldn't I be, Karissa?"

"I, uh... I don't know." She reaches down and picks up the spatula again. "You look kind of, uh..."

"Kind of what?"

"Upset."

Upset.

That's putting it mildly.

Inside, I'm a fucking mess.

"I'm fine," I lie. Blatantly. She can tell I'm not fine. "How are you?"

"Fine." She eyes me warily. "Seriously, are you okay? Did something happen?"

Did something happen? Yeah, something happened. My gaze shifts to the envelope as I shake my head. "Do you trust me, Karissa?"

"Uh…" She hesitates, tossing the spatula in the sink. "I'm trying to. I trust you won't hurt me, if that's what you mean, but as far as really trusting you… I don't know. I guess I do. Why?"

"Just curious," I say, strolling into the kitchen. "And do you think I should trust you?"

"Of course."

"Because I started to," I say, "and that wasn't easy for me. It took a lot for me to give you my trust again."

"I know," she says, her voice quiet. "You can trust me."

"So there isn't anything you want to tell me?" I ask. "Nothing you want to get off your chest?"

Her brow furrows at my line of questioning. "No."

"Nothing at all?"

"No, nothing." Her expression is full of confusion. "What is this about, Naz?"

Wordlessly, I stare at her, before opening the envelope and reaching inside. Holding it up, I pull out the top photograph, just far enough for her to see what it is. She stares at it blankly for a moment before her eyes widen with recognition. Her gaze darts straight to me, panicked, that fear returning.

The knife in my chest is being twisted.

"Where did you get that?" she asks. "Who took it?"

"Kelvin. You remember Kelvin, right? The bouncer from the club? I suppose some of those times you felt like you were being watched, you actually were."

Her eyes widen even further. "You had me followed? You said you didn't. You lied to me!"

"I lied to you?" I ask incredulously, shaking the photograph in her face. "You told me I could trust you."

"You can," she says. "That's not what it looks like. I don't know what he told you, but it's not what it seems."

"It isn't? Because it seems to me, Karissa, like you got caught talking to the police."

"I didn't get *caught*. It wasn't like that."

"It wasn't? Because I don't remember you telling me about it. I don't remember you coming to me."

"That's because you were hurt," she says, shaking her head as she turns the stove off, abandoning whatever she's cooking. "Jesus, Naz, you'd just been shot! You had enough to deal with. I was trying to be strong... for you, for me... for *us*. I was trying, okay? And every time I left the house, every time I went somewhere, those detectives were around. So I talked to them."

"You talked to them."

"Yes, when you were injured."

"When I was injured," I say. "You talked to them."

"Ugh, stop that!" she growls. "Stop repeating me. I went there because they wouldn't leave us alone. I went there because you were hurt, Naz, because you'd been shot, and I wanted to know what they were doing about it. So I asked, and then they asked me to help you, so I told them what I knew."

Anger, sometimes, is bitter cold.

It's harsher than red-hot rage.

There's the blue.

"You told them what you knew?"

"I told them who shot you."

I step toward her, tossing the envelope beside the stove as I go toe-to-toe with her, backing her up against the counter. "You don't *know* who shot me."

"Yes, I do," she says, her voice shaking. I can tell she's trying to hold it together. "I'm not an idiot. Just because you don't tell me things doesn't mean I can't figure them out on my own. I know who shot you."

"And you told them."

"I did," she says. "I told them, because it was better than the alternative."

"What, exactly, is the alternative, Karissa?" I ask, looking down at her. "Tell me why you really did it. Tell me why you talked to the police."

"I just told you why," she says. "If it went any further, one of you would end up dead. I couldn't just let that happen. So I told them my mother shot you, I reported her to the police, because I'd rather her be in jail than in a grave!"

These words aren't what I wanted to hear.

I hoped for a denial.

A stitch of repudiation that I could cling to.

I needed her to tell me it was a misunderstanding.

That she would never talk to the police.

But she's confirming one of my worst fears.

"And the other stuff," I say. "Why did you tell them it?"

"What other stuff?"

"Come on, Karissa... you just told me you weren't an idiot. Don't act ignorant now. They know things... things they wouldn't know unless somebody told them. Things I did. Maybe I haven't flat out told you about them, but like you said, I don't have to. You can put it all together yourself. So tell me, sweetheart, did you tell them how much of a monster I am? How I killed your father... how I killed your professor?"

The color drains from her face.

She knows I did it, but I never blatantly confessed to her before.

"I didn't say anything."

"So you didn't tell them I was coming after your family? You didn't tell them about the man at the body shop? You didn't tell them about the man who didn't come home from Vegas with us?"

"I didn't," she whispers. "I swear."

"And you expect me to *believe* you?"

"Yes."

"Why would I?"

"Because I'm telling the truth."

I want to believe there isn't more, that she didn't spill every dirty detail, but the evidence is stacked against her and she's already confessed to part of it. I want to believe in her.

I'm not sure I can.

"I didn't do it," she says. "Whatever they know, it didn't come from me. I didn't tell them anything about you. I told them my mother shot you. That's all. I swear. I wanted to stop all of this. It didn't want anyone else to die! I thought if they arrested her, she'd be safe. I thought you'd be safe. I was trying to save both of your lives!"

"And you endangered yours in the process *yet again*," I say, laughing bitterly as I back up a step. I need some room to breathe... to *think*. Running my hands through my hair, I growl with frustration, trying to purge the aggression that's building beneath my skin. "Do you know what happens to people who rat? Do you know what we do to them? Christ. You're supposed to lawyer up—that's what you do. You keep your mouth shut and they go away. Because that man? Jameson? He doesn't give a shit about me. He doesn't care about your mother, or you. He doesn't care about anything. All you gave him was validation. You gave him the justification he wanted to continue. The only person you helped is *him*."

"I didn't mean—"

"It doesn't matter," I say, cutting her off. "Don't say it unless you mean it. How many times have I told you that? Huh? You said it, and now you have to stand by it. And now I have to..."

Her voice trembles as she asks, "Have to what?"

Turning, I head for the door, not answering that question.

What am I supposed to say?

Now I have to decide who else will die because of this?

Chapter Twenty-One

There are worse things than being alone.

Being lonely, for one.

It's torture, being in a room with someone, breathing the same air, but feeling miles away. The isolation you feel, sharing a bed with someone you can't connect with, is insurmountable. Some people get off on casual sex, they relish in the physical pleasure, but that's never been enough for me. I've slept with a few women since my wife died, casual flings that ended as quickly as they started.

I got nothing out of it.

Afterward, I'd lie in bed beside some woman as she bathed in a post coital glow, coated in sweat and body fluids, and feel nothing but desolation. *Disgust*. It reeked of desperation.

It was always the loneliest moment of my life.

Until now.

Karissa's lying in bed beside me, both of us wide-awake. I could reach over and touch her if I wanted, run my rough fingertips along the curves of her soft frame, but succumbing to the temptation feels a lot like surrendering. Sex, with her, always had passion, toeing the thin line between love and hate. Touching her tonight would be dangerous. I could just as easy condemn her as I could forgive her, wrapping my hand around her throat and forgetting to let go.

Sighing exasperatedly, I sit up, my feet hitting the floor beside the bed. I run my hands down my face. I'm exhausted, physically and mentally, but I'm not going to get any sleep.

The moment I stand, her voice calls out to me. "Ignazio?"

Not Naz. *Ignazio.*

I think she knows that gets to me.

"Not right now," I say as I head for my closet. "I can't do this with you right now, Karissa."

She says something else, but I don't stick around to hear it. I grab a suit and walk out, putting it on and pulling myself together as I head downstairs. It only takes me a few minutes, and I slip on my shoes in the den, grabbing my keys before heading outside.

I lock the door behind me.

I need some space.

I need some answers.

I need to fucking *think*.

It's five in the morning, and there's not too much traffic on the streets as I drive around the outer boroughs before heading to Manhattan. I'm not sure where I'm going or what I'm even doing, ending up in Hell's Kitchen before dawn. I drive through the old neighborhood, the streets I ran growing up. The streets where Johnny Rita was my best friend, where Carmela was like a sister to me, where I fell in love with Maria.

They're all dead now.

All three of them.

Depends on who you ask, I might have all of their blood on my hands.

I pull the car in a spot along the street and get out but don't bother to feed the meter. I have no change on me. I stroll down the sidewalk, toward the old brick townhouse, oddly a shade lighter than the rest of the places on the block.

It's dark, no lights on, but it doesn't matter.

I have no intention of going inside.

I hesitate in front of it, staring at the chipped paint of the black front door, before I take a seat on the grungy steps leading to it. I sit in silence under the dim outside light, gazing around the neighborhood.

After a few minutes, the door behind me unexpectedly opens. I don't turn around, don't bother to look. I can feel eyes boring into the back of my head. Footsteps descend the steps and pause on the sidewalk in front of me.

My eyes slowly move up, meeting my father's steely gaze.

"I've seen you more this summer," he says, "than I saw you the past few years."

"I didn't come to see you," I say. "I figured you'd be at work already."

"So, what, you came for your mother?"

I can hear his anger in that question.

"No, I'm not going to bother her."

"So why are you here?"

I hesitate before deciding to go with honesty. "I don't know."

He nods, his harsh expression softening, like me not knowing makes perfect sense to him. He shoves his hands in the pockets of his khakis, stained from years of working in them. I gaze at him curiously, surprised he's lingering. I know it isn't because he enjoys my company. He's probably afraid I'll try to break in.

"Funny, seeing you out here, sneaking around in the dark, given you've always been scared of it."

The blunt way he says that makes me bristle. "I'm not afraid of the dark anymore."

"Of course not," he says. "It's not the darkness that's terrifying, it's what you might find in it. And it doesn't scare you anymore, Ignazio, because it *is* you. You're what's terrifying in the darkness."

He says it matter of fact, but he doesn't sound scared.

I don't terrify him.

To him, I'm just what's left of that little boy, the one who used a nightlight because he couldn't sleep in the dark. I'm a desecrated corpse.

"Can I ask you something?" I ask my father. He doesn't say anything, but his unchanged expression is as good as permission. "You ever talk to the police about me?"

"Yes."

No bullshit.

No denial.

I laugh bitterly to myself, shaking my head as I look away from him.

"They come around sometimes, asking questions," he says. "I tell them we don't know nothing. I know your reputation, Ignazio, but it's not my business to repeat what I hear. That's between you and your maker."

"You are my maker."

He scoffs. "You know what I mean."

"I know," I mutter, leaning back on my elbows. "So you never considered actually turning me in? You've threatened to a few times."

"I never threatened to turn you in," he counters. "I just protect what's mine. I'm not a coward, Ignazio. You won't harm what I love. But the rest is on you. Has nothing to do with me. I don't seek out trouble. I don't want it. That's why I ask you to stay away."

Nodding, I push off from the steps and get to my feet. "I probably shouldn't be here."

I step down, stopping in front of him.

"Is there a reason you're asking me that?"

I consider just walking away, but what the hell? I need to get it off my chest, and his opinion of me certainly can't get worse. My father won't hold back and maybe, I think, the brutal honesty is what I need.

"Karissa, the woman I was with that day..."

"Johnny and Carmela's kid?"

"Yes," I say. "She went to the police."

"She rat on you?"

"She swears she didn't."

"And you don't believe her?"

"I don't know."

He stands there for a moment before taking a seat exactly where I'd just vacated. "Now answer me something, Ignazio... you say this girl knows the kind of person you are? That she knows the history between you and her parents?"

"Yes."

"And she swears she didn't rat on you?"

"Yes."

"Why?"

That question makes me stumble. "Why what?"

"Why didn't she rat on you?" he asks. "Seems to me she has all the reason in the world to. We protect what we love. So why didn't she rat on you?"

"That's a good question."

"Why'd she talk to them? What was her explanation?"

"She told them Carmela attacked me."

His eyes widen with surprise. "She ratted on her mother?"

"So she says," I respond. "Says she thought it was the perfect solution to keep us all safe, but she risked herself doing it. Who's going to protect *her* now?"

"You." He says it with no hesitation. "Like I said, we protect what we love."

"I'm not sure I can do it."

"Come on, Ignazio. You're a lot of things, things I don't like, but I was always proud of your courage. You didn't get my integrity, but you got my guts. Seems to me if anyone can protect her, it would be you."

"But Ray—"

He cuts me off with the bitterest laugh I've ever heard, the kind that tightens my chest.

"Raymond Angelo," he says, shaking his head. "Never liked that guy. Don't like who he is, don't like what he turned you into."

"He didn't turn me into anything."

"Didn't he?" he counters. "Way I see it, he created this demon... created it, and fears it, with the way he tries to keep you under his thumb. But you don't owe him anything. It doesn't matter what Angelo thinks or what he wants. You got that girl into this mess."

"I didn't—"

"You did," he says, a hard edge to his voice. "She wouldn't be in this situation if not for you. You carry some of the blame. And if something bad happens to her, you'll carry that blame, too. I raised you to be a man. A *man*. Not this."

He waves his hands my way to prove his point.

"But there are rules," I say, "rules we follow."

"Bullshit," he says. "You think someone like Raymond Angelo respects rules? He makes it all up as he goes to suit his own needs. Because that's all he cares about: himself. He doesn't care about this neighborhood or these people, and he doesn't care about you. You think these police don't care? Take a look at who's around you, because they don't care, either."

Months ago, I would've come to Ray's defense, but I don't have it in me at the moment. My silence doesn't slip past my father, who laughs to himself as he climbs to his feet. Without saying goodbye, he starts to walk away, making it a few feet before turning back to me.

"You want some advice, Ignazio?"

Hesitating, I nod.

"People make mistakes. They do things sometimes that you don't like, that you wouldn't do. But that doesn't mean you should give up on them, that you should write them off. Because nobody is hopeless as long as they're still breathing."

"That's good advice."

"It's something your mothers been telling me for years," he says. "I haven't been able to listen, myself, but maybe you'll prove to be a better man than me."

"Unlikely."

He laughs. "Yeah, you're right. But Ignazio? Make *your* choice, not Angelo's. Because I guarantee Angelo's choice only benefits him."

I stand there, watching as he disappears down the street. Once he's gone, I head toward my car, wanting to be gone before my mother wakes. I drive back toward Brooklyn, considering my father's words.

What would I do if it were *my* choice?

I'd do everything in my power to make Karissa happy. I'd walk through fire, burn every broken bridge and sever every tainted tie to give the woman what she deserves. I'd give her the world, not take it away. I'd protect her life, not end it.

If it were my choice, I'd say fuck Ray.

Fuck his rules.

Fuck his plans.

The sun is starting to rise when I make it to my neighborhood, a strange sort of resolve settling through me, like my choice has been made without me even having to make it.

Like there wasn't even a choice at all.

My father was right, as much as I hate to admit it.

I feel relief, but the sensation doesn't last. The second my house comes into sight, my stomach bottoms out, my insides plunging.

The police are here.

A car sits in my driveway, in my usual spot, while another is double parked at the curb. I swing into my driveway, nearly side-swiping the unmarked cruiser, the back of my Mercedes sticking out into the street. Climbing out, I slam the door, rushing toward the house, my heart racing.

Not good.

Not good at all.

Not fucking good.

The front door is unlocked, the knob turning smoothly. As soon as I shove it open, I nearly run into the back of a man. Before I can say a word or even get a good look at my surroundings, the sound of hysterical sobbing slams right into me. My eyes dart toward the source, seeing Karissa. She sits on the couch, hands covering her face, crying as a familiar man sits beside her.

Jameson.

In my house.

On my couch.

With Karissa.

"What's going on here?"

The second I speak, Karissa chokes on a sob. She lifts her head up, meeting my gaze. Her eyes are bloodshot and her face is splotchy, distress weighing her down. She opens her mouth, her words cracking as she forces them from her lips. "My mom," she cries. "She's dead."

I don't react for a moment, trying to force down the anger that rushes through me. It mixes with the unexpected swell of regret inside my gut, making me feel sick. They came to notify her. They put together the pieces.

"Get out of my house," I say, eyes darting between the officers. "Now."

They try to argue, but I cut them off.

"I'm asking you nicely to leave my property," I say. "It's within my right to remove you."

"Remove us?" Jameson asks, slowly climbing to his feet as the others walk out. "Is that a threat, Mr. Vitale?"

"No, it's a fact."

"Is that so?"

"It is."

He nods, strolling my way, and pauses right in front of me. He stares dead in my eyes, unwavering, unblinking, not an ounce of apprehension in his expression. He has me this time, he thinks. He's got me all figured out. But he doesn't know me like he believes he does, or he'd know there's no way I'm ever going to be taken down by a man like him. We're enemies.

Men like me?

We see the end at the hands of a friend.

"You want to know what I think?" he asks.

I don't respond. I don't move. I don't care what he thinks about anything.

"I think it's curious," he continues, not needing any urging, "that you don't seem the least bit surprised. A woman you grew up with, your fiancée's mother, is dead, and you're not surprised at all, are you?"

Again, I say nothing.

"Curious," he says again. "It's almost as if you already knew."

He slips past me, and I watch as he makes his way out the door, closing it behind him. The crying has quieted, strained silence overtaking the room. I turn back to the couch once we're alone, meeting Karissa's gaze.

Horrified eyes regard me.

She heard what he just said.

"You knew." Her bottom lip trembles as she tries to hold herself together, but she's failing horribly. She's a flimsy house of cards that's about to collapse under her own weight. All it'll take is a single breath, the force of a few wrong words, to sending her crashing down. "You... Oh God, *no*... you didn't. Tell me you didn't!"

Tears stream from her eyes, coating her cheeks. Wordlessly, I step toward her, ignoring the fact that she flinches when I come close. Sitting beside her on the couch, I pull her into my arms, not loosening my hold when she tries to shove me away. Her quiet tears once more turn to hysterical sobs as I hold her tightly, restraining her.

"Tell me you didn't do it," she cries, fighting me. "Tell me it wasn't you!"

"Shhh," I whisper into her hair. "It's going to be okay."

"No!" she yells, choking on the word. "Tell me! Tell me you didn't do this, that you *wouldn't* do this! After everything we've been through, everything *I've* been through, tell me you wouldn't do this!"

She doesn't wait for me to tell her.

She knows, deep down, I can't.

I don't want to lie, and she doesn't want to hear the truth.

The silence is filled by her sobs as her hostility wavers, giving way to the devastation. She cries into my chest, her body violently shaking in my arms. I try to console her, but my words only make it worse.

The guilt nags at me until I can hardly breathe. The pain that coats her seems to seep into me.

I did this.

There's no way around that.

I caused this.

"I'm sorry," I whisper. "I'm so sorry, Karissa."

Those words bring back her anger, kick-starting her rage. She hits me, shoves against me, slipping out of my arms when I'm momentarily stunted by her aggression. She climbs to her feet, still crying, her eyes wild and face flushed.

"Are you?" Her voice trembles. "Are you *sorry*?"

"I am," I admit, surprised by how much I mean those words. "I never meant—"

"You never meant to hurt me," she says as she throws her hands up, masking her pain with the fury I can see burning in her eyes. "You're not sorry you hurt *her*, are you? You're not sorry you killed her, that you took her life, that you took her from me, are you? No, you're not! You're not sorry at all!"

"Your mother wasn't innocent."

"She's not innocent? None of us are innocent! My mother made mistakes, my mother wasn't perfect, but she was my mother! She was my... my mom... she was *my mom*. You killed her, you took her from me, and all you can say is she wasn't innocent? *What's wrong with you?*"

Too much, I think.

Way too much for either of us to ever understand.

"Tell me this is a sick joke," she continues, pleading with me, her emotions shifting so quickly I can hardly keep up. "Tell me this isn't real. Tell me she's not dead. You told me if I went with you that day, if I didn't wake her up, you'd let her live. And I did... I went with you. I've stayed with you. I did everything I could to save her. I wanted her to live. I even turned her into the police! Tell me that wasn't for nothing. Please. Tell me she isn't really dead!"

Her words make that guilt consume me, turning my insides to ice, freezing my muscles as I stare at the trembling mess of a woman in front of me. Is that why she stayed with me? Why she opened herself back up to me? Was it just to save her mother?

Was it never about me? About *us*?

The questions Ping-Pong around in my head, fueling bitter thoughts that nearly fly from my lips. The sense of betrayal is so frigid I'm afraid those answers might make me break, snap right in half like an icicle.

"Please," she whispers, wrapping her arms around her chest like she's trying to hold herself together. "Tell me this isn't real."

Sighing, my gaze drops from hers. "I'm sorry."

Before the last syllable is from my lips, Karissa hits the floor, her legs giving out on her. Her cries shake the room, rattling my fucking brain. Closing my eyes, I run my hands through my hair, gripping handfuls and pulling, trying to distract myself with the pain. Tears sting my eyes, tears I don't want to cry, tears I don't want to feel. I don't want it. I don't want any of this.

I wanted justice.

All I got was more heartbreak.

They say when seeking revenge, dig two graves, one for you and one for them. I've buried them all, disposed of bodies and left a trail of charred remains in my wake, and now all that's left is my own grave.

And I dug it, all right... dug it so deep there's no fucking way out of it.

No way out of it, and I'm seconds away from dragging a woman I love into it with me yet again.

"Go." The word is from my lips without a second thought. I *can't* give it a second thought or the selfish monster inside of me will stop it, with stop this moment of weakness. "Go. Now. Before I can't let you go again."

"What?"

Her voice is tear-filled and full of confusion. I open my eyes, looking at her. The sight of her distress hurts.

I have to look back away.

"Leave, if you want. If you want out, go. I won't come after you."

"You won't?"

I try not to be hurt by the hope I hear in her question.

Try, and fail.

It fucking hurts.

· "I won't," I say. "If you want to leave, I'll let you leave."

She stares at me, expression blank, as she tries to come to terms with what I'm saying.

"I don't want you to," I tell her, the words spilling out of me, a hitch in my voice. I've never felt so vulnerable in my life, cracking myself open for her. "Letting go of you will kill me. So I'm asking you to stay... to stay with me. It's my turn to ask you to stay this time. But it's up to you. I can't make this choice. You're going to have to make it. Stay or go."

She slowly pulls herself to her feet and takes a step back. One step. That's all it takes. My insides break.

"Don't ever come back," I tell her. "Never come around here again. You walk out that door, Karissa, for both of our sakes, you can never come back here."

She hesitates.

One.

Two.

Three seconds.

And then she turns around.

I close my eyes again. I don't watch as she leaves. I can't.

As soon as she's out the door, those tears burning my eyes break free.

I cry for the first time in twenty years.

So this is grief...

 ⌒◞◟⌒

Cobalt is quiet this afternoon.

Kelvin stands watch at the door, as usual, back to averting his eyes as I walk past. I ignore him, strolling through the club, straight toward where Ray sits with a few others. They all look up as I approach, silence befalling them. The man sitting to Ray's left vacates the leather seat, no words necessary. I sit down wordlessly, my expression stoic.

"Gentlemen," Ray says, clearing his throat. "Why don't you give me some time with my son-in-law."

So many years later and he still calls me that.

It makes us family, more family than these other schmucks, but that doesn't make much of a difference at the end of the day.

He'd fuck me over worse than the others, if anything.

He already has.

The men mutter amongst themselves as they disperse, while Brandy, ever-present these days, stays seated with Ray. The waitress approaches then, holding a bottle of pale ale, but I hold up my hand, refusing it.

"Double scotch," I tell her. "Single malt."

She hesitates. "Do you... do you want me to *pour* it?"

"I'm assuming that's still the bartender's job, but if that's what tickles your fancy, sweetheart, have at it."

She gapes at me for a second before nodding and disappearing with the beer. I turn my gaze from her to Ray, who eyes me warily. Even Brandy seems to be taken by surprise, as if the girl actually knows me enough to be caught off guard by anything I do.

"Scotch," Ray says. "Walking on the wild side, are you? Drinking my liquor... next thing you know, you might actually start eating my wife's cooking again."

"I just might," I say, eyeing Brandy, watching as she makes a face at the mention of Ray's wife. "Speaking of, when's the last time you spent any time with Martina? Every time I see you now, you're with *her*."

Brandy's expression twists again, this time marked with anger as she glares at me. Ray cuts his eyes at her, shrugging slightly as he takes a sip of his own drink. "We do what makes us happy."

"No, we do what we're supposed to do," I counter just as the waitress returns with my drink. I take it from her, gulping some of it down. It's like fire in my frazzled veins. "Or at least, that's what I was always taught. We do what we must, not what we want."

Ray eyes me warily, ordering the waitress away when she tries to get him another drink, waiting until the woman is gone before responding. "Something you want to talk about, Vitale? Something happen with that, uh... situation?"

"She won't be a problem anymore," I say, drinking more to burn the feeling out of my chest. "She's gone."

"Gone where?"

I cut my eyes at him, sipping the liquor. He's curious, that much is clear. He wants to know if she's dead, but he doesn't want to come out and ask me.

"Doesn't really matter," I say coldly. "She's gone like the rest of them."

He mulls it over for a second, tapping his finger against the rim of his glass. "What did it?"

"I came home yesterday and the police were there," I say. "Jameson was at my house... *in* my house."

"So you dealt with it."

"I dealt with it."

It's not a lie, technically.

It's not my fault if he misconstrues what I'm saying.

"Ah, see, I knew it," Ray says smugly, nodding to himself, a slight smile touching his lips. "So now you see."

Yes, now I see...

Now I see what a self-righteous bastard he is.

Now I see how dangerous he can be.

Now I see that my father was right, that Raymond Angelo isn't someone I should look up to, that this isn't the type of man he raised me to be.

My hands will never be clean. I'll never erase what I've done, and I don't want to. If you're still looking for an apology about that, you need to look elsewhere. My one regret is Karissa—the pain I caused her, the way I hurt her, after I swore I wouldn't. She got the only apology anyone will get out of me. But she's gone now, and I've got nothing left to give.

"Now I see," I tell him, finishing my drink before setting the glass down on the table. "And now I'm out."

He gapes at me as I stand up. "You're out?"

"I got everything out of it I can get, Ray. I bled it dry, and now there's nothing left for me. I finished what I started, what you needed me to do... what I needed to do... and now I'm done."

"You think you can just walk away?"

"I don't think I can," I say. "I'm *going* to."

I hold my hand out toward him, to shake his. He stares at it for a moment, his expression hard, before he meets my eyes. He takes it, gripping firmly, almost to the point of pain.

It doesn't faze me, though.

He could shoot me in the face, and I wouldn't flinch.

"She ruined you," he says.

"She didn't ruin me," I say. "She just made me realize there wasn't anything left to salvage in the first place. I died with your daughter, Raymond. I'm the walking dead, and nobody loves a monster. *Nobody*."

I pull my hand from his, eye shifting to Brandy. She's watching me curiously. My eyes trail over her. She's showing more skin than she's covering.

I turn back to Ray, shaking my head. "Appreciate what you have, while you have it. God knows I wish I could've kept what I had."

I walk away, walking out, not bothering to say goodbye.

I know this isn't the end.

The end will be a bullet to the head.

Nobody walks away, but I'm going to.

Maybe I'll get a day.

A week.

A month.

It won't matter, though, because the end will come eventually. I'm living with a ticking clock strapped to my chest, counting down the seconds I have left.

But then again, I've been living that way for decades.

I drive around for a while, not ready to go home. I haven't been home since she left, since she walked out that door and didn't look back. It hasn't even been a whole day, but it feels like an eternity. She took nothing except her purse, leaving her clothes and phone behind. I wish I knew where she went, or what she's doing, just so I know she's safe, but a promise is a promise.

She's resilient.

As long as she stays away from this godforsaken place, she'll make it.

I have to believe that.

I end up in Hell's Kitchen an hour later, standing on the front steps of my parent's townhouse. I hesitate before knocking quietly, tapping on the old wooden door. I hear my mother's voice inside calling out, saying she's coming. I lean back against the railing, crossing my arms over my chest as I wait.

A moment later, the door opens, my mother appearing. Michelle Vitale is beautiful, looking so much younger than her sixty years, and I know it's natural. It's the kind of beauty that comes from years of unconditional love and a lack of stress. It's what my staying away does for her. As much as she might miss me, and love me, I know she's better off away from the reality of my life. I know it, and my father certainly knows it.

It's why he doesn't want me near her.

But I can't help myself today.

There's no cure for life's ills quite like your mother's smiling face.

She beams when she sees me, gasping with surprise, and instantly pulls me into a hug. Her grip is tight. I hug her back.

She has a way of making me feel like that little boy again, and not just the shell of him. *All* of him.

"Ignazio!" she says. "What a wonderful surprise!"

"Mom," I say, kissing her cheek. "You look as beautiful as ever."

"Oh, you keep your flattery," she says, blushing as she swats at my chest. "Come in, come in… I was just making some lunch."

I hesitate before stepping inside. She shuts the door behind me, making a point to lock it. They never did that when I was growing up, never bothered to lock their doors, just like they used to not worry about security at the deli. Just like there, I wonder if this is a sign of the times changing or if it's something my father did because of me.

I follow her to the kitchen, plopping down in a chair at the small table.

My mother's a spitfire, gossiping and chatting away like no time at all has passed since she last saw me, treating me as if I'm here for lunch every day. She treats me like I belong.

I miss that.

Belonging.

I listen, happily, her voice putting me at ease, and I chime in when she asks something, but otherwise I just let her talk. She's interrupted after a few minutes by the phone ringing, and she scurries to the living room to answer it. I sit in silence for a moment, looking around. Everything still looks like it did years ago.

She returns, spooning some spaghetti onto plates, and turns to me with a smile. "I hope you're hungry."

I return her smile as she sets the plate in front of me, joining me at the table with a plate of her own. I bow my head instinctively as she says a quick prayer before I grab my fork, stabbing at the pasta.

"This isn't poisoned, is it?" I ask, taking a bite.

She laughs, reaching across the table to smack my arm. "You know better than that, Ignazio. Who in the world would try to poison my boy with spaghetti?"

I shrug a shoulder. "You'd be surprised."

She launches back into gossip again. I just enjoy the company and the homemade meal. My plate is practically licked clean when I push it away, leaning back in the chair. I'm about to thank her, the words on the tip of my tongue, when there's a pounding on the front door. My muscles tense as she lets out an exaggerated sigh, pushing her chair back to stand.

"That's probably your father," she says, rolling her eyes. "He always forgets his house key."

"Were you expecting him for lunch?" I ask.

"No, but I'm not surprised he's here," she says. "That was him that called a bit ago... he was so surprised when I told him you were visiting. He thought I was pulling his leg, said he couldn't believe you were here."

My stomach sinks as she says that.

She thinks his surprise is good.

I know it's not.

I push my chair back and stand up. I follow her, hearing the familiar voice as soon as she opens the front door. It's not my father, no, but he sent somebody. I expect no less.

"Ma'am, is Ignazio Vitale here?"

Jameson.

My mother seems flustered. "Uh, yeah, sure." She turns to call for me, but I'm already standing there. My eyes meet Jameson's as his dance with amusement. Any reason to harass me is a field day to him.

"I'm assuming my father called you?"

Jameson nods.

"I wasn't aware petty trespassing was your jurisdiction."

"We also have a few questions for you."

"Of course you do."

"Trespassing?" my mother asks. "Who's trespassing?"

"I am," I tell her, leaning over to kiss her cheek again. "Thanks for lunch, Mom. It was great seeing you."

I step out onto the porch as an officer pulls out his handcuffs.

"Can you do that when she's not looking?" I ask. "Out of respect?"

My question is ignored, unsurprisingly, as I'm thrown against the railing, my arms forced behind my back. Once I'm handcuffed, I'm dragged toward a nearby car. I glance back at my mother, lingering in the doorway. She's horrified, eyes wide. She looks so much older now, just like that.

I should've just stayed away...

I don't say anything on the drive to the police station.

Nor do I say anything once we get there.

As usual, they wait until my lawyer arrives to even try to question me. We sit in the small dingy interrogation room, my arms crossed over my chest, as Jameson and his partner, Andrews, sit across from us.

"What is this about?" my lawyer asks. "I hope it's not to ask the same questions as before. My client knows nothing about the murder of Daniel Santino."

"Or John Rita... or the murder of John's wife, Carmela? He knows nothing of them either, right?"

"I'm sure if my client had any information about them, he

would've come to you. But just because they used to be acquainted doesn't mean he knows what came of them."

"What about their daughter, Karissa?" Jameson asks, looking dead in my face as he speaks. "Does he have any information about her?"

"What about her?" the lawyer asks.

"We have reason to believe she's missing."

"Missing?" The word is from my lips instantly. My lawyer shoots me a glare that tells me to be quiet, as usual, but I can't help myself. Not when it comes to this. "What makes you think she's *missing*?"

"We received a report that—"

"A report," I chime in, cutting him off. "Someone filed a missing person's report? Because you just saw her yourself less than twenty-four hours ago, detective, so I'm not quite sure why your department would take a report on an adult who was just seen last night."

He pauses, glaring at me. "We received information from a source."

"A source."

"Yes, a source."

"And what did your source say, exactly?" I ask. "Because I can assure you, she isn't missing, and there's no reason for anyone to think she is."

"So is she at your house?" Jameson asks. "Because we went by there and nobody answered. She also didn't attend her classes today."

"She left."

"She left," he repeats, and I suddenly understand why it annoys Karissa when I repeat what she says. His condescending tone makes me want to punch him. "Where did she go?"

"You'd have to ask her."

"How can I get a hold of her? Where can I find her?"

"You're the investigator," I say. "Investigate."

He glares at me with so much hatred it almost makes me smile.

Almost. He leans forward, across the table toward me. "Is she dead, Mr. Vitale? Did you kill her?"

"Why would I do that?"

"Because she let us into your house yesterday," he says. "Maybe that was what finally did it for you."

"You think I'd kill her for talking to you?" I ask, mimicking his movements and leaning forward. My lawyer tries to stop me, interjecting, but I ignore him. "If that's the case, shouldn't I have killed her long ago, when she *first* started talking to you?"

His brow furrows, and I see a hint of genuine confusion in his expression. He's struggling to recall when she talked to him. That tells me right away that Karissa had been telling the truth. Had she been his source, he would've purposely kept his expression blank.

"The fact of the matter, detective, is that Karissa's alive, so whatever your source told you is bullshit."

"So you didn't take care of her for talking to the police?" he asks. "Raymond Angelo didn't want you to get rid of her?"

"Raymond Angelo isn't the boss of me."

"Ah, right, because you walked away."

The moment he says that, it all clicks into place. He's practically reciting my conversation from this morning word-for-word. He had a bug planted there, but it wasn't the electronic kind. Ray sweeps for them daily, carefully controls who comes in and out of that place. No, he had a bug in the form of a rat. His source.

There was only one other person there.

One that's always there.

Brandy.

"I have nothing else to say." I sit back in my chair as I turn to my lawyer. "You want to handle this?"

"I'm trying," he grinds out, clearly annoyed I even played along with the detective's questions, but it gave me what I wanted. He goes into his usual spiel—charge him or release him, stop hassling my client or you're looking at a lawsuit—before I'm brought back out of the interrogation room.

For the first time in my life, with as many times as I've been dragged down here in handcuffs, I'm booked into the system.

Second Degree Criminal Trespass

"That's a bit much, isn't it?" I ask as they fingerprint me. A misdemeanor. "My mother invited me in."

"Your father said you were asked more than once to stay away."

"So he's pressing charges."

"He is."

Despite myself, I laugh.

Go figure.

Leave it to my father to make sure the first black mark goes on my permanent record. I can't even be mad.

Not really.

He warned me.

Repeatedly.

Chapter Twenty-Two

The feed plays normal speed, most of the screen obscured because it's nighttime, but there's enough light in that one section of the back lot to easily make out what's happening. I watch myself collapse to the ground behind Cobalt, watch as the spray of bullets fly at me from the shaky gun just a few feet away. Even in the fuzzy video, it's not hard to make out her face, not hard to identify who it was that attacked me that night.

As soon as the last shot goes off and Carmela turns to run, I rewind the feed, starting it all over again.

I've been sitting here for what feels like a long time. Too long. Hours, maybe. I don't know. I just keep watching the same portion of video, like maybe one of these times something will change, like maybe it'll make me feel something other than this desolation. Like maybe my regret will fade and I'll feel justified again.

It's not working.

I can't get the look on Karissa's face out of my head.

Sighing exasperatedly, I close my eyes and lean back in my chair at my desk in the den. I scrub my hands down my face. I need to purge this frustration, purge this aggression, before I fucking implode.

My house is quiet, too quiet. I used to appreciate the silence here. But today it feels less like peace and more like penance. The silence isn't a gift. It's punishment.

Opening my eyes again, I look at the laptop just as Carmela panics and turns to run. I reach for the button, to rewind it a few minutes, to watch it all over again, when something catches my eye. On the corner of the screen, I'm stumbling to get in my car, but my eyes right now are trained on Carmela, fixed on a flash of something hitting the ground as she runs.

She dropped something.

I rewind it a few frames before rerunning it again, freezing the frame and zooming in. My stomach clenches, my chest tight, when I make out my keys falling from her hand. She doesn't stop for them, doesn't pick them, disappearing into the darkness and leaving them there.

No.

That's not right.

It can't be.

Did she come back?

Did she return just for the keys?

I hit fast forward, staring at that spot, watching as chaos erupts in the lot, people running onto the scene to try to figure out what happened. Time whisks away, an hour, almost two, before somebody finally stumbles upon my keys.

It's a man.

I hit play again, watching as he turns toward the camera.

Kelvin.

Disbelief seizes me as Kelvin tosses the keys to someone else, someone with their back turned to me, but I don't need to see a face to recognize Ray. He palms my keys for a moment before slipping them in his pocket and walking away.

I hit stop, the screen going black, putting the den into total darkness.

Ray had my keys the whole time.

That son of a bitch *toyed* with me.

I reach across the desk, to where Karissa's phone lay, and pick it up as I contemplate what to do about everything. I run my thumb along the jagged crack down the center of the phone, guilt-ridden that I never got around to buying her a new one.

I'm a terrible boyfriend.

A terrible fiancée.

An even worse husband.

I'm not a good man. I prove it over… and over… and over again.

I press the top button, relieved when it actually turns on. I swear the thing has more lives that a cat. Opening her contacts, I scroll through them, not surprised to find a listing for Brandy.

I understand now why the girl tried to befriend Karissa.

She was trying to get to me.

I can't help but wonder now if Ray knew. Does he know who the rat really is? Did he plant the seed, bring her in on a scheme, and use her to make sure it all ended the way he wanted it to? After what I saw, I wouldn't put it past him.

If I'm not a benefit, I'm nothing more than a hindrance, a roadblock he'd be all too eager to clear to get where he wants to be. *Sentimental* only runs so deep.

I don't take well to being disrespected, nor do I take well to being manipulated. I'm not one of his playthings. But if he wants to make this a game, I'll happily participate. I'll gladly show him how these things are played.

Brandy lives in an expensive high-rise in Manhattan, a penthouse suite, with a doorman and the highest security money can pay for. Ray foots the bill, of course. He pays for everything. It makes it nearly impossible to get to her. No way to slip in and out without being seen. I'm not much worried about being caught. I just don't want to be stopped.

I can't go to her, so she'll have to come to me.

Pressing the call button, I listen as it rings... and rings... and rings. I'm about to hang up and try again when the line clicks. "Karissa?"

"Brandy," I say calmly. "It's Ignazio Vitale."

"Oh, uh... Vitale. Hello. What can I, uh... what can I do for you?"

"Actually, I thought I could do something for you," I say. "I was cleaning out the house, you know, of all of this stuff... Karissa had a lot of things, things she won't need anymore, so I thought maybe you might like to comb through it, see if there's anything you want."

She hesitates. "I, uh... I don't know."

"Look, it's been a rough couple days. It's never easy finding out someone's ratting you out to the police. So I need to do this. I need to... make what happened worth it. I don't want any of this to go to waste."

"Okay." She still sounds hesitant, but it's not a denial, so I'll take it. "I guess I'll... I'll see you soon."

"Great."

I hang up, staring at the screen for a moment before setting it down on the desk. Reaching into the bottom desk drawer, I pull out a pair of black leather gloves and slip them on my hands.

Then I wait.

I wait a half hour, then forty-five minutes. An hour passes, and another, before I hear a car pull up in front of my house. I step outside, not at all surprised to find Kelvin behind the wheel, with Brandy climbing out of the passenger side.

Hands in my pockets, so not to alarm the man, I stroll toward the car, plastering a smile to my face. It unnerves him. I see it in his eyes.

"Go on inside," I tell Brandy. "Bedroom is upstairs to the right. I'm going to catch up with Kelvin."

Brandy heads right in. She wouldn't dare pass up an opportunity to snoop. No rat would.

I wait until she's gone before focusing on Kelvin.

"Go ahead home," I say. "I'll take her back later."

"But—"

"Leave," I tell him. "Brandy and I have some business to attend to, if you know what I mean."

"Oh, uh, sure," he says, nodding. "I get it."

He thinks he gets it, but he doesn't.

"And I'd appreciate your discretion," I say as he starts the car up. "I know Ray signs your paycheck, but I'm not one you want to cross. Got me?"

"Yeah, I got you," he grumbles, avoiding my eyes. "Have a good night, sir."

"Oh, I will," I say. "The best I've had in a while."

He speeds away, squealing tires, and I laugh to myself as I head inside. I shut the door behind me quietly, listening intently.

I hear the noise upstairs in the bedroom.

I creep up the stairs slowly, not making a sound as I head down the hall, pausing in the open doorway. I lean against the doorframe, crossing my arms over my chest, and watch as Brandy digs through the closet.

My closet.

She shifts through my clothes before focusing on the top shelf, zeroing in on the metal shoebox-sized container. She grabs it, and I cringe as she pulls it down, nearly dropping it, the contents clanking. She sets it on the bed, trying to pull the top off.

Through the darkness, I see her make a face when she realizes it's locked. "Damn it," she grumbles. "Where's the key?"

She turns around and freezes when she spots me standing there. Her eyes widen in horror as she inhales sharply, holding the breath. She looks like she's about to piss herself.

"Wrong closet."

She exhales shakily. "I, uh... I just, I thought... I mean..."

She continues to stammer as I push away from the doorframe,

pulling my hands from my pockets. She starts trembling when I come closer, her eyes fixating on the gloves I'm wearing.

"You know, Karissa once asked me what was in this box," I say. "I told her nothing. Not true, of course, because there's obviously something in there, but it wasn't exactly a lie. It's nothing she needed to worry about."

"I didn't know," Brandy says right away. "I was just looking, and I saw it, and I didn't know."

She has no excuse. We both know it.

She's just hoping I'll let it slide.

"Ask me what's in it," I say. "Go ahead... *ask*."

"What's in it?"

"How about I show you."

She tenses when I reach past her to open the drawer on the bedside stand, pulling out one of Karissa's discarded bobby pins. I bend it, holding it up toward Brandy.

"You see, there is no key to this box... there was, once, long ago, but I got rid of it. The only way to get into it is to force your way in."

It takes a moment for me to break into it, finding the right combination of movements to get the lock to disengage. It pops open, and I pull the lid off, setting it aside. I watch Brandy as her eyes curiously shift toward it, her brow furrowing when she looks inside.

"It's my life," I tell her. I haven't opened the box in a long, long time, since I locked it years ago. "Or the life I used to have, anyway. After my wife died, I locked the little we shared in this box and tucked it away. The rest I burned. I buried the memories under a mound of rage, and I continued on, forgetting this man." I motion toward the box. "Because I became this one instead." I motion toward myself.

She eyes me warily.

I shift the papers around on the top of the box—marriage certificate, Maria's death certificate, the deed to the house we owned—to weed through the rest of the contents. Maria's something old, something new, something borrowed and something blue from the wedding, and a few of her prized possessions, pieces of her I wasn't yet ready to let go of back then. There's a rattle in here, the only thing we ever bought for the baby... the only thing Maria had a chance to pick out. Photos, lots and lots of photos, and finally, at the very bottom, I fish out our wedding bands. I hold her engagement ring up, the diamond shining as it hits the moonlight streaming through the window.

"You know what I did to buy this ring?" I ask. "Do you know what an eighteen-year-old kid does to afford a diamond this big?"

She shakes her head.

"I promised things to Ray," I say. "Anything he wanted, anything he needed, and I was there. I told him I'd do anything for the money, so I could give his daughter the ring she deserved, and he made me work for it. I'd come home at night with bloody knuckles and lie right to her face about how it happened. But I never killed a man. I never took a life. He never asked me to... until after I got the ring. After we were married, he told me there was a rat that I needed to deal with for him. I didn't know what that meant then. *Deal with them.* But I do now, and I'm sure you do, too."

She nods.

She's trembling, scared about why I'm telling her this.

Good.

"He told me I still owed him, for the money he gave me for the ring, but if I did this one thing, my debt would be paid. So I agreed. And he looked at me that day, and he said, 'Ignazio, you have to kill your best friend.' And I couldn't do it. Rats had to go, but man... my best friend?"

Shaking my head, I slip the engagement ring in my pocket before closing the box again, leaving it lying on the bed. I stare at the top of it, trying to contain the emotion opening it conjured inside of me.

"I couldn't do it, but I guess Johnny could. It took me almost twenty years to return the favor, but I did it, finally, and now my debt is paid. And I learned a valuable lesson that day, one I'll never forget."

"What?" she asks quietly.

"You take out the rat before it can jump ship."

Before she can react, my hands are around her throat. I shove her into the wall, knocking her head against the plaster so hard it makes a dent. Her eyes bulge as she fights me, but I don't waver. I hold tight until her blood vessels burst and her heart stops beating, stealing her last breath.

I put her in the trunk and drive north, to the house tucked into the woods. I knock on the front door well after midnight, much to the dismay of Carter. He stares at me with disbelief before wordless getting the key to the incinerator, passing it over before going back to bed.

I'm not doing this to cover my tracks or conceal my crime.

Ray will figure it out.

I want him to.

I just want to make sure there's nothing left for the man to grieve.

He toyed with me.

I'll take his Baby Doll from him.

Chapter Twenty-Three

Grief doesn't go away.

You can ignore it all you want, shove it down or swallow it back, pretend it doesn't exist, but it's there. It stays there, lurking in the shadows, living way down in the depths, feeding off of anger, just waiting for the day it can rise up and take control.

No, grief doesn't go away, ever, because grief becomes a part of you.

It roots into your system, infecting your bloodstream. Grief pulsates in every beat of your heart and clouds around you with every breath from your lungs. Grief swims behind your eyelids every time you blink. It lives in every word you speak.

Grief is a fucking leech.

I know, because I'm grieving.

I ignored it for years, masked it with rage, but nothing I did made it go away. The moment I stopped and opened myself up again, dropping my guard to let myself feel, the grief seized hold.

The grass is an unnatural vibrant green that seems to glow brighter under the dismal gray sky. Water glistens from the ground, the wetness seeping through my shoes as I stand in it. I've been here for twenty minutes, I think. Twenty hours. Twenty days. Does it even fucking matter?

It's the first time I've come here in twenty years.

I know that for a fact.

The marble in front of me still looks brand new, the name etched on it bold. *Maria Angelo Vitale*. Fresh flowers lay on top of it. A few long stemmed pink roses. They were her favorite, I think. I'm not sure anymore. My memory's failing me. Today, it's her favorite flowers. Tomorrow, it's her face. I've already lost the sound of her voice. I've lost so much. Why couldn't I keep that?

The rage took it, I think. It got misplaced in my pursuit of revenge.

It didn't do her memory justice, like Ray said.

It did us all an injustice, but especially me.

It stole the only bits and pieces of her that I could keep.

I take a few steps closer, pausing right where I stood the day she was lowered into the ground. I'm wearing the same suit again.

I might burn it after this.

"Been a long time," I say. "A long, long time."

My voice is low but it seems to carry with the breeze. There's no one else here this morning, no one in this old cemetery, but it seems wrong, like the wind is stealing the words only meant for her. It pisses me off. Irrational, maybe, but since when am I rational?

I wanted to kill an innocent young woman simply for being born.

"I don't know why I'm here," I admit. "I don't know if you'd want to see me, or what you'd think of me if you were still here. I don't know, Maria... but I know I miss you. I've spent twenty goddamn years missing you, angry that you never had a chance... I've been so fucking angry that I forgot how to live. I'm trying to remember, but it's harder than I thought. I feel guilty. Guilty, because I let myself be happy again. It wasn't for long, but I felt it. It's easy to forget the grief, you know, when you ignore its existence. But it came back, and now I'm fucking grieving."

Pulling the diamond ring from my pocket, I stare at it under the dull sky before stepping forward, setting it on the headstone beside the flowers. I wonder who left them. Her mother? Her father? A friend who actually remembered things about her?

"You should keep the ring," I say. "You should've been buried with it. I wasn't thinking back then... they took it off of you, and you were already in the ground when I remembered it. Someone will probably come along and steal it before the day is out, but that's nothing new. They steal everything. It's yours, though, not mine, so I'm giving it back to you, but this time with no vows."

I take a step back, once again eyeing the flowers. They feel wrong somehow. Maybe it's because they're pink.

Peach flowers were her favorite, I think.

"Goodbye, Maria," I say. "Part of me will always love you, but it's time for me to go now and finally try to deal with this grief."

I give the gravesite one more look before walking away. I trudge through the damp grass to where my car is parked along the curb and start the drive home.

It's been one week.

One week since Karissa left.

In seven days, she could be anywhere, deep in the south or way out west, somewhere that's not here.

Somewhere far away.

It's been a long week.

I can't sleep.

I'm numb physically, emotionally spent. I have nothing left to give. Paranoia consumes me. Every gust of wind is a warning; every rustling leaf is a threat. I'm tired, so tired. I just want it to end.

I park in the driveway when I make it home, climbing out and closing the door. I slowly make my way to the house, pulling out my house keys and unlocking the front door. Carefully, I push it open, freezing with my hand on the knob when I hear a noise in the distance, animated voices coming from the den.

The television.

It's on.

I haven't turned it on all week.

I don't watch it.

It doesn't interest me.

Nothing here interests me.

My skin crawls, sickness brewing in the pit of my stomach as I let go of the doorknob. Slowly, I take a step back. I'm so fixated on the goddamn television that I hardly hear the rustling behind me, the faint sound of someone shuffling through the grass.

It's close when I hear it, too close.

Too fucking close.

I'm unarmed.

I'm too late.

Turning around, the first thing I see is the muzzle of a gun, pointed right at my face from just a few feet away. Ray holds it, gripping tightly to the weapon, his finger on the trigger.

I stare him in the eyes.

He looks unfazed.

Anger.

All I see is anger.

I recognize it, because for a long time that was all I felt, too. It's the look I saw every time I encountered my reflection in the mirror.

"You've been in my house," I say. "Looking for me, I suppose."

He shakes his head. "I didn't go in there. Didn't have to. Your car was gone. Knew you'd be back eventually."

He's lying, I think.

He has to be.

Somebody's been in there.

It wasn't me.

"I'm surprised you're here," I say calmly, trying to buy myself a moment to think. "I thought it would be Kelvin, maybe one of the others. Getting your hands dirty isn't really your thing."

"Yeah, well, a man does a job himself when he's got a personal claim to it."

"So it's personal."

"You know it is."

His hand is steady. It doesn't shake.

He's going to shoot me.

I know it.

And he's not going to miss his target.

This isn't an idle threat or meant to send some message. He's a man on a mission and his mission is murder. The end always comes at the hand of a friend. I should expect no less than the man who was like a father to me.

"Go on," I say, my voice steady. I feel no fear. I probably should. Maybe it's the monster in me that isn't afraid of death. Living terrifies me more. Living is fucking hard. I've already died once. "Do it if you're going to do it. Put a bullet in my head. Make your daughter proud."

His anger flares. "She was too good for you."

"She was," I agree, "but she loved me, nonetheless."

Ray's finger presses against the trigger, close to squeezing it, as I continue to stare him in the eyes. There's something wrong with me, I think. I should be pleading for my life. I should be praying I live. My heart should race. I should break a sweat. Something. Anything.

But I feel nothing.

Again, there's nothing.

Nothing until I hear my name.

It's hesitant, spoken behind me in the house, a faint whisper in that familiar voice I never thought I'd hear again. *Naz*. It's just my imagination, I tell myself. I didn't really hear it.

Except I did.

I heard it, and I hear it again. *Naz*.

This time Ray hears it, too.

It's real.

His gaze shifts past me, into the open doorway, his anger giving way to surprise. I turn quickly, catching a pair of soft brown eyes, hesitant but devoid of fear. She can see me but she can't see him. She thinks I'm alone. She thinks I'm just standing here.

She isn't afraid of me.

Not anymore.

Karissa.

She isn't sure what to think of my silence as she takes a step toward me and speaks yet again. "Ignazio?"

My heart skips a beat before hammering hard in my chest, my thoughts suddenly racing. *There's* the feeling. *There's* the fear. *There's* the adrenaline. It washes through me all at once until I'm drowning in it, but it's not for me. No, not in the least. It's for *her*.

No.

No.

Fuck, no.

She's not supposed to be here.

Karissa steps toward me.

So does Ray.

My gaze bounces between them, frantic.

It's only seconds, those brief seconds where the world stops turning, when you stare down the barrel of a gun that you know is going to take everything from you. Your life, maybe, but certainly your reason to live. But it only lasts seconds before the gun shifts.

Ray aims over my shoulder, into the doorway. His finger squeezes the trigger as I scream, lunging at him. The gunshot goes off, loud in my ear, a small explosion that rocks the air around me. I hit him a second too late, knocking him to the ground, familiar rage consuming me. We struggle as I fight him, getting my hands on the gun, beating him with it to get him to loosen his grip before turning it around on him. I don't hesitate. I don't even think about it.

I grip the gun.

I pull the trigger.

A second after the gunshot goes off, I hear the sharp inhale, the sucking in of air from lungs desperate to breathe. My eyes are on Ray, as he lays on his back in the grass, immobile. He's not breathing.

It didn't come from him.

No.

God, no.

My eyes dart to the doorway of the house when the sound hits me again. I don't see Karissa. She's not standing there anymore. But I can hear her.

I hear her when she gasps.

When she tries to breathe.

Pushing away from Ray, getting to my feet, I drop the gun in the grass and rush inside, nearly collapsing as soon as I step in the foyer. Blood streaks the white linoleum surrounding Karissa. She lays flat on her back, clutching a wound on her chest, trying to keep the blood in but it's seeping out too fast. Dropping to my knees, I pull her into my arms, forcing her weak hands away from the wound. I tear her shirt open, getting it out of the way. The wound is near her rib cage and it's sucking air every time she inhales.

Shit.

I put her hands tightly against it again, looking down at her. "Hold right there, okay? I'm going to get something to stop the air."

I run to the kitchen, throwing things around as I sort through cabinets, finding a roll of plastic wrap. I grab some medical tape from the drawer and run back to Karissa, grateful she's exactly how I left her. I drop to the floor, pulling her hands away, and tear off some plastic wrap. I cover the wound, taping it tightly, before I search through my pockets to find my phone.

With one hand, I press firmly on her wound, while I use the other to dial 911. My heart still races as her bloody hands grasp my arm, holding on to me. Tears streak her cheeks, her breaths panicked gasps as she stares up at me. The dazed look is already in her eyes.

"Deep breaths, baby," I tell her, my voice cracking, as I cradle the phone in crook of my neck. "Try to relax. The more excited you get, the faster your heart pumps and the more blood you lose."

"911, what's your emergency?"

"I need an ambulance right away," I say. "Nineteen year old female with an open chest wound from a gunshot."

I rattle off the address, and the dispatcher tries to give me instructions, asking me to stay on the line until help arrives, but I drop the phone, letting it hit the floor beside me, not bothering to hang it up. I still clutch tightly to her wound, trying to slow the bleeding, as my free hand brushes the hair from her face.

"Naz," she whispers. "Naz..."

"It's okay," I tell her, continuing to smooth her hair as I stare down at her. "I've got you. Just keep breathing, okay? You're going to be okay just as long as you keep breathing for me. You think you can do that?"

She nods weakly.

"Just keep breathing," I whisper, relishing every breath she takes, no matter how strained. "Just keep breathing."

She tries. Fuck, I can tell she's trying, but each inhale brings on a grimace of pain. Her face contorts with a cry as I brush away her tears. "Naz..."

"No," I say, shaking my head. "Don't try that bullshit. Don't *Naz* me. You just keep breathing and you're going to be fine. I promise. You can't... I can't lose you. I need you to keep breathing, Karissa. Help is coming soon. Just hold on for me."

Two minutes.

Four minutes.

Ten minutes.

A fucking century.

I don't know how long it takes before I hear the sirens in the distance, the lights flashing as they pull up in front of the house. It's the police first, then the EMS. People swarm the house, officers and medical personnel. Someone grabs ahold of me, pulling me away from her. Karissa turns her head my way when I'm dragged from the foyer, and I don't hear her voice, but I watch as her lips move, mouthing my name.

Naz.

I'm dragged outside. It's chaos.

Another century passes.

Maybe it's just a minute.

I don't know.

I don't know anything.

"Just keep breathing," I whisper to myself. "Keep breathing."

I blink, and officers surround me.

Another blink, and Karissa's being hauled away.

I try to force my way past the crowd, trying to get to her, but I'm restrained. There are too many people here. Where the hell did they come from? No matter how much I scream, how much I fight, the ambulance leaves without me, tearing through the street at full speed, sirens blaring.

A few more blinks. People are talking to me. Their voices are garbled. I can't fucking think. I grip my hair tightly, pacing in a circle, not saying a word except "keep breathing."

I don't know when it happened, but suddenly Jameson is there. Crime scene tape surrounds my house. I'm standing on my front step, covered in blood, my hands shaking. He stands in front of me, a concerned expression on his face. He's a blurry mass, and I blink to clear my vision, realizing I'm crying.

I'm fucking crying.

Again.

"I have to go," I say, trying to step around him. "I have to get to the hospital. I have to be there."

He steps in my path, half a dozen officers flanking him, blocking my way. I glare at him, nostrils flaring. I can feel the tears burning my eyes. It's pissing me off more than I'm already pissed.

"You want to stop me?" I ask, taking a step toward Jameson. "I dare you to try. I *dare* you."

The man shows no sign of anger, his troubled gaze leaving mine to look around. His attention settles on the lump in the grass covered in a white sheet.

"Just tell me what went on," he says before turning to me again, his expression earnest. "What happened?"

I hesitate.

"He shot my fiancée," I say. "He wanted us dead."

"So you killed him."

"So I stopped him," I correct him. "Justice was already served, Jameson. Not like you'd get any for me, anyway, but your work here is done. I did it for you... *again*."

He nods before stepping aside. "Go ahead. I'll have some questions for you later, but go on, get to the hospital."

I step past him, grabbing my keys as I head for my car.

"You're just going to let him go free?" Andrews asks with disbelief. "He just confessed to killing him, and you're letting him walk?"

"It was self-defense," Jameson says. "I want him behind bars as much as you, but we don't want to look like the bad guys here."

I get in the car, spinning tires as I speed away. I left my house wide open, crawling with police, but I don't care. Not anymore.

They can search every inch of it if they want.

They can burn it down for all I care.

Chapter Twenty-Four

Hospital waiting rooms are Purgatory.

It's that place, between Heaven and Hell, where you're forced to wait for your time, for word as to where you go next. It's not pleasant. In fact, it's torture. But you sit there, and you cling to hope, telling yourself it's not that bad, because you know it could always get worse.

Because you know it just might.

The room is brightly lit, the florescent lights above me flickering and hurting my eyes. Every blink burns. Every muscle in my body aches.

A kid screams in the corner. His mother sobs. An old man keeps sneezing. A woman won't stop talking. The noises surround me, a haze of chaos that makes my ears ring as I grip my hair tightly and stare at the door.

I stare.

And stare.

And fucking stare.

Just waiting for it to open, and for them to give me the final judgment.

Heaven or Hell.

Life or death.

It feels like I'm strapped to a gurney with a needle in my arm, except I don't know if it's a hospital room surrounding me or if it's actually an execution chamber.

A few more minutes.

I keep breathing, in and out, over and over, praying she is, too. *Just keep breathing.*

The door swings open eventually and a doctor steps out. Everyone around me stares at him, looking hopeful, but he stares right at me, his expression blank. He pauses before stepping toward me, appearing nervous.

My stomach sinks.

No.

No.

Don't say it.

Don't tell me she's gone, too.

Don't tell me her last word was my name.

"Mr. Vitale? Can I speak to you in private?"

I look away from him, glancing around the room. The mother is crying again. The kid is still screaming. The old man blows his nose as the woman tells him about her goddamn canker sores.

It's already Hell, I've decided, not Purgatory.

"Just say it," I tell him. "Get it over with."

"If you insist."

"I do."

"She's in recovery."

It takes a few beats for those words to sink in. I look at him again. "*Recovery?*"

He nods. "It was touch and go for a bit... punctured a lung, fractured some ribs, but we repaired the damage. She was lucky you were there when it happened. Your quick thinking saved her life."

I should feel relief from that, but I don't.

I didn't save her life.

I almost had it taken from her.

"Thank you," I say. "Can I see her?"

"Soon," he says. "She's still unconscious, but she'll be moved to a room in a little while. The nurse will come for you as soon as you can go in."

It's three hours later when they come get me.

I know for a fact this time, because instead of staring at the door, I stared at the clock. In that time, the old man got good news, the chatty woman fell asleep, and the mother was told her world would never be the same again.

The nurse leads me to a dim room in the ICU. I pause in the doorway, staring at the bed. Karissa lies completely still. She's breathing, but not on her own.

She's on a ventilator.

"You can have a few minutes," the nurse says, "but then I'm going to have to ask you to leave. Visiting hours are already over, so you'll have to come back tomorrow."

The nurse walks away, and I stand there in the doorway, watching her, listening to her heartbeat on the monitor. I don't wait for the nurse to come back.

I just leave.

I don't go far, though, ending up back in the waiting room. I camp out in a chair in the corner, getting no sleep. People come in and out all night long and well into the next afternoon. I wander around the hospital occasionally, passing the minutes in a daze.

I'm standing along a far wall near the ICU twenty-four hours after Karissa was brought in, still wearing the same clothes, covered in her blood. I stare out the window, into the parking lot, watching as the cars come and go, when someone approaches from behind. "Mr. Vitale?"

I turn around, coming face-to-face with the doctor who delivered the news to me yesterday. He stalls when he gets a good look at me, stammering a moment. "You've been here this whole time?"

"Yes."

"You should go home," he tells me. "Get some rest."

I glance down at myself and shake my head. "There's nothing there for me."

"At least get cleaned up," he says. "Let me get you a pair of scrubs. We have showers you can use."

I want to argue, to refuse, but a shower sounds good right about now. I follow the man to the locker room on the next floor. He hands me a pair of dark blue scrubs, telling me to take my time.

I stand under the warm spray for a long time, washing the red tint from my skin, trying to absolve myself of the memories but they haunt me. Every time I close my eyes, I see her ashen face, the stunned look in her eyes, the blood gushing from beneath her skin.

I shut the water off eventually, drying off and pulling on the scrubs. I discard my suit right in the trash before walking out. I stroll around the hospital again and head back to the ICU. I make my way to Karissa's room, pausing outside the doorway.

She's awake.

The machines are still beeping but the ventilator is gone. A nurse stands beside her bed, checking her vitals, as Karissa shifts around a bit. I watch curiously, quietly, waiting until the nurse is done. The lady walks out, flashing me a smile.

Once she's gone, I slowly step inside the room, watching her. Her eyes drift toward me. I'm not sure what to say. An apology is on the tip of my tongue, another fucking apology, but she breaks the silence and speaks first.

"Stealing scrubs again?"

Her voice is scratchy and faint, but she's joking around. It instantly sets me at ease, relieving the tension I've carried in my muscles since yesterday. I stroll closer, encouraged by the fact that she didn't tell me to get the fuck out. "You said we borrow them, remember?"

"I remember."

"So I'm trying out this look again. The black suits just aren't doing it for me anymore."

"I like it," she says, smiling softly. "You look... doctor-y."

"Doctor-y," I repeat, pulling a chair closer to her bed and sitting down. "I'll have to remember that."

Her smile wavers a bit as she stares at me. She reaches her hand out toward me, and it shakes when she tries to hold it there. Sighing, I grasp ahold of it, pressing it between both of my hands. Her skin is ice cold.

"You scared me, sweetheart," I say quietly.

"I'm sorry."

"Don't apologize," I say. "Never apologize to me. This isn't your fault... it's mine. If anyone should be apologizing, it's me."

She slowly shakes her head. "The doctor says you saved my life."

"I put you in that situation to begin with," I say. "You shouldn't have been there. You left, and I told you not to come back... I said if you walked out, to keep going, to never come back. Why were you there? What were you *thinking*?"

Her voice is even quieter now as she answers. "I missed you."

"You missed me," I say, laughing with disbelief. "Seriously... you missed me?"

"Yes."

"Why?"

She stares at me again. She doesn't answer.

"You should've been rejoicing. I told you I wouldn't come after you, and I didn't. You were free and clear."

"That's the problem," she says. "I knew you weren't coming."

"I thought that's what you wanted, Karissa. You wanted me to let you go, so I let you go."

"I thought that's what I wanted, too, but what I wanted was the option. I wanted to have a choice. I wanted you to ask."

"I did ask."

"No, you didn't. You said you were asking me to stay, but you never asked. You never do."

It makes no sense to me. It's a petty argument. It doesn't matter how I worded it... if she wanted to go, she would go, and she did. She left. And I don't understand why she would come back.

"I missed you," she says quietly as I stroke her hand. "I didn't expect to miss you as much as I did. I missed talking to you... missed the way you tease me, the way you look at me. I hate the things you do... I hate parts of you, monster you can sometimes be, but I don't hate the man I fell in love with. And he's the one I missed."

"I'm not a good man, Karissa."

"You're not a bad one, either, Ignazio."

It's the same argument all over again.

"I thought you hated the way I look at you."

"I do," she says, "but I love it, too."

Shaking my head, I let out a deep breath and lean down, kissing the back of her hand. "You should run far, far away from me."

"I know I should," she says. "I wish I could."

"You can."

She shakes her head and looks away from me, staring up at the ceiling. Her blinks are slow, heavy.

"I don't know why I came back," she says. "I don't understand any of this, but maybe I'm not supposed to. I shouldn't be here, but I am... I shouldn't love you, but I do. You have problems, Naz. There's something *seriously* wrong with you. But maybe there's something wrong with me, too, because no matter how much I try to hate you, or how much I want to stay away from you, I can't. I love you, but I don't understand... I don't understand why you'd do it, why you'd do that to me, how you could bring yourself to hurt me when you're supposed to love me, too."

"It wasn't about you."

"How can you say that?" she asks, her voice growing a little louder, stronger. "She's my mother."

"I didn't want to do it, Karissa," I say. "I didn't enjoy a second of it."

"And that's supposed to make it better?"

"No," I say, looking down at her hand in mine, my eyes tracing the IV stuck to her arm. "Nothing I say will ever make it better, Karissa. What's done is done, and it can't be taken back. I don't expect your forgiveness... I'm not even sure you *should* forgive me. Forgiveness... that certainly wasn't something I was capable of."

She's crying, quietly, silent tears streaming down her cheeks as she continues to stare at the ceiling. "She didn't know... about what he planned, about what he did, until afterward. She told me that, and I believe her. She didn't know until it was too late."

"That might be true," I reply, "but she spent years after it with the knowledge of what he'd done, and she protected him. She chose him. Despite what he did, she refused to turn her back on that man."

"Like mother," she whispers, "like daughter."

I stroke her hand for a moment, my thumb rubbing circles along her skin. "I'm not saying what she did warranted what I did. I'm not trying to justify it. I'm just saying, your mother made her decision. She knew what it would mean for her. She shot me. She knew this game would end with one of us dead, and I'm regretful it was her, Karissa... I am... but I can't be sorry it wasn't me."

She inhales deeply, as if to calm down, as she closes her eyes. "I don't know what I'm supposed do. They're holding her... she's in Watertown, and they tell me I can come, that I can... have her, but I don't know what I'm supposed to do."

"You lay her to rest."

"Where?"

I'm quiet for a moment, mulling over that question, before I let go of Karissa's hand. She lets it hover there for a second before pulling it back onto the bed, resting it against her chest.

"I have a place," I say, running my hands down my face.

She turns her head to look at me. "You have a place?"

"St. John's Catholic Cemetery in Queens. I own a plot there."

"You do?"

"Yes," I say quietly. "I think your mother would like it. Johnny was buried there months ago, so she wouldn't be far from him."

Karissa says nothing, but she isn't arguing against it, so that counts for something.

"I'll make the arrangements for you," I say, standing up. "You shouldn't have to do it."

I start to walk out when she calls my name.

"Naz, why do you have a plot there?"

"I bought it long ago," I say hesitating near the doorway to look back at her. "It's where Maria was buried."

"But don't you—?"

"I don't need it," I say before she even has to ask that question. "I don't belong there. Not anymore. Maria's life was marked by violence... she should be able to rest in peace."

⤷⤸

It's two weeks later when Karissa is released from the hospital.

Two weeks later when we stand in the damp grass of the quiet cemetery, in front of the shiny black casket placed over the freshly dug grave. The reality of the situation surrounds the gravesite, a stark reminder of where life led us all. Carmela lived her life in hiding, and her death feels much the same.

Isolated.

There's nobody here.

Nobody to share memories.

Nobody to say goodbye.

Nobody, that is, except me and Karissa, along with a preacher and the guys from the funeral home. In the distance, over the hill, I can see the unmarked police car, but they're not going to come closer.

They're just watching.

Watching me, because despite it all, they're still determined to bust me for something.

"Shall we, uh, get started?" the preacher asks, as the strained silence surrounding us grows thicker.

Karissa doesn't respond. She stands right beside me, wearing a plain black dress, so close her arm brushes mine. Her head is down, eyes fixed on the grass, hands clasped in front of her. She sways a bit. She shouldn't be on her feet. But she's stubborn... so damn stubborn.

She ignored me when I told her to find somewhere to sit.

Tears linger in the corner of her eyes. She just wanted someone to care, someone to show up... somebody else who wasn't me. She wanted her mother's life to matter to somebody other than her.

Sighing, I turn away from her and glance around, freezing when I see someone approaching in the distance. Surprise runs through me.

My father.

He wears his usual work clothes, khakis and a white shirt, his grungy apron still tied around his waist. He came straight from the deli, I realize, and he forgot to take it off in his rush. He's clutching a bouquet of flowers, and when he gets closer I see they're pink roses.

Pink roses.

My gaze shifts toward the adjacent gravesite. The ring is long gone, unsurprisingly, but the roses remain in place. Wilted, sure, but they're still there.

And I think I know who gave them to her.

My father keeps his head down as he walks up, grumbling to himself as he approaches. Karissa's head snaps up at the sound of his voice, her eyes widening as she stares at him.

"Sorry I'm late," he says to nobody in particular. "Time got away from me."

"Not a problem," the preacher says, taking his hand to shake it, seeming damn relieved to have somebody else show up. "We're glad you could be here."

My father nods, turning away from the man, and places the flowers on top of the casket before stepping back. He clasps his hands in front of him, refusing to meet my eyes as he stands there, waiting.

The preacher starts.

There isn't much to say.

He reads off the skewed facts of Carmela's life, making the woman a caricature none of us standing here recognize, before clearing his throat and looking at the three of us gathered, struggling for something more to say. "Do any of you have a story you'd like to share about Carmela?"

"I got one."

My father's voice draws my attention back to him. The preacher waves his direction, giving him the floor.

"I knew Carmela since she was just a little girl," he says, motioning toward his knees. "She was about this high, you know, a short little thing, and spunky. She used to come by the deli every day on her way home from school and I'd ask her how her day was, and it didn't matter how good of a day she had, she'd always tell me something bad. She was a complainer, that one. And I'd give her a cookie, you know, one of the ones we make fresh. I'd tell her no worries, tomorrow will be better. It's been a lot of years since I saw her... last time, she came by the shop, and I asked her how her day was and she said she'd just found out she was having a baby, so she wasn't gonna complain even if she could. She took a cookie and left. Never saw her again. To this day, every time we make Snickerdoodles, I think about her. Those were her favorites."

Tears stream down Karissa's cheeks, but she smiles. "She used to make them for me."

Silence overcomes the air around us again. The preacher clears his throat before moving on.

It's over as quick as it starts.

Afterward, my father approaches, taking Karissa's hands in his own. He kisses her cheeks, smiling, giving her the warm greeting she didn't get last time.

"Come by the deli sometime," he tells her. "I've got some cookies with your name on them."

"Thank you," she whispers. "I will."

He lets go of her, motioning toward me with his head. "Just leave this one at home next time."

The preacher pulls Karissa away then, and my father turns to me, meeting my eyes. He stares me down for a moment, not a stitch of apprehension.

"Pink roses," I say.

He shrugs. "They're your mother's favorite, so I figure I can't go wrong with them."

He turns, hesitating when I call out to him. "Look..."

He holds his hand up to stop me. "Save it, Ignazio. Whatever it is, I don't want to hear it." His gaze flickers to Karissa briefly before he turns to glare at me. "Just don't make me visit another woman's grave because of you."

My father walks away, and I think, as he disappears from the cemetery, that this is probably one of the last times I'll ever speak to him.

"Naz?"

I turn around when Karissa says my name and immediately pull her into my arms, hugging her tightly.

"Are you ready to get out of here?" I ask.

"Yes."

She gives one last long look at where her mother will forever rest before turning away. We head to my car and climb in, and I watch the rearview mirror as we pull away, waiting for the police cruiser to follow me, but it turns the other way.

They don't come after me.

Someday, but not today.

I breathe a sigh of relief, reaching over and taking Karissa's hand, giving it a squeeze.

I don't go home.

Karissa doesn't question it.

I drive north, out of the city.

She watches out the side widow, still holding my hand, but she remains silent. Maybe she's afraid to ask questions. Maybe she just trusts me to take her somewhere safe.

I don't know, but I appreciate her silence.

It's more comfortable than I expect it to be.

Dr. Carter's place is dead quiet, no cars around, no people anywhere. I pull the Mercedes right up front and cut the engine as Karissa eyes the building with confusion. There's only a small sign along the side, but her eyes zero in on it.

Dr. Michael Carter

Veterinary Services

"You're kidding me," she says, her eyes turning to me. "I thought he was a doctor."

"He is," I say. "A doctor of veterinary medicine."

"You got shot, you nearly died, and instead of calling 9-1-1, you made me call a fucking *vet*?"

Her disbelief makes me laugh, but I don't comment. Instead, I open the car door. "Come on, there's something I want to show you."

She gets out of the car after me and I lead her straight out back. The moment I round the corner, I hear the growling and pause, glaring down at a pair of beady brown eyes as they glare at me.

"Killer!"

Karissa gasps, pushing away from me to run to him. His growling ceases instantly as he grows excited at the sight of her, jumping up and down. Karissa drops to her knees, wrapping her arms around the dog as she starts sobbing.

She loses it.

She cries long and hard.

She's in pain.

Torture.

I can feel it emanating from her.

It exists deep down in her soul.

Torture to her Soul

It's not about the dog, I know. It isn't even really about her mother, and it certainly isn't her father. It has nothing to do with him. It's not about me, or her, or anyone else. Not about Daniel, or Paul, or Ray. It's about life, and how cruel it can sometimes be.

How unfair life is.

All of us have a hand in it.

We do what we have to do, take what we have to take, and sometimes we hurt people we swear we won't hurt, but we do, because life makes us.

It's a dog eat dog world.

We're all monsters, when it comes down to it.

Her eyes meet mine.

She mouths the words 'thank you'.

I do nothing but nod.

I don't deserve her gratitude.

But she's the kind of woman who is grateful, anyway.

Epilogue

I'm going to tell you something that a wise man once told me: *it's not the darkness that's terrifying, it's what you might find in it.*

I was always afraid of the dark as a child, afraid monsters would sneak into my room at night, but now I know there's nothing to fear. Not because monsters don't exist. They do. I've seen them. I've encountered them. One attacked me as I slept.

I even became one myself afterward.

No, the reason there's nothing to fear in the dark is because real monsters lurk in the light, too. They hide in plain sight. The trick is to find them before they can get you.

I'm not a good man.

I'm not.

I know.

But Karissa tells me maybe I'm not a bad man, either. I'm the kind of man who easily slips between the dark and the light, the kind of monster who walks along the shadows.

Through the darkness, I stare at where Karissa lays beside me in the bed. She regards me warily, eyes guarded and nervous as she waits for a reaction. I'm panting, trying to catch my breath, trying to calm down and purge the memories from my head.

I hate these fucking nightmares.

Seconds pass as she waits me out before there's a noise out in the hallway, something scratching against the bedroom door.

Panicking, I don't even think about it as I protectively grab ahold of Karissa, forcing her behind me. My heart stalls as I stare at the door, feeling her hands on me.

"Relax," she whispers, grabbing my arm. "It's just Killer."

Killer.

It takes a moment for that to sink in, but I don't relax, my muscles taut and shoulders tense. I offer Karissa a small smile as she leans over, lightly kissing my lips.

I kiss her back as she runs her hands along my face, wiping the sweat from my brow. She questions nothing. She asks nothing of me. I give her the world and for that, she offers trust. We both know I don't deserve it.

I never will.

But I'm grateful, and I show her.

I climb on top of her, kissing her deeper, more frenzied. It's instinctive, as she opens herself up, spreading her legs to accommodate me. I'm inside of her right away. With her, there's never any hesitation.

I've learned my lesson.

I find peace in the darkness sometimes now. I find peace with her. I'll never forget, but she makes me feel like it's okay to remember. It's okay to remember the pain and fear. It's okay to admit the darkness terrified me.

Because I found some light in it.

I found her.

The scratching at the door continues, followed by growling when Karissa starts to make noise. She might trust me, but Killer certainly doesn't. He takes her moans of pleasure as signs of distress and tries to break the door down to get at me.

Since you're so good at keeping secrets, I'm going to tell you one:

I had another fear as a child.

Just one other.

Goddamn dogs.

BONUS

scene

Karissa

The sports bar is utter chaos.

Every booth is packed, asses planted in all of the stools, as servers run back and forth and bartenders dish out beer after beer. Naz is still sipping on the same one he ordered over thirty minutes ago. I imagine it has to be piss-warm by now, but it doesn't seem to bother him.

He doesn't seem to *notice*, for that matter.

He sits across from me in the small wooden booth, posture relaxed but expression faded. The man's here physically, but his mind is somewhere far, far away. Where? I don't know. I'd ask, but he probably wouldn't answer.

He'd just tell me not to worry about it.

That's what he always says these days when I ask things, when he can tell I'm starting to overthink everything again. *Don't worry about it.* I try not to, but it's hard, given what we've been through, given who he is.

Or who he used to be...

"You're out?"

"About as out as a man like me can possibly be."

"What does that even mean?"

"Don't worry about it. Just know I'm done with all of that."

Out.

Done with all of that.

Hardly.

Over the past year, there have been incidents. Quiet phone conversations and middle-of-the-night disappearances, none of which he ever offers explanations for, leading to days of obsessively cleaning his finally-fixed car or being more paranoid than usual. The cops have come around more times than I care to count, asking about situations and people Naz always feigns ignorance about.

Out, for Naz, certainly hasn't been cold turkey.

Clearing my throat, I pick up the bacon cheeseburger the waitress shoved in front of me a moment ago when she ran past. I take a bite, dramatically rolling my eyes back in my head. Jesus Christ, it's Heaven on a bun. I'm surprised I don't hear trumpets playing in the distance as I chew, wiping the grease from my face when it runs down my chin.

Best burger ever.

"I swear, I could eat these every day," I say. "Breakfast, lunch, *and* dinner."

Naz's eyes drift my way at the sound of my voice. He's not eating. He says he's not hungry. "I'm not sure that would be good for your health."

"Yeah, but you'd still love me if I gained, like, seven hundred pounds, right?"

A small smile tugs the corner of his lips as he regards me, just enough to show off a hint of his dimples. "Right."

"See? No problem."

"Sure, until you had a massive coronary from the clogged arteries. I already worry about you getting diabetes with as much chocolate as you eat."

I roll my eyes instead of commenting, taking another bite as he laughs. I swallow it down with what's left of my Coke just as the waitress comes speeding by. She skids to a stop, grabbing my empty glass with a smile. "Refill, darling?"

"Yes, please."

She turns her attention to Naz. "Another beer?"

He shakes his bottle. *Empty.* "Sure."

The waitress scurries away, returning moments later with our drinks. The cap is already off Naz's beer bottle, but he barely gives it a look before taking a sip.

I smile, unable to help myself, as I stare at him. His mind drifts again, his attention elsewhere, but I don't mind. Not really. It gives me a chance to watch him like he usually watches me.

I'm sure, if people knew us, if they knew our history... if they read the fine print that accompanied our story... they'd wonder how I could even be here right now. How I could sit at this table, across from this man, and breathe the same air he breathes, sharing the same space that he occupies. They'd wonder how I could look at him and feel anything besides hatred. How I could see him and not wish him dead.

The truth is, sometimes I wonder those same things.

It makes me wonder if there's something wrong with me. Is it some sort of sickness I've caught? Delirium. Delusions. Maybe it's Stockholm syndrome, or maybe it's a disease I was born with. Not contagious, but genetic, something my mother passed on to me. I see an echo of her in myself. I'm stumbling down the same path she long ago got lost on, a path that reaffirmed her undying love for a man that had been marked for death.

I wonder if this is how she felt, facing the realization that the man she'd chosen to give herself to was the same man who took so much away from her. I wonder if she felt as I feel, if she saw what I see: a flawed man, a tortured soul, a shred of hope inside what everyone else finds utterly hopeless. I wonder a lot, but I'll never have any answers, never get a chance to ask my questions, thanks to the man sitting across from me.

Some days, I'm still so angry about what he did, about how he hurt me, but other days... days like today, when I watch him in silence and see a hint of the vulnerability he usually keeps locked away... I'm afforded a sick sense of relief. Relief that I'll never have my questions answered, that I'll never have to know just how fucked up we all really are.

I finish eating as he sips his beer, staring off toward the nearest television screen. Football is on, the noise from the crowd loud but the silence that surrounds the two of us is comfortable.

After my burger is gone, I shove my plate aside and gaze at the screen. I know nothing about sports. There's a green team and a blue team and they smash into each other like the waves of a tumultuous sea, mixing and mashing and doing whatever the hell they do to score points.

I don't know.

I don't get it.

"I need a job."

My attention darts right to Naz when he says that. "What?"

Sighing exasperatedly, he leans back in the booth, his eyes shifting to me. He stares at me, hard, but his expression remains passive.

After a moment, he shrugs.

"A job," he says again. "Something."

"Do you...? I mean, if it's about money, I..."

He cuts me off with a laugh and takes a swig of his beer. "We're good on money. Our children are good on money, as are their children, and their children's children. It isn't about money."

I gape at him. That was a whole hell of a lot of hypothetical children he just threw in there for a man who hasn't uttered a word to me about us potentially having a family since the last time we stepped foot in Sin City. "If it's not money, then..."

"I just need something," he explains, not looking at me now, his eyes drifting along the wooden tabletop between us. "You have school. You're going to have something someday, a *career*, and I've got nothing."

"You have plenty," I say, although I know exactly what he means when he says he has *nothing*. He has no focus, no goal, nothing he's working toward anymore. The man spent his entire adulthood hunting something, and now that it's been caught, he's just standing there, stagnant, unsure which direction to go.

"You asked me once what I would've done with my life had I not lost everything," he says. "I was thinking about that earlier... thinking about what kind of man I'd be if Johnny hadn't turned on me."

"Did you figure it out?"

"I don't know," he says, finishing off his beer before setting his bottle down. "I was a punk kid. Sure, I was in college, but who knows how long that would've lasted, considering I was already working odd jobs for Ray back then. I just wanted to be everything my father wasn't… I didn't want to have to work myself to the death just to pay the bills. I didn't want to turn out like Giuseppe Vitale. So I think maybe, regardless, when all was said and done, this is exactly who I'd still be. Even if Johnny hadn't done what he did, somebody, somewhere, probably would have, and I still would've become this man."

His voice has a dejected tone to it, like that realization knocked the wind from his sails.

"You think it was fate? That you were just born to be this way?"

"No." He meets my eyes again. "I'm saying my choices would've eventually led me this way. I can only blame myself, and I'm sorry what me being this man has done to everyone I've ever loved."

Those words send a shockwave through me.

Never, in a million years, did I expect to hear him say that.

I'm not sure how to respond.

"So yeah…" He motions toward the waitress, requesting our bill. "I need *something*."

He pulls out some cash, tossing it on the table, before standing up. He reaches for me, and I stare at his extended hand for a moment, shell-shocked.

Did he *seriously* just say that?

Holy shit.

Ignazio Vitale actually accepted blame.

Naz lets out a light laugh as I shake off my stupor and take his hand, climbing to my feet. He links our fingers together, squeezing gently, as the two of us stroll out of the busy sports bar and onto the floor of the MGM Grand.

I didn't expect to come back here, to see this place again so soon after our last visit. The casino is busy, and it's still pretty early on a Friday night, but instead of hanging around down here with the crowds, we head up to our Skyloft penthouse.

Same exact room as last time, too. It all feels familiar, yet so utterly different. This time, there's no Brandy, no Ray, and no guy Naz is going to murder at the end of the day (one can hope, anyway). There's no business to attend to (that I'm aware of), nothing planned (that he tells me about), no expectations except just existing in the moment.

No expectations except for being together.

I like it so much better this way.

As soon as we reach the room and Naz opens the door, I see a bottle of champagne in a bucket of ice sitting on the table, a platter of chocolate covered strawberries beside it. Smiling, I stroll over to the table, plucking a strawberry from the platter and holding it up, waving it toward Naz as he approaches.

"For someone concerned about my impending diabetes, you sure spoil me with this stuff a lot."

He smiles as he pops the top off the bottle of champagne and grabs two glasses, pouring a bit in each. He holds one out to me, keeping the other, as I take a bite of my strawberry. "I'm not in the business of denying anyone anything. I definitely don't deny *myself*. Sure, it might kill you someday, but I'm certainly not one to judge. Everything I do is bound to catch up to me, and when it does..." He shrugs, taking a sip of the champagne before smiling playfully. "I'm sure there will be hell to pay."

"For you?"

"Or them."

"Who's *them*?"

He steps toward me and I instinctively tense, glass of champagne in one hand and half-eaten strawberry in the other, as he grasps my chin, pulling my face up toward him, his thumb tracing my bottom lip. His expression changes right before my eyes, the playfulness draining as that look creeps into his eyes. *That* look.

The monster.

He's peeking out at me.

"*Them* is anybody who dares get in my way," he says, voice low, and I can't help but shiver as those words wash over me. Fear. Excitement. Terror. Exhilaration. The sensations battle for control of my body, twisting my insides and making my knees weak. I'll never for a moment doubt he means that, and as frightening as it is, knowing what he's capable of, knowing what he wouldn't hesitate to do, my sickness relishes the security. He'd kill the whole world, burn it to the ground, but that part of me believes him when he says he'd protect *me* from harm.

He's not bulletproof. I know he's not. But I think, now, he's grown shatter-resistant. After everything, Naz isn't an easy one to crack. Someday, when he dies, whether it happens tomorrow from a bullet or sixty years from now from old age, Naz will go out standing, fighting. Nobody will ever break him again.

His eyes scan my face, slowly and methodically, like he's studying every contour, before his gaze settles on my mouth. He licks his lips, and mine part in response, releasing a shaky exhale. My eyes drift closed as he kisses me softly, and I moan from anticipation, expecting him to deepen it, but instead I'm met with laughter against my lips.

Opening my eyes, I watch as he takes a step back, his expression once again light. The monster is gone. Naz tips his glass toward me before downing the rest of it and turning away.

"Enjoy your strawberries," he says. "I'm going to take a shower."

Fucking tease.

I gape at him until he disappears before eating the rest of my strawberry. I hear him moving around on the second floor of the suit, hear the water turn on in the bathroom. I stand here, listening to the noise for a moment, scowling.

I should stay down here.

Really.

I shouldn't follow him.

Shouldn't *bother* him.

It's not like he asked me to come along.

Not like he invited me.

So I should stay right where I am. I should drink all the champagne and eat all the strawberries and just say fuck him, the teasing bastard.

I should.

I don't.

I guzzle what's in my glass before setting it down and heading for the stairs. I tread lightly, tiptoeing toward the upstairs bathroom. The door is cracked open, and it doesn't make a sound when I slowly push on it to slink inside. The lights are dim, the air hazy from the steam from the shower, the mirrors and glass coated in a thin layer of fog, but I can make him out standing beneath the spray.

His back is to me as he lathers his hair with shampoo, the strong, all male, *all Naz* scent wafting toward me. Jesus, the man always smells as good as he looks. It's sinful, like just breathing him in is enough for a girl to need to shout out some Hail Mary's.

Hail Mary, full of Grace, let this man fuck me tonight...

"I'm not surprised."

The sound of his voice causes my muscles to tense. His back is still to me. He hasn't so much as even glanced my direction, but I can't help but wonder if he knows I'm here.

I say nothing.

I don't know what to say.

I'm not surprised?

Is he talking to *me*?

He rinses out his hair, as casual as can be, like he hadn't said a word. After a moment of silence, Naz turns around, his eyes meeting mine. He steps toward the glass, using his hand to clear away some of the fog.

I try to keep eye contact.

I do.

I try.

Really, I try hard.

Hard.

But my traitorous eyes have a mind of their own; my body does whatever the hell it wants. My gaze drifts down his chest and along his scars, following the trail of hair right to his cock.

Yep, definitely hard.

His laughter is sharp, drawing my eyes right back to his, knowing I've been caught ogling him.

"That's you," he says. "Exhibitionism is *your* kink, jailbird, not mine."

I feel my cheeks flushing. He curves a finger, motioning for me to come closer as he pushes open the glass door. Hesitating, I step toward him, as he casually leans against the wall of the shower, crossing his arms over his chest. I feel like a child about to be scolded for spying, with the way he's looking at me, expression serious, eyebrow cocked. He looks almost **irritated**.

Ugh, why does that excite me more?

"Is there something I can do for you?" His eyes scan me like I did him just a moment ago. "Is there something you need?"

The insinuation is clear, although his tone is anything but playful. There's a hard edge to the words. When he meets my eyes again, I see his have darkened. The monster's back, and he's feeling testy.

The rational part of me screams to get the hell out of there and leave the man to shower in peace, but I won't listen. I know it, and so does Naz. He cocks an eyebrow, waiting on my response.

I can't get any words to form.

"Well?" he says after a moment. "Are you going to answer the question, or am I going to have to *force* it out of you?"

I open my mouth to saying something, **anything**, barely getting out a syllable when Naz snatches ahold of me. Oh hell, he's not even **waiting** on my answer. The words morph into a shriek as he yanks me fully clothed into the shower with him. The water is hot... Jesus, it's practically **scalding**. I'm surprised it doesn't burn my nipples off.

He shoves me under the spray in front of him, slamming the

glass door. The water clings to my dress, weighing down the material, soaking through to my skin. I try to push past him, to get away, but he's too strong. His body pins me there, forcing me back against the wall. His hands grasp my thighs, pulling me up, and I gasp from surprise, wrapping my arms around his neck as I hold on for dear life.

"Like I said..." His lips ghost along my jawline before pausing beside my ear. "I'm not surprised."

"Are you ever?"

"No."

He pins me against the shower wall, one hand firmly around me, keeping me in place, while his other snakes between us, finding its way beneath my soaked dress. My breath hitches when he rubs me through the thin fabric of my panties before his hand slips beneath.

Oh shit.

Oh shit.

Oh holy fucking shit.

His fingers are rough, calloused, and he's not at all gentle about his movements, rubbing hard, sending strong jolts of electricity through my body.

"So wet," he murmurs.

"Well..." My nails dig into the skin at the back of his neck as I cling to him, my body tense from the sensations running through me. "We *are* in the shower."

Naz laughs darkly. "You know what I mean, sweetheart."

He pushes a finger inside of me, then another, as his thumb finds my clit. I bite the inside of my cheek, trying to be quiet, but it's pointless. I bite so hard I taste blood. He knows every button to press, every inch of skin to touch, to shove me right over the edge and into oblivion. With just a hand, the man has me climbing the wall, panting, squirming, desperate for more.

More.

More.

More.

"Is this what you want?" he asks. "Is this what you need?"

I shake my head, closing my eyes, as I relax back against the wall. Water streaks my face, raining down on me, my eyes burning, mascara running and makeup streaking, but I'm so damn close to orgasm already I can't even care. "More."

"How much more?"

"So much more," I murmur, feeling the pressure mounting, every inch of me tingling. Heat viciously attacks me, inside and out, battering my skin while straining my muscles. Naz's lips find my neck, and he sucks on it, making me gasp as he bites the tender spot below my ear. His fingers pump with fervor as I grind against his hand, getting closer... closer... closer...

"Oh God, so close," I groan, tilting my head more as his lips make their way around to the front of my neck. He bites my throat, hard, the skin vibrating around his mouth as I let out a piercing scream at the unexpected jolt of pain. My body tenses in reaction as he curves his fingers, finding that spot.

That spot.

I explode, pleasure and pain and tension and release and every fucking thing my body has ever contained igniting in a ball of flames that sparks right between my legs. I bang my head against the tile, pain shooting through my skull.

Before the pleasure even wanes, Naz lets go of me, dropping me back to my feet. My knees buckle, and I nearly hit the tile, unprepared, but Naz keeps me upright. He drags me to the other side of the shower before I can even catch my breath, spinning me around so my back is to him.

Naz presses me up against the massive glass wall that looks down onto the first floor of the suite. The material of my dress slaps against it, adhering to it just like it clings to my trembling body.

He says not a word—not a syllable, not a sigh, not even a whisper against my skin, as he yanks down my panties and lifts me up enough to thrust inside of me. I gasp, and he pauses at the sound, before steadying himself, stabilizing me there, to pound into me. He fucks me so hard, so brutal, I almost cry, the mix of pleasure and pain intense, unexpected. Jesus, I wasn't prepared for *this*. One arm pins me to him at the waist while his other hand finds my throat.

I suck in a deep breath, shakily exhaling when my lungs feel like they might burst, over and over. It's torture, waiting for something, waiting for the dizzying sensation of him blocking the flow of air, waiting for his fingertips to press against my jugular. I'm distracted, waiting... waiting... waiting... for the asphyxiation.

It doesn't come.

I feel like *screaming*.

"Naz..." My voice is a growl. "Please."

I don't even know why I'm begging. Do I want him to do it? I don't know. *I don't know.* I just wish he'd put me out of misery, Jesus Christ, just do it or don't. The taunting is too much, the imminent threat of his hand on my throat stirring up the adrenaline until my vision blurs.

Fuck, I don't know what I want.

He seems to know though, his hand shifting, squeezing just enough to make me gasp for air.

Within seconds, orgasm rocks through me, and he lets go as I suck in a deep breath, crying out his name. He thrusts into me so hard I'm surprised the glass can sustain the force, surprised it doesn't crack under the weight of the two of us, as his body shudders.

He drops me fast, letting go of me and backing away. I'm caught off guard, hitting the tile with a bang. I wince and look over at Naz, watching in shock as he strokes himself, fast, hard, coming down the shower drain.

It's been a long time since he's done that, pulled out like that, coming somewhere except for inside of me. *A long, long time.* His eyes are closed, mouth parted, head tilted back as his breaths come out haggard. He's stunning, there's no doubt about it, but the sight of him nags at me.

Something's wrong.

He's holding back.

After his body calms down, he opens his eyes, dropping his gaze to look at me. The faded, distracted look from earlier is back, his brow furrowing at the sight of me on the shower floor. "Are you okay?"

I nod slowly. "I think I broke my ass, but otherwise…"

He reaches for me and pulls me to my feet, dragging me back under the spray of water. He strips me, yanking off my heavy, soaked dress, discarding it in the corner of the shower, before his hands explore my skin. He caresses and massages, grabbing the soap and gently washing every inch of me before shampooing my hair.

I just stand there, letting him do it.

He doesn't speak, but this feel a hell of a lot like an apology.

Afterward, he takes a washcloth and runs it across my cheeks, wiping the skin around my eyes. I can see the black smears on the cloth from my makeup. "I look like a raccoon, don't I?"

A smile touches his lips. "You're beautiful, baby. Don't fret it."

I roll my eyes, but he doesn't give me much of a chance to argue. He shuts off the water and opens the shower door, stepping out. Grabbing a robe from the hook on the wall nearby, he drapes it around me, rubbing my arms as he kisses my forehead.

"Why don't you go pour us some more champagne?" he suggests. "I'll be right behind you."

I head downstairs, just as he told me to.

It takes him a while to follow.

Naz is distant the rest of the night. Again, he's here physically, but his thoughts are far away. I ask him more than once if he's okay, but he just repeats his mantra. *Don't worry about it.*

Naturally, I worry.

And worry.

And worry.

I lay in bed that night, *still* worrying.

I fall asleep worrying.

I dream about it.

I'm worried.

Something jolts me awake in the middle of the night. The room is dark, shadows befalling everything, the only light from the crack between the curtains letting the glow from the strip shine through. I'm on my back, and roll over, blinking away the sleep, but freeze when I see Naz's side of the bed is empty.

This isn't the first time I've woken up to find him missing.

Every time, I hope it'll be the last.

Sighing, I sit up, rubbing my eyes. Working, I assume. I guess he's here for work, after all. I'm about to climb to my feet when something shifts, startling me. I gasp, faintly making out the form in the darkness. Naz is sitting on the edge of the bed, still stark naked, his head down as he stares at the floor, hands clasped in front of him.

It takes a moment for my heart to calm down, for me to push back the swell of alarm. I swallow thickly, my voice cracking when I call his name. "Ignazio?"

He lets out a deep sigh, shifting position, turning his head my way. I can't make out much of his face in this darkness, but I know what it would look like if I could.

Troubled.

"I was a fool, Karissa." He speaks low, just above a whisper, the words strained. "Such a fucking fool."

"Why?" I pull the blanket up around me as my chest starts aching, tightening at his distressed tone. "What did you do?"

"Nothing," he says, sighing again before amending. "Everything."

I wait, but he doesn't elaborate.

He offers no explanation.

"I don't understand."

Shaking his head, he looks away from me. "I'm not surprised."

My confusion runs deep, my worry only growing as he stares at his hands fisted in his lap. The silence is stifling. There's so much more to say. I know there is... I just don't know what.

What am I supposed to say?

Before I can come up with something, Naz stands. I think he's going to leave, that he's going to walk away, and his name is on my lips to stop him when instead he turns my way.

All that escapes is a gasp of surprise.

Naz drops to his knees. No, to *a* knee. Just one. Right there, beside the bed, completely naked in the darkness. The man gets on a single knee beside me. My thoughts are a hellacious blizzard I can't see through to get a grasp on my surroundings. I don't know where I stand. I feel like I'm floating, hovering, my feet no longer on the ground. Knocked on my ass by this man for the second time today.

"Naz," I say, my voice with a panicked edge to it. "Oh God, Naz, what are you...?"

"Just be quiet and let me do this, okay?"

"But—"

"Please, Karissa."

Please. The man said *please*.

That alone silences me.

"I've been thinking about doing this all day," he says. "All fucking day it's been pestering me. Should I do it? Should I not do it? I didn't know what was the right choice. I *still* don't know. But I can't think about it anymore. So I'm doing it, and hoping like hell *you* know the right choice, because I don't."

I'm speechless.

Fucking speechless.

Naz opens his hand, and in his palm is a ring. I can't see it in the darkness, not really, but I can tell it's modest, not at all like the ring he gave me once before. That ring was gaudy and extravagant. This ring looks nothing like what he'd choose.

It looks more like what I would.

"You threw away the last one I bought you," he says quietly. "I could buy a hundred more like it. A hundred more flashy diamonds, bigger, brighter, each ring more expensive, but it would mean nothing, because it would just be a ring. A ring I bought with money I earned doing things I'd never want to admit to you. I wouldn't marry me with a ring like that either. I wouldn't marry the kind of person that bought that kind of ring."

"Naz..."

"Just... *don't.*"

I shut up again.

"So I went to my father," he continues, "and I asked him for the ring he used. He worked himself half to death saving up to buy it, and it took him years. *Decades.* I was a teenager by the time he could finally afford a real ring. And it was *nothing*, barely a carat, but it was a lot for them."

My stomach sinks. *His mother's ring.* Michelle Vitale died a few months ago, passed away unexpectedly in her sleep. I never got the chance to meet her, but I went to the funeral with Naz... and although he kept his distance, not going too close, never once approaching his father or participating in the services, I know it meant a lot to him that he could be there. That he got the chance to say goodbye.

He blames himself, though.

I know he does.

Death takes away everyone I love, he said to me that day. My only response was, *I'm here to stay.*

"I went to him, and asked him for this ring, because this ring means something. This ring was bought with money a man worked hard to earn, for a woman he loved more than anything. This ring is a sign of respect, and loyalty, and honesty. This is the kind of ring given by a man with integrity, a man like my father... a man, I realize, I was a fool for not wanting to be like. I asked him for it, and I expected him to say no, but he gave it to me. He gave it to me, and he said, 'if you do it, you gotta mean it, and it's gotta be right'. And I mean it... God knows, I mean it... but I don't know if it's right."

He stares at the ring for a moment before meeting my eyes.

"I'm not a good man," he says, "but I'm trying. I'm trying. I can't make you any promises of perfection. I can't promise I'll be what you deserve, or what you need, or even what you always want. All I can promise is that I'll love you until the day I die, and I'll spend every moment I'm alive trying for you."

He pauses, eyes studying my face.

"So I'm asking you to..." Shaking his head, he lets out a groan, backtracking. "Will you marry me, Karissa?"

He looks at me like he thinks I might say no.

Like he *expects* me to say no.

I should.

I know I should.

Rationally, I should reject him, run away from him, stay as far away from the man as I possibly can. But love is anything but rational. Love is ugly, and messy. Love makes no fucking sense. And I love him, as impossible as that may be.

I love him.

It's ridiculous.

But when I think about my life now, I can't imagine him not being in it. When I think about my future, I always picture him. This man is down on one knee, stark naked and vulnerable, and I could kick him while he's down, I could hurt him just a fraction of how he hurt me, but I would only regret it, because this, I think, is right. As wrong as it actually is, it still feels right to me.

"I will," I whisper. "I'll marry you."

Relief overcomes his expression as I hold out my hand. He slips the ring on, and it's slightly too big, but it feels like it belongs on my finger. Standing up, he leans toward me, hands on both sides of the bed beside me, as he smashes his lips to mine. He kisses me hard, kissing me deeply, climbing over top of me.

"Now," I whisper against his mouth, wrapping my arms around him. "I want to do it now."

"You want it?" he asks, lips leaving mine to trail my jawline, down to my neck. He kisses the center of my throat, where he left a bite mark earlier, as he presses himself against me. He's hard. "You want that, baby?"

I shiver, running my fingers through the hair at his nape. "Uh, yeah, but I meant I want to get married."

He pulls back, raising his eyebrows. "Get married? Now?"

"Yes," I whisper. "Tonight."

"But—"

"Be quiet," I say, cutting him off, covering his mouth with my hand as I laugh. "You want me to pick a date, right? Well I pick one. Today."

He looks stunned, but he doesn't argue, a small smile tugging the corner of his lips. He leans down toward me, leaving a light kiss against my lips. "Anything you want, Karissa. It's yours."

Hours later, after the sun has risen, Naz and I stand in the small chapel at the MGM Grand. There are no guests, no friends, no family, just strangers as witnesses and a man licensed to marry us. I don't wear a wedding dress. Naz doesn't even wear a suit. Just me, and him, and the simplest vow.

I promise to love you forever.

It's the only promise we've got.

After the man declares us husband and wife, Naz grabs a hold of me, yanking me toward him, and kisses me deeply, nipping at my bottom lip. I pull away, blushing, as Naz starts to tug me toward the exit of the chapel.

"Come on," he says. "We have a marriage to consummate."

"Is that right?"

"Absolutely," he says, his voice low, gritty. "I think I'm going to fuck you outside the Bellagio, in front of the fountain, somewhere where the whole world can see."

Acknowledgments

There's an old proverb that says it takes a village to raise a child. I'm of the belief that it takes the same to make a book. So many people were instrumental to the process, both directly and indirectly. I appreciate all of you, everyone who has discussed these characters or contacted me with theories or even just sent words of encouragement.

To Sarah Anderson, for spending countless hours listening to me complain when Ignazio Vitale just wouldn't cooperate. This story went through multiple drafts in various voices before we finally ended up here, where we are today, and I owe you so much for your unyielding patience when it seemed like every damn day I needed talked off a ledge.

To my family, for being the best support system a woman could ask for. I love you all. To my mother, who would've read this book and probably wondered where she went wrong with me (ha). It'll never seem real that you're gone. I still wake up every day and expect to see your face. And to my father... again, if you read this book, we're going to pretend these things didn't come from my brain. Thank you for always encouraging me.

To Nicki Bullard... you've been my best friend for most of my life. We both love broccoli and hate green onions. You're the Companion to my Doctor, the Castiel to my Dean, the crossbow to my Daryl. What would I do without you?

I want to say a special thank you the bloggers, who dedicate so much time to the books they love. It's truly humbling that out of millions of books, you choose to read mine. Thank you.

To everyone else: don't let anyone dull your shine. Love what you want to love. Do what you want to do. Read what you want to read. Life is way too short to live it for somebody else. Be *you*. You're beautiful.

Printed in Great Britain
by Amazon.co.uk, Ltd.,
Marston Gate.